THE DARKENING SKIES

When Sara Pallister's father dies leaving the farm bankrupt, she is reluctantly taken into the household of her narrow-minded Uncle Alfred and his wife Aunt Ida in the mining town of Whitton Grange. Determined to make Sara pay her way, Uncle Alfred hires young Raymond Kirkup and his aunt Louie, and through them the Dimarcos, owners of the popular local ice-cream parlour. As war approaches and hostility increases towards the Italian Dimarcos, Sara finds herself irresistibly drawn to leather-jacketed, motorbike-riding Joe Dimarco...

THE DARKENING SKIES

THE DARKENING SKIES

by

Janet MacLeod Trotter

Magna Large Print Books
Long Preston, North Yorkshire,
BD23 4ND, England.

British Library Cataloguing in Publication Data.

Trotter, Janet MacLeod
    The darkening skies.

A catalogue record of this book is
available from the British Library

ISBN   0-7505-2460-X

First published in Great Britain 1993 by Headline Book Publishing

Copyright © 1994 Janet MacLeod Trotter

Cover illustration © Len Thurston by arrangement with
P.W.A. International Ltd.

The right of Janet MacLeod Trotter to be identified as the author of
this work has been asserted by her in accordance with the Copyright,
Designs and Patents Act, 1988

Published in Large Print 2006 by arrangement with
Headline Book Publishing Ltd.

Magna Large Print is an imprint of Library Magna Books Ltd.

Printed and bound in Great Britain by
T.J. (International) Ltd., Cornwall, PL28 8RW

To Graeme and Amy
– for the joy you bring

Chapter One

'*April 21st 1939. Today Sid Gibson asked me to marry him.*'

Sara Pallister stared at the words she had just written in the old exercise book she used as a diary, chewing on the end of her pencil, recalling her surprise. They had been sitting on the wall below the old lead mine, dipping their feet into the burn. It was cold as ice. Heather was burning over on Thimble Hill and they had been watching the fires spreading in the wind. At least Sara had been.

All of a sudden Sid had said, 'Do you want to get wed?'

Sara had laughed, 'To who, like?' As Sid flushed scarlet she had realised the farmer's son was serious. He wants to marry me! she thought with incredulity, re-reading the stark words laid out in her bold script.

She had had this daydream for years about being proposed to up on the fell, among the heather. Her dream lad was tall and dark and full of passion, like Heathcliff in *Wuthering Heights* which Sara had read so often her mother complained the pages were falling out.

But Sid, Sara thought with dissatisfaction, had a round face and straw-coloured hair. She knew her father and Sid's father would be pleased at the Pallisters and the Gibsons coming together

11

after generations of being neighbours. And Bill's Mary would say good riddance and have her out of the house as quick as a flash, Sara thought, glancing across the large kitchen-cum-parlour at her sister-in-law. Mary was too mean to stoke up her own fire, preferring to come round here and help herself to her mother-in-law's cooking and have a gossip.

'John Lawson's got the sack from the slaughterhouse,' Mary was saying. 'Turning up drunk he was – and he with a bairn to support. Beth was a fool marrying a waster like John Lawson.'

Always poking her nose in is Mary Emerson, Sara thought, resentful of the criticism of her friend Beth. Her mother was too soft to tell Mary to mind her own business and just now Sara was too preoccupied with Sid's proposal. At least Mary did not know about her and Sid, Sara thought, hugging her secret.

She thought back to that moment on the wall again.

'I'll think about it,' Sara had said and Sid had leaned over and kissed her. His mouth had been dry and tasted sweetly of hay and Sara's long, wispy hair had blown in the way.

Sara wondered what it would be like being married to Sid. They would have to live with his family so he could help his father with the farm and it would be a life of fetching and carrying and she would never get to see the world like her brother Tom in the army.

Imagine never leaving Rillhope, Sara thought in dismay, or at least never getting beyond market day at Lilychapel most of the year. She might

12

never see Bishop Auckland or Durham again! Sara realised with a painful yearning that she longed to see more of the world. She wanted to see the dance bands she heard on her mother's gramophone and go to the pictures to see Clark Gable. She wanted one of those hats that came down over one eye and looked like they would slide off your head. But Sid Gibson did not understand this.

'You'll change once you're married,' Sid had told her like a doctor reassuring a sick patient, 'lasses do.'

That evening, Sara would have told her brother Tom, whose leave was almost at an end, about the proposal but a row blew up at the supper table. It was over the Germans marching into Czechoslovakia, though Sara was vague as to where it was or why it should cause so much bickering between Tom and her father.

'He's done it now, Hitler has,' Tom declared. 'He'll not be happy till he's scrapping with us an' all.'

'Don't talk daft,' Mr Pallister fretted, pushing away his food with disinterest.

'Well, we can't ignore Jerry for ever,' Tom continued, despite the signs of his father's darkening mood. 'They've got away with too much for too long. There'll be a scrap.'

'Chamberlain won't allow it!' his father snapped.

'Chamberlain!' Tom scoffed. 'He's got his head up his backside.'

'That's enough!' his father cried and pushing back his chair stormed out to the byre, leaving the family subdued.

The next day was Sunday and Sara peered out of the kitchen window at the rain spattering the daffodils, thinking glumly that Tom's leave finished tomorrow. She would miss him and the way he defended her when Mary got on her high horse about how she did not help around the house enough! Tom looked so grand in his Durham Light Infantry uniform, a real soldier, Sara thought proudly, watching him polish his boots. Even so, she wished he would not upset their father with his talk about another war with the Germans.

Last night her father had spent most of the evening sulking in the byre with the sickly lambs. These days he was always moody and their mother constantly warned them not to get in his way. He had not whistled round the house for weeks with all this talk of war, Sara thought, and then there were those letters from the bank she had overheard Mary and Bill discussing about the farm owing money. But why worry? Sara reasoned. Banks had plenty of money, so why should they mind if their small farm borrowed a bit?

'Put that blessed diary away before your father sees it,' Lily Pallister fussed at her daughter. 'And find Chrissie – make sure she's washed her face. Hurry up now!'

Sara slipped her notebook under the hooky mat by the solid oak sideboard and rushed into the scullery. Pulling on a pair of mud-splashed Wellington boots and covering her head with her gaberdine coat, she ventured outside into the pouring rain. She slithered along the flagstones

14

in front of the farmhouse and dived into the adjoining barn, knowing her younger sister would be with the lambs.

'Chrissie! Haway we'll be late for chapel,' Sara panted, peering into the nearest stall.

'Smoky won't take his milk this morning,' Chrissie looked up from her crouched position in the straw, her straight brown hair falling across her eyes. Sara had known her thirteen-year-old sister stay in the barn all night keeping vigil over the tiny bleating lambs, coaxing them to drink from a bottle.

'You'll have to leave him now,' the older girl said more gently, 'but I'll come and help you feed him after chapel. Mam's going light we're not ready.'

'Dad says I can keep Smoky as a pet if he pulls through.' Chrissie's pale face broke into a smile.

'That's grand.' Sara took her hand and pulled her up, thinking how soft her father was under his gruff exterior. He had paid for Bill and Mary's wedding last year because Mary's parents had been means tested and were getting public assistance. Furthermore, Richard Pallister did not insist that his sixteen-year-old daughter went out to work. No wonder he's in debt to the bank, Sara thought with a twinge of guilt.

The girls hurried back to the house and Sara made Chrissie wipe her face with a damp flannel while she combed the straw out of her tangled hair, before binding it into pigtails. Her own long, honey-coloured hair she bound in a pink ribbon then fixed on her green beret at a jaunty angle, glancing at her mother to see if she

15

noticed. But she was bending over the range, her all-enveloping apron protecting her frayed best dress from the cinders.

Down the stairs clattered her father and Tom, the one in starched white collar and old-fashioned black three-piece suit, the other in the khaki of his DLI uniform and polished black boots. Tom's face was ruddy with scrubbing, but her father's chin was nicked from shaving. It was not like him to allow his razor to become blunt. He reached for his sombre black hat, ignoring her look of concern.

'Fetch the Bible, Sara,' he commanded as they gathered in the doorway. 'Tom, help your brother hitch up the trap.'

Tom winked at Sara as he passed and pulled her beret over her eyes.

'Gerr' off!' his sister complained and rushed to the mirror.

'Do as your father says, Sara,' her mother said with a twitch of a smile as she pinned her blue hat to thick brown hair, 'and straighten up that beret. You're not going on a fashion parade.'

Chrissie giggled as their father led them out into a fresh deluge of rain and ran for the trap which Bill had waiting outside. Mary was already perched on a bench under the slim protection of a canvas covering, her round face prim under her purple crocheted hat. The other women and Tom squeezed in beside her while Richard Pallister took the reins beside Bill. The stocky Dales pony, Bluebell, set off at a quick trot down the track, shaking the passengers against each other in the old carriage. Cath, the Pallisters' sheepdog, ran

16

barking a farewell behind them until they reached the first gate, then she turned and trotted back to her kennel in the yard.

'Likely Sid Gibson'll be there already,' Tom teased Sara.

'So?' she answered unconcernedly, her fair face colouring.

'He's become quite religious since I was last home.' Tom winked.

'That's enough, Tom,' Lily Pallister said, but her smile was indulgent. 'The Gibsons have always been good chapelgoers.'

Mary joined in. 'I saw you coming back from Rillhope mine yesterday with Sid Gibson. You seem to be seeing a lot of him lately.'

'Am I?' Sara replied, giving her sister-in-law a dismissive look. 'I thought you were too busy with all your housework to notice what other folks do.'

Chrissie sniggered into her hand, but Mary was quick to retaliate.

'So you are courting, then? It would explain why you never have time to feed the hens, wouldn't it, Mrs Pallister?' She gave a knowing look to her mother-in-law, but the older woman did not respond. Mary persisted, 'If you're serious about Sid Gibson you'll have to bring him round for tea, won't she, Mrs Pallister? Better than sneaking around the beck in all weathers – it's not seemly.'

'That's up to Sara, our Mary,' Lily Pallister replied evenly, unruffled by their bickering. 'Sid's always welcome at Stout House.' She squinted at her plump-cheeked daughter through the rain. Sara flushed under the scrutiny.

'I just went for a walk up the beck, and happened to bump into him,' she said defensively. 'Can't a lass go for a walk without being watched?'

'Aye,' Tom agreed, 'Sara's always been one for walkin', nowt wrong with that.' He scanned Mary's thickening figure with his blue eyes. 'Looks like you could do with a bit exercise, yourself. Too much of Mam's home baking, eh, Mary?'

Mary gave him a hostile look and turned back to Sara. 'It doesn't do to lead a lad on, mind,' she continued to needle. 'If you're courting you should come right out with it and say so.'

Sara looked at her with derision, encouraged by Tom's jibe. She had a good mind to blurt out that Sid Gibson had proposed to her, she had not had to do the proposing like Mary had to Bill. Her dull, sensible sister-in-law had caught her brother like a fly in a spider's web at the spring fair two years ago and he had put up no resistance. They had been married within the year and since then Mary Emerson, the unemployed quarryman's daughter, had strutted around Stout House as if she owned the place.

But Richard Pallister put an end to their squabbling. 'I'll have no more o' your noise, or I'll skelp the lot o' you,' he barked over his shoulder.

Sara pursed her pink lips and swallowed her retort, silenced by her mother's warning look and her father's black mood. Exchanging grins with Tom, she turned to survey the rain-soaked valley. Mist rolled off the top of the fell, hiding the steep fields of grazing sheep and blurring the criss-cross of dry-stone walls. Below them was Rill-hope, a huddled row of cottages and a cluster of stone barns that held the slaughterhouse and Dickson's garage. The river, peaty brown from its race down the hillside, chuckled and foamed past the cottage doorways with their white-washed lintels.

No one spoke as they passed the Gibsons' farm. A couple of hens pecked forlornly on the open stone steps up to the farmhouse door, otherwise Highbeck was deserted. A shiny tractor stood ostentatiously at the gate and Sara saw Bill glance at it enviously as they rattled by in the cart.

Twenty minutes later they drew up in front of the Lowbeck Methodist Chapel that served the scattered communities of this remote part of upper Weardale. It was a solid stone building, only distinguishable from some of the farm buildings around it by its large, plain windows and discreet board that proclaimed the times of the services and Sunday School classes. Parked in front of its iron railings was the schoolmaster's gleaming blue Austin and next to it the even grander red Ford belonging to the butcher. Sara noticed Sid's battered bicycle propped against a tree and wondered if he would ever drive something as exotic as these cars.

Clambering down from the trap, she followed her parents into the chapel and they filed into the Pallisters' boxed pew, three rows from the front. She caught sight of Sid off to the right as she sat down, but was too far forward to look at him during the long service without craning round.

'Beth Lawson's wearing a new hat,' Mary murmured at the beginning of the second hymn. 'Don't know how she can afford it with a new

19

bairn to feed and clothe and John out of work.'

Sara marvelled that her sister-in-law noticed such details and, stifling a yawn, her mind wandered as the congregation sat and steamed quietly, their clothes drying out in the warmth of the hall. In her mind she was up on the fell in warm spring sunshine, walking hand in hand with a young lover. She tried to picture him as Sid in his Sunday best with his thatch of fair hair ruffled in the breeze, but it was Clark Gable who smiled at her, just like he did in the magazine picture her friend Beth had given her.

At one stage in the service the wind must have picked up outside, because smoke began to blow back down the flue of the old stove and Tom stood up on the bench to open the vent. Sara saw him nod and grin at one of the Metcalfe sisters from Thimble Hill Farm while he was turned around. She was proud that her brother was the most dashing young man in the chapel, dressed in his uniform.

After the service, Sara detached herself from her mother who was chatting to Mrs Gibson and slipped through the crowd outside the chapel to see her friend Beth.

'I need to talk to you about som'at,' she whispered with a grin.

Beth's squint eyes widened with interest. ''Bout what?'

'Can't speak now.' Sara walked her to the gate. 'Can I call after dinner?'

'Aye,' Beth nodded, 'we can tak' the bairn for a walk if the rain eases off. He might gan to sleep if he's pushed in the pram.'

'Where is Daniel?'

'Mam's got him, but he'll be bubblin' for his feed.' She put a hand to her swollen breasts and winced. 'Greedy little babby.'

Sara looked with concern at her friend's tired face. A year ago, she and Beth had run around together without a care in the world, until John Lawson had gone courting the giggling Beth and tempted her up on to the fell during the long summer evenings. Now the spark was gone from Beth's funny brown eyes and her talk was all of babies. If this was what marriage and mother-hood did to a lass, Sara thought with panic, she wanted none of it.

So when Sid Gibson sidled up to her as she said goodbye to Beth, she gave him a cool look.

'Mornin', Sara.' He touched his cap with an anxious smile.

'Sid...' Sara gave a brief nod and turned back to Beth. Her friend's look was enquiring, but Sara's face was impassive.

Sid cleared his throat. 'Thought I'd go up the beck later – see if there's any more lambs come in top field.' Sara felt a flush of embarrassment at such an obvious invitation in front of her friend. She glanced around to see if any of her family were watching. Her father sat alone on the trap, fretting to be off. Mary sheltered under a nearby tree talking to Jane Metcalfe but managing to keep one eye on her and Sid.

'I'm going visitin' this afternoon,' Sara murmured back.

'Oh.' Sid sounded disappointed. 'Well, likely I'll see you at the lecture here Wednesday evening.'

21

'Aye,' Sara nodded and Sid moved off to collect his bicycle.

'You courtin'?' Beth whispered. Sara flushed pink. 'Then why don't you speak to the lad?' her friend chided.

'I'm that mixed up about him,' Sara hissed back. 'I'll see you later.' She turned quickly and ran to the waiting trap, while Beth waddled over to her father's joinery van, looking as if she were still pregnant with her newborn baby. There was no sign of her husband John. Probably sleeping off his hangover after market day in Lilychapel, Sara thought with disapproval.

As the Pallisters set off up the valley to return to Stout House, they passed Sid Gibson wobbling in the wind on his ancient machine and Sara felt a stab of remorse that she had made no arrangement to see him later that day. She wanted his company when he was not there and yet was somehow irritated by it when he was.

Bill and Mary came in to Stout House for a Sunday lunch of mutton and potatoes and spring cabbage and carrots, followed by Lily Pallister's homemade rhubarb and meringue pie. But there was no leisurely nap beside the large kitchen fire for Sara's father that afternoon, as he and Bill ventured out into the wind and rain to count the lambs in the high fields. They went off, grim faced, with Cath yapping excitedly at her father's heels, obeying his whistle.

After washing up, Sara announced she was going out to see Beth.

'You'll catch your death in this weather,' her mother fussed, glancing out of the small windows at the billowing black rain clouds whipping across the hills. 'And you've been sneezing these past two days. Best stay indoors and keep warm, pet.'

'I'll not be long,' Sara answered, pulling on her gaberdine mackintosh and pushing her hair inside her beret. Her mother sighed with resignation, aware that if Sara was determined to go out, she could not be stopped.

'Going up the beck are you?' Mary paused over her knitting to enquire.

'No,' Sara muttered. 'I'm going down to Beth's, not that it's any of your business.'

'I'll walk you down.' Tom jumped up from his seat, eager to escape the tedium of a Sunday afternoon at home.

'Be back in time for tea the pair of you,' their mother said, 'else your father'll have something to say.'

They hurried out of the back door into the buffeting gale that had increased all day.

'Mary's knittin' those yellow bed socks for you,' Sara told Tom as they rushed down the track and her brother laughed.

'She means well most of the time. You shouldn't let her bother you. You're like a fish to the bait every time.'

'It's all right for you to say,' Sara grimaced, 'you're leaving the morra. I've got her every day making me life a misery. Mary hates the sight of me – always has done.'

'She's just jealous, that's all,' Tom tried to explain.

'Jealous?' Sara answered in surprise. 'What for?'

23

''Cos you've always had a happy family and plenty to eat, even when money's a bit tight,' Tom answered. 'She's come from a slum house in Stanhope and knows what it's like to have the means-test man go through all her possessions.'

'Aye, I know.' Sara felt humbled. 'But why does she pick on me?'

'Perhaps it's because you're the bonny one.' Tom grinned and gave her a playful push, 'Or perhaps because you're the laziest lass this side of Lilychapel.'

Sara pushed him back and Tom set off down the hill with his sister in pursuit, shouting and laughing in the wind. As they arrived, breathless, by the Rillhope cottages, Tom stopped and fished out a battered packet of the cigarettes he was forbidden to smoke at home. He turned his back into the wind and attempted to light one.

'There's one way you can get away from Mary,' he suggested, his match going out. 'Give a bit encouragement to Sid Gibson. It's plain he fancies you.'

'He's asked me to marry him,' Sara blurted out.

Tom gawped at her as another match fizzled and then laughed. 'Well, there you are then. You can be Mrs Gibson of Highbeck soon enough – Dad's bound to agree.'

'Aye,' Sara answered without enthusiasm and turned to knock on Beth's door. Tom's cigarette caught alight and he dragged on it hard. Turning up the collar of his army coat he said, 'I'll see you in a bit.'

'Where are you off to?' Sara asked suspiciously.

'Thought I'd get myself a cuppa at Thimble

Hill,' he winked. 'Jane Metcalfe asked me after chapel.'

'Soldiers!' Sara gave a wry smile. 'Ta-ra, then.' The door opened and John Lawson's bleary red eyes blinked at her in the rain. Beyond him Sara could hear the shrill wail of his baby son.

She spent an hour in Beth's kitchen, helping change Daniel's nappy and making tea while her friend fed her baby and John went back upstairs to sleep. To Sara, Daniel was ugly; a sallow, crinkled creature who fretted and cried or dribbled sick down his discoloured dress. She did not understand why people made such a fuss over babies and she was impatient to gain her friend's advice. Eventually they got round to the subject of Sid Gibson.

'Well, should I accept him?' she asked.

'He's a canny lad,' Beth considered, 'and he doesn't drink.' She looked up to the ceiling and pulled a face at her absent husband. 'And he'll get Highbeck Farm one day – you'll have a decent house to call your own.'

'So you think I should say yes?' Sara looked troubled.

'Aye,' Beth nodded, patting the wind out of Daniel. 'You'd be daft not to.'

Sara dropped her gaze. 'But I don't think I'm in love with him.'

Beth snorted. 'Love! Look where it got me.' There was an edge of bitterness in her voice. 'You've the chance of a good lad – tak' it, I say. There's no one else round here half as decent as Sid Gibson.'

'Aye,' Sara sighed, her green eyes sad. 'I know

he's a good'un, but...'

'The trouble with you, Sara, is you're too romantic by half. Looks in a lad aren't everything, believe me.' Beth's tone became sharp. 'It's no good sittin' around waiting for Clark Gable, 'cos he doesn't live around these parts and he's never likely to.'

Sara burst out laughing at the idea. 'If only!' she giggled. Then looking at the clock on the mantelpiece, she leapt up. 'Eeh, I'll have to be off. Come up to the house during the week, won't you? Mam's longing to see Daniel.'

'Aye, if the weather improves.' Beth stood up with Daniel cradled in her arms. Sara thought, for the first time, they looked contented and right for each other. 'So, what will you say?' Beth was curious.

'What I'm expected to say, I suppose,' Sara said resignedly. She slipped into her wet mac and shivered in its dampness. 'I'll see mesel' out, don't come to the door, it's blowing a gale. Ta-ra then, Beth.'

'Ta-ra,' the young mother replied, smiling at her contrary friend and doubting that she would ever do what was expected of her.

The large kitchen table was covered in a starched white linen tablecloth and spread with cold meat and pickles, drop scones, gingerbread, fruit cake and bread, butter and jam. Lily Pallister dispensed an endless supply of hot tea from the large china teapot, an heirloom from the Victorian Pallisters. But Sara, preoccupied, picked at her food without enthusiasm. The chill of the walk back still made her shiver in spite of the cosy warmth of the large kitchen, its windows now shuttered against the battering wind.

Afterwards, Bill and Mary went to their cottage next door and Richard Pallister went out in his oilskins to have a last check on his labouring ewes.

'Stay and rest by the fire,' Sara's mother coaxed. 'They'll manage without you for one night, Dick.'

He shot her a strange look, almost guilty, Sara thought. But her restless father would not be detained. 'Stop fussing, woman,' he snapped and went out.

When they had all gone, Tom went over to the old gramophone and lifted the lid.

'You know you shouldn't, Tom,' his mother protested half-heartedly. 'Not on a Sunday.'

'Who's going to hear us?' Tom laughed without concern and chose a record from its battered dust cover. He cranked up the machine.

'What if the minister was to call?' Lily Pallister laughed nervously.

'Oh, let us listen, Mam,' Sara urged, pausing over her diary writing. 'It's Tom's last night.'

Her mother acquiesced and began to hum tunefully to the strains of Jack Buchanan.

'Haway and dance, Sara.' Tom pulled his sister up from her prone position in front of the roaring fire. Together they waltzed to the crooner and, when he finished, Tom played the popular songs he had brought home the previous Christmas.

Their mother, unable to resist the music, abandoned her mending and joined them, dragging her youngest daughter around the room. Chrissie giggled, glancing nervously at the scullery door, lest her stern father should suddenly reappear to admonish them all for their ungodliness. They shuffled around the large table to the strains of 'These Foolish Things' and Sara's favourite hit from two years ago, 'I've Got You Under My Skin'.

'It's so romantic,' Sara sighed as they danced to a halt.

'Aye, Mrs Gibson,' Tom whispered cheekily.

'Shut your gob!' Sara pushed him away with an embarrassed snort. But the thought had occurred to her as she glided around the firelit kitchen, mellowed by the music. She imagined herself being escorted up the chapel aisle in a white satin dress such as Princess Marina had worn for her marriage to the Duke of Kent. Waiting for her would be her gentle Sid, his soft hazel eyes full of admiration at the sight of her. He would whisk her away in a covered carriage pulled by elegant horses and she would smile charmingly and throw coins to the children and Mary Emerson. She would say goodbye to her childish pinafores and take up the role of married woman. Her heart beat a little quicker at the thought of being intimate with Sid Gibson and the memory of his tender kiss the previous day. As the voice of Jack Buchanan had rolled sensuously into the room, Sara had determined that on Wednesday evening, after the lecture on the Romans in Britain by the schoolmaster, Mr Banks, she would say 'yes' to Sid Gibson.

Her musings were interrupted by a heavy banging on the front door. Somebody was already inside the porch, his bulk silhouetted against the frosted glass of the inner door. Her mother rushed guiltily to shut the gramophone, while Tom went to answer the knocking.

'Minister must have heard us after all, Mam,' he joked.

A squall rushed in to the room, preceding their visitor. In the half-dark of the dreary day, it was difficult to make out the stout figure in the doorway enveloped in black oilskins and cumbersome boots. Sara was the first to identify him.

'Sid!' she gasped, blushing at his sudden appearance as if her daydreams had conjured him to her side. He had come for her answer now, unable to wait until midweek. But the look of alarm on his face dispelled her smile of pleasure.

'Sorry t' inter'up, Mrs Pallister,' he gabbled out of breath, hardly acknowledging Sara. 'Can you come quick, Tom?'

'Aye.' Tom did not stop to ask why, but unhooked his father's old greatcoat hanging on the back of the wide farm door.

'What is it, Sid?' Lily Pallister asked anxiously, her amiable face creasing in concern.

Sid hesitated a moment, then plunged on quickly. 'I saw a man go int' beck, up by Rillhope mine. I can't get to him on me own.'

'Richard!' Lily's hand flew to her mouth. 'He went up that way.'

'Aye,' Sid nodded grimly. 'I saw him gan.'

'Quickly, Tom!' his mother begged.

'I'll call for Bill,' Tom said already halfway out of the door. 'Haway, Sid, show the way.'

For the first time Sid looked at Sara and she thought his eyes reproachful.

29

'Go fetch Dr Hall, Sara,' her mother ordered.

'I'll go on the bike,' she offered at once.

'Best get him to ring for the ambulance at Lilychapel,' Sid said ominously and left.

Sara rushed into the scullery, seized her damp coat and raced out into the gloom. To her surprise she found Cath leaping with concern in the yard, barking frantically.

'Poor Cath.' Sara calmed the dog a moment. 'Did you come back to warn us?' Then it struck her; the sheepdog was chained up and straining to be free of its shackles. Her father had not taken her with him when he'd left to do his rounds.

With no time to puzzle over why Cath had been left behind, Sara took Tom's old bicycle from the byre, mounted it unsteadily and wobbled off into the icy wind. Twice, freewheeling down the hill, she was blown off and badly scraped her knees and elbows. But the thought of her father, trapped on the rocks at the foot of the tumbling beck in the drenching rain, spurred her on to Lowbeck.

It was dark and she was soaked through by the time she reached Dr Hall's stone house, sheltered by a wall of beech trees in the middle of the village. She hammered frantically on the front door for what seemed like an age, but there was no reply. Rushing round the side of the house, Sara saw a chink of light spilling through the curtains of a downstairs room. She battered on the window, trying to stem the panic rising in her throat.

'Please let him be in! Please!' she cried to the wind. The back door opened.

'Who's there?' a woman's voice called nervously.

'Mrs Hall,' Sara sobbed with relief, 'we need the doctor. It's me dad.'

'Sara Pallister, isn't it?' The young woman regarded the agitated girl, her long hair plastered to her face and rain dripping off her nose and cheeks. 'Come in, you look exhausted.'

'Please, Mrs Hall, I just want the doctor,' she persisted, her mud-spattered legs rooted to the spot. 'Me dad's gone in the beck. They think he's badly hurt.'

'I'm afraid Dr Hall isn't here,' the young doctor's wife answered in concern. 'He's away to assist at a birth in Lilychapel.'

Sara's head flopped forward and she let out an agonised wail of desperation. Her knees felt as weak as a newborn lamb's after her cycle ride and it had all been to no avail. Her father was lying unconscious on the desolate fell and she could do nothing to help him.

'You can come in and wait for my husband,' Mrs Hall suggested, quite at a loss. Sara's head went up at the sound of the woman's helplessness. She must control herself and not give way to the waves of hysteria that threatened to engulf her. She swallowed hard.

'Please ring for the ambulance in Lilychapel,' she ordered. 'Tell them to come up to Stout House – that there's a man badly injured. I must get back and help me mam when they bring him in.'

'Yes, yes, I'll ring at once,' the young woman agreed with relief, thankful that this bedraggled girl was not going to have hysterics in front of her. 'But you'll come in and have a hot drink before you go?'

'No ta, Mrs Hall.' Sara resisted the warmth beckoning from the open door and turned on her heels and ran back into the night, clambering once more on to Tom's bicycle.

By the time she got to the steep climb up the hillside to Highbeck and Stout House, it was quite dark. Sara, abandoning the heavy framed bicycle in the ditch, trudged the final mile. Cold and soaked and utterly exhausted, she fell in at the back door. She could hear voices in the kitchen and as she entered she saw the room was full of people.

'Sara!' It was Mrs Gibson who gasped at her half-drowned appearance. 'Eeh, take off those wet clothes at once, you poor lamb.'

Dazed by the sudden heat of the kitchen and the crowd of people around the long table, Sara stood nonplussed. As her neighbour pulled at her sodden coat, it dawned on her that there was somebody lying motionless on the bare table. She could not make sense of anything she saw.

'Dad?' she croaked. Then her heart lurched as she caught sight of her mother's stricken face, Bill's arm about her shoulders. Chrissie was blubbering into Mary's lap in the chair by the fire. Sara felt her knees buckle. Suddenly Tom was there beside her, his handsome face ashen with shock.

'He was dead when we got to him,' he choked in explanation. Sara held on to him, quite numb to his words. For the first time she realised the body on the table was covered in a white sheet. 'Sid's gone for the minister,' Tom added, 'and to look for you.'

'Mrs Hall's ringin' for the ambulance,' Sara said, 'it'll be here shortly.' She could not take her eyes off the humped shape on the kitchen table. If she pulled back the sheet, perhaps it would not be her father after all. She looked around for him. Mary was in the corner crying and rocking Chrissie in her arms. Her mother was holding the dead man's hand and Mrs Gibson was asking her if she wanted a cup of tea.

Suddenly someone started to scream, a strangled high-pitched cry like an animal in a trap. It rang in Sara's ears until everyone's eyes were on her. Tom's arms came about her, holding her tight and Sara realised it was she who cried out.

'I tried to get the doctor!' she sobbed. 'He wasn't in, Tom, he wasn't there!'

'It wouldn't have made any difference,' Tom tried to calm his sister. 'The fall broke his neck. He'd gone before Sid came to fetch us.'

The airless room began to waver before her. Tom's voice buzzed in her ears. Sara leaned into her brother's shoulder and fainted.

Chapter Two

Sara lay listlessly in her bed. Of the past week she remembered little, except a confused jumble of voices in her pounding head. Dr Hall had come and leaned over her and held her wrist and put a cold hand to her sweating forehead.

'Bad dose of 'flu...'

'Aye, out in damp clothes ... the shock, poor pet.' It was her mother's concerned voice.

'Old Gibson died o' 'flu...' Mary said.

'Hush now!' Lily Pallister commanded.

It surprised Sara to see Dr Hall, because he was supposed to be delivering a baby. Then it struck her that it was her father he should be attending to and not her, so she had grown agitated and tried to tell him that her father was lying at the foot of the beck bleeding to death. Death... Dead... Suddenly the memory of that body on the kitchen table had leapt into her mind and with searing pain she remembered her father was gone.

At this very moment they were burying him in the cemetery at Lowbeck after a service at the chapel. Sara had protested that she was well enough to go and pay her last respects, but her mother, under instruction from Dr Hall, would not allow her to venture down from the icy bedroom she shared with Chrissie. As far as Sara could see, Dr Hall believed in fresh air and fresh

34

vegetables as the best remedy for all ills. So the rags that had insulated the room from draughts all winter were removed from the window and blasts of chilly spring air swept out the mustiness.

Earlier that morning she had listened to the assembled family praying and hymn singing in the large kitchen below, before her father's coffin was borne out to the waiting hearse. Sara had lain and wept alone, gripped by grief that she could not see her father buried and remorse that she had not demonstrated her love for him more. As the funeral party left, Sara had dragged herself to the small window and watched them depart. She felt a spasm at the sight of her mother's defeated face. Under her black hat she was grey and featureless in the lukewarm sun, older than Sara had ever seen her look.

For Richard Pallister Lily Cummings had become Mrs Pallister and left her home and the cosy pit village of Whitton Grange for the bleak isolation of Weardale, putting up with all its hardships from wild weather to the suspicion of her as an incomer by the surrounding farmers. They still treated her differently, Sara thought, but she did not doubt that her undemonstrative father had loved her mother equally. You could see it in the quiet way he studied her across the kitchen table or the muted laughter she sometimes heard through the bedroom wall. How cruel for such love to be wiped out by one careless slip of the foot. Or had it been careless? Sara shuddered at another possibility, that her father had stepped off the cliff willingly. His mood of late had been as foul as the weather and why else would he have

35

left Cath behind chained up at the house?

Mrs Gibson, left in charge of Sara, found her shivering and in tears at the window and bustled her back to bed. Sara fell asleep, overwhelmed by weakness, until the sound of returning family awoke her again.

Tom was the first to come up to see her. He sat in silence on her bed, holding her hand for several minutes.

'I so wanted to gan to the burial,' Sara whispered miserably.

'I know.' Tom squeezed her limp hand, sapped of its usual strength by the 'flu that had struck his sister. 'It was a grand send-off – chapel was burstin' – folk had to stand outside.'

'He was that popular, wasn't he?' Sara gave a wistful smile.

Tom nodded. 'He was a real Pallister, folks have always respected the Pallisters – good chapel people. I reckon I'm the black sheep.'

'No,' Sara protested. 'Dad was right proud of you in your uniform, no matter what he said about not wanting you to fight a war. You're one of the Faithful Durhams just like him.' Tom smiled at her gratefully. 'It's me who's the black sheep, I should've been there,' Sara added feeling her eyes blur with tears once more.

'You can't even walk to the door.' Tom shook his head. 'It's more important you get your strength back – Mam'll need you to be strong, once I've gone.'

Sara lay back feeling the weakness shaking her body. She knew Tom was right but it did not ease the frustration she felt at her immobility.

'How long can you stay?' she asked with eyes closed. She dreaded the time Tom's compassionate leave must end and she would be left with her distraught mother and younger sister. Through the fog of her fever she had heard Chrissie crying under the bedclothes every night for what seemed like hours.

'I'm back in barracks the day after tomorrow,' Tom said quietly.

There was a sad, shared silence between them, then Sara dared to ask what had been preying on her mind. She needed to know if Tom harboured the same black thoughts as she did.

'How could it have happened, Tom? How could a strong man like Dad have fallen into the beck?'

'He must've lost his footing, it was that muddy from the rain and blowing a gale.'

'But not Dad!' Sara pulled herself up. 'He knew every inch of these hills.'

'It was an accident,' Tom said with a fatalistic shrug.

'He shouldn't have gone alone,' Sara fretted, 'why wasn't Bill up there with him? And why didn't he take Cath? It was all wrong.'

But Tom misunderstood her anxiety. 'It's not right to blame Bill,' he answered sternly. 'And he wasn't alone, was he? Sid saw him go up, but he couldn't have stopped him falling all that way, no one could, it just happened in seconds.'

'I hate that beck now!' Sara's voice grew querulous. 'I never want to go up there again, Tom, never.'

Tom reached over and hugged his sister to him and she gave way to her grief.

'I wish I could've hugged him before he went out that evening, like I used to as a bairn,' she cried. 'It's terrible not being able to say goodbye, isn't it?'

'Aye,' Tom choked, 'but it's ten time's worse for Mam.'

'Oh, poor Mam!' Sara sniffed. 'I'll help more around the house and the farm, I promise.' She felt better as she spoke her words of resolution. 'At least Bill can carry on with the farm. He and Mary will move in here, likely?'

'Don't pull such a long face,' Tom smiled. 'Mary's been canny while you've been ill, sitting up night-times watching over you.'

'Has she?' Sara asked in surprise.

'Aye,' Tom insisted. 'Anyways, you'll be moving out once you're married to Sid, won't you?' His blue eyes looked teasing. Sara's wan face turned a faint pink at the mention of Sid's name. 'He's been round every day to ask after you,' Tom persisted.

'That's nice,' Sara answered bashfully, 'Sid's all right, isn't he?'

'Aye, you could do worse,' Tom agreed. 'He's downstairs now.'

Sara felt nervous at the thought of Sid so close by when she still had not given him an answer to his proposal. 'Who else has come?' Sara quickly changed the subject.

'All the neighbours are in and the minister and the Halls, and Aunt Freda and the cousins are over from Teesdale. Oh, aye, and Uncle Alfred's come up from Whitton Grange,' Tom told her.

'That's grand. Mam'll be pleased to see him

after all this time.'

Tom grimaced. 'He says he can't stop and he's getting the afternoon train back from Lowbeck. Just staying long enough to stuff his face full of Mam's pies and Mary's baking.'

'You don't like him, do you?' Sara asked. 'I thought he was canny the time he took us all to Redcar.'

'That was years ago,' Tom scoffed. 'He's not bothered with us since he became overman at the pit. You should see the airs and graces now! To him we're just farm labourers, common as muck.'

'No! Uncle Alfred wouldn't say that,' Sara defended

Tom snorted, 'He as good as said so to Mr Gibson! And he never had time for Dad when he was alive, so why's he bothering now?'

'For Mam's sake, of course,' Sara answered, 'he's her brother, after all, and she needs his support.'

'Well, she's not getting much of it – just a lecture on how she should never have married a sheep farmer,' Tom scowled. 'He's even got the cheek to take money off her to buy a present for his snotty-nosed daughter who she's never seen since her christening. And at a time like this, when she'll need every penny she can lay her hands on. It's down right disgustin'!'

Sara had never heard Tom so angry. 'We will be able to stay on at Stout House, won't we?' Sara asked worriedly. She had always pictured the family staying on for ever in this house, as generations before them had. Despite the winter dampness and the rattling windows, she loved its familiar uneven floors, its creaking doors and the large, homely kitchen below with its dark polished furniture and roaring fire. It had been built by Pallisters four generations ago, when the mottled sand-coloured stones had gleamed with newness and the blue and white china stacked on the dresser had been a wedding gift to the first Mrs Pallister. In time, it would all be Bill and Mary's, to pass on to their children and children's children. But this talk of no money made her uneasy.

Tom hesitated before answering. 'Things'll work out, I'm sure.' He got up quickly. 'Mary'll bring you up some egg-and-bacon pie.' He swung open the complaining door and gave a half-hearted smile, 'I'm away to talk to Jane Metcalfe.'

Later, coming out of a doze, the half-eaten pie still on the wooden chair by her bed, Sara became aware of subdued voices below the open window.

'It may come to that.'

'He should've provided for you. I can't take on such a responsibility – I've a wife and daughter of my own. And there's Colin, too.'

'I'm not asking much – just this one favour,' a woman's voice pleaded. 'I'm a widow now, it's going to be hard.'

'You always did spend too freely, Lily,' the man replied in flat blunt tones, 'you'll have to cut your cloth to fit your coat.'

'My bairns have had precious little, Alfred, life up here is no summer picnic, I'll have you know.'

'Didn't I warn you not to go off with Dick Pallister? I could see a mile off he had no business sense. These hill farmers are little better than peasants herding a few sheep – there's no living to be made here now the lead mines are closed.'

'Dick was a good man,' her mother protested. 'I'll never regret the choice I made.'

Sara felt her eyes sting and she hauled herself out of bed to see what was happening. Creeping up to the window she peered out. Her mother was hidden below the eaves of the stone roof, but she could see the heavily jowled face and receding black hair of her uncle, Alfred Cummings.

'Then you're as daft as you always were, Lily,' he scorned. 'What's he done for you? Left you with a crumbling house and a farm up to its ears in debt, that's what. You're lucky the bank hasn't made you bankrupt.'

'I'll manage well enough with our Bill's help,' her mother insisted stoutly. 'I'm just asking you to give the lass a bit start in life, Alfred, while we sort things out with the bank. If it doesn't suit you and Ida, you can send her home. *Please*, Alfred.'

The small man in the neat black coat furrowed his bushy eyebrows and sucked in his cheeks with disapproval. Finally he wagged a finger at his younger sister, 'She'll have to go out and work mind. I can't have Ida running around after her like you do. Not even coming to her father's funeral, tut!'

'She's been very ill this last week!' Lily Pallister's patience almost gave way. 'I don't want to lose two of them do I, for pity's sake?'

Sara felt her knees shaking at her mother's words. They were arguing over her! Her head swam as she tried to make sense of the conversation she had overheard. Was her mother about to send her away? And what did Uncle Alfred mean saying all those hurtful things about her father and the farm in debt?

Below, the scullery door opened and someone else appeared. It was Tom.

'I'll take you down to the station now,' he said curtly.

'Good lad,' Uncle Alfred nodded and fixed on his black bowler hat with precision. 'At least one of your family shows some promise,' he grunted as Tom went across to the stable to fetch Bluebell and the trap. 'Army's a good living for a fit young lad like Tom – long as there's no war.'

'So your answer's yes?' Lily persisted.

'We'll take her for a few months,' he grumbled. 'But if she proves idle I'll send her packing.'

Sara watched as her uncle clambered up in to the trap without a goodbye kiss to his sister. Tom flicked the reins and Alfred clung on nervously as the vehicle gave a violent lurch forward and Bluebell trotted off down the track.

Sara groped her way back to bed, giddy nausea overwhelming her. She lay shivering under the covers for what seemed like an age before anyone appeared. As the watery evening sun fell in a shaft through the window, there was a tap at the door and her mother entered.

Freed of her dark bonnet, her brown hair sprang thick around her ears and forehead. Her pale brown eyes were dark-shadowed and her smile weary in her square, pallid face.

'How are you, pet?' she asked softly.

'Better,' Sara lied, feeling sick with dread at the recent revelations below her window.

'You've hardly touched the pie,' her mother chided.

'I've not much appetite.'

'No, poor lamb.' Her mother stroked her brow with a cool hand. 'We'll go together to the cemetery when you're feeling stronger, just the two of us.'

'Thanks, Mam,' Sara answered hoarsely. 'I wish I'd been–'

'Don't, pet,' her mother cut short her words of regret and they clung to each other, her mother rocking her in comfort.

'What'll happen now?' Sara whispered into her mother's shoulder. The rocking stopped. 'Are things worse than you thought, Mam?'

'Mr Clark came from the bank on Wednesday,' her mother's voice was steady.

'He could have waited till Dad was buried!' Sara was indignant.

'Mr Clark hadn't heard about the accident,' her mother replied gently. 'It seems he'd arranged to see your father that day. There was a letter, I remember it coming week before last...' Lily's voice trailed away as she puzzled over something.

'What did Mr Clark say?'

'Bill spoke to him mostly.' Her mother was evasive.

'Tell me, Mam,' Sara urged, clutching her mother's hand. 'I'm sixteen now, I should know about the affairs of the family. Don't treat me like a bairn.'

'No,' her mother sighed, 'perhaps that's been

my trouble. I've wanted to keep you all close to me, so you didn't have to grow up too quick like the young'uns at Whitton Grange.' She stroked her daughter's lank fair hair. 'But now you'll have to be grown up.'

'Meaning?' Sara regarded her mother with glazed green eyes.

Lily took a deep breath. 'The farm is badly in debt, has been for years it seems. That's why your father sold off his herd of Shorthorns couple of years ago. Mr Clark suggests we rent the house out – you know, to shooting parties or hikers who want to be up on the moors. Me and Mary'll do the cooking for them. It would mean having to share the cottage with Bill and Mary, but just until we got enough income from the house to pay back what we owe to the bank. And it means we won't have to sell up or leave the farm – at least not yet. He's really been very good about it.'

'Good about it!' Sara exploded. 'Making us give up Stout House? But it's been in Dad's family for generations.'

'I know.' Lily's face creased in pain as she nearly gave in to her own distress. 'But we have no other choice. Otherwise the bank will make us bankrupt. They're only trying to make things a bit easier because of your father's ... death.'

'How are they making things easier by turning us out of our home?' Sara's face flushed with indignation. Her mother gave her a harrowed look.

'Do you want to see the bailiffs come in and auction off what's been in Pallister hands for a century and see us begging for public assistance?

44

'Cos that's the alternative!'

'Of course not,' Sara replied quickly, flinging her arms around her mother's neck. 'I'm sorry.'

Lily steeled herself to carry on. 'So you are going to have to help the family too, Sara.'

'How?' she asked, drawing back warily.

'There'll be precious little room next door for me and Chrissie, so you're to go to Uncle Alfred and Aunt Ida's for a while. It'll be easier finding work there than up here – and we'll need you to work now, pet, every bit will help.' Sara's stomach churned at her mother's words. 'Aren't you the lucky one going back to Whitton Grange?' her mother attempted to joke. 'I've been hankering after the place since I left! Haven't I always bored the neighbours to tears with stories of my days there as a lass?'

'Aye,' Sara answered with a forced smile. 'But Uncle Alfred – what does he think?'

'Oh, he'll be pleased to have you.' Sara knew that for a lie. Her mother continued with forced brightness, 'And you'll be company for Ida. Uncle Alfred's going to enquire about a job for you. It'll all be just grand. They've got a nice house now, by all accounts, overman's house near the green. Three bedrooms and electricity in every room – and a bathroom with an inside toilet, imagine that! And you can come home for visits once you're settled in a new position. Mind you, once you've seen the bright lights of Whitton you'll not want to come home, but!'

'I will,' Sara insisted, smothering her mother with an embrace, knowing the older woman was hiding her grief in a bold show of good humour.

She was still too weak and confused to work out whether she wanted to go away to the pit village down the valley. The violent changes of the past few days were far too sudden for her to comprehend. Should she tell her mother of Sid's proposal now? Sara could no longer think straight, and before she could find the words to tell her secret, her mother was tucking her up in bed and leaving with the half-touched plate of pie.

'I'll pop up with a hot drink later.' She blew a kiss from the doorway and was gone.

It was two weeks before Sara was well enough to go outside again. For the first few days she walked around the fields close to the farm, helping Bill count the lambs. At first she felt light-headed and fragile from the unaccustomed exercise, but gradually she felt her old strength and energy return.

Soon she was walking to the store at Rillhope with eggs from her mother's hens to sell and helping Mary spring clean Stout House in preparation for letting. Bill, with the help of Sid and Mr Gibson, worked on repairing the roof where it leaked into the scullery.

'Given a lick of paint Stout House'll look just grand,' Lily Pallister said stoically as the women sorted through the dresser in the kitchen.

'It seems a shame to leave this in the house,' Mary said, holding up an embroidered table-cloth.

Lily sighed, 'That was my mother's. We embroidered it together before I got wed. Take it next door if you like.' Mary smiled in approval and put it to one side.

Sara shifted restlessly, flicking closed the lid of the box full of possessions that were going for auction at Lilychapel next month. She hated to see her old home dismantled and portioned off and the furniture rearranged to suit strangers.

'I'll go and meet Chrissie from school,' she announced.

'But we've got two more drawers to sort,' Mary said.

'You're better at this than me,' Sara replied and disappeared outside.

'Let her go.' Lily gave her daughter-in-law a warning look. 'She'll be off to Whitton shortly so she might as well enjoy her last few days.'

'Then she'll find out what hard work is all about,' Mary muttered.

Lily watched her daughter dash past the window, her pale gold hair lifting in the breeze and felt a pang of loneliness at the thought of her going. Sara, who looked achingly like her father but was most akin to her in mood and character, would leave a gaping hole in her life when she took the bus to Whitton Grange, Lily thought...

Sara found Sid trundling his old bicycle down the track towards Highbeck. She had seen him leave Stout House with his dirty tweed jacket slung over one shoulder, the repairs to the roof finished. She had avoided him while recuperating from the 'flu, unsure what to say to him. But the words could no longer be delayed.

'Sid!' she cried, running after him. 'Wait on!' He turned and stopped.

'Sid...' she came to a breathless halt at his side, her flyaway hair escaping its ribbon to lick her face. 'How are you?' she felt suddenly foolish, as he returned her look with puzzled blue eyes. He nodded. 'Can I walk with you?' Sara asked, her throat turning dry.

'Aye,' he agreed and began pushing his bicycle again.

She felt a pang of remorse at having avoided Sid; the last thing she wanted was to hurt him.

'Strangers are coming to Stout House next month,' she told him, attempting to draw him out. 'We've nearly sorted everything – it'll need a wagon to take all the stuff for auction. Mam and Mary are going to cook and clean for the visitors, did you know?'

'Aye.' Sid slid her a cautious look, 'Bill said.'

'What else did Bill say?' Sara asked, dreading his reply.

'That you're ganin' to Whitton Grange to live with your uncle.' Sid's voice was flat. Sara slipped a hand on to his arm.

'Come up to the mine with me, Sid,' she asked, her green eyes pleading, 'I can't tell you about it here.'

With a sigh he abandoned his machine and followed her over the stile. Together they climbed the hill and jumped the stone wall that bordered the beck, following the path that snaked upriver to the disused lead mine. Wild primroses were already sprouting out of the rocks about them and the trees were forcing out tiny emerald green buds. Their footsteps echoed against the rock walls of the ravine that used to provide a natural stable for the ponies that worked the mine.

Hopping the stepping stones, Sara led the way to the broken-down wall that marked the entrance to the old washing floor where the lead had been sifted from the stone. Years ago, the large water wheel had been removed for use elsewhere. High above them a curlew gave a mournful, throaty whistle as it dived into a current of air and was swept eastwards. Sara shivered to be so close to the place where her father had died, just a few hundred yards further up the beck. She could not come here alone, but with Sid she felt safe.

'I have to go and find work.' Sara sat on the wall and spoke quietly. 'Mam needs the money I can send home and it'll be one less mouth to feed. And if it means we can save Stout House for future Pallisters then I don't mind going.'

'And what about us?' Sid's tone was reproachful. Sara took one of his rough, grimy hands in hers.

'Before the accident I might have said yes to you, Sid.' She smiled at his ruddy face wistfully. 'But now I'd be marrying you for the wrong reasons. I can't turn me back on the family now and escape its problems – I've promised Mam I'll help out and I will. Uncle Alfred sounds a right stick in the mud, but I can stand up to him.'

'Aye,' Sid smiled ruefully, 'I don't doubt you can.'

'And it won't be for ever,' Sara tried to sound optimistic. 'Uncle Alfred said he'll only have me a few months anyroads.'

'It sounds a long time to me,' Sid said, twisting his cap between strong hands.

'You'll have a bit peace without me around,' she smiled.

'Are we still courting?' Sid's question was almost inaudible.

Sara regarded him with frank green eyes. 'I'm not ready for marriage yet, Sid,' she said softly. 'I'm only sixteen and I've got to find me feet in the world. I've been gaddin' about like a silly bairn full of fancy ideas about filmstars. But life's not going to be like that, is it? I've only come to see that since Dad...' Her eyes pricked as she thought of her father, she could not bring herself to use the word 'died' in this haunted spot.

Sid nodded resignedly and jammed on his cap. 'I'll miss thee, lass.' Sara turned her face up to his and they kissed briefly, affectionately on the lips. She felt a wave of tenderness for Sid, so physically strong, yet so gentle and mild mannered with her.

Sliding off the wall, Sara whispered, 'Will you show me where Dad – you know – please, Sid?'

He looked at her, aghast, for a moment. 'I don't think–'

'I need to know where, before I go,' she insisted.

Sid flushed but he took her hand and led her up the sheep's path that clung to the edge of the beck. Five minutes later they reached the top of the ravine where the waterfall plunged deafeningly on to the black slimy rocks below. Today the water sparkled like liquid silver in the early May sun, not like that fateful Sunday, Sara thought, when it must have roared and fumed in a brown, boiling cascade.

'He was standing on the far side.' Sid pointed grimly. 'I was coming up the path below.'

'But what was he doing there?' Sara asked perplexed. 'The ewes were two fields away. Was he after a stray?'

Sid shrugged, uncomfortable with the question. 'More than likely.'

'What happened next?'

Sid gulped. He could not describe to her the picture that had plagued him since that twilit afternoon. The light had been bad and it was raining hard, so he must have been mistaken. Yet try as he may, he could not get the thought out of his head that Richard Pallister had hurled himself off the top of the ravine into the turbulence below. Sid had tracked his movements across the fell, trying to pluck up the courage to ask the farmer's approval in marrying his daughter. But Pallister had acted strangely, not checking on his sheep at all as he roamed the rain-sodden moors, before suddenly switching direction and heading for the beck. He had called up to Sara's father, but the noise of the waterfall had drowned his appeals. The man had looked up to the sky and shouted something, then jumped.

Sara's eyes watched him keenly, awaiting his answer, as if she, too, suspected there had been no accident.

'He slipped,' Sid replied in a small voice. And took with him my chances of marrying his daughter, Sid thought to himself with bitterness.

Sara's distressed face looked down at the rushing water. 'There wasn't any hope, was there, even if I'd found the doctor?'

51

'None,' Sid assured her.

Sara gulped back tears, banishing the vision of her father plunging to his death. The place held no fears for her now, just a desperate emptiness. For the first time she was swept with relief that she would soon be leaving Stout House behind and the grief that rang around its walls. The strange world of Whitton Grange might frighten her, but nothing would remind her of the loss of her dear father as did this desolate beck and the rugged hills around.

'Thanks, Sid,' she whispered. 'I best be gettin' back.'

Descending in silence to the stile by the farm track, they parted.

'I'll see you before I leave,' Sara promised, pushing strands of hair out of her face.

Even in her old, darned school skirt and green jumper unravelling at the sleeve, Sid thought her beautiful. He nodded and watched Sara rush back up the dirt road to Stout House. He saw, with regret, that Sara Pallister did not look back.

Chapter Three

Changing buses at Stanhope marked Sara's final farewell to the Dales. Leaving behind the solid, sandy-coloured farmhouses and the rugged patchwork of fields dotted with quietly grazing sheep, she was suddenly swamped by the bustle of the market town.

'Parker's is o'er there,' a man answered Sara's anxious question as to which bus would take her to Whitton Grange. 'Green dirty one,' the man nodded and hurried on.

Clutching the small suitcase that her mother had brought with her as a young bride to Stout House, Sara scurried across the street, dodging the traffic of farm carts, milk lorry, butcher's van and bicycles.

'Going all the way to Durham, pet?' asked the beaky-nosed driver.

'Whitton Grange,' Sara croaked, her throat dry and tight with crying.

'Right you are,' he smiled and grabbed her case, helping her on board. Already seated were two middle-aged women nursing shopping baskets, a young mother with a fractious baby hidden in a frilly coat and hat and three men bent over the same newspaper. Sara was struck by the thought that she recognised nobody; for the first time in her life there was no familiar face to which she could turn and share her apprehension. Feeling the pressure of fresh tears building up behind her eyes, she sat down quickly and stared through the window at the chaotic street outside.

'Visiting family, are you?' the bus driver asked pleasantly.

Sara gulped and nodded, but could not trust herself to speak.

'I'm a Whitton Grange man m'sel,' he smiled and began lighting a cigarette. 'What's your family's name?'

Clearing her throat Sara managed to say, 'I'm a Pallister – but me Mam's family are Cummings. I'm going to stop with me Uncle Alfred.'

'Alf Cummings?' the driver blew out a ball of smoke. 'Overman at the Eleanor?'

'You know him?' Sara asked.

The man grunted. 'We used to scrap when we were lads – always fighting was Alf Cummings – bad-tempered bugger, your uncle.' The driver grinned. Sara flushed at his bluntness; she could not imagine her serious uncle being involved in anything as unseemly as a fight. The driver continued, 'So you'll be Lily Cummings's daughter?'

'Aye,' Sara said, feeling a rush of gratitude at his interest. 'You know Mam, too?'

'Bonny lass, your mam was,' he flicked ash out of the open window. ''Course, haven't set eyes on her for years. Married a farmer, didn't she?'

Sara's eyes stung with tears as she nodded. 'Me dad died last month. That's why I have to gan to me uncle's – he's going to find me a job.' Seeing her distress, the bus driver patted her shoulder briefly.

'Sorry, pet. Must be hard on you.'

54

Then a flurry of last-minute passengers arrived with luggage, children and two dogs and he flicked his cigarette butt out of the window and went to help them on board.

Sara shuffled up to make room for a young man in naval uniform and she thought of Tom back with his regiment. Only last week the wireless had announced the introduction of conscription for twenty- and twenty-one-year-old men. Until then, she had taken no real notice of the talk of war on the Continent or Tom's heated arguments with their father over Germany's occupation of Czechoslovakia. Oh Dad! He would have been appalled at the preparations for war; he had forbidden any talk of preparing a shelter from air attack in the old lead mine. But her father was not here to dispute with this young sailor, would never be there to protect his family again and his going had overshadowed all other concerns about what might be happening beyond Stout House. And although the sight of a uniform was unnerving, Sara could not imagine war coming to this busy market town with everyone hurrying about their business in the spring sunshine.

The bus coughed and revved into life and they edged their way through the town with noisy splutters from behind. Sara watched the fells suddenly unravel into gentle, rolling hills covered in woods and untidy hedgerows rushing along beside the road. The countryside was studded with tightly packed redbrick villages sending up smoke from their chimneys and gathered around spinning pit wheels.

The sun through the window was hot on Sara's

face and the bus stuffy with the smell of humans, dogs and cigarette smoke. By the time it had wound its way around outlying communities dropping off and picking up passengers and provisions, Sara felt queasy from the unaccustomed motion. The sailor, whose name was Frank Robson, was telling her he had been visiting an aunt in Stanhope before going to join his new ship, his training finished. Her throat watered ominously, but she fought back the urge to be sick. She nodded or shook her head in reply to his chatter and it was with relief she heard the driver call to her that the next stop would be Whitton Grange.

Taking her mind off her sickness, Sara craned for a better view of her new home. They were passing a pretty stone-built church set in a leafy graveyard, its noticeboard proclaiming it as St Cuthbert's Parish Church. She was struck by the number of trees camouflaging the town. On the nearside stretched a wooded dene, its trees bursting with fresh, lime-green leaves and, beyond it, an impressive row of grand redbrick villas isolated from each other by high garden walls. Sara was quite astonished by what she saw, not in the least expecting to find such wealth and grandeur in a mining town. Her spirits raised a fraction.

But as the bus chugged nearer to the town itself, she noticed that the stream through the dene was shiny with oil and a rusting coal tub and other debris lay piled on its banks. A railway track ran parallel to the road and a labouring engine pulling full trucks of coal panted past with a piercing whistle that made Sara jump.

'You'll get used to it,' Frank the sailor said with amusement. 'You'll find the country too quiet after a bit, believe me.'

Sara gave an anxious smile and peered at the rows of blackened brick houses marching up the hill as the bus turned and groaned at the incline. Each terrace was belching smoke into the blue sky, an acrid haze that pinched the nostrils and covered the town in a veil of grey. The bus eased along a wide street lined with shops, their faded, striped canopies shading windows packed with tins of pilchards and semolina, displays of tea and cigarettes. An ironmonger's had pails and brushes hanging outside its door and a strange-looking metal contraption blocking the pavement, advertising itself as a modern washing machine.

Groups of men stood chatting in the sun, dressed in suits of dark blue and black with large caps shading their faces. The driver hooted with impatience as shoppers crossed the road in front of the bus.

'South Street!' the driver called as the bus juddered to a stop outside the imposing entrance to the co-operative store. Across the road, people were queuing for a cinema proclaiming itself in brash lettering to be The Palace. Sara craned to see what film was showing. Cary Grant and Carol Lombard were starring in something, but she could not see the name. The young woman with the baby alighted, her child now asleep in her arms, the driver handing down her carpet bag.

'Where do you want to be?' he asked Sara.

'South Parade – by the green.'

He nodded. 'I'll drop you off on the way out–

couple more stops. Just sit tight.' He swung into his seat again and they pulled away, sending puffs of dust into the crowds of Saturday strollers.

After South Street the road narrowed and the houses seemed to close in about the bus as if to stare curiously at its passengers, Sara thought. Grubby children stopped their skipping and football games to watch and wave, while hot-faced women came to their back doors and blinked in the strong sunlight. She saw small shops on every corner and a pale boy standing on one leg outside a barber's, sucking a bright orange stick. The noise of voices calling in play wafted in through the window and a strange hissing and clanking of machinery that Sara could not locate.

They stopped outside a large, square chapel and the fresh-faced sailor stood up.

'I hope you like Whitton,' he smiled at Sara. 'The people are canny.'

'Ta.' Sara smiled back nervously. 'And good luck on your ship.'

'Enjoy the rest of your leave, Frank.' The driver put out his hand as the young man swung down his duffle bag.

'Ta-ra, Mr Parker,' he grinned and disappeared down the steps.

The bus stopped again at the top of the town just past some tall iron gates which led into the pit yard and revealed the source of the deafening, incessant noise. Towering above them were the massive buildings around the pithead, housing the engines that drove the caged wheels. They whirred furiously and steam hissed, while through the gates Sara glimpsed a trail of wagons shunting across a zig-zag of tracks and a pile of freshly-cut timber waiting to be moved. This must be the Eleanor pit where her uncle worked, Sara thought. Or was it the Beatrice? She was not sure. From up the valley she had seen the two Whitton Grange pits straddling the hillside like grim sentries keeping watch.

Four men climbed on board and Sara smothered her gasp of horror. They were filthy black. Red-ringed eyes stared out from coal-blackened faces, their lips strangely pink and moving rapidly as they greeted Mr Parker. The bus driver seemed unconcerned when they sat their damp grey trousers down on his seats and continued their conversation. They were smallish men but broad-backed in their dusty jackets, with dirty strips of material around their coal-engrained necks in place of ties.

'Grand day,' one of them said, offering the driver a cigarette from a battered tin.

'Champion,' agreed Mr Parker, accepting the gift. He lit up before starting the engine again. 'Grange were winning two-nil 'gainst Waterhouses when we went through,' he reported.

'Bloody great!' The younger smoker clenched his fist in triumph. 'We'll win the Pitmen's Cup next week.'

'Bet two bob we don't,' grunted a stoop-backed older man, aiming a spit out of the open door.

'Five,' the young man grinned.

'Done!' They shook on it.

'Half a day's wages!' a third man exclaimed in a reedy, wheezing voice. 'You're daft, the pair o' you.'

Sara stared at their large, dirty, callused hands.

She was used to seeing earth-ingrained working hands, but these men looked as if their whole bodies had been rolled in black flour. They smelt of rock and sweat, a musty, mineral smell.

She was so transfixed by their appearance and their strange talk of tub loading and other mysteries of their craft, that she did not realise the bus had stopped for her.

'South Parade, pet,' Mr Parker prompted, lifting down her case. Sara eased herself past the miners, hoping her best summer frock of pale blue flowers would not catch their dirt. The young one touched his cap at her ironically, reading the distaste in her face. Sara blushed and climbed hurriedly down the steps.

They were outside a row of modern semi-detached houses with tiny, neat gardens that faced on to a rough patch of ground that Sara took to be the green. Two skinny dogs with arching backs and pointed snouts were running across it ahead of a bulky youth in a too-tight jacket.

'There's your cousin, Colin Cummings,' the driver pointed to the dog owner. 'Never apart from those whippets, that lad.' Sara stared at the retreating figure, but did not recognise him as the gangling boy she remembered from their distant holiday in Redcar. 'Tell your uncle, Parker was askin' after him – the old bugger!'

'Aye – thanks,' Sara stuttered in confusion, but returned his friendly smile. The tired engine of the bus revved once more and, with a wave from Mr Parker, roared off towards the dene, carrying its passengers to the Durham road.

Sara turned nervously and looked along the row

of tidy houses, their windows modestly covered in frilly nets against prying eyes. Number sixteen stood before her. The Cummingses lived at number thirteen. She gulped, dismissing the unlucky connotations of a dozen and one. Walking slowly up the street, she spotted the dark blue door of her uncle's respectable residence, its front garden bedecked in straight rows of yellow pansies, behind them a crop of faded daffodils ruthlessly chopped off at the heads. Sara found her palms sweating and her grip on her case slippy. Her heart beat quicker the nearer she stepped. She tried to think of the good things her mother had told her she would find – piped hot water and an inside toilet and her seven-year-old cousin Marina to befriend. But all she could think of was how hemmed-in the house seemed, how orderly its pocket-sized garden, pinned in the middle of this large sooty sprawling town that the locals called a village.

Sara told herself to show a bit of Pallister spirit. She would *not* be over-awed by this noisy place or its confident worldly inhabitants. Raising her small chin and taking a deep breath, Sara flicked open the catch on the blue-painted gate and marched up the path, aware of a downstairs net curtain disturbed out of its correct position. Sara knocked on the front door.

Joe Dimarco roared up Hawthorn Street on his motorcycle with Pat Slattery whooping on the pillion at the scattering backlane footballers. They spluttered to a halt outside number 28, home of their boxing coach, Sam Ritson, and dismounted.

'Afternoon, Mrs Ritson!' Joe called as he strolled through the backyard, catching a glimpse of Sam's wife Louie at the scullery sink of the colliery house. 'Mr Ritson at home?'

'Hello, lads,' the tall woman with the pasty round face replied, pushing back a wave of fair hair that had escaped its grip. 'Sam's in-by,' – she nodded beyond the scullery door – 'he's off to a meeting, shortly.'

'How you keeping, Mrs Ritson?' Joe asked pleasantly, pausing before going further. Louie smiled at the lanky youth with the lively dark eyes and goggles pushed up over spiky black hair. Of all Sam's 'boys' who drifted in and out of their dilapidated home and its smoke-filled kitchen, she liked Joe, the chatty Italian, best, but tried not to let it show.

'Oh, full of busy, Joe, thank you. How are your family – I hear Domenica's getting married soon?'

'Not soon enough!' Joe grinned. 'That's all my sister ever talks about – Pasquale Perella and the wedding! Mam and Granny Maria are just as bad. You would think no one had ever got married before.'

'Well, it's a special time for a lass,' Louie reproved, wiping her hands on her faded apron and hiding a smirk. 'Don't you go spoiling her fun. Hello, Pat,' she acknowledged the other boy. 'How's your mother?'

'Not too grand, Mrs Ritson.' Joe's red-haired friend pulled a face. 'And my sister Minnie's home again – more hindrance than help.'

Joe saw Louie sigh with concern that Pat's sister should have once again left her bad-tempered husband Bomber Bell and gone back to the Slattery home. Pat was the seventh in a family of eleven and Joe had no idea how many relations his friend had, just that he seemed to have far more than his fair share.

'I'm sorry. Tell Minnie I'll be over to see her next week,' Louie said with a warning look, bustling them into the kitchen. 'You'll have a glass of ginger beer, lads?'

'Aye, that'd be grand, Mrs Ritson,' Joe smiled, stooping slightly to avoid the low doorway.

He glanced round quickly and saw, with relief, that Louie's Bible-thumping, white-haired father, Jacob Kirkup, was not occupying his worn arm-chair by the range. The old man, with his fierce blue eyes and tremulous voice, always made Joe feel he had sprouted devil's horns and a forked tail in his presence.

Sam Ritson sat at the kitchen table, brawny-shouldered in his vest, drinking a cup of tea and concentrating hard on a copy of the *Daily Herald*. He was barely forty, yet his square-jawed face was channelled with age, his dark hair receding in two peaks across his scalp.

'Lads,' he grunted at their arrival, his dour expression showing no surprise.

'Going down the club this afternoon, Mr Ritson?' Joe asked, straddling a stool at the table. Since he and Pat had been runny-nosed nine-year-olds they had haunted Sam's boxing gym, watching him teach the older boys how to fight with discipline and aggression. Then it had been their turn and they had learned how to handle themselves in fist fights in the damp, leaking hut on Daniel Street that passed for a gym and which the club shared with the Pentecostalists.

'Got a lodge meeting,' Sam shook his head. 'There's a lad speaking who's just been released by Franco's fascists – fought in the civil war. And there'll be discussion about this conscription business.' Sam waded into the subject that was uppermost in his mind. 'There'll be a formal protest from the union, of course – people say it makes war more likely – but I'm not so sure Churchill doesn't have a point this time – bullies need to be stood up to...'

'Churchill!' Louie scoffed as she entered with two glasses of home-made ginger beer. 'Sam Ritson. I never thought I'd hear the day when you'd praise him!'

'I'll never forgive him for the harm he did us in '26,' Sam was defensive. 'I'd've tipped him in the Thames for helping to break our strike, if I'd got my hands on him then, so I would. But this foreign business is different, Louie. Look at the way the Nazis have persecuted the trade unions – and what do our government do? Bugger all, that's what!'

Joe took the proffered glass from Mrs Ritson and exchanged an amused glance with Pat. It had been like this in the Ritson household for as long as they had been coming here, begging Louie's biscuits and making themselves at home by her fireside, playing cards with her nephew Raymond Kirkup in this cramped musty cottage when it was too wet to kick a football against the wall in the backlane.

Over the years they had half listened to Sam's political outbursts against the government and coalowners who had kept him unemployed for most of the decade, and against the fascists in Spain and Germany. Joe and Pat had helped him in door-to-door collections in support of Spanish workers, then Czech workers, Austrian political refugees and German Jews, not because they understood half of what Sam said, but because they admired him for his robust strength and loved him for the unsentimental way he took an interest in lads like them, when everyone else was belting them for getting in the way.

'It could've been me – that Spanish prisoner – he was with the International Brigade.' Sam reverted to his original topic. 'An unemployed pitman,' he added pointedly, as Louie refilled his cup.

'Don't start that again,' she said wearily.

Three years ago, as fourteen-year-olds and willing pupils in Sam's boxing club, Joe and Pat had taken Louie's side and protested against Sam going to Spain to fight for the Republicans. They had won, but a thwarted Sam had disappeared for a month on a hunger march to London and then stood unsuccessfully in the 1937 elections for the Independent Labour Party. Bad-tempered in defeat and frustrated by his impotence, Sam filled his idle days with political crusades and took out his anger on the boxing bag. Louie had once let slip that the coalowners, the Seward-Scotts, would never let Sam work in any of their mines again, after his leadership in the 1926 strike. For years he had been known as Red Sam Ritson, feared even within the union for his radicalism and in the boxing ring for his right-hand punch. Sam was a rebel who had once been imprisoned and Joe, forever in trouble with his law-abiding parents, came close to hero-worshipping him.

Only once, when Joe was thirteen, had his adoration of Sam Ritson been tarnished; when the Italians bombed their way into Abyssinia. Joe's Italian parents had sent precious money and jewellery to finance the Italian effort, swelling with pride that their country was now returning to its days of Roman glory, while Sam had fulminated against the butchering of defenceless Africans by fascist thugs. Joe's loyalty to his family had led him into a bitter argument with his coach, bragging about Mussolini being a modern-day Roman emperor. Sam had battered him relentlessly with evidence of Italian atrocities and Joe, his pride and feelings severely wounded, had withdrawn and stayed away from the club for several months.

Only when Louie had invited Joe round for tea on her nephew Raymond's eleventh birthday had they patched up their quarrel in front of a cosy fire in Louie's homely, threadbare kitchen and Joe had volunteered to deliver leaflets for one of Sam's endless causes. So Joe knew better than to enter the fray when Sam's temper was roused.

'Raymond playing footy tomorrow?' Joe changed the subject.

'Aye,' Louie nodded, pouring a second cup from the stewed pot and allowing herself to sit for a minute. 'Boys' Brigade. He's out practising now. Either of you playing for the Catholics?'

'Not picked,' said Pat.

'I'll be working,' Joe answered, slurping at the pop.

'Shouldn't you be out now selling that ice-

66

cream of yours – on a sunny afternoon like this?'
Louie asked suspiciously.

'I am,' Joe laughed, unconcerned. 'Pat's helped
me fix up a drum on the motorbike – like a
sidecar. We're on our way to the park for a bit of
business.'

'To watch football, more likely!' Louie commented with a wry smile.

'I thought you were going to the club?' Sam
stood up and pulled on his shirt. He was a head
smaller than Joe, but his muscled body was alert
and powerful. The boys stood up too.

'Later,' Joe said, finishing off his drink in a gulp.
'If my slave-driving father ever gives me a minute
off.'

Louie snorted. 'Mr Dimarco's one of the
kindest men I've met – and I don't know how he
puts up with you racing around on that motor
machine all day long. You live the life of royalty.'

Joe laughed, enjoying her teasing disapproval.

'Haway, Joe, let's go and put Raymond off his
practising.' Pat pulled at his arm. 'Ta for the
drink, Mrs Ritson.'

'Off you go and keep out of trouble.' Louie
waved them out of her kitchen.

'Ta-ra, Mrs Ritson,' Joe smiled. 'Mr Ritson.'

'I'll come out with you,' Sam said, putting on
his jacket. 'Be back for tea, pet,' he told his wife
and led the boys into the yard, his mind already
on the afternoon's agenda.

'Want a lift, Mr Ritson?' Joe asked. 'Pat can
walk.' Pat stifled a protest.

'Nowt wrong with my feet, is there?' Sam
answered with a grunt, unimpressed by Joe's

67

ancient but cherished Triumph. 'You lads should do more walking – I used to walk ten miles a day as well as a hard day's graft before they closed the Cathedral pit by Ushaw.' They had heard him say so dozens of times before, but Joe could not remember ever seeing Sam dirty from pit work like old Jacob Kirkup or Pat's elder brothers. Pat scrambled back on to the bike with relief.

'I'll be down the club Monday. Thinking of putting on a fight for the Carnival, if you're interested?'

'Aye!' the boys answered together. Joe pulled down his goggles and started up the noisy machine. He revved it for a moment in front of an admiring crowd of curious children, enjoying the attention, and then swerved around, scattering them like startled chickens. He picked up speed down the bumpy terraced street and rode off in search of excitement and Olive Brown, last year's Carnival Queen.

Chapter Four

Sara's knock on the freshly painted door of 13 South Parade was answered at once by a small girl with plaited brown hair and a quizzical frown. She stood defensively on the sanded doorstep and stared hard with close-set blue eyes.

'Are you Sara?' she demanded suspiciously.

'Aye,' Sara smiled, although nervousness tugged at her stomach. 'And you must be cousin Marina?'

The girl continued to appraise her with shrewd eyes. 'I'll get Mam,' she said at last and closed the door. Sara hardly had time to recover from this rebuff when the door opened again and Aunt Ida appeared. She was smaller than Sara had remembered, but the crinkly brown hair and pale blue eyes set close to the bridge of her nose were unmistakably Aunt Ida's.

'Come in, Sara,' she said hastily, but without reproving her daughter for her rudeness. 'You must be tired after your journey. It's too hot out there for my liking. Is that all the luggage you have?' Her florid face showed surprise. 'Never mind, come away. Colin!' She turned and called timidly over her shoulder, 'Come and help Sara with her case.'

Sara did not like to say she had seen Colin escaping across the green just moments before. 'You'll be sharing a room with Marina and I'm sure you'll get on like a house on fire. Colin!'

Sara nodded, but caught sight of her young

cousin's resentful face peering round her mother's crisp pink-and-yellow patterned frock.

'That boy's never around when he's needed – always under my feet when he's not,' she fussed.

'I can carry it,' Sara insisted, looking around with interest.

The small hallway was decorated in green and orange triangles and the gleaming, polished floor was covered in a strip of carpet with orange and brown swirls that snaked away up the steep staircase ahead of them. A small table displayed a large black telephone and a note pad beside it, otherwise the floor was empty. Everything seemed to have taken to the walls, Sara thought in astonishment. They were covered in embroidered pictures and china ducks in flight, while the high dado rail was crowded with jugs in the shape of fat-faced men and jolly monks jostling for space. Catching sight of herself in a round, gilded mirror Sara was dismayed to see her pink face perspiring and her fair hair trailing loose under her beret.

'We'll have a cup of tea in the parlour,' Aunt Ida continued to prattle. 'Just leave the case at the foot of the stairs and Marina can show you your room in a minute. Father'll be back shortly from the Institute – plays billiards there every Saturday – but he's never late for tea. Your Uncle Alfred doesn't like anyone being late for tea.' She threw Sara a look of caution. 'Come in and sit down.' She pushed open a cream-painted door into a brightly lit room flooded with the afternoon sun.

It was crammed with furniture and ornaments and lamps with fringed shades and clocks and photographs in pigskin frames. 'I'll warm the pot.

Marina – take Sara's beret.' Marina remained clinging to her mother's dress. 'Go and sit with cousin Sara, now, Marina pet.'

Reluctantly her daughter allowed herself to be coaxed from behind the screen of pink and yellow cotton. Aunt Ida hurried away and Sara sat on the edge of a floral-patterned seat listening to the clink of china cups in the kitchen. Marina swung her legs back and forth between the arms of two chairs, without taking her eyes off Sara. Sara took off her beret and smoothed back damp hair.

'Your hair needs washing,' the young girl commented.

Sara flushed, but answered quickly, 'Aye, I know. I'd like to have a bath before chapel tomorrow. Always bath on a Saturday night at home.'

Marina laughed loudly as if she had said something amusing. 'We don't go to chapel.' She assumed a superior air. 'Mam and me go to St Cuthbert's. It's for posh people, but you can come with us if you like. The Seward-Scotts go to St Cuthbert's – they sit in the gallery.'

Sara had no idea who the Seward-Scotts might be, but from Marina's tone she knew she ought to be impressed.

'Uncle Alfred goes to chapel though, doesn't he?' she asked, trying not to appear ruffled by the girl's condescending manner.

'Daddy doesn't go to church or chapel unless it's Christmas or somebody dies or there's a christening. He goes to the club on Sundays – not the men's club – the officials' club – the posh one.' Marina's small, narrow face allowed a smile of satisfaction. 'We can't start Sunday dinner

71

until Daddy comes home.'

Aunt Ida bustled in with a huge tray of cups, tea plates and mounds of scones and sandwiches and a large sponge cake with orange icing.

'Can I help?' Sara asked, unnerved by her aunt's frantic activity.

'Pull out that table over there, Sara,' her aunt indicated with her thin eyebrows, 'and put the flaps up.' Sara arranged the gate-leg table as instructed. She took the starched white tablecloth from under her aunt's arm and spread it out. Aunt Ida glanced worriedly at one of the clocks, a dainty carriage clock on the mantelpiece with Roman numerals.

'Father will be home any minute,' she said as if to reassure herself. 'He likes the tea just so – not too stewed – but not too weak. Men hate weak tea, don't you find?'

Sara had never given it a thought, but did not say so.

'And cousin Colin?' she enquired. 'Will he be having tea with us?'

'Oh, that lad!' Aunt Ida said with exasperation. 'He pleases himself. He'd rather eat in the yard with those wretched dogs, given half a chance. I've tried to teach him proper manners, but he'll not be taught. His own mother was far too soft on him, of course, God rest her soul. Spare the rod and spoil the child, I say. Father's the only one he takes heed of, does Colin.'

Sara did not remember Uncle Alfred's first wife, for Aunt Susan had died when Sara was quite small. But her mother had told her that Uncle Alfred had soon married Ida, the housekeeper, who had come to help him look after his young son.

That must have been when they lived in a small terraced house next to a butcher's shop. Sara's only recollection of visiting there as a small girl was of strings of sausages displayed in the window like garlands.

Aunt Ida turned to see Marina poking her finger into the butter icing on the sponge cake. 'Marina, poppet, don't spoil your appetite.' Marina licked her fingertip and then reached out for a thin drop scone spread with butter and jam. She shovelled it into her small, round mouth. 'Well, just the one,' Aunt Ida said weakly. 'But don't let your father catch you.'

The older woman left the room to fetch the teapot. Marina swallowed hard and quickly reached for another scone, defying Sara with mischievous blue eyes.

'You heard what your mother said,' Sara warned. But Marina stuck out her small pink tongue, then crammed the whole scone between elastic lips. Sara itched to smack her insolent face, but Aunt Ida returned with another trayload and placed the tea and hot-water jug on a side table with the milk and sugar and cups of pink and white china. If she saw Marina's bulging cheeks, she chose to ignore the disobedience.

A door slammed and a voice called, 'I'm home!'

Aunt Ida's hands flew to pat her permed hair, though not a strand was out of place. Sara wished she had had time to rearrange hers and wash her sticky face.

'Daddy!' Marina flew to the door, her scone digested in seconds. She jumped up at the small, stout man who entered and demanded, 'Have you brought me anything? What have you got behind your back? Show me, show me!'

He teased her a second more and then produced a package with a laugh. 'For my little pet!' He kissed her head, but she had turned away and was already tearing at the brown paper bag. He turned to his wife and asked curtly, 'Tea ready?'

She nodded anxiously towards Sara hovering in the corner and Alfred Cummings's face creased into stern lines as he saw her.

'So you're here,' he grunted.

'Aye.' Sara gave him a nervous smile. 'Mr Parker the bus driver said to send his best,' she said, trying to win his approval. She wondered if she should give her uncle a kiss? He had not come to see her at her father's funeral, when she had lain upstairs full of misery. He was little more than a stranger. Sara stuck out her hand instead.

'Parker?' he answered suspiciously, ignoring her gesture.

'Aye, he said you used to be friends – as lads.' Sara dropped her hand, feeling foolish.

'Oh, aye, Parker,' Uncle Alfred repeated with disinterest. 'Still driving that clapped-out old bus.' He turned away from his niece. 'Get the tea poured, Ida,' he said and waved an imperious hand.

'Yes, Father!' Aunt Ida smiled and rushed to unveil the teapot, beginning the ritual of pouring and adding milk. With dainty pincers she dropped four sugar lumps into Alfred's cup and handed it to her husband as he settled himself into a deep armchair with lace antimacassars protecting the flowered upholstery.

74

'Milk and sugar?' Aunt Ida asked, turning to Sara.

'Just milk, thank you.' Sara squirmed at the formality.

'Pass me them sandwiches, lass,' Uncle Alfred ordered. As Marina was now absorbed in eating the strands of red liquorice that her father had bought her, Sara assumed he was speaking to her. She handed him a plate which he piled high with dainty triangular sandwiches of white bread with their crusts cut off. Sara felt a twinge of longing for her mother's thick wedges of homemade loaf spread thick with cheesy farm butter and honey from the hives at Thimble Hill.

'How's your mother?' Uncle Alfred asked at last, through the churning of paste sandwiches.

'She's managing, thank you,' Sara replied. 'But it's a good job our Bill's around to help with the farm. And Mary, too – she's going to cook for the visitors who come to Stout House.' Sara had not imagined that she would miss her bossy sister-in-law, but at that moment she did.

'Well, I've got work for you, young lady,' Alfred grunted. 'Dolly Sergeant can do with a bit help in her grocery shop. She's a widow – old Sergeant was a marra of mine. It'll just be stacking shelves and doing the running around, but.'

'Father,' Ida murmured, 'there's plenty time to tell Sara about Dolly Sergeant's shop when she's had a bite to eat. Help yourself to the sandwiches, Sara.'

'No time like the present,' her husband scowled. 'The lass should be grateful she's got som'at so soon. I'll not have her getting in your way, Ida, or spoiling the running of the house. And you'll be that busy with preparations for the Carnival.'

'I'm sure Sara will be a help around the house, not a hindrance.' Ida smiled at her shyly. 'Won't you, dear?'

'Of course,' Sara replied, trying to hide her dismay at the future they had planned for her.

'Well, make sure you are,' Alfred gave Sara a stern look. 'Now, pass us a piece of that orange cake.'

Sara's appetite deserted her in the face of her uncle's hostility; she knew his response to taking her in had been lukewarm, but she had not expected this abrupt coldness. She struggled to see some resemblance to her mother's kindly face, so quick to bestow an encouraging smile or conspiratorial wink, but there was none. Uncle Alfred's eyes might be the same pale brown, she thought, but they were small and hard like polished brown nuts. Sara chewed disconsolately on the starchy bread, watching Marina twirl liquorice around her fingers and snap bits off in her mouth, returning her look with a satisfied smirk.

Somewhere a door banged open and then shut with the same violence, setting the thin china rattling in fright. Aunt Ida jumped, and Marina looked round warily at the parlour door. Muffled barking subsided as heavy footsteps clumped along the passageway and the noisy intruder entered. A large young man lumbered into the room, his long, lugubrious face set impassively below a shaggy fringe showing the indentation of where his cap had been. Heavily jowled like his father, Colin Cummings looked older than his seventeen years, yet his nose was button-shaped like a little boy's and his blue eyes showed youthful resentment at the sight of his elders.

'What time do you call this?' Alfred barked at his son, startling Sara who was expecting to be introduced to her cousin.

'I had a meetin' with the trainer.' Colin's reply was defensive.

'Tea is always at five o'clock,' his father glared. 'If those bloody dogs are more important than your own family then you can go and eat your tea with them.'

Colin stood for a moment as if unsure of his father's threat. He glanced at Sara and she saw a flood of embarrassment rise from his thick neck into his flaccid cheeks. Her throat dried up at the thought of his humiliation, this huge, ungainly youth being treated like a naughty schoolboy in front of his newly arrived cousin. She felt pity for him and it must have shown because his face set in a scowl at her.

'Go on, get out!' his father ordered, flicking crumbs off his striped waistcoat and wide worsted suit trousers.

Colin's small mouth drew in as if bottling up a retort and he retreated from the room. Aunt Ida said nothing, quickly asking Sara if she would like her teacup refilled. Sara handed it over without a word, a tense knot gripping her stomach. Marina drew closer to her father's knees and began to chatter about a visit to the park. Uncle Alfred smiled down at her, with an indulgent pat on her head, as if nothing had happened.

A few minutes elapsed, then Ida asked, 'Shall I

clear away now, Father?' Her smile was nervous as she sought her husband's approval. He nodded. Sara saw her aunt put the remaining sandwiches on to the tea tray.

'I'll help you,' Sara volunteered at once, not relishing the thought of being left alone with Marina and her surly father. Uncle Alfred gave a further nod of approval and she followed Ida out of the airless parlour, bearing the half-demolished cake.

'He doesn't mean anything by his outbursts,' Aunt Ida whispered to her in the safety of the passageway. 'It's just Colin can be so awkward. It's his own fault, silly lad. Come and I'll introduce you.'

Sara entered the small kitchen behind her aunt. It was decorated in bright yellow tiles and black linoleum, with a view from the sink into the backyard where some dishcloths were drying on a washing line. One side of the room was taken up by a large white stove with gleaming metal hoods over the hotplates and the remaining walls were lined with orderly cupboards painted in primrose yellow. A door led off into a walk-in pantry where plates of cheese and cold meat were covered in domed frames of white netting.

Colin sat hunched on the back doorstep, fondling the heads of two fleshless, skinny-faced dogs. They looked mean and ugly, Sara thought, compared to Cathy, her father's gentle-eyed sheepdog.

'This is your cousin Sara,' Ida told him. 'Say hello, Colin.'

'Hello,' he mumbled, half twisting to look at her, but not leaving go of his hounds.

'Hello, Colin.' Sara's smile was tentative. One

of the grey dogs barked at her in suspicion.

'Easy, boy,' Colin quietened him and he snuffled in to his palm.

'What are they called?' Sara asked.

'This one's Flash and this one's Gypsy.' They licked as they heard their names. Sara could not tell them apart.

'I like dogs. Can I touch them?' She stepped forward. Flash growled.

'They don't take to strangers easy like,' Colin warned. Sara put out her hand to the quieter dog. It sniffed at her curiously. She patted Gypsy's head and got a lick in return.

'I don't like to touch them myself,' Ida shuddered as she cut some meat from the cold knuckle of ham taken from the larder. 'Animals are such dirty creatures – I won't have them in the house, will I, Colin?' She shoved a plate of food towards him. 'Now don't let them have any of it – they're greedy beasts for all they're as skinny as string beans.'

'Me dad had a working dog,' Sara smiled wistfully. 'Cathy. Bill's got her now. I miss her a lot.' Colin nodded as if he understood. 'Are yours just pets?' she asked.

'Na,' he answered with aggression in his voice, 'these are workin' dogs an' all. I'm going to race them once they're trained. Flash and Gypsy are ganin' to make me plenty money one of these days.'

Sara saw Ida roll her eyes in disbelief.

'One of these days you'll land yourself a proper job like your father,' she insisted, 'instead of hanging around with gypsy trainers and the like and looking for easy winnings.' Colin threw her a resentful look which she missed as she swept the ham back under cover in the pantry.

'I'll show you upstairs, Sara,' said Ida when she returned, 'then you can have yourself a wash. Father goes out to the club in the evening, so you can have a wander round the green – get your bearings. We'll have a cup of cocoa when he comes in before bed. Father doesn't like anyone staying out late – not after nine. He says it's always a bad lot out on the streets after nine, doesn't he, Colin?' she added pointedly.

He ignored her, munching hungrily on a piece of ham, and Sara again sensed their mutual hostility.

'I'll see you later, then,' Sara said, thankful to be able to escape upstairs. Colin watched her go with expressionless blue eyes, his long jaws working on the food. As she turned to take the stairs, she noticed his gaze was still on her. Picking up her case she hurried after her aunt.

The second door on the upstairs landing led into a small back bedroom with a view through pink curtains to the backlane and the rows of terraces beyond. A large single bed covered in pink and white patchwork and occupied by a one-eyed teddy bear and a floppy-eared toy dog took up the centre of the room, with a chest of drawers and a narrow wardrobe fighting for the remaining space. At the foot of the bed, blocking the full opening of the door, was a truckle bed made up with crisp linen sheets and old blankets that gave off a spicy smell of mothballs.

'This is Marina's room.' Aunt Ida squeezed past the low bed to allow Sara to enter. 'And

yours now, of course. Bathroom's next door –
and the toilet's next to that,' she added with a
proud smile. 'There's plenty hot water for a
wash. Just make yourself at home, Sara. The top
two drawers are for your things and there's
hanging space in the wardrobe.' She gave Sara's
small case a doubtful glance.

'Thanks, Aunt Ida,' Sara smiled. 'I think just
one drawer will do.'

'Well, I'll leave you to it.' They manoeuvred
round each other so Ida could leave. She hesitated
a moment, a thin hand on the doorframe. 'I hope
you'll be happy here,' she said, uncertainty tinge-
ing her voice. 'I'm not good at saying these things,
but I was sorry about your father going. Father
didn't–' she stopped. 'Your Uncle Alfred never
thought he was right for your mam – thought
farming was too hard a life for her. That's why he
may seem a bit cross at your coming. But he'll
come round – just as long as you help about the
place and don't get in his way. And don't answer
back,' Ida added with a worried frown. 'He can't
stand cheekiness.'

'Aye,' Sara nodded, quite subdued. Her aunt's
face relaxed at her compliance.

'I only met your father the once – at our wedding,' Ida mused softly. 'A gentleman if ever there
was one. You're very like him in looks,' she touched
Sara briefly on the arm, 'two peas out of the same
pod.'

Sara felt her eyes water suddenly at Ida's kind
words, but her aunt closed the door and was
gone before she could respond. Gulping back the
tears in her throat, she stepped over the truckle

bed and stared out of the window. Colin's dogs lay in the yard below half inside their outhouse, backs nestling against each other as they dozed. She wrestled with the stiff window catch and pushed open the glass to allow a whiff of the evening breeze into the stuffy room.

In the backlane she saw Marina standing alone, eyeing a group of girls playing a skipping game. She chewed on something while they sang their rhythmic song and took it in turns to jump into the moving rope. Beyond, she could see a stretch of street with people milling past, calling out to each other, laughing, entering the grand-looking shop on the corner. The evening sun was shining off its window, so Sara could not see what treasures it stocked, but the gold lettering of the shop sign was visible, boldly declaring it as 'Dimarco's – Superior Ice Cream'.

She felt a flood of different emotions at the strange sights and sounds of this bustling town; fear at being so far from home and the people she loved, apprehension at the thought of working for Dolly Sergeant, curiosity at the world beckoning outside, a twinge of excitement that she was sixteen, in a new place where anything could happen, even romance.

Then someone, unseen, went by whistling. It was an ordinary whistle of a popular song, but it tore off the protective layer in which she had bound her grief for her dead father. He had been a whistler of songs and of secret messages to his dog Cath and the familiar sound pulled unmercifully at her heart. Sinking on to the unsteady bed, Sara buried her face in her hands and wept.

Chapter Five

It was stiflingly hot. Sara lay on top of the rickety bed in her nightgown. Marina, who was snoring loudly in the high bed, had not wanted the window open and Aunt Ida had asked Sara to keep it shut in case the young girl caught a chill. But Sara had drawn back one of the curtains and a street lamp cast light into the room so she could see to write her diary. It was the first time she had scribbled in it since her father's death and she found the familiarity of confiding in it a comfort.

It was so noisy here, Sara wrote to herself. People were still shouting and singing to each other along the backlanes, setting off a chorus of barking from Colin's whippets and other dogs around. She could hear two cats screaming and spitting in a fight on a neighbouring roof and always there was the monotonous hum of the pit. And Marina snoring... Sara sighed in annoyance. She had not known it was possible for a seven-year-old to snore like an old engine and she would have to endure it for *months*.

She longed for the comforting sound of Chrissie's even breathing in the bed next to hers, but tonight her sister would be sharing a bed with her mother in Bill's tiny cottage.

A motorcycle roared past and Sara craned for a better view. Marina stirred and her breathing altered. In the lamplight, Sara could see two boys on the back of the bike laughing as they skidded over the rough lane. The portly, aproned proprietor with the large moustaches at the ice-cream shop came out and shouted at them. There were lights still on inside the cafe though the clock on the landing had just struck eleven. Who was still buying ice-cream at this late hour? Sara wondered in fascination.

'What are you doing?' a small voice accused from the bed above. Marina was awake.

'Nothing,' Sara whispered, thrusting her diary under the covers, 'I just can't sleep.'

'You woke me!' Marina's voice was petulant.

'I didn't,' Sara protested. 'It must have been that motorcycle.'

'I don't like sharing a room with you,' the young girl complained. 'I wish you hadn't come.'

Silently, Sara wished the same. 'Go back to sleep,' she coaxed, trying to keep the hurt out of her voice.

In the distance she could hear the soft whistling of a train. Was it going back to Weardale? she thought with yearning. How I miss Mam! At that moment, Sara would have given anything for her mother to be there or her to be home. What was she doing here? she thought bleakly.

It was hot and noisy and impossible to sleep, and the Cummingses didn't want her, except, possibly, Aunt Ida. Money, came the dull answer in her head, that's why I'm here, to earn my keep.

The motorcycle revved again, somewhere further away in the dark.

'I can't sleep now,' Marina fretted, 'and it's all

84

your fault.'

Sara pulled a face in the dark. 'Would you like me to sing you to sleep?' she asked, willing herself to be patient.

'No!'

'Suit yourself.' Sara drew the curtain and lay down under the sheet once more.

After a minute of silence. 'What can you sing?' a muffled voice came from under the pink quilt.

'Bobby Shafto,' Sara suggested.

'No.'

'Blaydon Races?'

'No. Something modern.'

Sara searched her tired brain. 'Teddy Bears' Picnic? Chrissie loves me singing that – I know all the words.'

'Yes,' Marina agreed. 'Sing that one.'

So Sara did. When she got to the end, her cousin requested it again. Then Sara sang Bobby Shafto because her mother had often sung it to her and it drew her closer to home. There was no protest from the pink bed and for the next quarter of an hour Sara sang softly to herself, the popular love songs she had heard on the gramophone. She thought of herself and Tom dancing to them when he was on leave only weeks ago, though it seemed in another age. And Sid, kind and bashful Sid, did he think of her at that moment? No, Sara thought ruefully, he would be sleeping soundly after a day's hard labouring she was sure. She felt a faint twist of regret that she had turned her back on the gentle farmer's son. Faced with months of living with the strange Cummingses, the idea of being married to Sid suddenly had greater appeal.

Don't be daft! she chided herself. She was going to work in a shop where she would meet people and she consoled herself with the thought.

Marina's breathing was regular once more. Sara lay longing for sleep, listening to the hours on the landing clock chime their way into early Sunday morning.

'Mam says you're to keep my room tidy,' Marina declared, tossing a pair of white ankle socks onto the floor as they made ready for church. 'And Daddy says if you make a nuisance of yourself he'll send you home.'

Sara grimaced in the frameless wall mirror as she pulled a brush through her long fair hair. She noticed her green eyes were dark-ringed and puffy from crying. She had lain awake for hours after it had grown too dark to write her diary, feeling quite alone and miserable.

Binding the front strands of hair behind her head and biting back a sarcastic reply, she said, 'Do you want a hand with your plaits? I'm used to tying up Chrissie's hair.'

Turning round she saw Marina considering her with hard blue eyes.

'Yes, you can help me,' she answered, holding up the yellow satin ribbons. Sara took them and began to plait the girl's thick brown hair into pigtails. 'Make sure the parting's straight at the back.'

'Does Colin go with you to church?' Sara asked, trying to be friendly. It had been decreed last night that Sara would accompany Aunt Ida and Marina to the Eucharist at St Cuthbert's.

'That's if you want to be religious,' her Uncle Alfred had said in a disparaging tone. The fact that Sara might like to attend the chapel as she was used to doing was never considered.

Marina giggled at the idea of Colin in church. 'Mam doesn't like him with her, not since he broke a cup and saucer at the parish sale-of-work. He's too embarrassing and he wouldn't want to come anyway.'

'So what does he do Sundays?' Sara asked, feeling sympathetic towards her hapless cousin.

'Sleeps, then takes Flash and Gypsy for a walk,' Marina answered. 'He's not bothered about anything but those dogs. I think they *smell*.'

Sara bound the ribbon around the end of the first plait. 'When did your dad stop going to chapel?' Sara asked. Her mother used to talk about her and Uncle Alfred being chapel-goers and attending all the functions in their youth.

'Daddy's never been to chapel,' Marina said dismissively. 'Only the common pitmen go to chapel. Posh people go to St Cuthbert's – or the officials' club like Daddy. He's a very important man.'

Or thinks he is, Sara thought to herself.

'Ow! Don't pull my hair, stupid.' Marina's face creased in a cross expression. Sara apologised, biting back words of irritation. What Marina wanted, Marina got, as far as Sara could see, but there was no point in antagonising Uncle Alfred's favourite. At breakfast Aunt Ida had attempted half-heartedly to tell her daughter off for kicking Colin under the table. Marina had blubbered that Colin had started it and Uncle Alfred had sent Colin out of the room and Ida had ended up saying sorry to Marina. No, dislike the girl as she did, Sara was resigned to placating her to keep the peace.

Uncle Alfred was reading a Sunday paper in the parlour when they descended, a cup of tea on the table beside him. There was no sign of the banished Colin.

'Give your dad a kiss,' he ordered. Marina ran forward and presented her cheek. 'Pretty as a picture,' he beamed, approving Marina's powder-blue dress with the yellow smocking. She wore a straw Sunday hat anchored around her small face with elastic.

Ida bustled in. Despite the warm sunshine outside, she wore a sensible blue coat buttoned up to her thin neck, and a felt hat skewered on to her wiry brown hair with a huge, pearl-headed pin.

'Ready, girls?' She gave her anxious smile. Alfred stood and pecked her on the forehead with a proprietorial kiss. 'There's more tea in the pot, Father,' Ida assured her husband.

'Aye, now be off with you, or you'll be late,' he shooed them out of the door. Sara followed her aunt, feeling relief at the gust of blustery air that greeted them. It smelt of cinders, but it was fresh compared to indoors. The green was deserted save for a mangy horse grazing beside some makeshift football posts.

They set off along South Parade, Ida nodding at a neighbour they passed on the way and Marina chattering about a skipping game.

'Nancy Bell got up to twenty. Of course I could've done better, but I didn't want to play.'

'Didn't you, pet?' Ida enquired.

'No, Nancy Bell's *common*. She lives in Oswald Street and doesn't have a proper bathroom, just an outside toilet,' Marina sneered.

'Didn't you used to live in Oswald Street?' Sara asked without guile, remembering the name.

'Yes,' Ida replied with a faint flush to her narrow cheeks, 'but we moved soon after Marina was born – when your Uncle Alfred was made an overman.'

'Well, Nancy Bell's still common – her dad's on the dole.' Marina was stubborn.

Ida did not correct her; instead she began a diatribe on the unemployed. 'Yes, men like Bomber Bell think the government owe them a job, but you don't get something for nothing. It's Father's hard work that's got us a nice modern house with a bathroom. Hard-work and sensible housekeeping. Standing around on street corners getting into trouble never got anyone a decent home. There are too many idle men in Whitton Grange who don't know the meaning of hard work.' Sara listened in astonishment to hear her aunt so forthright. 'Father says half the men hanging around the labour exchange don't really want to work – they're just there for a bit of idle gossip. Like Colin, for instance. He's been left school for three years and he's never done a proper day's work in his life!'

'Could Uncle Alfred not get him a job at the pit?' Sara tried to be helpful. The idea turned her aunt's face magenta.

'Well, he would have done, of course,' she exclaimed, 'but three years ago they weren't taking

89

on young boys at the pits. Colin wasn't suited to the idea, any road – he wanted to go and work on a farm among dirty animals. Naturally, Father wouldn't allow it – he wanted Colin to get a steady job and get on. But not our Colin, he's as lazy as they come.'

Sara thought the criticism of her cousin harsh; he could hardly be blamed for the lack of jobs in the town.

'Farming's just as important as working down a pit,' she said. 'And a lot less dirty, to go by the men who got on the bus yesterday.'

Ida looked at her with bafflement in her close-set blue eyes, but chose to ignore the interruption to her moralising.

'Of course, Father says if there's war, they'll all have to get off their haunches and do their bit for King and Country – aye, even communists like Bomber Bell and Sam Ritson.'

'Don't let's talk of war,' Sara begged and ended the conversation and Marina skipped ahead.

Turning into the wide road Sara had seen yesterday from the bus, their steps echoed around the empty high street, its shops closed and shuttered and the cinema queues gone. A dog sidled past, sniffing at the drains and the breeze picked up a page of discarded newspaper and whipped it in a crazy dance down the road.

They crossed over and walked along a side street, emerging onto the Durham Road bordering the dene. Metal-hard pavements gave way to an uneven track along the verge, glinting black with coal dust. The sound of voices came once again and Sara saw swathes of church-goers gathering on the steps of a cavernous gothic building of brash red bricks. Small girls in elaborate white dresses lent a festive air to the crowd. Ida called Marina to her side.

'Catholics,' Marina announced with disapproval, raising her pert nose in the air. Her mother took her hand and crossed over the road, avoiding contact. Sara hurried after them, puzzled.

'Looks like something special,' she suggested, curious at the throng of people.

'First communion, I suspect,' Ida mumbled.

'We don't mix with their sort,' Marina spoke loudly. 'Daddy says they're always drunk and gambling on a Sunday. And they don't wash properly. There's a Catholic in my class and *she* smells.'

Sara wanted to laugh at such nonsense, but the nod of agreement from her aunt indicated that she shared such prejudice.

Ida made another pronouncement, 'Your Uncle Alfred doesn't hold with Roman Catholics – they've been known to give him trouble at the pit. They're not quite … respectable.' She blushed at the word.

Sara glanced back at the jovial parishioners, dressed in their Sunday best and wondered why they had been condemned out of hand by the censorious Cummingses when it was obviously quite respectable for her uncle to spend the morning drinking at the officials' club. Farmers, unemployed, Catholics; was there anyone her relations approved of? she wondered with impatience.

Aloud she said, 'Well, our postman's a Catholic and he's as respectable as they come.' No one answered as Ida quickened their pace towards the trees and an insistent peal of bells. Marina stuck out her tongue at Sara, without her mother noticing.

'And *he* doesn't smell,' Sara added, with a glare at her cousin.

A last row of cottages petered out and the squat tower of the old parish church emerged above a frill of pink cherry blossom and fresh green leaves. Frail petals were scattered along the path that led from the lych-gate to the church door. Over the clang of bells, Ida greeted fellow parishioners and filed into the cool church beside a large, elderly woman in a close-fitting hat.

'Good morning, Mrs Cummings,' she wheezed. 'Good morning, Marina. How are we today?'

'Good morning, Mrs Naylor.' Marina smiled back sweetly at the lady, formidable in a green tweed coat that bound in her large bosom.

'Mrs Naylor,' Aunt Ida said nervously, 'this is Alfred's niece, Sara Pallister, who's come to stay with us.' She pushed Sara forward.

'Oh! How do you do?' Mrs Naylor held out a gloved hand, giving Sara an appraising look with brown eyes that sagged in her puffy face. 'Will you be with us long, Sara?'

'A few months, I think,' Sara replied, trying not to wince from the crushing handshake she was receiving.

'Mrs Naylor's the under-manager's wife.' Ida's voice was full of deference. Sara knew she was supposed to be impressed, but could think of nothing to say, so she just smiled.

'Well, it's nice to have another Cummings in

the fold,' Mrs Naylor nodded. 'Such a good family. Your uncle's a well-respected member of the community, I hope you know?'

'Aye,' Sara said without enthusiasm, resenting being called a Cummings. Mrs Naylor turned away with a regal wave and headed for the front of the nave. Ida let out a breath and bustled Sara into a pew halfway down on the left. Shivering in the gloom of the old building, Sara thought of the coldness of dead centuries emanating from the grey stones. The church was cluttered with memorial slabs and moth-eaten flags and the prone bodies of two ancient knights petrified on their tombstones. Yet there was beauty, too, in the splashes of vivid colour from the freshly arranged flowers and the gold-embroidered altar cloth. Huge candlesticks glinted in the light of their flames, giving off a powerful smell of burning wax that was at once familiar. With a stab, Sara realised it conjured up the smell of candles in her bedroom at home.

The church filled up and the service began. It was all a mystery to Sara, as to when she should stand or sit, chant or remain silent. Everyone else seemed to know the incantations and responses that echoed around the lofty roof, the organ spurring them on to greater praise. Marina sniggered at Sara's confused bobbing and by the end, Sara's back and knees ached from all the kneeling. No one in her chapel at home ever kneeled.

When Ida followed a stream of people up to the altar for communion, Marina nudged her and whispered, 'That's Sir Reginald.' A tall, distinguished man with greying hair and trim moustache marched stiffly back down the aisle. He looked expressionless, like a lead soldier.

'Who's Sir Reginald?' Sara asked under her breath.

'Sir Reginald Seward-Scott.' Marina's look was impatient, as if Sara should know. 'The coal-owner. He's the most important man in Whitton Grange. And that's Lady Seward-Scott – isn't she pretty?'

Sara watched a thick-set woman with permed red hair rippling under a green slouch hat, striding behind her husband. She was expensively clad in a silk dress and short jacket, but Sara thought her unremarkable. They disappeared through an arched side door that led on to the gallery steps.

'They live at The Grange,' Marina whispered under cover of the shuffle of communicants. 'It's the poshest house I've ever seen. I've been in and had mince pies at Christmas with the Sunday School.' She shook her pigtails with importance. 'And Lady Seward-Scott let me ride one of her ponies at the summer fete last year. She *spoke* to me. I want to be like her when I grow up.' Marina's face shone with admiration.

A woman behind them prodded Marina in the back and told her to be quiet. Marina glared at the interruption, but ceased her gossiping.

As they emerged into the sunshine again, Sara glimpsed the Seward-Scotts climbing into a large black Bentley waiting at a side gate. The sleek, polished car moved off with a becapped driver at the wheel and the mine owner and his wife marooned on the back seat, looking aloof and disinterested. It was as if they had been attending a quite different event, cordoned off from the rest of the congregation, Sara thought. That was the kind of hat she wanted, Sara decided, thinking of Lady Seward-Scott's emerald-green one, but she did not feel any envy for the woman as she sped away with her stern husband.

'There's tea in the hall,' Aunt Ida explained, 'but I want to get home to get the dinner on. You don't mind missing it, do you? Uncle Alfred will be home shortly.'

Sara curbed her feelings of curiosity and they trouped off in the direction of the village.

But Uncle Alfred did not appear shortly, despite Aunt Ida's constant glances towards her array of clocks. She spent the rest of the morning busying herself about her small, neat kitchen, preparing the vegetables, checking on the sizzling joint of roast beef in the oven and mixing up batter for Yorkshire puddings. Sara thought her aunt seemed happiest when ruling her own domestic empire, and the juicy aromas filling the warm house confirmed her competence as a cook.

Sara debated whether to slip out of the house for a wander around the town, but Ida set her to laying the table in the dining-room with all the best china and cutlery and then to stirring a thick custard to top a massive trifle. With that done, Ida allowed them a welcome cup of tea. Finally, one o'clock chimed on the small grandfather clock on the landing and Sara wondered when lunch would begin. The tantalising smells wafting out of the kitchen were making her stomach growl.

'It's ten minutes fast,' Aunt Ida told Sara as if

she had spoken her query aloud. All the same, Ida went to glance out of the parlour window to see if her husband was in sight.

When one o'clock struck simultaneously in the hallway and parlour, Marina was called in off the street to wash and tidy. Colin materialised from the backlane to fetch scraps to feed his dogs.

'Mind you give yourself a good scrub before dinner,' Ida warned him. He gave a surly affirmative and retreated into the yard without another word.

Sara watched her older cousin from the open back door, round-shouldered in his tight jacket that strained at the seams around his armpits. He looked ill-at-ease under his grubby cap, a great lump of a youth who did not seem to know where to put his massive hands or over-large, dirty boots. In comparison, his dogs were lean and swift in their movements, alert and aggressive to sound or touch, inquisitive and softly padding.

Colin turned to catch her eyeing him. 'What you staring at?' he asked with suspicion. Sara flushed.

'Nothing,' she assured quickly. 'Hello, Gypsy.' She reached out for the friendlier of the two skinny hounds. The dog sniffed at her, hoping for food. She patted its bony head. 'Have you had a nice run this morning?'

'Aye,' Colin answered for the dog, 'she's been with Adamson – the trainer. Coming on canny. Adamson says Gypsy'll be a better runner than Flash when she's bigger. Got more brains,' Colin said, his lugubrious face lifting in a half-smile.

Sara nodded, seeing the tenseness in his hunched figure relax a fraction. Then Aunt Ida's voice came shrill from the parlour.

'Father's at the top of the street! Quickly now!'

Colin's look darted to the door as if some avenging spirit were about to sweep through it. His face went as blank and secretive as shuttered windows.

Marina came flying down the stairs. 'Daddy's here! Daddy's here!'

'Get washed this minute!' Ida ordered her stepson as she scurried into the kitchen to reinspect her steaming vegetables. Sara felt her insides churn with nervousness at the behaviour of the Cummingses, so that by the time Uncle Alfred threw open his front door and swept in like some conquering dictator, she, too, was tongue-tied with apprehension.

Rosa Dimarco stood outside St Teresa's watching two small girls having their photograph taken. She was reminded of her own first communion, when she had been the centre of family attention. Her parents kept a photograph on the sideboard of a wide-eyed girl with a short, dark fringe peeping from under a veil, an innocent in a long white dress and white gloves, an ornate cross on her flat chest. Rosa Dimarco, aged eight. Half her life time ago, Rosa recalled with a sigh and smiled at the young girls preening with importance, as her mother handed them small gifts of sugared almonds. The next important event at St Teresa's would be her sister's marriage, Rosa thought, and lately the talk among the women of the family had been *only* of Domenica's forthcoming July wedding. When would it be her turn? she wondered impatiently, falling in behind her mother and elder sister as they discussed the elaborate arrangements yet again.

'Has Papa asked Uncle Davide to play his accordion yet?' Domenica asked, flicking back her well-groomed, light brown hair. 'And has he organised the band? There must be plenty of dancing. Isn't that right, Rosa?' she laughed excitedly at her sister.

'Yes,' Rosa nodded bashfully. Domenica seemed so grown-up and sophisticated these days in her flowery dress with the large sash belt and frilled waist over her hips. Her shoes were high-heeled with ankle straps, and round earrings adorned her earlobes below her short, bobbed hair. Sunderland had changed Domenica from a gauche, unfashionable village girl into a young woman engaged to be married to Pasquale Perella, heir to two ice-cream shops on Wearside.

'There will be plenty of dancing,' their mother smiled, her tight black bun of hair nodding in agreement. 'Don't pester your father about it – he has enough to organise as it is. And Father Guiseppe will be visiting next week.'

The visiting Italian chaplain would be coming to check that the marriage arrangements were going according to plan, Rosa thought. He would take mass in their flat above the shop and counsel Domenica on the importance of motherhood. It would be the second time in three months the austere priest had paid them a visit in the remote outpost of Whitton Grange. Last time it had been to see to the baptising of baby Linda, newly born to Rosa's eldest brother Paolo and his shy wife

Sylvia. It had been a great family occasion with a sit-down lunch for thirty in the Dimarcos' cafe and Italian friends and family had travelled from as far away as Glasgow.

An appearance from Father Guiseppe would mean her brother Joe would have to behave himself for a whole day, Rosa thought with amusement. As if her other brother had read her mind, he came tearing past on his motorcycle, sending up dust from the road. Somehow, he had managed to attach a drum of ice-cream to his vehicle like a sidecar. He went past tooting and waving, an impudent grin spread beneath a huge pair of goggles.

'That boy!' Anna Dimarco coughed from the dust and lapsed into her village dialect. 'How did I nurture such a devil? Always so noisy on that terrible machine.'

Domenica and Rosa exchanged amused glances, knowing how their mother doted on her middle son.

'At least he's off to sell ice-cream somewhere,' Domenica remarked in English, understanding but seldom speaking the dialect peculiar to her parents' district of Cassino in Central Italy.

As her mother and sister reverted to their previous discussion about the wedding, Rosa watched Joe disappear towards the dene and felt envy at his freedom to go where he pleased. This rare trip to church was one of the few ways she escaped the strictures of home since she had left school and even now she was accompanied by her mother and sister. She seldom ventured beyond the house or shop and since her sister-in-law Sylvia had given birth to baby Linda, Rosa had been in charge of her two-year old nephew Peter and rarely got to serve in the cafe anymore. Now her sister Domenica had returned from helping look after the young family of a sick cousin in Sunderland and the small terraced house, containing the ice-cream shop, felt as if it would burst with relations.

But Joe escaped and stayed away all day long; where, Rosa did not know. Their father put up with his waywardness so long as he returned with his ice-cream churn empty and handed over the takings. Then Joe would roar off to meet his friends again, like the jovial and ginger-haired Pat Slattery or skinny, pale-faced Raymond Kirkup.

I have no friends, Rosa thought with regret. The girls she had known at school had left to go into service in the south of England and she had lost touch with them all. Not that she had ever played with them much outside of school, because she had always been needed to help at home or look after her baby brother, Bobby, while her mother worked in the shop.

'Smile, Rosa,' Domenica's bright voice broke into her thoughts. 'You're supposed to be happy, thinking about my wedding.' The older girl slipped an arm through her sister's.

'Sorry,' Rosa grinned, 'I am.'

'Well, here's something to cheer you up. Pasquale's *compare* is looking for a wife and he's extremely handsome!' Domenica winked. Rosa blushed at the implication she might be interested in Pasquale's best man, or he in her.

'Who is he?' Anna quizzed her daughter, as

they turned into Pit Street, her small brown eyes full of interest.

'Emilio Fella,' Domenica replied. 'He's working for Mr Perella – I met him at a dance at the *fascio* – very charming.'

Rosa had tired of hearing Domenica go on about the social gatherings at the Italian club and the trips to the seaside the *fascio* had organised. But she was interested to hear more of the handsome Emilio.

'I've not heard of him,' her mother interrupted, her neat features frowning. 'Who are the Fellas and where are they from?'

'They're distantly related to the Perellas, I think.' Domenica gave a vague wave of her hand. 'Emilio and Pasquale fought together in Abyssinia. Now Emilio's helping run a billiard hall in Seaburn.'

'That's all very well,' Anna's voice was impatient, 'but where're the Fellas from back home?'

Domenica gave Rosa a heavenwards look behind her mother's back and Rosa's grimace was sympathetic. Their mother's tone implied there would be stiff questioning about the mysterious Emilio.

'Valvoni region, I think,' Domenica replied, adding quickly, 'he's not been over from Italy long – but Mr Perella has given him responsibility of the billiard hall already.'

'A stranger,' Anna clucked, her look dubious. 'We shall need to find out more about this Emilio Fella. It's most odd of the Perellas to allow a stranger to be Pasquale's *compare*.'

Domenica began to insist, 'He's not a stranger,

he's–' But her mother cut her short.

'Look, there's your grandmother still peeling vegetables,' Anna pointed ahead. 'Stop her before she skins every potato in sight.'

Domenica's protest subsided as they drew near to the ice-cream parlour on the corner of Pit Street and Mill Terrace. Their grandmother sat on the pavement outside, lapping up the spring sunshine like a somnolent cat, a huge bowl of white-fleshed potatoes cradled on her black-skirted knees. Her crinkled face, under a sweep of grey hair, broke into a smile as they approached.

'Nonna Maria,' Rosa ran up to the elderly woman, 'let me finish those.'

'No, no, my little kitten,' her grandmother answered in her Italian patois, shooing her away kindly, 'they are all done. You go and see to Peter, he's been crying for you ever since you left. Sylvia can't comfort the poor little thing and he won't let her feed the baby.'

Rosa smiled with satisfaction to think she was so indispensable to her nephew. She might be short of local friends, but she was an important member of the Dimarco family and she felt a warm security in their midst.

'I'll go and find him,' she smiled. She darted ahead of the other women through the shop. Already there were customers sitting at the marble-topped tables, nibbling ice-cream or sipping pop, though it would be after lunch before large numbers of villagers would flock into the parlour to pass their Sunday afternoon. Rosa had seen them come and taste the delights of their homemade ice-cream, whole families dressed in their Sunday best and young girls in groups eyeing the single boys. A place of courtship and romance for so many, Rosa thought restlessly, while she was hidden upstairs looking after the family.

Her brother Paolo smiled at her as he brought out a tray of hot drinks from behind the counter.

'You're needed upstairs,' he indicated with a nod, his broad face amused.

'I'm going,' Rosa assured him and dived round the counter. In the backshop she halted abruptly at the sight of her father sitting drinking coffee with the impassive police officer, Sergeant Turnbull. Turnbull was a regular visitor and not averse to a game of cards after the shop closed for the night, but Rosa stopped shyly at sight of him.

'Rosa!' Arturo Dimarco greeted his daughter with a broad smile. 'Fetch Signor Turnbull another cup of coffee.'

'No, I must be on my way.' The fair-haired policeman rose and straightened his jacket. He reached for his cap. 'Just been hearing all about the forthcoming wedding,' he said to Rosa, looking her over with appraising blue-grey eyes. 'Over thirty people expected, your father tells me. You Italians know how to celebrate, I'll give you that.'

Rosa nodded, tongue-tied. She did not like the way he studied her whenever she came into the room; she always felt uncomfortable in the tall man's presence.

'Signor Turnbull,' Arturo rose regally, immaculate in starched white shirt, striped tie and waistcoat above his gleaming white apron. 'You would do us a great honour if you were able to attend our daughter Domenica's wedding – you and your wife.'

The boyish-faced policeman lost his serious poise for a moment as he gawped at the cafe proprietor. Rosa saw her father's strong-jawed face beaming in anticipation. Her heart sank at the invitation, certain he had just thought of the idea on the spur of the moment, carried away with bonhomie towards his distinguished guest on this bright spring Sunday.

'That would be most kind,' Turnbull grunted, flushing above his dark blue uniform. 'But you have enough to feed as it is.'

'You are our friend, Signore.' Arturo spread his hands in a generous gesture. 'We do not count the cost on our daughter's wedding day! So you will come, yes?'

'Well, um, thank you. The missus will be delighted, I'm sure,' he muttered and made swiftly for the back door. Regaining his poise as he donned his cap, the sergeant became businesslike.

'Remember to have a word with that son of yours about riding his motorcycle over the crossing.'

'*Bene*, Signor Turnbull,' Arturo nodded and showed him out with a firm handshake.

'Such a good man,' he told Rosa as the policeman left, 'and he takes such an interest in all our family. He asks after each one of you. That is a good man,' he repeated.

'What was he saying about Joe, Papa?' Rosa asked.

Her father gave an impatient grunt. 'Making

trouble for the Sergeant again – riding his motorcycle where he shouldn't. Next time Signor Turnbull will take it away and it will serve him right. See how much your brother Joseph likes pulling a cart like a horse – like your brother Paolo had to do before we had the shop!'

Rosa saw the signs of her father's rising temper, slow to boil but red-hot when roused and no one could annoy him quite so consistently as her brother Joe. Swiftly she changed the subject.

'I'll go and help Sylvia upstairs.'

Arturo relaxed at his daughter's eager face and patted her dark head in affection.

'*Bene*, little kitten,' he smiled, 'Peter cries for you all morning – off you go.'

'Yes, Papa,' Rosa skipped towards the staircase in obedience.

Chapter Six

Sara escaped from 13 South Parade as soon as the washing up was done and her Uncle Alfred had fallen asleep in his chair beside the parlour fire. The fire blazed on this warm afternoon, making the stuffy room more airless than usual and her uncle's alcoholic snores rumbled rhythmically with the gentle tick of clocks.

She was still shaking from the ordeal of this first Sunday lunch with the Cummingses. Uncle Alfred's original boozy good humour had evaporated as soon as Colin had asked him for some money.

'You'll get nowt till you get rid of them dogs and find yoursel' a job,' he grumbled.

'I'll never get rid o' them!' Colin's reply was stubborn.

'If there's war there'll be jobs,' his father continued as if he had not spoken, 'then you'll have no excuse for hanging around like the idle bugger you are.'

Sara cringed as her uncle grew expansive on the subject. 'Aye, we'll show the krauts who's boss – the English bulldog. War'd be good for the lazy devils who won't work around here. Spot of army discipline to put some backbone int' them, 'stead of scrounging off the dole. Aye, a short sharp war to send the Hun packing mightn't be a bad thing. It'll come,' he predicted, shovelling potato and gravy into his mouth, 'they've already made plans to take on more lads at the Eleanor – we're gearing up for extra production.'

Sara thought how horrified her father would have been to hear Alfred talk about war, his tone almost gleeful. She looked around at the others. Colin's head was down as he ate, dodging his father's criticisms. Marina played with her food without interest, while Ida sat tense but said nothing. They're all afraid of him, Sara thought with sudden clarity – even Marina was withdrawn.

'Me dad said there should never be another war with Germany,' Sara piped up, finding her voice at last. 'Not after the Great War. He said no man should have to go through all that again and if we'd learnt anything by it, then it's that fighting never gets us anything but misery.' Sara faltered at her uncle's derisory look. Ida's face was anxious at her defiance and Colin had stopped his steady munching to stare at her. 'He used to say that to our Tom, any road,' she faltered, her throat drying.

'Well, he was wrong!' Alfred thumped the table with his fist clenched around a knife. 'You would think we'd lost the Great War the way men like Pallister complained about it. They make me sick, these bleeding-heart conchies.'

Sara flushed, furious at the slight to her father. 'Me dad wasn't a conchie – he fought with the Durham Faithfuls!'

'And so would I have done, if I'd been old enough,' Alfred barked, his thick black brows collecting over his red nose like thunderous clouds.

107

'I was itching to get out to France, but I was still training when they blew the whistle. Your father always thought himself above me 'cos he fought with the DLI and I didn't. Well, I proved mesel' a man by ganin' down the pit and now I've got all this to show for me hard work.' He gestured to the laden table and the comfortable room. 'What's Dick Pallister left but a bankrupt farm and my sister in poverty? That's all he ever was – a penniless farmer.'

Sara felt her face engulfed in red indignation. She glared at her uncle, but she could not trust herself to speak.

'Father,' Ida tried to calm her husband, 'we mustn't speak ill of the dead.' Alfred shot her an angry look and she smiled nervously. 'Have some more roast potatoes, Father – they're your favourite. Marina, pass Father some more tatties and tell him how Mrs Naylor was asking after him at church this morning.'

The girl did so, making a big show of putting them on his plate. Alfred seemed mollified by her action and the mention of the under-manager's wife, but his mood was still belligerent and simmered dangerously with each course. By the end of the beef and Yorkshire pudding he was berating Colin for his slovenly appearance and Sara for her red-faced silence; serving trifle Ida dropped some jelly on the tablecloth and was given a lecture on thrifty housekeeping. He even snapped at Marina when she got down from the table without asking permission.

'I work my backside off to bring meat to this table, young lady,' he shouted, 'so the least you can do is sit there till we're all done!'

'Father!' Ida murmured in weak protest at his language, but her look was timid. Marina slunk to her mother's side, chewing the end of her plait, her face petulant.

'Get the tea made, Ida!' Alfred pushed back his chair, stood up, and belched loudly.

Ida hurried into the kitchen, shooshing Marina before her. 'You go out and play, pet, and give Father some peace.'

As Alfred left the room, Sara caught Colin's look of disgust on his half-washed face. She began to clear the table, still fighting back tears of outrage at her uncle's harsh words about her father.

'I hate 'im,' Colin muttered under his breath, but loud enough for Sara to catch. 'He shouldn't have spoken to you like that.' She glanced up, surprised by the venom in her cousin's voice and saw him regarding her with his doleful brown eyes. For the first time she felt the stirrings of friendship for her sullen cousin, grateful for his sympathy.

'I don't care what he says,' she answered with spirit, tossing her fair hair over her shoulder. 'And I'd tell him so, if I didn't need the job he's found me and a roof over me head. Aye, I'd tell him his fortune and be off sharp!'

Colin glanced warily at the closed parlour door across the passageway. 'Aye, I've wanted to do that plenty times,' Colin admitted, keeping his voice low as he helped her stack the plates.

'Why don't you?' Sara encouraged. 'I don't know why you put up with the way he treats you.

Me dad was kinder to the rats in the barn.' She stopped, seeing him flush puce and look away from her critical eyes.

'I don't have a choice, do I?' he answered defensively, hunching his shoulders. 'I've no job and no money.'

'Sorry, Colin,' Sara touched his hand lightly, regretting her impulsive words, 'I can see how it is.' She quickly gathered up a pile of crockery, eager to get the chores finished and get out of the house. So she did not notice the way her cousin flinched under her touch, or the way he watched her go with a flicker lighting his eyes.

Walking across the village green Sara turned up a steep street called Daniel Terrace and found the gates to the Memorial Park. Immature cherry trees were in full blossom and the park was busy with pit folk enjoying the fresh air. Young couples strolled arm-in-arm, while others went past pushing rattling old prams. A game of bowls was going on behind a screen of hedges, the flat green like a luxurious carpet. A row of old miners, sitting on a bench like scraggy crows, gave a commentary between throws, one of them shooting spit into the hedge after each pronouncement. The call of children at play rang around the open fields and Sara carried on, feeling her spirits lift as she mingled with the holidaymakers.

The noise of a game of football drew her towards the far field. Quite a crowd had gathered to watch and their cries were vociferous.

'Who's playing?' Sara asked a tall woman among the onlookers who could see what was happening. She thought how much her brother Tom would have enjoyed this lively spectacle.

'Boys' Brigade 'gainst the Catholics,' she replied eagerly. 'Boys' Brigade are one-nil up. My nephew's playing.' As she turned away, there was a roar from one end of the pitch as someone scored. 'Oh dear, they've equalised,' the woman cried. 'Haway, Raymond!'

Sara stood back, lifting on to tiptoes to try and get a better view without success. Deciding to work her way around to one end, she stepped back further without looking and, as she did so, a noisy revving and tooting behind made her jump violently, twisting her ankle. A jabbing pain shot up her leg and she bent down to clutch it. Turning, she saw a young man skidding across the grass on a motorcycle, whooping with delight and circling the pitch. Attached to his cycle was a battered drum which claimed to be trans- porting 'pure ices'.

'Watch where you're going!' Sara called after him in annoyance, but the youth did not appear to hear and carried on his flamboyant progress. Sara sat down and rubbed her ankle.

'You all right, pet?' the fair-haired woman in the pudding hat who had spoken to her before asked as she bent over. 'That lad's got no sense sometimes,' she tutted. 'Good family, but that one's wild as they come.'

'Aye, I'm all right.' Sara stood up again with the woman's help. 'Ta very much.' The older woman had a kind, plain face with light blue eyes and a large mouth that smiled readily.

'Who is he any road?' Sara asked, craning to see

where the motorcyclist had gone, vexed that he had not stopped to see how she was.

'Joe Dimarco,' the woman answered with a cluck. 'He's canny when he's not causing bother. Father runs an ice-cream shop on Pit Street. Nice man. Mr Dimarco gave us free ice-cream for our chapel picnic last year.' She squinted at Sara. 'You not from round here, then?'

'No,' Sara flexed her ankle, 'I'm from up Weardale. But me mam's from Whitton Grange. I'm stopping with me uncle.'

'Oh, and who's that?' she asked with interest.

'Alfred Cummings – overman at the Eleanor. Do you know him?'

The woman's face clouded as the smile died on her face. 'Aye,' she said stiffly as the motorcycle circled again, this time carrying a red-haired passenger shouting support for the Catholics.

'Watch yourselves, lads!' the woman wagged a finger at them. 'You nearly knocked this lass over.'

The rider braked and stopped. He shouted over, 'Sorry, Mrs Ritson.' Then, with a grin, 'Would you like some ice-cream – freshly made this morning?'

Mrs Ritson waved a hand at him. 'No, but this lass deserves one.' She put a hand on Sara's shoulder. 'What's your name, pet?'

'Sara. Sara Pallister.'

'I'm Louie Ritson.'

The cyclist parked his bike and clambered off. His passenger slid away quickly to watch the end of the game, with a nod at the tall woman. Sara watched, embarrassed now by the attention, as the dark-haired Joe Dimarco made a grand gesture of opening his drum of ice-cream and, taking a cone from a box strapped to the back of his vehicle, scooped a generous dollop on top.

'For the young lady,' Joe presented her with the cone, giving a bow. *'Ciao, bella.'*

Sara blushed at the foreign words, suspecting he was mocking her for creating a fuss. Well, he had given her a fright, she thought crossly, and bent to give her leg another rub before accepting his peace offering.

'Are you hurt?' he asked, but she could not tell if there was real concern, hidden as he was behind his cycle goggles.

'Ankle's a bit sore,' she scowled at him.

'Here, take this,' he ordered, thrusting the cone into her hand. A moment later he had removed his tattered jacket and spread it on the grass for her to sit on. 'Gan on, sit down. I can see it's painful to stand.'

Sara hesitated, unsure if he teased her or not.

'Please,' he insisted.

She lowered herself on to his jacket, clutching the ice-cream with as much decorum as she could manage.

'Ta,' Sara said coolly. He gave a broad grin.

Then, pushing his goggles off his face, she saw him properly for the first time. His face was slim, the bones pronounced under his sun-darkened skin, his brown eyes large and lively between black lashes. They were laughing at her, as she'd suspected.

'Eat it before it melts,' he encouraged and Sara began to lick the frozen ice. It was so long since

113

she had eaten one, she had forgotten how good it tasted. Joe turned to watch the football once more. Sara ate and slid glances at Joe Dimarco while he was not looking.

'Your Raymond's playing well today,' he said to Mrs Ritson.

'Not well enough it seems,' the woman pulled a face, 'but he tries that hard. Doesn't get much time to practice these days, mind.'

'Mrs Sergeant still cracking the whip, is she?' he laughed.

'Don't be cheeky,' Raymond's aunt replied, but could not help smiling. Sara wondered if they could be referring to the Mrs Sergeant who was about to become her employer, but she was concentrating too hard on eating her ice-cream with delicacy to break into the conversation. It was delicious, rich and creamy and tinglingly cold on her tongue. She had never tasted anything quite as good as this before.

'Do you like it?' Joe turned suddenly to ask her. Sara wiped a bit that was dribbling off her chin and sucked at a trickle spilling over her fingers.

'Aye, it's grand, thanks,' she answered, her indignation beginning to thaw.

He nodded, satisfied. 'Dimarco's make the finest ices in County Durham. Nowt better, eh, Mrs Ritson?'

'I wouldn't know,' the woman laughed. 'I've hardly been out of Whitton since I was wed.'

'Take it from me, then,' Joe winked. 'I've ridden all over the county selling the stuff. And I better gan now and sell a bit more, else the boss will have me guts for garters, won't he?'

'Not your father – he's too soft on you by half,' the woman teased.

Sara was intrigued by Joe's broad Durham accent, belying his swarthy foreign appearance. All at once, she was reluctant to see him go.

'D'you make it yourself?' she blurted out, ice-cream melting on to her dress and hands. 'The ice-cream, I mean?'

'Every morning, before the sun is up or you are out of your bed, I bet,' he declared. Sara found herself blushing at the suggestion and dived for another bite of her cone. It crumbled drastically, half of it splashing her dress before landing with a splat on his jacket lining.

'Sorry!' She flushed pinker, grabbing for her handkerchief to wipe up the mess.

'I told you to eat it quickly,' he said with amusement. 'It doesn't matter about me coat.' She was only too aware of how gauche and hot-cheeked she must seem to Joe Dimarco when she wished to appear calm and composed.

'It'll wash off easy,' the practical Louie Ritson assured.

Sara stood up, cramming the rest of the cone into her mouth before she did any further damage. At that point, Joe's red-haired companion reappeared and pulled his arm. 'Gan on, the copper's coming.'

They all looked round to see a tubby, uniformed constable panting up the slope towards them.

'It's only Simpson,' Joe sounded unconcerned. But his friend was restless.

'Haway, Joe, you're not supposed to have the

bike up here. He'll nick you this time.'

'All right,' Joe acquiesced with a shrug. Sara picked up his jacket and gave it a shake. She held it out to him.

'Ta,' said Joe. Then, 'What's your name?'

'Sara Pallister,' she said, more dignified now all traces of the ice-cream had been removed from her face.

'*Ciao*, Sara,' he winked, briefly touching her hand as he took his jacket. Sara felt a frisson of excitement. Don't be daft, she told herself silently, he's just a Whitton lad, not a Heathcliff or Clark Gable. Still, quite a good-looking one, she had to admit.

'Ta-ra, Mrs Ritson,' Joe raised a hand in farewell. The boys headed back to the motorcycle, Joe swinging into the saddle in one swift, lean movement and pulling his goggles back over his eyes. He kicked the bike into life again and they roared off, waving at the portly policeman who was gesticulating as they passed.

'Eeh, I hope they're not in any trouble,' Mrs Ritson shook her head. 'They're canny lads, a bit high spirited but that's lads isn't it?'

Sara thought of her brother Tom and some of his escapades. 'Aye, that's lads,' she sighed dreamily, looking after the disappearing motorcycle and licking her lips for the last traces of Dimarco's ice-cream, feeling wicked and satisfied as if she had tasted something near to forbidden fruit.

Rosa's nose wrinkled as the smell of Granny Maria's cooking filled the kitchen. The old woman was stirring the tomato sauce that would cover the small, potato-filled dumplings, while Domenica cut freshly made bread and salami for the evening meal. Rosa had helped her sister-in-law Sylvia put the babies to bed and now they were waiting for her father to close the shop so that the family could eat their late meal together for once. It was the first time since Domenica's return that they would all be gathered round the long table; normally they ate in shifts while taking it in turns to work in the cafe.

'I'll go and help Papa tidy the shop,' Rosa volunteered, seeing her mother was busy preparing pies to sell the following day.

'And find your brother Bobby,' her mother called after her, pausing over her rolling pin. 'Remind him he has school tomorrow.'

Rosa descended the steep stairs into the backroom of the shop. Buckets of boiled milk stood covered and cooling, in preparation for the next day's ice-cream making. The smell of the milk mingled with the sourness of strong cheeses, the earthy smell of olives and sausages stored in shadowy recesses and the rich aroma of coffee beans and sugar in their dusty sacking. She loved the comforting smells of their home and shop, and the feeling of safety that they instilled in her. No one else's home that she had ever visited, smelt quite as safe.

Paolo was sweeping the cafe floor and her father stood at the open door bidding goodnight to his last customers.

'I'll mop,' Rosa told her eldest brother. He smiled and nodded. She fetched the bucket and mop from the back scullery and filled it with water from the cold tap over the stone sink.

'Bairns asleep?' Paolo asked after his children, as Rosa returned.

'Peter's sleeping like a top, but Sylvia's still trying to settle Linda. She's a greedy lass your daughter.'

Paolo gave his grave smile. 'She has a good Italian appetite,' he said with pride.

Their father came in from the pavement and pulled down the blinds. 'It's been a good day and I'm ready for supper.' He grinned at his daughter and patted his solid stomach. 'Umm, you can smell Nonna's pasta down the street.'

'Bobby's missing,' Rosa said. 'Shall I go and find him?'

Arturo shook his head. 'It's dark now.' He went to the door again and called for his youngest son. Moments later, a grubby-faced boy darted in at the door, his face, hands and knees smeared in black grease.

'Bobby, you're filthy!' Rosa screeched. 'Get yourself scrubbed this minute,' she demanded with sisterly authority.

Her father laughed and put an arm round the boy's weedy shoulders. 'Is Paolo's bicycle in a thousand bits, Roberto?'

'No, I've fixed it,' he chirped, his look triumphant.

'*Grazie*, Bobby,' Paolo murmured.

'*Bene.*' Arturo ruffled his brown hair. 'You will make a good engineer when you grow up. Maybe one day I'll let you work on my van, yes?'

'That would be canny,' Bobby beamed. 'Paolo,

can I ride your bike to school t'morra?' he asked his brother with a pleading look.

'*Si*, if you're careful,' Paolo replied, wiping down the counter.

'Now, wash!' Rosa fussed. 'Supper's ready.' Bobby pulled a face but his father gave him a playful cuff.

'Do as your sister says, Roberto.' The boy ran ahead with Paolo, giving him a detailed explanation of what had been wrong with his bicycle.

'What about Joe?' Rosa asked her father cautiously, as he bolted the shop door.

'He can sleep on the street for all I care!' Her father was suddenly angry. 'That boy! Where does he spend half the day?'

'But Papa–' Rosa's protest was interrupted by banging on the front door. Arturo lifted the blind to see Joe's face peering out of the dark. He let him in with a curse.

'Where have you been?' Arturo demanded, his craggy face frowning. 'You should be here with your family, not chasing around the streets with Whitton boys. Domenica has been home a week, but she's hardly seen you. She's forgotten what her brother looks like.'

'I promise I'll take her to the pictures next week, Dad,' Joe smiled, pulling off his jacket.

'Don't Dad-a me!' his father shouted, working himself into a temper. 'Are your family not good enough for you that you have to spend every minute away from the house? Huh? Can't you help your own father and brother in the shop for one day? Is that too much to ask?'

Joe shrugged and turned to Rosa with a

119

heavenwards roll of the eyes, as if to say he had heard it all before. Rosa was silent but beseeching in her look, not wanting the family evening spoilt by a familiar row between her brother and father.

'Papa...' Joe turned to his father and looked contrite. 'I'm sorry I'm late. I was giving Pat Slattery a lift home and his mam asked us in for a bit chat.'

Arturo gave an impatient gesticulation. 'His mamma! Are you now a Slattery not a Dimarco? Are you Irish not Italian, huh?'

'I'm Durham born and bred,' Joe answered, winking at Rosa, knowing the comment would infuriate his father. 'Like Rosa here – and Domenica – and Bobby.'

'*Madonna!* Don't you forget you are a good Italian underneath the English, eh?'

'Papa,' Rosa intervened bravely. 'Nonna Maria's pasta is ready. Let's go and eat.'

'Umm, gnocchi!' Joe exclaimed, kissing the end of his fingertips in delight. 'I'm always a good Italian when it comes to food.'

'*Bene.*' His father grew calmer at the thought. 'Come, my little pussycat,' he said to Rosa, 'let's not keep Nonna and your mother waiting.'

He led them through the backshop and up the dimly lit staircase to the flat above. The table was spread with a white cloth, the cutlery glinting in the artificial light and the rest of the family were seated, waiting for the steaming pasta to be served. Arturo called for Paolo to open some red wine and Rosa went to help her mother and Domenica serve out the food.

The intimate living-room, with the kitchen at one end, became fuggy with the smell of food and the press of bodies around the table. The chatter grew noisy as the wine and pasta were demolished and the men sat back, rosy-faced and mellow, to smoke their cigarettes. Rosa revelled in the cosy warmth of it all. At times like this she did not care if there *was* a world outside these homely walls.

Granny Maria dozed in her chair and Peter woke with the hubbub and came to sit on Rosa's knee, yawning and trying to stay awake. Eventually Sylvia picked him from her lap and took him back to the bedroom which he shared with his parents and baby sister.

Rosa looked at her mother's tired face. They would all be up early to help mix the ice-cream and prepare snacks for the pitmen coming off night shift. Paolo and Joe would wheel a barrow up to the pit gates to catch the tide of hungry and weary miners, selling them cigarettes and pies and the early morning newspapers that her father would fetch in his van from Whitton Station.

'Let's get Nonna to bed,' Domenica nudged Rosa and they coaxed the old woman out of her seat and into the small backroom they shared over the backshop. The narrow window was thrown open and a scent of honeysuckle drifted in from the white-washed yard below, where their mother's pots of flowers stood in a tight cluster.

Later, with the sound of the men's voices still rumbling beyond the door, Rosa sat up in the bed she shared with Domenica and whispered excitedly about the wedding.

'Does Emilio Fella have a lass?' Rosa asked shyly.

'So you *are* interested?' Domenica said gleefully, as she slipped out of her cotton dress and hung it carefully behind the door.

Rosa glanced away. 'I was just asking,' she mumbled.

Domenica pulled on her nightgown and began to brush out her short wavy hair.

'Emilio Fella doesn't have a lass,' Domenica informed her. 'Not a serious one anyway.'

'What does that mean?' Rosa's interest in the mysterious Emilio was roused.

'Well, Pasquale says he's been seen at the pictures with a local girl, but it's nothing serious. He's not courting an Italian lass and that's what counts isn't it?'

'Oh, I see,' Rosa brightened. 'And is he very handsome?'

'Very,' Domenica laughed. 'If I hadn't already met Pasquale...'

Rosa giggled, 'Ssh, Nonna might hear you.' Then she became dubious again. 'But what about Mam? She didn't seem to think much of the Fellas.'

'Mamma doesn't know anything about them,' Domenica was dismissive. She climbed into bed beside her sister.

'Exactly,' Rosa worried. 'So she'll be against him from the start.'

'Stop worrying.' Domenica kissed her on the head like a child. 'I'll get Pasquale to do some investigating. I bet the Fellas are impeccable Italians with lots of land and no sons but Emilio to pass it on to.'

'Pigs might fly,' Rosa giggled again with excitement.

'Yes – and lots of pigs.' Domenica stifled her laughing as their grandmother stirred.

The girls turned back to back and snuggled down. Rosa drifted into sleep trying to imagine what it would be like living in an Italian village as the proud possessor of a herd of pigs. She hardly knew what life was like outside Pit Street, let alone beyond the horizon of Whitton Grange and County Durham, so how could she possibly imagine what Italy was like?

Still, Granny Maria talked about it longingly and her mother and sister-in-law Sylvia had been born and brought up there, so it couldn't be that difficult to adapt, could it? she thought drowsily as sleep enveloped her.

Chapter Seven

'And you're to wash your own overall,' Mrs Sergeant wheezed at Sara, 'so keep it clean. You can start by sweeping the storeroom – you'll find the brush and pan behind the door. I'll call you if I need a hand in the front.'

Sara nodded, in awe of the large shopkeeper with the mop of white hair around her grey-skinned face. She had dark down on her cheeks and upper lip that gave her a masculine appearance, her square frame sexless in a vast starched white overall. Sara scurried into the back of the shop without a word.

She was halfway through sweeping the dusty storeroom with its stacked wooden crates of pop, tea chests and boxes of unpacked groceries, when the back door banged. A thin youth, swamped by a huge cap, came in whistling. When the cap was removed, Sara saw a lad with auburn hair and a pale face who looked a year or two her junior.

'What time do you call this, Raymond Kirkup?' Dolly Sergeant boomed from the shop. The boy pulled a face, then, noticing Sara, broke into a broad grin.

'Morning, Mrs Sergeant – lovely day, isn't it?' he called back.

'Get in here, this minute!' his employer thundered and Raymond took off his jacket quickly, exchanging it for a work coat hanging on the door.

'I can tell the Sergeant-Major is full of the joys of spring,' Raymond whispered to Sara as he passed. 'I'm Raymond, but I can't stop.'

'I'm Sara,' she smiled back, thankful she would have an ally against the grumpy grocer. This must be Raymond, the footballer whose aunt, Mrs Ritson, she had spoken to yesterday, Sara realised.

Presently, her job done, Sara crept into the shop where Mrs Sergeant was instructing Raymond on his morning errands.

'The lass can help you make up the parcels,' she jerked her head at Sara. 'Perhaps she can stop you getting them wrong for a change. I don't want Mrs Naylor ringing up complaining you delivered Greek currants instead of Californian sultanas again.' Mrs Sergeant gave him one of her severest looks.

'No, Mrs Sergeant, I can't think how such a terrible thing happened,' Raymond answered, his thin face pained. But the mischievous look in his bright blue eyes showed Sara he was teasing the humourless woman.

'Well, get on with it,' she ordered with a fat finger.

'Haway, Sara,' he beckoned, 'you read out what's on the list and I'll gan up the ladders.'

As she read out the names of the goods that had been ordered over the telephone by Mrs Sergeant's more well-to-do patrons, Sara had time to look around the cramped, old-fashioned shop. From floor to ceiling, its shelves were stacked with tins of cocoa, corned beef, pears, syrup, baking powder, dusty packets of tapioca, teas and sugar, while brass-handled drawers hid explosive

125

mixtures of curry powder, matches and cut plug for pipes. Under glass cases on the counter were displays of her finest boxes of biscuits; Nice and Cream Crackers, and a large selection of cigarettes, including packets of Players, the brand Tom had been smoking on his last visit home. Behind the counter a cold slab held neat parcels of butter wrapped in greaseproof paper and a side of pink bacon waiting to be carved by an ancient slicer.

'Half a pound of – tea,' Sara struggled to read the spidery writing.

'What kind?' Raymond asked from halfway up the ladder.

'Ass – something,' Sara blushed.

'Assam!' Mrs Sergeant barked, watching over them closely, despite the interruption of two customers.

'Sorry,' Sara stifled a giggle as she saw Raymond grin.

'When you're done,' the shopkeeper said sternly, 'you can make up some packs of sugar in the back.'

'Yes, Mrs Sergeant,' Sara answered meekly. This was worse than having her sister-in-law Mary bossing her around, she thought.

As Raymond escaped on his bicycle to make his deliveries, Sara was sent into the storeroom.

'Use the royal blue paper for granulated and the dark blue for caster.' Sara watched the woman's quick, dexterous movements as she cut the correct size of paper and made it into a bag, pouring in a shovel of sugar and sealing it. The shop doorbell announced a customer and Sara was left puzzling over the art of packaging, while

126

Dolly Sergeant went to answer it.

More intent on listening through the half-open door to Mrs Sergeant fulminating at the visitor over the new air-raid shelter being built in the school playground, Sara struggled to copy the regimented bags of sugar lined up at attention on the shop shelves.

'...too far for me to walk to with my bad back.'

'Yes, Dolly, but I suppose it makes sense to have it there for the bairns.'

Sugar began to seep from the bottom of the misshapen bag and spill on to the floor. Sara cursed inwardly and started again.

'I can't bear to think what a war would do to my business. It's been bad enough these past few years having to run the place without Billy – and half the village out of work.'

'Let's pray it doesn't come to war,' the unseen woman answered. 'Give me a twist of black bullets an' all, Dolly, the bairn's got a sore throat.'

'On the account?'

'Aye, I'll settle up at the end of the week. You'll be looking forward to the Carnival, then. First in the rhubarb jam last year, weren't you, Dolly?'

Sara paused with scissors in hand at the mention of the Carnival. It must be a big event, she thought, everyone who had come into the shop that morning had talked about it, yet it was not until the end of the month.

'Yes, but I don't know if it's worth it – I'll not get away from the shop – I haven't managed to go since my Billy died.'

'That's a shame and you being such a good jam maker. Could that young lad not mind the shop?'

'Raymond!' Dolly Sergeant expostulated. 'I'd not leave him in charge of a pot of tea. Mind you, I've got a new lass started this morning, so if she's any good... And as long as Raymond's out the road – I'll not stand for any nonsense while my back's turned, I know what the young'uns are like these days.'

Sara, flushing with annoyance at Mrs Sergeant's derogatory remark, heard the customer ask who the new girl was, but the shopkeeper, suspicious at the quiet in the storeroom, closed the door before she answered.

A few minutes later the doorbell tinkled again as the customer left and Sara braced herself as the solid shopkeeper swept into the room. She shrieked at the mess Sara had created with the sugar, castigating her for the waste of the precious commodity. She was unceremoniously discharged from sugar duties and set to sweeping up again. Then, for the rest of the morning Sara was banished up the ladder to dust the top shelves and wipe over the tins of toffee and mustard powder that shared the same quarters. Sara was mystified by Mrs Sergeant's classification of goods; they appeared to be grouped together by the colour of their packaging rather than content. She was doubtful if she would ever be able to find anything if asked.

At twelve-thirty precisely, Mrs Sergeant closed the shop for her lunch hour and despatched Sara home. There was no sign of Raymond.

'Be back by twenty-past-one, sharp,' she ordered and, securing a purple trilby hat on her white hair, set off for her house in Oswald Street.

Sara was reluctant to return to South Parade in case her uncle was there. Marina would be home from school and Ida would be fussing over dinner and not wanting her in the way.

Moreover, her appetite had deserted her and the thought of the morose Colin loafing around, too, convinced Sara that she would wander the village instead.

After half an hour of meandering the town and its warren of identical streets, Sara found herself in Pit Street and was excited to discover Dimarco's cafe on the opposite corner. If only she had some money with which to go in and order a treat from its sparkling windows under the gaily striped awnings, Sara thought wistfully. There had been no mention of remuneration from the formidable widow grocer and Sara had not dared ask when she was likely to be paid her first wage.

Still, she could gaze in at the sophisticated cafe and watch its patrons guzzle ice-cream. She sauntered over pretending to study the array of chocolates in the window, far superior to Sergeant's dull bottled jars of boiled sweets and leaden toffees. Mouth-watering, these were studded with coloured crystallised flowers and encased in beribboned boxes, their lids raised to entice the sweet-toothed.

Glancing into the cool interior of the parlour, Sara did not like to admit that she half hoped for a glimpse of the handsome Joe Dimarco. On one side of the cafe, wooden booths housed marble-topped tables and coloured glass in the partitions threw shards of red and blue light on to the spotlessly clean tiled floor. Some tables were occupied by people drinking tea and eating pies and a stocky young man with a thin moustache was hurrying to and fro with a tray, but there was no sign of Joe.

A large silver machine with taps and handles gleamed on the polished counter, and behind it stood the mustachioed proprietor she had spotted from Marina's bedroom window. From the hissing machine, he dispensed coffee and jokes with a genial, beaming face to the customers. A woman with hair tightly scraped back in a bun was pouring chocolate drops from a curvy-shaped jar into a cone of paper for a child at the counter.

A voice startled her from behind. 'You can't afford to go in there!' Sara jumped round guiltily and saw Raymond standing at the kerb with his bicycle, his large cap pushed back on his copper-coloured hair.

'Just looking,' Sara replied, with a lift of her chin. 'Where've you been all morning, any road?'

'Got a puncture,' he grinned. 'Bobby Dimarco's been fixing it for me. His people run this place. I'll treat you to an ice if you like.'

Sara was touched by the youth's ready generosity, for she was sure Mrs Sergeant would not pay him enough for such luxuries.

'No, I couldn't,' she refused half-heartedly.

'Have you had any dinner?'

Sara shook her head.

'Haway, I'll buy you an ice-cream,' Raymond insisted, propping his machine against a lamp-post. Sara followed him eagerly.

'Hello, Mr Dimarco,' Raymond greeted the proprietor, 'Mrs Dimarco.' She nodded at him.

'Good afternoon Raymond,' the burly Italian replied with a smile. 'What can I do with you?'

'I'll have a chocolate ice with monkey's blood please,' he replied.

'What's monkey's blood?' Sara asked, pulling a face.

'That's the red syrup,' he laughed.

'And the young lady?' Mr Dimarco inclined his head towards Sara.

'Vanilla, please,' she smiled shyly, enjoying his deferential manner.

'A good choice,' he nodded wisely. Mrs Dimarco disappeared to fetch some more glasses.

'Your Bobby's just fixed me bike,' Raymond told the rotund cafe owner as they waited. 'So if you want me to do any deliveries for you after work, just say the word.'

'*Grazie*, you're a good boy, Raymond,' the man thanked him. 'My Joseph may need some help at the Carnival. *Va bene*, I come and say the word then.'

Mrs Dimarco reappeared and served them ice-cream in tall glasses with long-handled spoons. 'Fourpence,' she smiled and Raymond handed over the money.

'You sit at the table,' Mr Dimarco insisted with a sweep of his hand. 'Enjoy your ice-cream.'

'Ta very much,' Raymond grinned and led Sara to a table by the door where the wood and glass partitions would not obstruct the view of passers-by. She realised he was enjoying showing off to her in front of the Dimarcos and perhaps hoping some friends might spot him sitting in the prestigious cafe with an unknown girl. Sara did not mind; she sucked happily on her spoon, unable to believe her luck in having two ice-creams in two days.

It reminded her of the football match and she told Raymond she had met his aunt, Mrs Ritson.

'Auntie Louie watches me in all weathers,' Raymond said proudly. 'Hates football but she always turns out to support me.'

'Do you live with your aunt, then?' Sara asked.

'Aye, ever since me dad died when I was a bairn.'Raymond volunteered the information without emotion. 'Mam's a famous actress and has to travel, you see,' he preened. 'She's been on the wireless an' all.'

'Never!' Sara gasped in admiration. She eyed her skinny companion in a new light. 'I'd love to meet a real actress. What's she called?'

'Iris Ramshaw.' Raymond's face shone with pride. 'It's her maiden name – actresses often keep their maiden name like that.'

'I've never heard of her,' Sara said, a touch disappointed.

'Well, she's famous,' Raymond maintained stubbornly. 'Mam has to travel about all o'er the place. But she comes home when she can,' he added with a wistful note in his voice.

Sara warmed to the boy's friendly confidentiality and found herself telling him about her own father's death, feeling the ache of emptiness ease a fraction as she spoke of him. She explained why she had come to live with her uncle.

'Alf Cummings?' Raymond's look hardened as he repeated the name. 'We don't have anything to do with him.'

Sara wanted to ask why, but was wary of antagonising her new friend, so she asked him about his own uncle instead.

'Uncle Sam's an important man in the union,' Raymond said proudly, 'and popular too – except with the bosses and men like Cummings. That's why he's been unemployed more often than not. Auntie Louie didn't want me to gan down the pit, so I took the job at Sergeant's – naff pay mind.'

Sara was on the point of asking about pay when Joe Dimarco strolled into the cafe and the question died on her lips.

'*Ciao*, Raymond,' Joe greeted him with a playful punch. 'Sorry you lads lost the match yesterday. Still, the saints were on our side,' he joked.

'Luck of the devil, you mean,' Raymond grunted. Joe laughed, unoffended.

'Waiting to see my sister, are you?' Joe's tanned face grinned. 'Well Rosa's washing nappies all day, so you're out of luck.'

Raymond's white face turned crimson. 'Get lost! I hardly know your sister! Any road, I divv'nt care about lasses – they're too much bother.' Then he caught Sara's quizzical look and added quickly, 'Not all lasses, mind. Joe, this is Sara, she's new in Whitton and doesn't know her way about. We just came in for an ice-cream.'

Joe swung round to look at her properly and recognition dawned.

'Hello again. I see you've got a taste for Dimarco's ices?'

'Aye, best in County Durham so they say,' Sara said dryly.

Joe laughed. 'And is your ankle any better?'

133

Sara blushed, realising she had quite forgotten about hurting it.

'On the mend,' she mumbled.

'So you know Sara?' Raymond interrupted, his face disappointed.

'We bumped into each other at the football,' Joe grinned, his dark eyes appraising. Then turning back to his friend he asked, 'What were Normy Bell and Scotty arguing with you about before the game started?'

'Nowt.' Raymond was reticent.

'Were they giving you a hard time again?' Joe demanded.

'No more than usual,' Raymond muttered. 'It's you that's bothering them – said I was to warn you off.'

'Why?' Joe laughed.

'You know why,' Raymond answered with embarrassment. 'Normy doesn't like you seeing Olive Brown – says there'll be trouble if you try and see her again.'

'I'm not scared of Normy Bell,' Joe was scornful.

'He's looking for trouble, Joe,' Raymond warned, 'and I don't see that Olive Brown's worth the bother.'

Joe clapped the other youth on the shoulder. 'Don't worry, I'll look after you, Kirkup.'

Raymond shook him off with embarrassment. 'Didn't say I was bothered about Normy or Scotty, did I?'

Sara, annoyed by talk of the popular Olive Brown, stood up. 'We better be getting back to the shop, Raymond.'

'Oh, so you're working at Sergeant's, too?' Joe asked, regarding her once more.

'Aye, it's me first day and I'm already in her black books for spilling sugar everywhere.'

'Joseph!' his father called across the shop. 'We have a business to run. Help Paolo while I speak to the traveller.'

'Know what you mean!' Joe touched her shoulder with a smile. She felt a ridiculous thrill at the gesture.

'Ta-ra, Raymond – Sara.' He left them.

Sara followed Raymond out of the parlour, glancing back.

'You like him, don't you?' Raymond nudged her playfully.

'Who?' Sara took on an innocent air.

'Joe Dimarco. You went all pink when he was talking to you,' the boy smirked. 'He has that effect on lasses.'

'Not me,' Sara pouted, then as casually as possible she asked, 'Who's Olive Brown?'

'Last year's Carnival Queen. Joe's been seeing her, but Normy Bell thinks she's his lass. If Joe's got any sense he'll leave her alone – Normy's a bad'n.'

Sara quashed her jealousy for the unknown Olive by changing the subject.

'And who's Rosa?' Sara grinned. 'The mention of her got you in a flummox.' She nudged him back.

'No it didn't!'

'Rosa, Rosa,' Sara sung the name aggravatingly. 'What a romantic name.'

'Haway,' Raymond gave her a shove. 'I'll race

you back.'

Sara responded to the challenge, chasing after the swift youth up Pit Street and into Mill Terrace. They fell against the back door of the shop just as Mrs Sergeant appeared round the corner in her pork-pie hat.

'Stand to attention,' Raymond muttered under his breath and Sara suppressed her urge to giggle. At least with Raymond around, working for Dolly Sergeant might not be such a drudge, Sara thought with optimism.

But by the end of the first week, life in Whitton Grange seemed bleak. Raymond spent most of the day out on his deliveries and Sara was left to the full wrath of Dolly Sergeant. Tuesday was a day of disasters; Sara managed to drop a box of eggs and then burst a bag of split peas which scattered into every corner of the shop. On Wednesday she lost the key to the spice drawer and on Thursday nearly injured Mrs Sergeant by letting go of a toffee tin from the top of the ladder. Her employer scolded and threatened her into a useless, fumbling idiot and Sara wondered, anxiously, if she would be out of a job by Friday.

At home, there was tension in the Cummings' household. Her Uncle Alfred had badgered Colin into going to see Naylor, the under-manager, as there were rumours at the Eleanor that boys were being taken on at the pit. When Colin returned unsuccessful, his father had been so incensed he had locked him out for two nights. Sara had seen him from her bedroom window, sleeping with his dogs in their kennel, his legs exposed to the night rain, and felt sickened by her uncle's heartlessness. She had gone out in her nightclothes and given Colin a blanket from her own bed, retreating, embarrassed, by his stuttering thanks and the dirty hands that reached out to touch her as he took her offering. But Marina had watched her go and relished landing Sara in trouble by telling her mother who reported it to Alfred.

'You'll spend your evenings in for the next week,' he had raged, his small brown eyes merciless, 'and do Ida's mending and any other jobs she can find for you. Do you hear?'

Her aunt had put her to making a new patchwork blanket to replace the one spoiled by Colin's dogs, so Sara had not been able to explore the town after work or hang around the ice-cream parlour which seemed such a popular haunt of the young. She thought now and then about Joe Dimarco and once heard a motorcycle roar down the backlane, but it was gone by the time she got to the window and she did not know if it was his.

Anyway, she concluded as she spilled out her feelings in her diary, he's probably never thought about me twice. Raymond says all the lasses fancy him, so why should he bother with me? she wrote. Then guilt gripped her to think that Sid Gibson probably still thought of her as his lass and yet she hardly thought of him. A letter had come from her mother, passing on regards from Sid and she had been engulfed with homesickness to read how much she was missed at home. She thought of her mother constantly.

To compound her unhappiness, Sara received a shock on Saturday afternoon. After Raymond received his wages, Sara had the temerity to ask for hers.

Dolly Sergeant gave her a thunderous look. 'I've handed them over to your uncle, you cheeky madam. You must know about the arrangement?'

'What arrangement?' Sara asked sharply, her frayed patience dangerously near snapping.

Mrs Sergeant drew herself up behind the counter where she was consulting her books. 'Mr Cummings thought it best we had an arrangement – so you'll have to speak to him about it.'

Sara looked at her, astounded. Suddenly, after all the disappointments and upsets that week, she was filled with anger.

'He doesn't have any right to me wages,' she protested. 'You should have given them to me!'

The middle-aged woman gasped at her boldness. 'He has every right,' she snapped back. 'He's giving you bed and board, isn't he? Besides, young lasses don't know how to handle money these days – you'd just throw it away going to the pictures or the dance hall, more than likely,' she spoke with disgust.

'But I'm supposed to be sending money back to me mam,' Sara persisted, defiantly.

'Well, that's your concern. You'll have to have it out with your uncle.' Mrs Sergeant stabbed the inventory with fingers like sausages, 'We have our arrangement and that's that. If I hear any more complaints from you, you can pack your bags and be off.'

Raymond came inside from winding in the tattered canopy to hear this last threat. He was swift to interrupt before Sara said anything rash.

'Finished, Mrs Sergeant. I'll be off, then. You coming, Sara?'

Sara nodded, stony-faced, as she pulled on her cardigan and stuffed her overall savagely into her string bag. The shopkeeper had gone back to entering totals in her account book.

'Be here sharp Monday morning,' she told them without looking up. 'If you're late again, Raymond Kirkup, I'll dock a day's pay.'

Outside, Raymond whistled with relief. 'And a happy weekend to you too, you old cow,' he said over his shoulder. Sara was still seething too much to laugh with him.

As they walked on, her companion warned, 'Do not cross the Sergeant-Major about brass again, mind. She's that touchy about her money. Your uncle'll give you some pocket money, won't he?'

'That's not the point. I don't want to be beholden to him,' Sara fumed. 'How will I ever be able to save money for Mam and return home, if Uncle Alfred keeps it all?'

'Is that what you want,' Raymond asked shyly, 'to gan home?'

'Aye, of course,' Sara said crossly. 'I *hate* Whitton Grange! I hate Sergeant's and I don't want to stop a minute more than I have to with the Cummingses. Me uncle's a bully and Marina's always whingeing on – and as for Colin and those dogs barking all night long!' She looked desperately at the lad beside her, realising how she dreaded returning to South Parade. 'It's not me home. I miss me mam and me sister Chrissie. And I've got a lad called Sid who wants to get wed.'

Sara flushed at her own words, not knowing why

139

she should mention him to Raymond. If she was honest, she had hardly given the quiet, dependable Sid Gibson more than five minutes' thought in the whole of this past week, let alone dwelt on marriage. But she was angry and miserable and adding him to her list of wants seemed to give strength to her case against Whitton Grange.

Raymond watched her in dismay, wondering whether to feel insulted by her attack on the village he loved. He pitied her, but what help could he be? Lasses were either moody like Nancy Bell in the next street, or mysterious like the shy and pretty Rosa Dimarco who sometimes came into the shop for household soap. This one, he glanced at Sara in awe, appeared to be both and he would do best to leave well alone.

'I'll see you Monday,' he said abruptly, abandoning the idea of asking Sara to his home, 'I've got footy practice.' He took off up Holly Street without a backward glance, head buried in his enormous cap.

I don't have any friends here, Sara complained bitterly to herself, even Raymond could not wait to get away from her. She realised she was close to crying and brushed at her eyes to prevent tears falling. Yet she would not give in to self-pity, she told herself harshly, or let the world see her unhappiness.

It was half an hour till tea-time. She would not go home immediately, not caring if her truancy got her into trouble. Turning round, she set off down the hill to wander along South Street and peer into the shop windows. Sara was drawn to the posters outside The Palace cinema, wretched that she had no money to buy a ticket for the matinee.

As she did so people began to stream out of the early performance of a George Formby film and Sara watched them enviously as they chattered. With a jolt she recognised Joe's dark head above the crowd, as he pushed his way into the street.

Sara pulled back her untidy hair and pushed it under her beret, conscious of how bedraggled she must look after a day clearing out the storeroom. An instant later he seemed to be looking her way and for a second or two they held each other's gaze. Joe was smiling and Sara's heart began to beat with excitement.

Then a pretty girl with wavy, bobbed brown hair and a fashionable pink cotton dress emerged at his side and linked her arm through his. It was someone other than Olive Brown, for Raymond had told her Olive was plump and fair.

Sara stood back, her rising hopes that he was about to speak to her dashed. A moment later, the young couple were beyond her, swallowed up by passers-by and the chance encounter was over.

Had he recognised her, or had she just imagined it? Sara gulped back the tears in her throat. What did it matter? she asked herself harshly. Joe Dimarco was a waster and a womaniser who, this particular Saturday afternoon, was courting an attractive brown-eyed girl in a pretty summer dress. Whereas she stood limp and grubby in a patched skirt and home-knitted cardigan, her hair a tousled mess under a green school beret. No wonder Joe Dimarco had ignored her. Best to forget all about him. Sara bit her lip in dis-appointment and walked away.

Chapter Eight

It was not until Sara had been at Sergeant's for nearly three weeks, that she first met Rosa Dimarco. Raymond was away delivering a parcel of quality Darjeeling tea to The Grange, with Mrs Sergeant's warning not to dawdle ringing in his ears. She made it sound as if the Seward-Scotts would be drumming their fingers on the tea table that very moment in anticipation of the smelly scented leaves, Sara thought with derision. But the speciality tea was one of the few items the illustrious coalowner's household ordered from Sergeant's and they would not be kept waiting a second more than necessary.

Dolly Sergeant was on the telephone in the storeroom and Sara was left in charge of the shop for five minutes when a slight, dark-haired girl came in clutching a small boy by the hand.

'Can I help you?' Sara smiled, admiring the newcomer's apricot-coloured dress and matching hair ribbon that set off her creamy skin and dark brown eyes. The chubby-faced infant was neatly dressed in velvet shorts and a yellow blouse. Something about them marked them out as different from the noisy, grubby children around Mill Terrace who usually came in for twists of sweets.

'We've run out of baking powder,' the girl explained. Sara turned and picked a tin off the shelf, enjoying the feeling of being in charge.

'There we are. Anything else?'

'Sweetie!' the little boy pulled away from the girl's hold and pointed at the solid jars of coloured sweets on the counter.

'No, Peter,' the girl answered with a shake of her head, 'you've been eating all morning.' She looked back at Sara with an apologetic smile. 'I'll take two tins of plums and a packet of pudding rice please. Oh yes, and a bag of blue.'

'Sweetie!' The boy began a more persistent cry, jumping up and down in his well-polished sandals.

'Be quiet, Peter,' the girl tried to hush him, her straight fringe falling into her eyes as she bent down. Sara thought that something about her was familiar but could not recall seeing her before. The child pushed her off, keeping up his demanding chorus. Sara leaned up and pulled the bag of rice off the shelf, then searched in vain for the plums.

'They're next to the tinned salmon,' the girl said helpfully.

Sara laughed, 'I've been here three weeks and I still can't work out what goes where.'

'Only Mrs Sergeant seems to know that,' the other girl smiled. Peter's shouts were growing so loud, Sara knew it was a matter of minutes before her employer appeared to reprimand the child for making her telephone conversation with Mrs Naylor impossible. Mrs Sergeant was not shy of scolding the local children for what she considered to be bad manners.

'Peter...' Sara leaned over the counter and spoke to him, '...would you like a piece of liquor-ice? Sweetie liquorice?'

'Yeth,' he lisped, triumphant.

143

'One bit won't do him any harm,' Sara said brightly and pulled a stick of the black confectionery from a box on the counter. 'There's a sugar mouse an' all,' she offered in a spontaneous gesture. 'We'll not tell the boss,' Sara grinned at the other girl. The boy sighed with pleasure at the sudden treats.

'Thank you,' the dark-haired girl replied. 'He's that spoilt, but it's not easy saying no to Peter.' She patted his head with affection. 'He's my parent's oldest grandchild and only grandson, you see. Paolo, my brother thinks the world of him, too. Daddy's bonny *bambino*, eh, Peter?' she cuddled the boy.

'You're one of the Dimarcos, aren't you?' Sara asked with sudden realisation. The girl had the same liquid brown eyes and engaging smile as Joe.

'Yes, how did you know?' the girl seemed surprised.

'Just guessed,' Sara blushed. 'I've been to your cafe with Raymond – you know – the lad that works here,' she added swiftly.

'Oh, yes, Raymond. He's canny, always laughing. Sometimes helps my father out if we're extra busy.'

'Is there anything else you need?'

'No, that's it, ta. Could you put it down on the account, please?'

Sara rummaged for the book. The Dimarcos must be good customers and prompt payers to be one of the chosen few for Sergeant's credit, Sara thought wryly.

She licked the pages as she turned them. 'Dimarco, Dimarco – ah, here you are.' A long list of previous orders filled the page and Sara wrote the new items into the book in her bold handwriting.

'I'm Sara, by the way,' she spoke as she wrote, not wanting the girl to rush away. 'Are you Rosa?'

'Yes.' The girl's open face showed surprise again. 'You seem to know all about us. We haven't met before have we? It's just I don't remember...'

'No, Raymond's mentioned you, that's all.' Sara glanced up slyly, but Rosa just seemed bemused. 'Were you at school with him?' Sara asked.

'Yes,' Rosa replied, 'but he was two classes below me.'

Sara looked at her more closely, realising she must be older than her girlish fringe and flat chest made her look. 'Do you work in your dad's shop now?' she asked, intrigued.

'Sometimes,' Rosa nodded. 'I do the washing up and clear the tables if it's busy. But usually I'm stuck in the house upstairs helping my mother,' she added wistfully.

'Well, you're not missing much,' Sara pulled a face. 'I think I'd rather be at home than doing shop work all day long. It's killing on me feet.'

'Are you related to Mrs Sergeant?' Rosa asked.

'No, thank goodness!' Sara whispered, glancing over her shoulder at the storeroom door. She could still hear the older woman gossiping on the telephone. Rosa giggled with her. 'Me uncle got me this job,' Sara continued. 'I don't come from round here – me family's from Rillhope, near Lilychapel.' Rosa's face looked blank. 'Up Weardale,' Sara elaborated. Rosa shrugged in ignorance. 'Well, anyway,' Sara gave up trying to

145

explain, 'I was brought up on a farm – I'm not used to a pit village.'

'No, it must be strange for you,' Rosa leaned on the counter, eager to chat. 'My family were farming people, too – in Italy – that's where my parents are from. But I've always lived in Whitton Grange – I don't know anything else. I think my mother would like to go back one day – but my father is happy here, so we'll probably stay for ever.'

Sara put her chin in her hands, her fair hair falling forward. 'You wouldn't want to go back, would you? I mean, you seem as English as me, if you don't mind me saying.'

Rosa shrugged with indecision. 'Perhaps when I marry...'

Sara smiled knowingly. 'Ah, you mean when some tall dark Italian whisks you away to his large mansion in Italy as his blushing bride!'

Rosa gasped at the idea. 'I think that only happens in the pictures,' she giggled.

'Aye, you're probably right,' Sara sighed.

'My sister Domenica is getting married to a handsome Italian, though,' Rosa confided, 'in July. She and Pasquale are going to have a big wedding with musicians and dancing. She talks of nothing else.'

'That sounds grand.' Sara felt excited by the news, although she did not know Domenica. In the storeroom, the telephone clicked to signal the end of the grocer's conversation. 'And will she go back to a big house in Italy?' Sara asked hastily.

'No, an ice-cream shop in Sunderland,' Rosa said and then both girls burst out laughing, just as Dolly Sergeant appeared at the door.

146

'What's all this carry on?' she boomed in her deep voice. Her criticism died as she saw the young Dimarco girl filling her shopping bag with groceries. 'Oh, good morning, Rosa.'

'Morning, Mrs Sergeant,' Rosa smiled politely. 'My mother says she'll be in to see you next week.'

The woman heaved her bulky body behind the counter. 'I'll look forward to seeing her,' she nodded in approval. 'Now, don't let the lass keep you from helping your mother.' Sara bridled at the way she was never referred to by name in front of the customers.

'Oh, Sara wasn't stopping me,' Rosa gave her most innocent of looks. 'She's been very obliging.'

Mrs Sergeant gave a humph of disbelief, but Sara felt grateful to the girl for defending her.

'Come on, Peter,' Rosa took her nephew's hand, ignoring the stickiness that was the only evidence of the vanished liquorice. The sugar mouse bulged in the boy's pocket.

'Here, give the bairn a couple of lemon chips.' Dolly Sergeant relented at the sight of the solemn child and plunged her fat hand into one of the large jars. Rosa held her hand out quickly and took the offering, as Peter squealed, 'More sweetie.'

'Thank you, Mrs Sergeant, I'll keep them as a treat for after dinner,' Rosa smiled engagingly, her glance at Sara conspiratorial.

'Ta-ta, Rosa,' Sara grinned, 'been nice talking to you.'

'Yes.' Rosa wheeled Peter around and led him to the door. ''Bye, Mrs Sergeant, ''bye, Sara.'

When she had left, Dolly Sergeant turned to Sara with a disapproving frown. 'You're not here to fraternise with the customers, lass. I can't leave you for five minutes and you're acting like the village gossip. Now get back in the storeroom and start unpacking those tins of pineapple.'

Sara checked her impatience and went without protest to the backroom. At least it was Saturday and early closing, she thought, just one more hour to pass.

Raymond appeared just as they were shutting up shop.

'I've met Rosa Dimarco,' Sara nudged him, as they shed their overalls in the storeroom. 'She thinks you're canny – always laughing, she says.' With glee, Sara noticed the youth glow pink.

'She wasn't talking about me?' Raymond scoffed.

'She was,' Sara insisted.

'Don't believe you!'

'Well don't, but it's true.' Sara pulled on her gaberdine, seeing through the dirty window that it had started to rain.

'Canny, did she say?' Raymond asked with a bashful grin.

'Aye,' Sara encouraged. 'She likes you. I said she was too good for you, mind, and too grown up.' Raymond looked aghast at the idea they should have been discussing him, then saw that she was teasing.

'Very funny!' he groaned. 'Still, I was going to call round to Pit Street to see if Bobby can fix me brakes. Squeaking all the way back from The Grange, they were.'

Sara laughed, 'You've got that parcel to deliver

148

to your Auntie Hilda at Greenbrae, remember?'

'I remember,' Raymond grinned, bundling her out of the back door, as Mrs Sergeant came to lock up.

'See you Monday,' Sara smiled at him and ran in to the rain.

All was quiet when she arrived home at South Parade. Uncle Alfred would be playing billiards at the club and Aunt Ida and Marina were visiting Mrs Hodgson, the vicar's wife, to discuss arrangements for the Carnival flower show and who would be serving teas in the Mothers' Union tent. Such social gatherings at the vicarage were the highlight of Aunt Ida's week, Sara knew from her aunt's anxious excitement over breakfast on such days. As Ida would be late back, Sara had been told to prepare the vegetables for Uncle Alfred's tea.

Bliss to have the house to herself for a few hours, Sara thought thankfully. But she had hardly removed her coat when the back door banged and Colin stamped in, trailing his muddy boots over the pristine kitchen floor. They regarded each other warily. Sara had hardly spoken to him since helping her cousin had landed her in trouble with Uncle Alfred and confined her to the house to do her aunt's wretched sewing.

'Afternoon,' Colin glowered.

'Want a sandwich?' Sara asked, feeling tense as she went into the larder for a hunk of cheese.

'Ta,' Colin grunted. He hung around, making her unease grow, his dull eyes watching her every move.

'You'll be taking the dogs out this afternoon?'

149

Sara broke the awkward silence.

At least he would not be around for long, Sara thought with relief. She prepared two cheese and pickle sandwiches and pushed one towards him on a plate.

'I'm taking mine in the front room,' she told Colin, eager to escape his presence. But he kicked off his boots and followed her along to the parlour like a possessive hound. Sara wanted to fetch her diary and record her meeting with Rosa, but she was not going to let Colin know she kept a secret correspondence with herself. No one in Whitton Grange was ever going to discover the things she wrote about them or their dismal town.

They sat at opposite ends of the room, the smacking and grunting of Colin's noisy eating disturbing the quiet.

'There's a practice race in the park this afternoon,' he startled her with the sudden announcement, his large jaws demolishing the bread and cheese. 'I'm putting Gypsy in.'

'Oh, that's nice.' Sara answered, trying to hide her irritation at his pig-like noises.

'And I'm showing her in the Carnival,' he said, dropping pickle onto his mother's new carpet.

'Good.' Sara's smile was tense; she wished he would hurry up and leave.

'Want to come up the park, then? I know Gypsy's your favourite.'

Sara looked at him in astonishment, embarrassed to see the expectant expression on his face. It was no idle question, but then Colin did not waste unnecessary words. She was about to say no, when it occurred to her she had nothing better to do but peel vegetables and return to the endless patchwork. Why should she not have a trip to the park in the fresh air, even if it was with her odd cousin? she reasoned.

'Aye, I'd like that,' she replied, licking the end of her fingertips.

Colin sprung up, a foolish grin spreading across his large face.

'I'll get Gypsy ready. Give you a shout when we're done.'

Sara nodded and watched him go. It was not that she disliked Colin Cummings, it was more a feeling of distrust. That was it, Sara decided, there was a darkness in Colin's brooding looks, a pent-up anger in his sullen mouth that disturbed her. He seemed at odds with the world. But at least, Sara reasoned, he appeared to like her and so his private grievances were none of her concern.

It was blustery in the park, with occasional splatters of rain that whipped off the low hills, shaking the yellow gorse in a frantic dance. But Sara enjoyed its freshness, her long hair coiling around her full face and her green eyes squinting into the pearly grey sky at the motley collection of dogs running around the field. It was the same uneven pitch that was used for football games, but the spectators today were grey-faced pitmen of indeterminate age who whistled their whippets to heel or spat knowingly into the wind.

Colin was soon immersed in the sport and Sara, growing bored and thinking she would not be missed, wandered off. Taking shelter behind a high hedge, she sat on a bench and watched the

151

outcome of a tense game of bowls. Enjoying the somnolent click of balls and muted comments, she fished out her diary and pencil from her coat pocket and began to scribble her thoughts.

'Sweetie!' a familiar voice cried and Sara looked up to see Peter running unsteadily towards her. Behind him came Rosa pushing a large pram.

'Hello again,' Sara greeted her. Rosa smiled and came over to sit beside her, manoeuvring the hooded pram next to the bench. Peter climbed up beside Sara and started searching her pockets. She quickly pushed the diary inside her gaberdine.

'Sorry, pet, I've nothing to give you,' Sara caught the pudgy exploring hands in hers. He giggled and tried to release the hold.

'Here, Peter, eat this,' Rosa handed him a banana, 'and leave Sara alone. She isn't made of sweets you know.'

'Is this another Dimarco?' Sara asked, peering into the boat-shaped pram.

Rosa nodded, giving the pram a gentle rock. 'Baby Linda, Paolo's daughter, she's four months old. Sleeping at last, thank goodness. She was yelling so much, my sister-in-law Sylvia was at the end of her tether, so I said I'd take her for a walk.'

'It's done the trick,' Sara smiled, looking curiously at the plump, peaceful face, all but hidden in a fancy frilly bonnet. 'My friend Beth has a baby boy Daniel about the same age. He gets on her nerves a bit, too.'

'You could bring him out for a walk when I bring Linda,' Rosa suggested with enthusiasm, 'we could meet in the park when you're off work.' Rosa liked this girl with the untidy hair and the expressive face and wanted to be friends.

'Oh, she doesn't live here,' Sara explained, 'she's at home in Rillhope.'

'Oh,' Rosa sounded disappointed. 'Is that far away?'

'Far enough,' Sara answered glumly. 'Twenty–thirty miles or so. But it takes most of the day on the bus, by the time you've walked into Lowbeck and then changed at Stanhope...' Sara broke off, seeing by the look on Rosa's face she might as well be talking about Outer Mongolia. 'It's a world away, Rosa,' she said sadly, 'and I've not heard from Beth since I came here. I've written but had no reply.'

'Expect she's been busy with her bairn,' Rosa suggested kindly. 'You'll hear from her soon I bet.'

'Aye, well, Beth was never any good at writing,' Sara said ruefully. 'At least you can go and visit your friends. Living in a town has its compensations, I suppose.'

'I don't have friends, really,' Rosa answered simply, 'just my family.' Sara watched her more closely, but her expression was uncomplaining.

'You must have someone,' Sara insisted. 'Who do you go to the pictures with?'

'I don't go,' Rosa said, leaning forward to pull the restless Peter on to her knee.

'Well, church then?' Sara persisted, seeing the delicate silver cross hanging from Rosa's neck. 'Don't you have socials?'

'We go to mass,' Rosa conceded, 'but we never get to the socials – the parlour is always open and we're working when everyone else is free. My parents don't take holidays. That's just the way it is,' she finished.

'I see,' Sara nodded sympathetically. 'My dad was like that I suppose – but at least the family had a bit fun, now and then.'

'I'm not unhappy,' Rosa became defensive. 'I love my family – I don't need anyone else. And sometimes we get together with the other Italian families in the area – at weddings and things – like Domenica's. That will be fun.'

'Aye, I suppose you're the lucky one having your family around you,' Sara conceded, feeling an engulfing loneliness to think how far away were her own loved ones. 'I miss me mam something terrible. I write to her every other day!'

'Tell me about your family,' Rosa urged, snuggling Peter on her knee.

Sara found herself unburdening to this simple girl, who appeared even more naive than herself about the outside world and yet generated a warmth and interest towards her that she found comforting. They sat for a long time, while Sara told her about Stout House and her happiness there until her father's death. Rosa pushed a lacy handkerchief towards Sara when grief for her father bubbled easily to the surface. She did not seem embarrassed by Sara's tears but prompted her to keep speaking. Peter wriggled off her knee and went to explore under the hedge and still Sara went on talking.

She spoke of her brothers and Chrissie and her tiffs with her sister-in-law, Mary.

'You're like me!' Rosa said with delight. 'I have a sensible older brother Paolo like your Bill, and Joe's the daft one like Tom.'

154

Sara laughed. 'Tom was always getting into trouble with me dad.'

'So does Joe,' Rosa grinned, 'but they still love each other. It's just in Joe's nature to be disobedient.'

'I think he'd get on well with Tom, then,' Sara smiled. The baby woke up and instantly began to whimper.

'Do you want a feed, *bombalina?*' Rosa rocked the pram vigorously. She stood up. Turning to Sara she asked unexpectedly, 'Would you like to come back to my house for a cup of tea?'

Sara hesitated a moment, thinking of the unpeeled vegetables, but the thought of going to the Dimarcos' house was too big a temptation to resist.

'I'd love that,' she agreed and went to extract Peter from under the hedge where he was playing with a dirty tennis ball he had found. Together the girls set off down the hill into the village, Sara quite forgetting Colin and Gypsy and the original reason for being in the park.

Colin noticed with fury the way Sara had slipped away, showing no interest in the dogs. She was just like the rest of the family, he thought with disgust, only concerned for herself. For a short while he had thought her different.

'Bloody lasses!' he cursed and spat as he watched Sara leave the park with Rosa Dimarco instead of returning to watch Gypsy. She was just as bad as the other girls, only concerned about gossip and not about his beautiful, sleek animals.

'Who's that with the Italian bitch?' It was

Norman Bell suddenly beside him with his ill-kempt mongrel, Baldwin, and his sour-faced companion, Scotty.

'Me cousin, Sara,' Colin flushed.

'What she want to hang around with foreigners for?' Norman asked with a jut of his blemished chin. Colin shrugged. 'Want a bit of sport?' Norman continued, his pale blue eyes challenging.

Colin slid a look at the cropped-haired youth with his name tattooed across his knuckles. If Norman Bell or his friend Scotty talked of 'sport' it meant only one thing.

'Where you going, Normy?' Colin asked.

'Dene. Got a quarry.' His smile was malicious. 'Coming then?'

Colin gave one last glance to where Sara had been sitting. She was gone. 'Aye,' he answered with a spit, his aggression stirring, and fell in behind the others.

Joe Dimarco stepped back as Olive Brown slammed the door in his face, leaving him speechless. Normy Bell had forbidden her to see him, she'd said, because his family were Italian and the Italians had just made a pact with the Germans. Joe fumed, wanting to dismiss Olive's foolish words. Normy's antipathy towards him had nothing to do with his family being Italian; Normy Bell hated his guts because he was a better boxer and Olive, last year's Carnival Queen, had chosen to go out with him instead of Normy. Nevertheless, Joe decided to detour through the dene on his way home and find out what was going on, unable to shake off his unease at Olive's warning, which still rang in his ears.

'Listen, Joe, you'd better watch out for Normy and the others. Don't say I didn't warn you. And Raymond Kirkup – he's another one in trouble. His dad was a scab and you shouldn't let him hang around with you.'

'I'll choose my own friends, ta very much!' Joe had shouted at her.

'Suit yourself,' Olive had answered, trying to close the door.

Suddenly suspicious, Joe had seized her arm and demanded, 'What do you know about Raymond Kirkup?'

Olive had protested, but Joe held on. 'Normy said something about a scrap in the dene. Now ger'off us!'

Ten minutes later, scouting along the oily burn, Joe almost gave up, finding nothing more sinister than a group of children knocking apples off the overhanging trees from Naylor's vast walled garden. But a nagging concern for Raymond's safety made him continue.

Reaching the disused railway siding at the head of the dene, Joe rode past the no trespassing sign where the fence had been torn down, dismounted his motorcycle and lit up a cigarette. As he blew smoke into the air and mused ruefully on Olive Brown's rejection, he heard muffled voices from one of the far abandoned carriages. Someone shrieked out in fear and a baying of dogs went up.

Joe ground out his cigarette and ran forward. He circled the rotting trucks and debris of the once-busy siding, searching for the source of the noise. Rounding a corner, he saw the ramp of one freight

157

van was down and inside he could see three shadowy figures lacing into a prone body doubled up on the floor. A couple of whippets snapped around the entrance, while a large, snarling black-and-tan mongrel worried at the victim's leg.

'Kirkups are scabs!' Normy Bell shouted and jabbed a heavy boot into the boy's guts.

'They're not–'

'Raymond Kirkup's a scab's bastard!' Scotty took the next swing with his foot.

'Ah-ya!'

'Your father was a bloody traitor scab! Come on, Colin, it's your turn!'

Raymond began to whimper.

'Where's your Uncle Sam to protect you now, eh, baby Raymond?' Joe saw Colin Cummings's ungainly figure loom over the defenceless boy. 'We're not good enough for his bloody club are we? Well let's see you fight now.'

'Please–'

Joe's stunned disbelief turned to sickening fear as Colin aimed a kick at Raymond's head and he heard the dull thud. The boy's arms went up in a protective reflex.

Long seconds seemed to pass as the others followed Colin's example, the rain of blows bringing sweat out on Joe's palms at their brutality.

'Tell your uncle that's what we think of his pissing boxing club,' Normy Bell screamed savagely. His bad-tempered dog barked and snapped excitedly.

Joe was paralysed with horror; any moment now one of the lynching gang would notice him and he would be next. Never before had he felt so afraid or so vulnerable. He dodged out of sight and crept back towards the motorcycle.

'Tell nancy boy Joe Dimarco he's next,' Normy jeered. 'Fancy having a dirty Wop as a marra.'

Joe stopped. Raymond had warned him about Normy and Scotty and he had told him not to worry. Joe had said he would protect his friend and now he was running away to save his own skin. What sort of friend was that? Joe accused himself. He jumped on his motorcycle, his anger igniting. These thugs had insulted his family and his race, they were scum who boasted of manhood by picking on younger boys and he would not be terrified by them.

Kicking his bike into life Joe swung round and roared towards the van. Nearly skidding as he turned sharply to confront them, he saw Scotty look up in astonishment at the sudden intrusion. The dogs stood alert.

'Leave him alone!' Joe shouted and revved.

'It's the Dimarco bastard himself.' Normy's eyes narrowed in hate. 'Let's have him.'

Joe did not wait to allow them to recover from their surprise. He rode up the ramp straight at Normy Bell.

Realising with incredulity that Joe had no intention of stopping, Normy jumped from the open doorway as the front wheel caught the side of his leg. His mongrel squealed in fright.

'You daft bastard!' Normy cried, hobbling out of danger.

Joe braked, pinning Scotty in the corner.

'Ah, me foot!' he whined in agony. Colin Cummings scrambled out of the way in a panic.

Joe turned and set off down the ramp, pursuing them across the empty yard, scattering them like frantic chickens. Raymond's attackers ran off into the dene, each looking out for himself. Colin Cummings, being slower than the others, was the last to flee through the broken-down railway fence and head for the shelter of the trees. His whippets raced ahead of him and Joe chased behind, threatening to run him down.

In his haste, Colin stumbled and fell, ripping his jacket at the shoulder. Joe circled him.

'Leave us alone, Dimarco,' he pleaded. 'It wasn't my idea. I didn't want—'

'Get up Cummings!' Joe cried at him. 'Before I run you over.'

Colin half scrambled to his feet, holding up his hands in protection.

'I didn't want to hurt the lad, honest!' Colin gabbled. 'It's just the others would think me soft if—'

'You're pathetic!' Joe shouted with disgust. 'You're worse than the rest of them with your whingeing. Get up, you're not worth fighting.' Colin got to his feet, breathing hard. 'But you go near Raymond Kirkup again and I'll ride this up your fat backside, do you hear?'

Colin's look was a mixture of loathing and fear. He turned without a word and ran in the direction of his vanished whippets.

Joe found Raymond sitting up clutching his leg, his left eye closed with blood and a swelling appearing on his brow.

'They could've killed you, the daft bastards!' Joe swore angrily. Raymond sat shaking; a

160

moment later he leaned over and was sick. Joe fetched a water bottle from his cycle and poured some on his forehead, then made him drink.

'They were waiting for me coming back from Greenbrae,' Raymond gasped at last. Joe shook his head in disbelief. The gang must have been watching his movements and known that Raymond took a parcel every Saturday afternoon to his Aunt Hilda who worked for the school-mistress at Greenbrae.

'Haway, let's get you home before they think of coming back.' Joe heaved him up. Raymond protested at the pain to his leg where Normy's dog had savaged him but Joe supported him to the cycle and helped him on the pillion. 'Your Auntie Louie'll fix you up...'

'Don't tell her what happened,' Raymond said stubbornly.

Joe looked surprised. 'Why not?'

'She'll just get upset I was picked on because of me dad being a blackleg,' Raymond fretted.

'But we'll get them back for you!' Joe felt bold in relief. 'Sam and me and Pat–'

'No!' Raymond was adamant. 'I'm grateful for what you've done, Joe, but I don't want a fuss made. Normy and Scotty'll just wait and get me again.'

Joe shrugged and argued no further. It was more important to see his friend home and cleaned up. As he pulled on his goggles he heard Raymond mutter, 'Why did my dad have to scab in the '26 strike? I hate him for it!'

Joe could not answer, for it had happened when he was a small boy. He knew that his own father

161

had nearly ruined his fledgling business helping out neighbours and extending credit to the strikers, so he understood Raymond's bitterness that his father should have betrayed his fellow pitmen. Shaken and subdued by the ordeal, Joe and Raymond headed back to the village.

Instead of tramping through the spotless ice-cream parlour, Rosa and Sara approached by the backlane where a farmer's cart stood waiting on the cobbles by an open gate. Out of it came the square-set young man who served in the cafe, rolling a vast empty milk churn before him.

'Paolo, this is my friend Sara,' Rosa said breathlessly, seeking his approval. The young man smiled shyly and nodded as Sara said hello, then his face broke into a besotted grin as Peter sprang towards him.

'Careful, little man!' He swung him up protectively, avoiding the metal churn. 'Have you been a good boy for Auntie Rosa, heh?'

'Good boy,' Peter mimicked. His father kissed him in delight.

'Come on, Peter, Daddy's busy.' Rosa grabbed him back and bundled him into the yard, his protests drowned by Linda's hungry cries.

'Ah, my little *pussetta*,' Paolo laughed and chucked the baby's cheek, making her cry even louder. 'Mammy's waiting for you, *bambina*.'

Sara followed Rosa as she steered the pram into a large yard with several outhouses. Immediately she was struck by its strangeness compared to the bare drab yards of the pit houses with their wash-houses and coal bunkers and tin baths hanging above moss-covered stone. Here, the brick walls had been white-washed and pots of coral pink Busy Lizzies sheltered in a corner, next to a rough wooden bench. Yet it was still a work-a-day yard. The door to one shed stood ajar, revealing large barrels and more milk churns.

'That's where my brothers make the ice-cream,' Rosa said, seeing Sara's curious glance.

'Do you have to help?' Sara asked.

Rosa shook her head and laughed. 'It needs to be stirred and scraped for hours – very hard work. You need strong arms like Joe's, not puny ones like mine,' she joked, bending her arm to show her lack of muscle. Sara felt a tingle at the thought of the brawny-armed Joe, with his sleeves rolled up, exerting himself over the barrels of ice-cream.

But Sara had no time to pause as Rosa led her across the yard, passing a small stable, pungent with the smell of horse manure and hay.

'This reminds me of home,' Sara said, sniffing the air nostalgically and feeling a pang of longing for her mother and Stout House.

'That's where Gelato lives,' Rosa told her. 'We don't use the pony much now – not since Joe got his motorbike – and my father has the van, so Gelato spends most of his time grazing on the green.'

'Oh? I've seen a black and white horse there – in front of my uncle's house.'

'That's Gelato. Peter likes to feed him, don't you, pet?' Rosa picked up the tiring boy.

'Lato,' Peter nodded, stabbing his fingers into his aunt's mouth.

'Funny name for a horse,' Sara said. 'Ours is

called Bluebell.'

'It means ice-cream in Italian,' Rosa laughed. 'My younger brother Bobby called him that when he was a small boy and the name stuck.'

Abandoning the pram in the yard, Rosa asked, 'Can you lift Linda out, please? Peter's tired and he might be awkward if I put him down.'

Sara, feeling nervous at the thought of touching the baby, pulled back the blankets and gingerly reached to pick her up. She was heavier than she had imagined and her dark eyes widened in astonishment as this stranger's face loomed near. For a moment she stopped her bleating and Sara cradled her tightly, fearful of dropping Paolo's precious daughter.

Rosa smiled, 'She won't break.'

'I'm not used to this,' Sara smiled anxiously. 'Am I doing the right thing?'

'Of course,' Rosa laughed, finding it strange a girl her age should be so ignorant of babies. She led the way into the backshop.

Sara gawped about her at the strange sights and smells that assaulted her senses. Clumps of mouldy-looking sausages and strings of onions and garlic hung from the ceiling like weird decorations, while tea chests and sacks of sugar, crates of pop and piles of long dusty loaves on top of chocolate boxes, crowded the stone floor. A creamy vanilla smell mixed with the deep richness of coffee from the parlour, and somewhere lurked the salty sweaty odour of old cheese. At a sink in the corner, a thin young woman with jet-black wavy hair was clattering dishes. She turned at the sound of their entry, rubbing her bony nose with the back of her wet hand.

'Rosa, thank you. Did Peter behave himself? It's time for Linda's feed. Come, little one,' she gabbled in her own language, stepping forward to take the baby. Sara gaped at her, jiggling the infant in her arms as she started to howl once more.

'Sylvia, this is Sara,' Rosa replied in English so her new friend could understand. 'She's been helping me with the bairns.'

'*Grazie!*' Sylvia smiled her thanks, plucking the babe from Sara's tense hold and cuddling her to her breast. The baby continued to cry. 'You come for drink, yes?' she asked Sara.

'Ta very much,' Sara agreed.

'Rosa, we're very busy in the shop,' Sylvia lapsed into a staccato of Italian dialect, 'can you finish the washing-up? Domenica is serving with your mother and Paulo is seeing to the milk. Joe is goodness knows where.'

'And Papa?' Rosa asked, depositing Peter and discarding her coat.

'He's upstairs with Father Guiseppe discussing the wedding arrangements.'

Sara looked between them, baffled by the alien tongue and wondering if Rosa was receiving a telling off for bringing her home.

'Is there anything I can do to help?' she asked, sensing the urgency.

'No,' Rosa reassured her. 'You go upstairs with Sylvia and the bairns and have a cup of tea with Granny Maria. I've just got to help out here for a bit – Saturday's are always busy for us.'

'Let me do that,' Sara insisted, reluctant to climb the gloomy stairs into the unknown without her friend. 'I'm not useless at everything domestic, you know. You go and help out front.' Sara had thrown off her gaberdine and pushed up her cardigan sleeves before Rosa could protest. Sylvia shrugged and nodded and Rosa dived into the shop with a hasty thanks.

As trays of dirty glasses and cups and dishes streamed in from the cafe, Sara felt an exhilaration in the mundane chore that she had never before experienced. The Dimarcos flew in and out, shouting at each other in a mix of English and Italian, fetching supplies of cigarettes and sweets, staggering in with a new barrel of ice-cream, making up exotic concoctions of ginger-beer and ice-cream, cream sodas and fruit sundaes and disappearing again into the bustling parlour.

The woman with the tight bun whom Sara recognised as Mrs Dimarco seemed taken aback to find her at the backshop sink but thanked her graciously and told her not to run away before she had been rewarded with an iced drink. Sara glowed with satisfaction that, for a short while at least, she was an indispensable member of the family team. For the first time since arriving in Whitton Grange, she felt needed and welcome.

When Mr Dimarco appeared on the dark stairway, he made an instant fuss of Sara, reprimanding his family for allowing a friend of Rosa's and a guest in the house to be allowed to wash up.

'You are Raymond's friend, yes?' Arturo Dimarco asked. 'I never forget a pretty face,' he teased.

Sara blushed coyly, loving the attention.

'Papa!' Rosa laughed.

'*Bene!* Rosa give Sara a cool drink – an ice-cream – whatever she wants.'

Sara sat down happily at the bare wooden table in the backshop with her friend while they sipped soda through straws and spooned delicious mouthfuls of homemade ice-cream.

'I could live on this stuff,' Sara grinned, relishing every sweet morsel. 'Even Aunt Ida doesn't make anything this good.'

The sudden thought of her aunt made her go cold and then flush hot with panic. She had quite forgotten the time. Glancing at a clock on the shelf above the sink she saw with horror it was well after four.

'Eeh, I'll be skinned alive!' she screeched at Rosa who looked up with alarm. 'Uncle Alfred'll be home for his tea and I haven't even peeled the potatoes. I'll have to go.' She jumped up, abandoning her half-eaten ice. 'Ta for the drink.'

'You'll call again, won't you?' Rosa asked anxiously, reluctant to see Sara go. She was enjoying the fuss being made of her new-found friend and knew her mother would be disappointed if Sara went before she had grilled her on every aspect of herself and her family.

'Aye, I'd like that.' Sara grabbed her coat.

'We could go for a walk tomorrow with the bairns,' Rosa suggested.

'Grand!' Sara agreed. 'Say ta-ra to your parents and Sylvia.'

Halfway to the door, she heard someone enter from the shop and turned in the hopes that it might be Joe. Her stomach knotted to see the pretty girl with the bobbed brown hair who had accompanied Joe to the cinema walk in carrying a tray of dirty dishes. Sara's enjoyment of the afternoon vanished. Joe's girlfriend worked here, too! The tall girl was obviously well in with the family then, she thought with crushing disappointment. No doubt she was from another Italian family; as Rosa said, they did not need outsiders like herself.

'Sara,' Rosa called out to her, 'wait a minute this is—'

But Sara fled out of the back door, unable to stop and be civil to the girl that Joe favoured. She flew across the yard, fearful of the furious reception she would receive at South Parade. If Uncle Alfred did not get his tea at five o'clock precisely, she would be making patchwork blankets for the rest of the year.

Paolo waved from the outhouse, but she ignored him, skidding across the cobbles, greasy in the fresh rain that had fallen while she had been busy inside. At the gate she almost fell into Joe Dimarco as he dismounted from his motorcycle.

For a moment his dark face gawped with surprise instead of his usual confident amusement. He grabbed her to prevent her falling and Sara coloured scarlet as his fingers dug into her upper arm.

'Running into me again!' he laughed.

Sara was about to laugh too, her heart hammering to be suddenly so close to him, when the thought of his pretty girlfriend just yards away made her stiffen. She shook him off.

'You should mind where you're going, Joe Dimarco,' she glared with her green eyes. He looked nonplussed by her rebuttal. 'And this is one lass who's not going to fall at your feet, an' all. You might think you're God's gift to lasses, but you're not as far as I'm concerned!'

He had nothing to say. Sara straightened out her coat and, anchoring her beret on her fly-away fair hair, stalked off down the backlane. She itched to look back to see if he watched her go, but resisted the urge. She had meant what she said; she did not care two pins for the tall Italian. Round the corner and out of sight, she picked up her heels and ran like the wind, trying to shake off the memory of his dark eyes and strong hands on her.

Joe stood, hands on hips, wondering what he had done to offend the plump-cheeked girl with the blonde hair to whom he had hardly given a second thought. He clicked his tongue against his teeth and shrugged. He was peeved by her rudeness, his feelings already battered after Olive's rejection and the brutal hostility of Norman Bell's gang in the dene. For the first time in his life he wondered if he really was different from his peers in Whitton Grange. Today he had certainly been made to feel so.

Shrugging off the uneasy feeling, he watched the strange girl disappear and admitted to himself that there was something about her petulant dismissal of him that stirred his interest; perhaps those haughty green eyes.

Turning into the yard he went in search of the answer to why this strange girl, Sara, had come running out of their back gate in such a hurry.

Chapter Nine

Sara clattered in the back door, bracing herself for a reprimand.

'Where in the world have you been, girl?' Ida fretted, her face pink in the steam of the kitchen.

'Sorry, Aunt—'

'It's a good job I got back early from Mrs Hodgson's. Father's in a fearful temper as it is — he's late for the billiards competition. Did you expect him to go out on an empty belly? Really, Sara, what were you thinking of?'

'I met a friend in the park—'

'It's no time for excuses — get yourself into the dining-room,' Ida interrupted.

Sara did as she was told, never having seen Ida so agitated.

'And where the hell have you been?' Uncle Alfred thundered from the end of the table. 'You should have been here helping your aunt, not galavantin' around the town.' He stood up and wiped his mouth, dressed in his best suit.

'Sorry, Uncle Alfred, I won't be late again,' Sara apologised.

'No, you won't, 'cos you'll stop in all of next week and help your aunt around the house, starting from tonight,' he ordered.

Sara bit her lip in frustration, glancing at Colin across the table.

'Oh, Uncle Alfred, I only went to the park to

see Gypsy race, didn't I, Colin?' she protested.

Colin glowered back at her. 'No you didn't – you went off with Rosa Dimarco,' he accused. 'I saw you.'

Sara blushed hotly, taken aback by his disloyalty.

'Dimarco?' Alfred frowned. 'One of them Italians? What you doing with the likes of her?'

'She's just a friend, Uncle Alfred – comes into Mrs Sergeant's. Mrs Sergeant thinks the world of the Dimarcos,' Sara added quickly. 'Such good payers, you see. Me and Rosa got chatting.'

He pursed his lips in disapproval. 'Well, I'll not have you gettin' cosy with foreigners – and Catholics at that. No, you just stop in the house with your Aunt Ida,' he nodded at his wife as she bustled in with a fresh pot of tea. 'I know what's best for you and while you're under my roof you'll do as I say. I've no time for another cup, Ida, I'm late as it is.'

He left with Marina and Ida following him to the door and making a fuss over his going.

'It's nice to know who your friends are,' Sara muttered at Colin.

'You said you were going to watch Gypsy.' Colin was petulant.

'You didn't have to tell him about Rosa, did you?' she countered.

'What you want to be friends with her for? She's not one of us. The Dimarcos are foreigners,' he said with disgust. 'They don't belong here.'

'Then neither do I, Colin Cummings!' Sara hissed back as Ida returned.

171

For the rest of the meal she remained silent and resentful. Once she had helped Ida wash up and set the breakfast table and Marina had gone to bed, Sara locked herself in the bathroom and wrote the events of the day into her diary, pouring out her fury at her Cummings relations. But it was to Joe Dimarco that her thoughts kept returning and the harsh words she had spoken to him in the back lane behind the parlour. On reflection, perhaps she had been a little hasty in her condemnation. After all, they hardly knew each other, so why should she be so bothered that the dark-eyed Joe was courting someone else? Sara sighed heavily as she closed her notebook for the night.

If Rosa had gone to the park on Sunday afternoon, she would have looked in vain for her friend, Sara thought with frustration, as she spent the afternoon helping Ida cut up and stitch together scraps of cloth into dolls' clothes to sell at the Carnival. Marina was bad-tempered and Colin bleary-eyed and morose, having come in late the night before and been boxed around the ears by his father. Only Ida was content, seeming to enjoy having Sara's forced company while she supervised her needlework and told her of the sewing sessions they had at the Mothers' Union.

'If you keep your nose clean,' Ida promised her, 'I'll take you along to Mrs Hodgson's sewing bee one of these days.' Sara paled at the thought but kept quiet.

It was a relief when Monday morning came and she escaped to the shop, anticipating Raymond's cheerful banter and Mrs Sergeant's familiar scowls. But she found her employer in a gale-force mood.

'He'll not be in today,' she snapped when Sara dared to ask where Raymond was. 'He's done som'at to his leg playing football – daft game, I say. Mrs Ritson called at home to tell me. I've a good mind to sack him on the spot. What use is he to me, hobbling around with a stick?'

'Will he be off long?' Sara asked in dismay.

'Better not be,' Dolly Sergeant bellowed, 'or there'll be hell on. He'll stand behind this counter if it kills him. But what I'm going to do with the deliveries, I just don't know.' She shook her head with worry.

'I'll take them,' Sara offered at once. 'I can ride a bike as good as any. Used to ride for miles at home – and the hills round here are nothing compared to up the valley.'

Mrs Sergeant gave her a dubious look. 'You're just a puny lass – you'll never manage all the groceries. It's heavy work.'

'Give us a chance, Mrs Sergeant,' Sara pleaded, relishing the thought of being out in the fresh air on the deceased Mr Sergeant's ancient bicycle.

The elderly woman sucked in her sallow cheeks. 'Well,' she considered, 'you can have a trial run to Greenbrae, in the dene. Do you know where I mean?'

'I'll easy find it,' Sara assured her. 'What do I need?'

Dolly Sergeant flapped a list of provisions and, snatching it, Sara hurried to collect the items off the shelves. She bound them up in brown paper and tied the parcels carefully with string, carrying them out to the bicycle in the yard, hidden among discarded crates, mouldering boxes and packing straw. Mrs Sergeant stood with hands on hips, instructing her where best to place the groceries. Tins and sugar went in the box on the back of the bicycle, while tea, eggs and a packet of wheat flakes were balanced in the basket on the front.

The machine wobbled precariously as Sara mounted, but she managed to steady it and launch forward across the yard. The seat was too high for her to perch on comfortably, so she stood in the pedals and called goodbye, not wanting to halt the momentum.

'Miss Joice's is the green door, next to the Naylors',' Dolly Sergeant cried, leaping out of the way.

'I'll find it!' Sara grinned and wove unsteadily out of the gate, leaving a troubled Mrs Sergeant shaking her mop of white hair.

'If you break those eggs you'll have to pay for them, mind!'

But Sara was rumbling down the slope towards South Street, gathering speed, whooping with joy at the motion and her unexpected freedom. Narrowly missing a coal cart, an arthritic man crossing the road and a hooting Parker's bus, she negotiated the hazards of the centre of town and headed for the Durham Road and the dene.

The morning was bright and blustery, the fresh breeze shaking the purple lilac and yellow laburnum blossom like Monday morning dusters clearing out the dreary weekend weather. The burnt, cindery smell of the village lessened as she took to the path through the dene and Sara gulped in lungfuls of air, privately thanking Raymond for injuring himself and giving her this chance to explore.

She found the large redbrick villa of Greenbrae, sheltering behind a screen of chestnut trees bedecked with candlesticks of white flowers. At the tradesmen's entrance, a cheerful, aproned woman with discoloured teeth and straw-coloured hair helped Sara carry in the parcels.

'You doing Raymond's job then?' she asked. 'Just put them on the kitchen table.'

'Aye, he's injured himself playing footy,' Sara panted.

'Footy!' the young woman guffawed. 'And I'm Vivian Leigh.'

'What do you mean?' Sara questioned.

'He's been in a scrap from what our Louie says. Raymond's my nephew, you see. Our Louie – that's my sister – is in a right panic he'll lose his job over it, so she's pretending it's a football injury. I'm Hilda Kirkup, by the way, but everyone calls me Hildy.'

'Sara,' Sara smiled briefly. 'Is he hurt badly?' she asked in concern.

'Bit bruising to the head and a nasty gash on his leg.' Hilda shook her head. 'But he's a tough'n'.' She cleared a space and dumped the sugar down on the huge, untidy wooden table. 'I've told Louie not to worry about him losing his job – that old dragon Sergeant'll not find many lads who'll work for the pittance she pays him – not with that many of them joining up just now. Queuing outside the DLI recruiting office they are.'

'Me brother Tom's in the DLI,' Sara told her. 'I

don't like to think there might be a war.'

'Who does?' Hilda sighed. 'My lad Wilfred's in the Terras – he'll be one of the first called up if it comes to war. Have you time for a cuppa? There's a fresh pot just made.' The bony-faced woman seemed eager to chat.

'Well, Mrs Sergeant won't miss me for a few more minutes,' Sara said, tempted to sit in the large kitchen with its huge black range. The smell of dried herbs and freshly made bread reminded her poignantly of her mother's farm kitchen, except this one was cluttered with piles of magazines and books, knitting patterns and half-made clothes strewn among the scales and baking implements. 'I don't want to keep you from your work, mind.' Sara glanced at the chaos. Hilda was unperturbed.

'Sit yourself down,' she said brightly, turfing a ginger cat out of a sagging armchair and flinging a half-sewn dress over the back. 'Miss Joice is no slave-driver – she won't be back till dinner time so I've got plenty time to do the washing.'

'Mrs Sergeant says Miss Joice is a schoolmistress,' Sara said, settling into her chair and feeling more at home with Hilda's mess than Aunt Ida's obsessive tidiness.

'Headmistress,' Hilda corrected, 'but she's canny – not the least bit strict with me. Mind, I've worked here since I left school, when old Dr Joice was alive. Now he was a *real* gentleman. Miss Joice never married, so there's just the two of us rattling around in this big house. Can you believe it?' she chortled. 'And if Wilfred Parkin ever gets round to popping the question, she'll have to find

176

someone else to look after this place.' Hilda's grin was wry. 'Are you courting?' she asked, handing Sara tea in a blue-and-white striped mug.

Sara flushed at the woman's directness, watching her open a tin of homemade shortbread and push it across the table. 'Not really.' She thought fleetingly of Sid, but he seemed so remote now, from another world. 'There was a lad at home – up Weardale – but...' Sara reached for a sugary biscuit to hide her awkwardness.

'So you're not from round here?' Hilda's deep-set blue eyes widened with interest.

Sara found herself repeating the story of how she had come to Whitton Grange and, as Hilda seemed keen to hear more, she told her all about her family and her life on the farm.

'Poor lass, losing your father like that,' she sighed. 'My mam died a few years back – she was always poorly. But me dad's fit as an ox. He was still working down the pit until three years ago when he retired. Now he walks around the villages preaching in the chapels – a proper John Wesley!' Hilda squinted over her mug. 'Jacob Kirkup, perhaps you've heard of him?' Sara shook her head. 'Your folk not chapel people?'

'My family are – the Pallisters,' Sara answered. 'But me Uncle Alfred likes me to go to the parish church with Aunt Ida. It's not really my cup of tea though – all that bobbing up and down.'

Hilda laughed, 'You should come to the chapel on North Street then – we'd be happy to see you. Our Louie goes regular – she sees that Raymond attends, too. Who did you say your uncle was?'

'Alfred Cummings,' Sara replied uneasily.

'Raymond says your family and Uncle Alfred don't speak.'

Hilda grimaced. 'Cummings is a bad word in Louie's house.'

'Why?' Sara wanted to know.

Hilda sighed. 'It all goes back to the '26 lockout.' For a moment she looked sad and reflective, then she smiled at Sara, a warm, compassionate smile that made her plain face interesting. 'It's water under the bridge – nothing for you to worry about, pet. These days, only men like Louie's Sam remember. Mind, Sam's had it hard – hasn't had a full week's work for ten years.'

'That must be terrible,' Sara said in concern. 'How on earth do they manage?'

Hilda shrugged. 'Louie cleans next door for the Naylors – Sam hates her skivvying for the under-manager but it helps put bread on the table – and now Raymond's working. But it's been hard for our Louie – I can't say it hasn't. And now my dad's retired from the pit, they have to pay rent on the pit house.'

They supped their tea in silence, as Hilda's mind seemed focused on the past. At least on the farm they had never gone hungry, Sara thought with thankfulness. She had been lucky in her upbringing in so many ways in comparison with the hardships these pitfolk endured. She was only just beginning to realise how fortunate she had been. Sara wondered why her mother had never told her about the poverty in Whitton Grange when she reminisced about the place. Surely it was something that could never be forgotten?

Then Sara remembered she was on trial as a

delivery girl and broke into Hilda's reverie.

'I'll have to be off – ta very much for the tea, Hildy.'

'Any time.' Hilda stirred herself and stood up with Sara. 'It's been nice having a bit natter – usually just the cat or myself to talk to around here,' she smiled. 'Come again, won't you?'

'I'd like that,' Sara agreed, 'I don't know many folk here. Just Raymond. And the Dimarcos – they've been friendly.' She did not know what suddenly made her mention them.

'Oh, the Italians on Pit Street?' Hilda sounded surprised. 'Wilfred sometimes takes me there if we're going to the pictures. They make the best ice-cream I've ever tasted.'

'Do you know them quite well then?' Sara asked lightly, as she pushed her hair into her beret to keep it off her face.

'No,' Hilda admitted, 'but Sam taught boxing to one of the lads – Louie's quite fond of him – what's his name? – goes about on a motorcycle...'

'Joe?' Sara felt butterflies as she said the name.

'That's the one. But the rest of the family keep themselves to themselves. Bit clannish, the Italians, Wilfred says. But they're respectable people – Mr Dimarco donates free ice-cream for the bairns' summer picnic every year. Mind you, the village give them plenty business in return – they have their own van and their own shop which is more than most of us have to show for years of hard work. No, the Dimarcos won't be short of a penny or two,' Hilda said with a touch of envy. She lifted the latch on the back door. 'And they'll make plenty out of the Carnival –

hundreds of folk'll be at the parade and the fair –
then there's the dance. You'll be going to that?'

'I doubt if my uncle will let me,' Sara said with
a resigned expression. 'And I've no one to go
with, any road.'

'*Everyone* goes to the dance,' the older woman's
voice sounded pitying. 'You could always come
along with me and Wilfred.'

'Thanks, but I couldn't do that,' Sara answered
hastily, leaving the haven of the warm kitchen.
Hilda was friendly, but she must be nearly twice
her age. Hilda and her man Wilfred would hardly
want a girl of sixteen tagging along, spoiling their
big night out, and the Carnival dance appeared
to be a big social occasion in this pit town.

'Raymond could take you.' Hilda suggested as
Sara climbed on her bicycle.

'Raymond?' Sara laughed. 'He's not interested
in lasses and dancing is he?'

'If he's like his father he will be,' Hilda smiled
wryly and waved her away. Sara felt a surge of
restlessness. Somehow she would find a way of
getting to the dance.

At closing, she decided to risk a telling-off for
being late home and go and visit Raymond. In
Hawthorn Street, she asked directions to the
Ritsons' home and found them near the top of the
steep street, hidden behind lines of flapping washing. Entering cautiously by the backyard, dodging
some well-patched shirts, she called at the open
back door. A bareheaded Louie Ritson popped
out.

'Haway in, lass,' she greeted Sara with a breathless smile. 'It'll be Raymond you've come to see?'

'Aye,' Sara nodded, following her into the cottage. 'How is he?'

'You can see for yourself,' Louie answered with a wave of her pink, chapped hands, showing her into the kitchen beyond the scullery. Sara stepped over a basket of washing waiting to be ironed and saw a white-bearded man sitting by the fire reading a newspaper. He nodded at her and Louie introduced him in a loud voice as her father, Jacob Kirkup. Beyond, Raymond sat eating fried egg and potato at the kitchen table. He looked up and grinned sheepishly, his head swathed in a thick bandage and his left eye a slit in a mass of purple bruising.

'Eeh, Raymond!' Sara winced.

'Pretty picture, isn't he?' Louie said with a click of her tongue. 'Won't tell us who did it, mind. Even Mrs Sergeant's not going to believe he got an eye like that playing football. I don't know what his mother would say if she could see him.'

'Well, she won't will she?' Raymond said defensively. 'There'll be nowt to see by the time she turns up at Christmas or whenever.'

'Sit yourself down, pet.' Louie pulled out a stool for Sara. 'Have you eaten?'

'I can't stop long. I'm just on me way home for tea, thanks all the same, Mrs Ritson.' Sara sat down.

'How's the Sergeant-Major?' Raymond asked, slurping his tea. Louie put a full cup at Sara's elbow. 'Missing me, I bet?'

'No,' Sara teased, 'I'm doing the errands now, so you can stay off as long as you like.'

'You are?' Raymond asked astounded. 'But

you're just a lass.'

Louie chuckled. 'Well done, pet. Perhaps he'll appreciate how important his job is after all.'

'There's not much point going back if Sara's doing me job,' Raymond complained. 'I can't be doing with standing in the shop all day with the Sergeant-Major breathing down me neck.'

'You're going back tomorrow, if we have to carry you in, lad,' Louie told him roundly. 'With your granda's stick you can manage well enough on a gammy leg. Isn't that right, Da?' she raised her voice to the elderly man but he did not hear.

Raymond pulled a face but the noise of footsteps and voices beyond the kitchen door put an end to argument. Sara turned to see a smallish thick-set man with receding hair and a strong jaw enter with a tall companion. It was Joe Dimarco.

'Got room for one more, pet?' Sam Ritson asked.

'Aye,' Louie answered without complaint, 'come in, Joe. Sam, this is Raymond's friend, Sara.'

Sara jumped up, quite unnerved by the unexpected arrival, glancing warily at the pitman, Sam Ritson, who was so at odds with her uncle.

'Sit yourself down, pet,' he said mildly. As she did so, she slid Joe a look.

He was watching her, his smile sardonic.

'Come to cheer Raymond's miserable face up?' Joe asked.

'Aye,' Sara answered, cringing to think of her rudeness to him on their last meeting. He swung on to the stool beside her.

'Rosa's disappointed you haven't been to see her,' he said.

'Tell her I'm sorry,' Sara blushed deeper, 'but me Uncle Alfred hasn't let me out since Saturday. I shouldn't really be here now.'

'Alfred Cummings?' Sam grunted. 'He's a fascist if ever there was one.'

'Now, Sam,' Louie warned, 'he's Sara's uncle.'

'You have my sympathy,' Sam retorted.

'Thanks,' Sara grinned, warming to his gruff humour. 'I better be off now and report to Führer Cummings.' Sam's face cracked in a smile at her joke. 'Ta for the tea, Mrs Ritson.' Sara stood up.

To her consternation, Joe followed. 'I'll see you down the road – I'm going your way.'

'There's no need–'

'What about your tea?' Louie asked dryly.

'I forgot Granny Maria's making pasta tonight,' Joe said airily. 'Sorry, Mrs Ritson. I'll see you at the club later, Mr Ritson?'

'Aye, we'll discuss the Carnival competition then,' he said, already tucking into his meal.

After they had gone, Louie asked Raymond, 'Has Joe finished with Olive Brown?'

'Aye,' the boy replied, gingerly sipping the thin soup his aunt had made him. Chewing was too painful. 'Looks like Sara's next on the list.'

Louie sighed. 'I hope he doesn't get her into any bother with her uncle,' she said dubiously.

'He's just walking her down the road,' Sam pointed out. 'Even an old bugger like Cummings can't mind that.'

'I worry for her living with that family – that terrible man,' Louie persisted. 'It's no place for a canny lass like Sara – she needs good company.'

'Looks like she's found it,' Raymond muttered.

'You've got enough to worry about with your own family, Louie,' Sam pointed out.

Jacob Kirkup rustled his newspaper and spoke. 'This German-Italian Pact is a bad thing,' he shook his white-haired head, 'a bad thing. You were right, Sam, we should have stopped them when they went meddling with the Spaniards.'

'Another cup o' tea, Da?' Louie shouted.

Jacob shook his head solemnly, sucking air through a gap in his bottom teeth. 'The barbarous hordes, Louie,' he said with a sad reflective look, 'they're on the march again, like in 1914 when...'

Louie exchanged glances with Sam. They knew he thought of his eldest son Ebenezer who had survived the Great War only to be estranged from his father by his scandalous liaison with a Seward-Scott. But Jacob would never allow Eb's name to be mentioned, let alone allow him across his threshold, even though he had later married his lover, Eleanor Seward-Scott, and had fathered a son, Rupert.

Louie laid a comforting hand on the old man's arm. 'Don't think about the past, Da. Have some more tea.'

'Why was Raymond beaten up like that?' Sara asked. They had walked the length of Hawthorn Street before she said a word, waiting for Joe's banter about the proposed boxing competition at the Carnival to end.

'Just bad lads picking on a weaker one.' Joe shrugged and Sara thought him callous in his lack of concern.

'And no one was there to defend him?' she said pointedly.

'He's going to have to learn to stand up for himself.' Joe's voice hardened. 'A few lessons from his Uncle Sam wouldn't do him any harm, but he doesn't care for fighting.'

'Neither do I,' Sara said with distaste.

'You surprise me,' Joe gave an infuriating smile. 'You seem to give as good as you get.'

Sara coloured.

'So why are you in your uncle's bad books?' Joe grinned. 'I'd like to see you answer Alfred Cummings back.'

'I got wrong for being late – and for meeting your sister,' Sara answered, sliding him a look.

'Rosa?' Joe said in surprise. 'Hardly a devil, that one.'

'Quite,' Sara sighed, 'but he doesn't seem to care much for your family.'

'The Cummingses don't care much for anyone,' Joe mocked.

'He'll not stop me being friendly to Rosa, mind, just because he's got strange notions about folk.'

'Good,' Joe said, as they turned into South Parade, 'I'd hate to think of you locked up and out of reach.'

Sara caught his wicked look and felt her cheeks go on fire.

'Better not see me to the door,' she gulped.

'Another time, then,' he smiled, but Sara had turned and was running down the street before she was seen with him.

Raymond hobbled in for work the next day but for the rest of the week Sara sallied out on the old black bicycle making the deliveries, while a subdued Raymond limped around the shop getting in Dolly Sergeant's way and taking the brunt of her criticism.

'She's driving me daft,' Raymond hissed to Sara as she returned after taking the special tea delivery to The Grange. Sara had been flabbergasted by her first visit to the secluded mansion of the Seward-Scotts, never imagining such wealth could exist. She had only seen the grandeur from the outside and there had been no friendly housekeeper to usher her in for tea as at Greenbrae, but the mine owner's house had sprawled in every direction, its steeply sloping roofs and turrets dominating the skyline.

'It took me ten minutes just to cycle up the drive!' Sara gasped, ignoring Raymond's complaints. 'I wonder how many servants they have to clean all those rooms?'

'The coffee beans have come in for Dimarco's,' Raymond told her and Sara's wonderings vanished at the mention of that name. 'I could walk round with them...'

'I'll take them on the bike,' Sara said quickly. 'You should rest as much as possible. Your Auntie Louie said so.'

'Rest!' Raymond protested. 'With the Sergeant-Major ordering me around all day. Me life's a misery, Sara!'

'Well, I've got a suggestion to cheer you up,' Sara plunged in with the idea she had been mulling over. 'Why don't we go to the Carnival dance together on Saturday?'

Raymond gawped at her. 'With you?' he sounded amazed.

'What's wrong with me?' Sara was offended by his tone.

'Nowt, I just don't like dancing,' he protested.

'You must do – your mam's a dancer,' Sara reminded him. 'I bet you're a canny dancer.' She gave him a winning smile.

'What you want to go with me for?' he asked, suspicious at the suggestion. 'I'm hardly going to be Fred Astaire with me leg all bandaged up.'

'Haway, Raymond, I just want to go,' Sara pleaded, 'and I don't know anyone else I can ask.'

'Charming!' Raymond grunted. 'I thought lads were supposed to do the asking, anyway.'

'Well, ask me, then,' Sara urged.

Dolly Sergeant shouted from the shop, 'Is that you back, lass?'

'Yes, Mrs Sergeant,' Sara called, then lowering her voice again, 'please, Raymond, you don't have to dance with me, just take me along. I haven't had any fun in ages. Rosa Dimarco might be there – your Auntie Hilda said everyone goes.'

'Ah, that's what this is all about, isn't it?' Raymond began to smirk. 'You think you might see Joe Dimarco at the dance.' Sara flushed with embarrassment at the mention of his name.

Dolly Sergeant grew impatient. 'Get yourself in here the pair of you!' she bawled.

'Coming!' Sara shouted back. 'Haway, Raymond, say yes?'

'I'll think about it,' he weakened. 'But you don't want to get any ideas about Joe. The Italians stick

187

with their own kind, Sara, just like Domenica's doing. They don't end up with local lads and lasses – I've been around them long enough to know that.'

'I don't know what you mean,' Sara said, turning scarlet and heading swiftly for the door.

'Besides, there are some people in the village who wouldn't like you gettin' friendly,' Raymond added mysteriously.

'If you mean Uncle Alfred, I don't give two pins.'

Sara dismissed his warning and rode eagerly over to Pit Street with the coffee beans, wheeling the bicycle into the back yard.

'Sara!' Rosa cried with delight, as she turned at the sink and saw the other girl entering the backshop.

'I've brought the coffee. I'm sorry I didn't come to the park on Sunday – I had to help me auntie,' Sara apologised.

'I'm glad about that,' Rosa assured. 'It was too wet to take the bairns out and we were that busy in the parlour I had to work all afternoon. Papa!' she called through the door. 'Sara's here with the coffee.'

Arturo Dimarco appeared in his long white apron. 'Sara, *grazie,*' he took the heavy package. 'How is Raymond?'

'Hobbling around and complaining he can't get out on the bike,' Sara grinned.

'Or playing the footy,' Mr Dimarco added. 'Poor Raymond...' he spread his hands in a sympathetic gesture. 'Rosa, get Sara something to drink. Lemonade, yes?'

'Thanks,' Sara nodded.

Rosa plucked a bottle from the top crate in the corner and pulled the stopper. When her father disappeared again, she asked. 'Are you going to the Carnival?' She poured them both a glass.

'I'll be working all day,' Sara answered glumly, sipping the fizzy drink. 'What about you?'

'Mamma says I can take Peter to see the fancy-dress parade,' Rosa answered with excitement, 'and Joe is in a boxing competition. Papa says he can enter as long as he sells lots of ice-cream at the dance.'

'Joe will be at the dance then?' Sara could have kicked herself the second the hastily spoken words were out.

'Yes.' Rosa glanced at her in surprise.

'It's just that – me and Raymond are going,' Sara stuttered, 'and I was hoping you'd be there too. They say it's a canny night out – the Carnival Queen starts the dancing and everyone gets dressed up.'

'Oh, if only I could,' Rosa gave a heavy sigh, 'but Papa would never let me.'

'Have you asked him?' Sara persisted, aware of how protective the Dimarcos were towards their youngest daughter.

'No,' Rosa admitted, 'but...'

'Suggest that Domenica goes with you, or Paolo and Sylvia – they can chaperone you,' Sara was persuasive. 'Tell him I'm going with Raymond – we can make up a party. Oh, go on, Rosa, do try!'

'Would you ask for me, Sara?' Rosa pleaded.

'If you want me to,' Sara agreed.

'Please!' Rosa nodded. 'I've never been to a big

189

dance before.'

'It'll be the first time I've been out in Whitton Grange, too – a chance to get dressed up – not that I've got anything grand to wear,' Sara pulled a face.

'You could borrow one of Domenica's frocks if you like,' Rosa volunteered. 'She brought a trunkful back from Sunderland.'

'Wouldn't she mind?' Sara asked, her eyes sparkling at the idea.

'No I'm sure she wouldn't, and you're nearer her height than mine.'

When Mr Dimarco appeared again with a cup of coffee, Sara nudged her friend. 'Let's ask him now,' she whispered.

'You ask!' Rosa blushed, suddenly nervous.

'What are you girls cooking, eh?' Arturo smiled indulgently, amused by their bashfulness. 'Tell Papa.'

'I was wondering, Mr Dimarco, if Rosa could come to the Carnival dance with me and Raymond?' Sara plunged in with her request. 'Domenica could come too and keep an eye – or Paolo and Sylvia, of course – it's such a special night – just once a year – and the Carnival Queen will be there, I just thought...'

'That you girls could see a bit of the dancing, eh? The girls in their smart dresses?' He looked amused.

'Please, Papa?' Rosa looked at him eagerly.

'And your uncle says yes?' Mr Dimarco asked Sara. Her heart missed a beat at the thought of Uncle Alfred. As yet, he knew nothing about her plan to go to the dance and it was not a confrontation she relished.

'Uncle Alfred won't mind,' Sara said evasively.

A knock at the back door interrupted their plea. Sergeant Turnbull loomed in the doorway.

'Come in, please come in!' Arturo beckoned their visitor. Rosa sat back in her chair and dropped her look. 'These girls are begging me to let Rosa go to the Carnivale, Signor Turnbull,' the large proprietor teased. 'Should I say yes? What do you think?'

The tall, fair-haired policeman removed his cap and looked across at Rosa with grey, considering eyes, while Rosa sat with head bowed.

'I don't see any harm in her going, Mr Dimarco,' he said coolly. 'She's quite a young lady now and we'll make sure there's no trouble. A father can be over-protective, I always think.'

Arturo spread open his hands and smiled. 'Then a loving father has nothing to fear?'

'Nothing at all. It's a respectable run dance, Mr Dimarco.' Turnbull's tone was vexed. 'Most of Whitton Grange are just as concerned for their daughters' well-being as you are, Mr Dimarco. You Italians don't have a monopoly on family virtues.'

'No,' Arturo Dimarco laughed in a baffled way. Sara did not like the way the police officer mocked Rosa's father in a way he did not understand.

'So we can go?' Rosa asked, her head shooting up.

'*Si*, you can go, little kitten,' he smiled. 'But only if Nonna Maria goes too. And we'll tell your mother when she has eaten and is in the good mood, yes?'

'Yes, Papa, thank you!' Rosa clapped her hands and grinned at Sara.

Arturo pulled out a chair for the grey-eyed policeman.

'No, I'm not stopping,' Turnbull refused. 'I've just come with a complaint about your son and his motorbike.'

'Joseph?' Arturo's face fell.

'He's been driving recklessly in the dene, by all accounts. Rode over Dick Scott's foot and narrowly missed Norman Bell.'

'Sante Guiseppe!' Arturo exploded. 'I will have the strong words with him, Signor Turnbull.'

'You better, Mr Dimarco, because if I get any more complaints, I'll have him charged and his bike impounded. Do I make myself clear?'

'*Si*, Signor Turnbull,' Arturo agreed at once, looking quite abashed.

'I must be off.' Sara rose feeling embarrassed to have witnessed the reprimand. For the first time, Sergeant Turnbull turned his methodical attention on her.

'You'll be Alf Cummings's niece?' He startled her with his deduction.

'Yes – sir,' she stuttered.

'I've seen you in church,' he explained. 'I'm friendly with your uncle and the missus attends the Mothers' Union with your aunt. Yes, your uncle and I are very good friends.'

'Oh,' Sara forced a smile and picked up her beret. 'Ta-ra, Mr Dimarco. Rosa, I'll call round tomorrow after work, then?'

Rosa nodded.

'*Grazie*, Sara.' Mr Dimarco waved her away

and she darted out of the back door, pleased to escape the searching eyes of the police officer. She emerged to find a young boy tampering with her bicycle.

'I thought I'd lower the saddle for you,' the sallow-faced youth announced before she could complain. 'I've seen you riding about and the seat's too high.'

'Thanks,' Sara laughed at his serious expression. 'Are you Bobby?'

'Aye,' he nodded, standing up. 'Try that.'

Sara hitched her skirt and climbed on. 'That's much better! Ta, Bobby. Raymond said you were canny with bikes.' The boy seemed pleased and Sara rode off, feeling mounting expectation at the prospect of the weekend ahead.

Raymond, after persuasion from his Kirkup aunts, agreed to take Sara to the dance. Broaching the subject with the Cummingses proved more difficult but Sara had prepared the way by being extra helpful around the house all week.

'What you want to go to the dance for?' Uncle Alfred demanded. 'I don't know what your mother would say,' he grumbled. 'No, I'll not allow it.'

Ida spoke up with temerity, seeing the disappointment on Sara's face. 'I don't suppose Sara's mother would mind. She always liked a dance herself.'

'And look where it got her!' Alfred glared at his wife. 'Married to a sheep farmer.' His face creased with disdain. 'No, I'll not have my niece going about with Red Ritson's nephew – you're not going and that's final.'

Sara took a deep breath to control her temper.

'It'd be the first evening I've been out since I came here, Uncle Alfred, I didn't think you'd mind me going out just once in a while. And I'll pay for the ticket myself out of the pocket money you allow me.' She forced herself to smile at him as she revealed her trump card. 'That nice Sergeant Turnbull was saying it'll all be quite orderly – no trouble.'

'Turnbull?' he looked at her across his pipe in surprise. Tapping it on the hearth he asked, 'Where did you meet him?'

Sara's heart skipped a beat. She did not want to tell him how the Dimarcos had befriended her, knowing her uncle would disapprove, but it would only be a matter of time before he heard about her visit there from the police officer.

So she answered carefully, 'When I was delivering coffee to that ice-cream parlour. Mr Turnbull was talking to the proprietor. They seemed friendly. Mr Dimarco's daughter Rosa is going, so it's all quite respectable. Mr Turnbull thought we should all go together – as long as you agree, of course, Uncle Alfred.'

'Turnbull said that, did he?' Her uncle considered, his indignation subsiding at the mention of the policeman. 'I'm surprised at him.' Sara waited, seeing the confusion on his face. 'No doubt he has his reasons for being civil to those foreigners,' he grunted. Sara held her breath. 'Well, just this once I suppose – and as long as you're back before eleven. And you're not to make a spectacle of yourself doing these modern dances. You're to behave yourself, do you hear?'

'Yes, Uncle Alfred,' Sara smiled, hiding her impatience.

'And I don't want you getting too friendly with this Italian lass, either.'

Sara feigned tiredness and escaped upstairs, exultant, before her uncle changed his mind.

Saturday seemed interminable as Sara was confined for half the day to the shop. She and Raymond had persuaded a reluctant Mrs Sergeant to agree to decorating the outside in festive greenery and flowers that Sara gathered from the dene. With Hilda Kirkup's help, she had been allowed some hothouse blooms from Greenbrae to display in the window and attract the admiring attention of passers-by. Raymond's leg had made a dramatic recovery, or so it appeared to a sceptical Sara as she saw him wobble off on the bicycle with produce for the Naylors, his head no longer bandaged, but his eye a glory of purple and yellow bruises. Ignoring his protests, she had bedecked the bicycle in coloured ribbon and daisy chains and told him to enter the competition for the 'best dressed bike'.

At ten o'clock Mrs Sergeant allowed her to stand at the shop door and watch the charity floats rumble past, bearing councillors and local dignitaries in fancy dress. The colliery band marched past, drums booming and brass instruments glinting in the sun, with villagers flocking behind. The Boys' Brigade came next, succeeded by a girls' jazz band playing jaunty kazoos. Sara yearned to be able to join in, waving at the throngs of holidaymakers rushing to see the children's fancy-dress parade and the three-legged race in the park.

'Go and watch the judging of the jam making, Mrs Sergeant,' Sara urged on her return. 'I can look after the shop for half an hour.'

To her surprise, Dolly Sergeant needed little persuasion to abandon her post to watch the judging. She returned, her jowly face triumphant, with a first prize in the jam and a third in the marmalade. Seeing that no catastrophe had occurred in her absence, Dolly Sergeant decided to allow Sara away early.

Sara rushed to the park to view the stalls and sideshows where boys attempted to knock coconuts from their perches and girls squealed with delight in the shuggy boats. Sara found Aunt Ida in the tea tent and in good humour, so was treated to a slice of sponge cake and a cup of tea, before dashing off to meet Rosa and try on one of Domenica's dresses.

For the first time, Rosa led her up the dark stairway to the Dimarcos' flat above the shop. Not knowing what to expect, Sara was struck by the spartan furniture in the living-room-cum-kitchen, functional rather than chosen for comfort. But the floor and table and large stove were spotlessly clean and there were touches of homely decoration in the lace coverings over the chair arms and arrays of family photographs proudly displayed on the mantelpiece and dresser.

Rosa's grandmother nodded at her with a toothless smile when Sara said hello. She had seen her knitting outside in the yard in the sunshine the day before, her face like a wrinkled plum. Then

Sara's stomach lurched as the tall girl at the stove turned around and she recognised the girl Joe had taken to the pictures.

'Sara's come to try on the dresses,' Rosa said brightly to the pretty girl with the short wavy hair.

'Hello, Sara,' she smiled warmly. 'It's nice to meet you at last.'

'Hello,' Sara replied, her voice tense.

'Domenica's looked a couple out for you,' Rosa continued, 'so come into our bedroom and try them on.' She led the way into a tiny back room with two narrow beds and a chest of drawers squeezed in behind the door.

'They're lovely!' Sara gasped, touching the cotton dresses laid out on the far bed. Then she realised she had seen one of them before; the waisted floral dress was the one Joe's girlfriend had been wearing as she came out of the cinema.

'This is Domenica's?' Sara asked, puzzled.

'Yes,' Rosa nodded. 'It's new but she doesn't mind you borrowing it for one evening. Ask her if you don't believe me.' Rosa jerked her thumb towards the kitchen.

Realisation dawned on Sara like the blinds being lifted from a horse's eyes. How stupid she had been!

'That's Domenica in there?' she almost choked with relief.

'Of course it is! Who else could it be?' Rosa asked baffled.

'Nobody!' Sara laughed with relief. 'Help me with the frock, Rosa.'

The first dress was too tight about the hips, but

the second was belted, with a wide skirt that flattered Sara's fuller shape.

'Is it a bit long?' Sara asked, glancing down at the green striped dress.

'No, it looks lovely on you – and your legs wouldn't suit anything too short,' Rosa answered candidly.

Sara laughed, 'That's honest.'

'Go and have a look at yourself in the mirror,' Rosa pushed her towards the door. 'There's one in my parents' bedroom.'

Sara did as she was told, emerging to the interested eyes of Domenica and her grandmother. The old woman said something in her own language and Domenica translated.

'She says it was made for you, green is your colour.'

'Thank you.' Sara grinned with pleasure at the grey-haired woman and hurried after Rosa. In the half mirror on the Dimarcos' bedroom wall, Sara admired the effect of the fashionable dress. The top was yoked and buttoned over the breast with small false pearls, the sleeves short over her rounded arms. It was gathered at the waist by a white belt and then flowed out over her hips, accentuating her womanly figure. With her hair brushed loose, Sara thought happily, she would look quite grown up.

Giggling, she and Rosa pushed each other back into the living-room. 'You try yours on now,' Sara grinned, piling her hair on top of her head. She stopped short, aware that someone else had come into the room.

In the open doorway Joe stood in rolled-up

sleeves, his muscled arms defined from the exertions of stirring a new batch of ice-cream. Wayward strands of his black hair stuck damp to his tanned brow and his grandmother shouted at him in Italian.

'Go away, Joe!' Domenica laughed. 'The girls are trying on their frocks for the dance.'

'Doesn't Sara look nice, Joe?' Rosa asked him innocently, proud to have a friend who looked as sophisticated as Sara suddenly did. Sara gulped and grew hot under his scrutiny, dropping her hands and letting her hair fall about her shoulders. For a few seconds he just stared at her as if he had never seen her before. Then he recovered his poise.

'*Bellissima*,' he smiled, continuing to regard her with admiring brown eyes. '*Very* beautiful.'

'Go, Joe,' Domenica commanded. 'Paolo's waiting for that ice-cream.'

'Paolo can wait – I need to sit down,' he grinned, pulling out a chair, still regarding Sara.

Granny Maria rattled off a sharp reply and he laughed, raising his hands in submission. 'I'm going, I'm going. See how I am ruled by these women, Sara,' he appealed to her. 'I'm free to do nothing.'

'And mostly he does nothing!' came Domenica's riposte.

'*Ciao*, girls, see you later,' he grinned and was gone. It was several minutes before Sara's pulse had returned to its normal pace and she left soon after to make ready for the dance.

Chapter Ten

To avoid the Cummingses, Raymond met Sara at the top of the street. He was glancing around nervously and fidgeting with his second-hand suit, his floppy cap pulled down over his black eye, when Sara appeared. He looked in alarm at her glamorous green dress, bare legs and honey-coloured hair loose and sleek over her shoulders. Raymond started walking as soon as she drew near to prevent the embarrassment of her slipping a hand through his arm.

'Free at last!' Sara grinned, falling in beside him. 'How's your leg?'

'I'll not be up to much dancing,' Raymond muttered.

'I hope you're going to cheer yourself up,' Sara nudged him. 'Rosa's looking forward to seeing you.'

'Well, I don't know why,' Raymond said, thrusting his hands deeper into voluminous pockets. 'I hardly know the lass – and don't you go pushing us together.'

He ducked his head as a group of lads overtook them. Sara shot him a surprised look.

'What's wrong, Raymond?' she hissed. 'You've been that nervy lately. There's not going to be any trouble tonight is there?'

'There's nowt wrong with me.' He quickened his pace.

Sara grabbed his arm and stopped him. 'There's something else,' she said looking directly into his face. 'I know you got beaten up the other Saturday and I want to know why.'

Raymond gave her a fierce look. 'I get picked on because me father was a scab – a strike breaker – the bosses' man. It's the lowest of the low in a pit village – specially a radical village like Whitton. And there are lads like Normy Bell and Dick Scott who'll use any excuse just to give someone a good hiding.'

'You mean you get the blame for something your father did years ago?' Sara asked, incredulous.

'Aye,' Raymond said tersely. He did not want to tell Sara of the threats against him for being friends with Joe Dimarco. He was scared, but Joe had saved him from a worse beating and he could not disown him. He would do anything for Joe now.

'And that's why your Uncle Sam and my Uncle Alfred don't get on – because of the strike?'

Raymond nodded. There was no point telling Sara that the enmity went deeper and that the Ritsons blamed Cummings for the death of Raymond's father.

'Why can't they let bygones be bygones?' Sara asked, feeling utterly depressed.

Raymond saw her sadness. 'Haway,' he brightened, shaking off his sense of foreboding, 'forget our uncles. Let's have a bit fun.'

Sara was pleased to let the matter drop as they joined the crowds of people making their way into South Street, heading for the grand Memorial Hall. Raymond slid her a look.

'I'll tell you some'at, though. It was Joe Dimarco saved me from a bad hidin' by Normy and his lot. Rode his motorbike right at them and they scarpered like frightened rats with him chasing.'

'Joe did?' Sara gasped. 'So that's what Turnbull was giving Mr Dimarco a hard time about.'

'Aye,' Raymond looked ashamed. 'Joe got into bother with the police for that 'cos Normy Bell's a cousin of Turnbull's and he knackered his ankle jumping over the dene. Serve the bugger right! I'd stick up for Joe in any fight, after he did that for me,' Raymond said with vehemence.

Sara felt a flood of admiration for Joe. Why had he not told her about his brave rescue instead of letting her think the worst of him? Sara wondered.

The carnival decorations above the closed shops and outside the public houses heightened the festive air in the dusty town. There were many who had been celebrating all day who were weaving about the streets, arm in arm, singing at the tops of their voices. As they reached the Memorial Hall, Sara caught her breath at the sight of the colourful flags and bunting almost hiding the solid building with its sweep of stone steps and pillared entrance. Lights shone from inside, beckoning in the dancers, and she rushed a limping Raymond up the steps in her keenness to be a part of the celebrations.

They made their way into the large hall, festooned in flowers and paper streamers, five musicians making ready to play on the far stage. Around the room, hard wooden chairs and plain tables had been arranged, with embroidered tablecloths hiding their bareness. Opposite the stage, open double doors led into a further room where Sara glimpsed long trestle tables covered with white linen cloths laden with sandwiches and jugs of juice.

'Sara!' someone called from a table in the corner and she turned to see Rosa waving them over. Already seated beside her were Domenica in a lemon skirt and white blouse and her sister-in-law Sylvia, looking demure but happy in a blue and white checked dress. Rosa was wearing the peach dress that suited her so well. Nonna Maria sat like a Victorian matron, swathed in black and presiding over her family.

'I didn't know the old witch would be here,' Raymond grunted.

'She's canny, come on,' Sara nudged him and he slunk behind her, hands firmly plunged in the pockets of his over-large suit.

Rosa made room for them on the bench beside her. 'Joe and Paolo are bringing in the ice-cream for the interval,' Rosa explained, putting Sara out of her suspense. 'Isn't it beautiful?' the dark-haired girl marvelled at the decorations above them.

'It's not as grand as the *fascio* in Sunderland,' Domenica said with a superior look. 'They had a ten-man band at the dances I went to.'

Rosa pulled a face and told Sara, 'Nothing's as good as Sunderland according to my sister. She can't wait to go and live there.'

'It must be an exciting thought,' Sara agreed, smiling at Domenica. She could understand Domenica's yearning to live in a sophisticated city and was impressed the older girl had been there. It showed in her style of clothes and her self-confident poise. 'What's the *fascio*?' Sara asked, intrigued.

'It's the Italian club,' Domenica explained with a condescending smile. 'All the families meet there socially. They have the best dances I've ever been to.'

'Have you been to many, like?' Raymond asked sceptically.

'Well no,' Domenica pouted. 'But I know they're the best.'

Rosa giggled. 'My sister's a know-all, Raymond. Are you feeling better?' she asked, abruptly changing the subject.

He flushed at her interest, still hiding beneath his grey cap. 'Aye, on the mend.'

Nonna Maria said something in Italian to Rosa and her chattering ceased.

'Here is Paolo.' Sylvia smiled shyly to see her small, dapper husband appear through the open doors of the supper room in a smart pin-striped suit and freshly shaven face, his thin moustache neatly trimmed. Sara's pulse began a rapid beating to see Joe at his side, a good head taller and not nearly so smart in a pair of old flannel trousers and open-neck shirt, with the tattered pigskin jacket he wore when motorcycling. It was torn and faded as if he had just scrambled through brambles, Sara thought disapprovingly. He had made no effort to dress up for the occasion, whereas she had spent ages on her appearance. Well, if he saw this dance as so unimportant, thought Sara, she would not let him guess how much she had been looking forward to it.

Paolo came and sat close to Sylvia and they exchanged a few words in Italian.

Rosa leaned towards Sara and whispered, 'It's the first time Sylvia and Paolo have been out anywhere since Linda was born.'

'They look happy,' Sara said, noticing the affectionate looks passing between the couple. While Rosa chattered about her niece and nephew, Sara was acutely aware of Joe beside her discussing the charity boxing competition with Raymond in which Joe appeared to have won his fight.

'Pat and the lads have just come in,' Joe nodded over to a group of youths standing at one side of the ball. 'Coming over, Raymond?' Joe asked. The younger boy accepted with alacrity, feeling quite out of his depth sitting among a group of girls talking about dancing and bairns.

Sara hid her disappointment as the boys crossed the room to speak to their friends. But soon her attention was diverted by the entrance of the Carnival Queen, dressed in flouncy pink and white with a huge headdress of flowers and attended by several other girls with garlands in their hair. The band played them in and then a square-jawed man in a smart suit was invited by the mayor to open the dance.

'I'm very pleased to be back in Whitton,' the important guest spoke stiltedly, 'and to – er – start the dancin'. I hope you all have a good night.' Amid enthusiastic applause, he went over to the Carnival Queen and, as the band struck up, they began to waltz around the hall.

'Who is he?' Sara quizzed Rosa. Her friend shrugged.

'He's a famous football star,' Domenica told them. 'Plays for Sunderland now.'

'Does Pasquale know him?' Rosa asked naively.

'No,' Domenica had to admit. 'Sunderland's a big place, you know. But Pasquale has seen him play, and I've seen his picture in the papers,' she added triumphantly and Rosa looked impressed.

Sara and Rosa were quickly immersed in the scene before them. Older couples took to the floor and executed perfect foxtrots, while the girls commented on their dresses and questioned Paolo on who was who, as most of them had patronised the parlour at some time or another. As the dance progressed, the youths of Whitton Grange grew bolder and began to cross the room to ask the opposite rows of single girls to dance. Sara glanced over surreptitiously at Joe and Raymond, but they were part of a crowd who had gathered admiringly about the professional footballer and were joining in a heated discussion with the ginger-haired friend she had seen riding on Joe's motorcycle, whom Rosa told her was Pat Slattery.

When Paolo and Sylvia danced a waltz, a young pitman came up to ask Domenica to dance, but she shook her head and told him she was already spoken for.

'The next time I dance will be at my wedding,' she sighed dreamily and began a litany of the arrangements which Rosa had heard countless times before. But Sara was eager to hear about Pasquale and the style of Domenica's dress and every detail of the romantic day.

'I'm so excited for you,' she beamed and Domenica seemed pleased at her interest.

'Can Sara come to the wedding?' Rosa asked unexpectedly. 'As my friend. You would like that wouldn't you, Sara?'

Sara was overwhelmed by her friend's genuine enthusiasm. 'I – I couldn't possibly expect...' she stammered.

'We would have to ask Papa,' Domenica said cautiously.

'Then will you ask him for me?' Rosa pressed her sister. 'Please, Domenica.'

Domenica was doubtful about inviting an outsider to such an important family occasion; after all, they hardly knew Sara and they knew her family even less. But Domenica wanted her young sister to enjoy the day, too. Having been away from home herself, she could see the restricted life at Pit Street was sometimes lonely for her sister. Soon she would be married and gone for good, Domenica thought, and deep down she was glad Rosa had found a friend to take her place, even if Sara was not from their community.

'I'll ask him,' Domenica conceded with a smile and squeezed her sister's hand.

'That's very kind of you.' Sara was breathless at their generosity. 'I'd love to come.'

Just then a woman called her name and Sara recognised Hilda Kirkup walking past them on the arm of a tubby red-cheeked man whom she took to be Wilfred. Hilda, in high-heeled shoes, towered over him by several inches.

'Are you enjoying the dance?' she asked Sara. 'I heard you were coming with our Raymond.'

'Aye,' Sara laughed. ''Cept I haven't danced yet. He's nattering about football over there.'

'Lads!' Hilda exclaimed. 'My Wilfred's just as bad, that's why I'm hanging on to him. Isn't that right, Wilfred?' The fleshy-faced man grunted. 'I'll send Raymond over, don't you worry,' the boy's aunt promised as they moved on.

Her words must have galvanised Raymond because, just before the interval, he limped dramatically to the table and asked her to dance. Sara felt wonderful, spinning around, feeling the skirt of her dress brush her bare legs as they moved amateurishly in a quickstep. Concentrating hard, she did not see Joe watching her from his position by the wall.

Sara appeared to have turned from a gauche girl into a lively young woman before his eyes, Joe pondered in amazement. Before, he had always seen her in darned clothes or gaberdine, her hair hidden in a green beret like a schoolgirl. But now he could see the plumpish curves of her sixteen years, flattered by the green and white dress and swaying in Raymond's awkward hold. Her long hair snaked over her shoulders, molten and glinting like liquid gold under the ballroom lights. Her green eyes sparkled with devilment, there was no other word to describe the look that lit her whole face, Joe thought with mounting interest.

His previous attempt to flirt with her had been half-hearted, but now he would ask her for the next dance, he determined, no matter what Domenica might say. His sister was forever badgering him to find a nice Italian girl with whom to settle down, but he felt in no hurry. He would have his fun first, and at that moment he could think of nothing more entertaining than dancing with Rosa's spirited friend, Sara.

But as he detached himself from the group of young men by the door, the interval was announced. Paolo caught his eye. With a reluctant glance in Sara's direction, Joe followed his brother into the supper room to help serve the ices.

When Sara and Raymond returned to their seats, Domenica and Sylvia had gone to help the Dimarco men and only Rosa and Granny Maria remained.

'That's finished me for the night,' Raymond groaned. 'It's harder work than footy.'

'Your leg's sore?' Rosa asked in concern.

'Rubbish!' Sara pushed him. 'There's nothing wrong with his leg that a few more dances won't put right. He was fit enough to skive off work and enter the bicycle competition this afternoon.'

'He mustn't overdo it, Sara,' Rosa warned, her pretty face creasing.

'I'm all right,' Raymond muttered, embarrassed by the attention. 'Let's go and get some grub.'

They joined the queues in the supper room and piled plates high with paste sandwiches and slices of corn beef pie, hard-boiled eggs and sweet tomatoes and took a plateful out to Rosa's grandmother. To quench their thirsts, they drank cupfuls of the homemade lemonade on offer. Later they went back for ice-cream and jelly, but to Sara's disappointment Joe was nowhere to be seen. How could he have left so early? she asked herself gloomily.

The dancing recommenced and the vast hall grew hot and airless as more revellers took to the floor and latecomers streamed in from the surrounding pubs.

Sara bullied Raymond through two more dances and, while they muddled their way through a waltz, she suggested, 'Ask Rosa for the next one. She's only danced with Paolo and Joe seems to have left without dancing with anyone.'

'Paulo said Joe's taking the empty tubs back home,' Raymond said, treading on her shoe.

'Ah-ya! Watch me foot,' she protested. 'Well, he's not hurrying back, is he? So let's forget about Joe Dimarco. Give Rosa a dance, Raymond – you'd make her night.'

'Give over,' he blushed. 'What would the old grandmother say?'

'Nothing,' Sara coaxed. 'You're just asking her for a dance not her hand in marriage.'

'Maybe I will...' Raymond mumbled.

There was a break for the announcement of raffle prizes and much sniggering from the ranks of boys when Raymond went up to collect a cheap necklace of sparkling beads and a bracelet to match. He stuffed them in his pocket and retreated, crimson-faced to the corner table.

'Suits your colouring!' Pat Slattery called out, amid guffaws of laughter.

As the band struck up for the final part of the evening, Sara gave him a nudge. 'I'll sit this one out,' she said and fanned her face with her hand.

Raymond cleared his throat. He felt goaded by the ribald remarks of his mates and was going to show them he could dance with one of the beautiful, remote Dimarco girls. So far there was no sign of Normy Bell or Scotty to intimidate him and Raymond felt brave.

'Would you like to dance, Rosa?' he spoke to the table.

Rosa glanced at her grandmother for permission. The white-haired woman nodded gravely and her sister said, 'Go on. We'll have to go home after this. We promised Papa to be in before the parlour closed.'

Rosa glanced at Sara, who was nodding encouragingly too. She stood up and took Raymond's hand, feeling a thrill to be asked to dance by someone who was no relation of hers, even if it was just pale-faced Raymond with his funny remarks. She was grateful to Sara for allowing her to dance with her partner.

Soon she was lost in the crowds on the polished wooden floor, shuffling around with her heavy-footed partner. He joked about his dancing expertise and made her laugh. Rosa felt quite light-headed as the music pulsated around them, drowning out the chatter of the dancers. For the first time in her life she felt grown up, no longer a youngest daughter or little sister, but a young woman at a carnival dance being paid admiring attention by a passably handsome boy in a hand-me-down suit. He was younger than she or Sara, but Rosa felt a stab of envy that Sara had found a boy as nice as Raymond to take her out. How would she ever meet anyone while she was cooped up at home every day? Rosa wondered with impatience.

The waltz ended and the moment of exultation passed. Reluctantly, Rosa allowed the rest of her family to lead her away.

'Come and see me in the shop next week,' Sara

told her.

'Yes,' Rosa promised, picking up her cardigan. 'And you must call round at the house – anytime.'

'Ta, I will,' Sara smiled.

As the others said goodbye and Granny Maria bustled them towards the main door, Rosa turned and called shyly, 'Thanks for the dance, Raymond.'

He nodded. 'Ta-ra, Rosa.' His cheeks under his auburn hair were flame-coloured. A moment later she was gone into the night.

Raymond and Sara looked at each other, both overcome by a mood of anti-climax. Sara looked at the large clock above the stage; it indicated half-past ten.

'I'll have to go soon,' she sighed. 'He's not coming back is he?' She did not have to explain whom she meant.

'Probably had to help his dad in the cafe,' Raymond tried to ease the disappointment. 'They'll be busy tonight.'

'He's not bothered about me, you don't have to be nice about it.' Sara gave a sad smile.

'You're a right one!' Raymond cocked his head. 'You ignore Joe when he's here and moan about him when he's not. How's he supposed to know you fancy him?'

'Who says I fancy him?' Sara tried to sound unconcerned.

Raymond just laughed. 'Here...' He dug his hand in his pocket, hating to see her glum, '...you have the necklace.'

Sara was touched by his gesture, but refused to take it. 'You give it to Rosa,' she pushed it back.

212

'She thinks you're canny, I can tell.'

'Do you think so?' Raymond swallowed. Sara nodded.

Just then there was a commotion at the door and Sara saw a group of lads forcing their way past the doorman. They were swaying with drink and one with a cropped head and a squint nose was shouting at the elderly attendant. Their mood was ugly and a menacing air blew in like a draught to the stuffy hall. With shock she recognised her cousin Colin looking belligerent among the troublemakers. Sara saw Raymond visibly pale.

'Is that them – the lads who beat you up?' she asked. He nodded.

'But Colin's with them,' she said nonplussed. 'You don't mean to say...?'

'Aye,' Raymond whispered, stiff-faced. 'Your cousin was there that day.'

'Never!' Sara said aghast. 'Why didn't you tell me?'

'Knew it would upset you,' Raymond answered.

'Oh, Raymond, I'm sorry – I'm so ashamed that a cousin of mine...'

'It's not your fault,' Raymond said, his throat painfully dry. He was only glad the Dimarcos had left.

But Sara was filled with revulsion that Colin had been part of such a brutal attack. As the band leader announced the next number, Normy spotted Raymond and came lurching across. Sara felt a sick tightening in her stomach as Raymond, clearly swallowing his fear, stood up.

'Where's Dimarco?' Normy asked, his face savage.

'Not here,' Raymond said, facing his intimidator squarely.

'Tell him we'll have him,' Normy snarled, making Sara shiver with fear. She caught Colin's look, but he glanced away awkwardly and she knew what Raymond had said was true. How she despised her cousin! He was no better than her bullying Uncle Alfred.

But Raymond stood his ground as a group of pitmen led by Wilfred Parkin migrated towards them, sensing trouble.

'Joe Dimarco could have you anytime,' Raymond answered with derision, filling out with confidence as he realised help was coming. Sara tensed and stood up beside Raymond as Normy Bell leered forward and spat at him.

'Scabbing bastard!'

A moment later, Wilfred and Pat Slattery had Normy by the arms and Sara watched dumbly as the drunken aggressor and his mates were forcibly jostled from the hall by the older men.

Raymond felt himself shaking, but did not want to betray his relief to Sara. For several minutes they just stared as the protesting youths were ejected through the swinging doors.

'Oh, Raymond,' Sara whispered with a shudder, touching his arm, 'you were that brave. What terrible lads!'

Raymond felt a flush of pride at her words, as his fright lessened. 'They're not worth the bother,' he grunted.

'Should we warn Joe?' Sara asked anxiously.

Raymond experienced a twinge of disappointment to see Sara's pretty face pucker in concern for Joe instead of him. 'Joe can handle himself,' Raymond answered stiffly. Then, not wanting her to worry, he added, 'And they're no threat, the state they're in.'

'Well, if you're sure...' Sara gulped.

'Haway, let's dance,' Raymond brightened, feeling bold after his stand against Normy Bell. 'It's a progressive. That way we don't get stuck with each other for the whole dance.'

'Suits me,' Sara laughed and nudged him, thankful that the moment of tension was passed. For all his boyish slimness and joking nature, Sara was impressed by the spirit Raymond had shown, while she had clamped up with fear. She slipped an arm through his as he led her on to the dance floor.

The hall was a seething mass of people and Sara's spirits soon revived as she passed in the huge chain from partner to partner. Raymond gave way to chubby Wilfred Parkin, whom she thanked for intervening and he was followed by a middle-aged pitman with black creases of dirt in his neck. Two further strangers came and went, then wiry Pat Slattery took her hand and swung her about with a bashful grin. To her surprise, Sara recognised her next partner as the freckle-faced sailor, Frank Robson, who had sat beside her on the bus when she had first arrived in Whitton Grange. He was dressed in his naval uniform and looked boyishly handsome as he smiled at her.

'Remember me?' he asked.

'You're on leave again?' Sara queried, with a smile.

'Family bereavement,' Frank explained, his face

sobering. 'My aunt in Stanhope.'

'I'm sorry,' Sara said, noticing the black band on his upper arm for the first time.

'Ta,' Frank replied. 'Aunt Flo always liked a good dance, so I knew she wouldn't begrudge me a couple of hours before I rejoin the ship.' He took a deep breath. 'How are you settling in?'

'Canny,' Sara answered, not going to add to his problems by telling him how difficult she had found adapting to this dirty town.

'You're looking well on it,' Frank told her, giving her a final polka before passing on.

'Thanks,' Sara smiled bashfully.

She turned to find herself facing Joe Dimarco. She heard Frank say goodbye and her own voice wishing him good luck on his ship, but she was only aware of the feel of Joe's arm slipping behind her back and his other warm hand grasping hers. He must have slipped in the back of the hall when all eyes were on the troublemakers at the main entrance.

He regarded her with dark eyes, his hair tousled over his perspiring brow. 'I may not be a sailor in a fancy uniform,' he said as he twirled her, 'but you're stuck with me now.'

Sara was engulfed in relief to see him unscathed, but would not say so.

'Thought you weren't bothering to come back,' she reproached.

'So you noticed I'd gone?' Joe grinned with pleasure.

'Raymond noticed,' Sara pouted, unable to look into his dark eyes without betraying her nervous excitement at his sudden reappearance.

'And that awful Normy Bell's been in here looking for you, too.'

Joe laughed, unconcerned. 'I got trapped in the cafe,' he explained. 'There was a rush when the pictures finished. I slipped out when Paolo got back – said I'd left something at the hall.'

'Oh, what was that?' Sara asked, struggling to appear calm when her heart hammered like the band drums.

'A bonny lass,' he said and turned her again. She felt the queasiness of failure grip her insides; he probably meant Olive Brown.

'Better go and find her, then,' Sara said with a lift of her chin and prepared to meet her next partner, who was moving towards her. But Joe did not let go.

'Pass on,' he told the confused man. He shrugged and shuffled round them.

Joe grinned at Sara's astonished face. 'The bonny lass I left was dancing with a skinny lad too young for her – with two left feet and a limp.'

'Oh aye?' Sara challenged him with her green eyes and mimicked his own words, 'So you noticed did you?'

'How could I not see the most beautiful girl in the room, *bellissima?*' He leaned towards her and brushed the word against her hair. Sara had no idea what it meant, but it sounded romantic. The strength drained from her knees.

The dance finished and they stood close, still holding onto each other. A waltz was announced and Joe pulled her to him as they set off across the dance floor without a word exchanged. The heat of bodies pressed about them and a saxophone oozed sensuous music, wrapping them in the melody.

Sara relaxed against Joe's shirt, her cheek resting on his shoulder and felt his arm tighten around her waist, squeezing her to him. She closed her eyes wishing the moment could go on for ever, savouring the bitter-sweet smell of perspiration and aftershave, and the closeness of his strong body which was causing her stomach to turn somersaults.

The saxophone wailed to a halt and immediately broke into a jazzy quickstep. They stepped apart but Joe held on to her hand. The clock showed it was quarter to eleven.

'I have to go home now,' Sara told him without enthusiasm. 'My uncle says I'm to be in by eleven.'

'I'll see you home,' he said, which was just what she wanted to hear.

'But what if Normy Bell's waiting for you?' Sara said doubtfully.

'We'll go out the back way.' Joe squeezed her hand.

Returning to the far table, Sara picked up her cardigan as Raymond arrived. Joe told him he would see Sara safely to her uncle's house. The younger boy did not hide his relief at being rid of the responsibility, diving off with a hurried goodbye to join his mates. He had no wish to be teased further about lasses that evening.

Hurrying down the back steps into the cool of the night, Sara felt Joe's arm reach around her as the dark enveloped them.

'This way,' he murmured, pulling her further

down the street.

'That's not the way home,' Sara answered with a twinge of apprehension.

'I know a short-cut through the dene,' Joe coaxed. She peered at his shadowed face as they passed under a street lamp. His dark eyes were challenging.

'I must be back by eleven,' Sara insisted stubbornly. He laughed softly and gripped her tighter.

'Are you frightened I'll turn into a rat, Cinderella?' he joked.

'Maybe,' Sara answered, a gurgle of nervous laughter rising in her throat.

'Well, here's your glass carriage, princess,' Joe pulled her to a halt by the kerb. 'This'll get you home fast enough, won't it?'

Sara gawped at the dark shape in the roadway. It was Joe's motorcycle. 'You want me to ride on that?' she exclaimed.

'Haway and swing your leg over, lass,' Joe laughed and pushed her forward. He clambered on and held out his hands to help her.

Sara only hesitated a few seconds, then, hitching up her dress, mounted the pillion of the slumbering machine.

'Put your arms round my waist,' he instructed.

This, Sara Pallister, she told herself excitedly as she slipped her arms about the handsome Italian, is the beginning of a real adventure.

Chapter Eleven

Sara's nervousness at balancing on the noisy machine gave way to exhilaration as they picked up speed along the Durham Road and she clung on to Joe's body, leaning into the bends as he did. The night breeze caught her hair and lifted it like the mane of a wild pony, whipping strands across her face. Above them the sky was clear, the pall of coal fires that usually hung over the village dispersed by the wind. A spattering of stars winked above the outline of the low hills and the bright disc of an almost full moon lit their way into the dene.

Joe rode along the cinder track, disturbing a courting couple who jumped back with fright, the man shaking his fist after them. They passed the grand villas of the well-to-do of Whitton Grange and emerged once more on the road snaking east towards Durham. He brought them to a halt and turned to speak over the throbbing engine.

'Do you want to gan up to The Grange and watch the posh lot through the big windows?' he asked.

'You can't do that!' Sara laughed, pushing hair out of her eyes.

'I've done it plenty of times,' Joe chuckled, 'and I've never been caught.'

'We haven't time,' Sara was half-hearted in her objection.

'Sit tight,' Joe ordered and turned to rev the motorcycle.

They took off along the narrow road like the wind. Sara gulped in the cool air and laughed out loud with sheer joy. The weeks of dislocation and homesickness were wiped from her memory for that brief period and all she could think of was how good it felt to be speeding through the Durham countryside on a fast machine with the most handsome and desirable lad she had ever set eyes on.

They headed up the moonlit drive that Sara had cycled on Sergeant's old pedal bike. Then, she had had to dismount and push it up the final slope, weighed down with groceries and puffing in the heat. Now the surroundings seemed magical and mysterious, a silver trail winding into the woods with the hoot of an owl to announce their intrusion. Holding her breath at Joe's audacity, she thrilled at the sight of the gothic mansion towering over them as they motored nearer, like some enchanted castle spilling golden light on to the gravelled drive.

Through large uncurtained windows, they glimpsed a throng of people in evening dress, milling around a vast room, the men in stiff black tails, the women shimmering in backless gowns that swept the floor. Sara noticed a group sitting round a table playing cards, before Joe swerved on the loose stones and almost threw her off as he righted the bike. From somewhere, dogs began to bark and the massive front door was thrown open.

'You're a terrible driver, Joe Dimarco!' Sara shouted in his ear, terrified as she clung on to him tighter. 'I'd never have got on this contraption if I'd known.'

Joe laughed in reply and accelerated down the drive as the baying of dogs pursued them. By the time they reached the village once more, Sara was laughing, too, the relief of escape making her light-headed. They stopped on the edge of the green and Joe switched off the engine, so as not to draw attention to their arrival. Nearby, the old horse Gelato munched in the dark and the calls from late revellers echoed across the rough, open ground.

'I feel like I've been flying!' Sara panted as she climbed off the bike, her legs weak as they touched ground again. Joe laughed and removed his goggles. They looked at each other a moment then Sara said, 'Raymond told me how you saved him. Why didn't you tell me?'

Joe shrugged, 'I don't feel clever about it– I should've kept a closer eye on him before – but I had other things on my mind.' Joe had no intention of adding that it was Olive Brown who had diverted his attention from the growing danger.

'Well, I think it was brave of you,' Sara said shyly. 'But don't you think he should report the attack?'

'That's not the way scores are settled in Whitton Grange,' Joe smiled ruefully.

The chimes of the church clock carried towards them on the wind. It was quarter past eleven.

'I'm late,' Sara gasped.

'I'll walk you to the door,' Joe offered.

'No,' she replied quickly, 'someone might be looking out. Me uncle would have a fit if he knew

222

I'd been riding on this.' She touched the bike.

Joe caught her arm. 'Can I see you again, Sara?' he said, his face suddenly earnest.

Her heart pounded as she heard herself reply. 'Aye, I'd like that. But I must go in now.'

'Tomorrow?' he pressed her.

'When?'

'Afternoon. I'm going into Durham with a drum of ice-cream. Come with me,' Joe suggested.

'I'll try and get away,' Sara promised, breathless at the thought of another escapade in Joe's company.

'I'll wait in the dene until two-thirty,' he told her and then, raising her hand to his lips, he planted a kiss on her fingers.

Sara gulped hard and pulled her hand away. 'Goodnight, Joe,' she whispered hoarsely and turned from him.

'*Ciao*, Sara.' She heard his low reply as she ran up South Parade. Outside number thirteen, she glanced back to see him still watching her. They waved. Opening the garden gate, Sara tiptoed up the path and let herself in as quietly as possible.

To her relief there was no one about, just her uncle's shoes and coat discarded at the foot of the stairs to indicate his revelries were over. The hall clock confirmed she was twenty minutes late. Slipping off her shoes, she padded upstairs without switching on any lights. Beyond the gentle ticking of clocks, she heard her uncle's thunderous boozy snore and wondered how her aunt could sleep on undisturbed.

Undressing in the dark, a small voice asked sleepily, 'Where have you been?' Sara's heart sank. Marina was still awake.

'To the dance, of course,' she hissed back. 'You should be asleep.'

'Tell me about it,' her young cousin demanded.

'In the morning.' Sara stole a look through the curtains. The lamps outside Dimarco's were still ablaze and she wondered how Joe would explain his prolonged absence from the parlour.

'I'll tell Daddy you were late coming in,' Marina threatened. 'I heard it strike eleven and you weren't here.'

Sara mentally cursed the meddlesome girl, but went over and sat on her bed.

'There was a big band on the stage and the hall was decorated with bunting. It looked wonderful. The Carnival Queen started the dancing,' Sara whispered.

'What did she wear?' Marina sat up in bed, full of curiosity.

Sara found herself recounting the evening in detail to her cousin, all except the final hour.

'Was there lots and lots to eat?' Marina asked.

'Plenty savouries – and jelly and ice-cream–'

'Jelly and ice-cream,' Marina interrupted, her tone envious. 'My favourite.'

'Well, if you're very good and go to sleep now, I'll take you to Dimarco's one afternoon,' Sara promised.

'Ooh,' Marina squealed with delight, 'and buy me a fruit sundae in a big glass?'

Sara nodded, thankful to see a smile lighting the girl's small, moody face. 'As long as you keep quiet about what time I came in,' Sara bargained, prepared to spend her meagre pocket money from Uncle Alfred to win Marina's compliance.

Marina weighed up the choice for a moment, but decided the lure of the forbidden Dimarco's was a greater pleasure than getting her big cousin into further trouble. She nodded in agreement.

'Snuggle down, then,' Sara instructed and leaning over, kissed her lightly on the forehead as her mother used to do to her.

'Don't do that,' Marina complained and made a fuss of wiping the kiss from her skin.

Sara turned away and pulled a face in the gloom. But settling down on her creaking camp bed, she grinned to herself in the dark as she reenacted the evening in her mind. Drifting off to sleep, she was cosy in the memory that Joe Dimarco wished to go out with her again.

On Sunday, Uncle Alfred came in late for lunch from the club and Sara fretted she would not be able to slip out of the house in time to join Joe in the dene. In the cold light of day, it seemed a mad ploy to run off with him into Durham alone. She hardly knew him and he had a reputation for being wild and irresponsible. What if they were spotted leaving the village on his motorcycle and the news was reported back to her uncle? Knowing the shortness of his temper and his prejudice against the Dimarcos, Sara suspected she would be thrown out of his house.

Yet her yearning to break out of the strictures of South Parade and visit the prestigious city of Durham with its grand houses and ancient cathedral, was too strong. Above all, she could not wait to be in Joe's company again, feeling a hungry ache in the pit of her stomach that only seeing him could satisfy.

At twenty-past two, Sara had finished the washing up and told her uncle and aunt she was going out for a walk. To her surprise, they did not question her on where she planned to go, Uncle Alfred being overcome with drowsiness and Aunt Ida assuming she was going to join Rosa in the park, but not wanting to mention her name in front of Alfred. That morning Sara had told her more about Rosa, overcoming Ida's apprehension by stressing how much Mrs Sergeant approved of Rosa as a polite and responsible girl.

'They do dress well, the Dimarcos,' Ida had conceded, 'and Rosa can't help being a foreigner, I suppose.'

'She's not foreign – Rosa was born in Whitton Grange,' Sara had answered impatiently. 'She's just a lass like me, Aunt Ida.'

'I can't say I'm happy, you being friendly with her,' Ida had been grudging, 'but I suppose there's no harm in it – as long as you don't go on about Italians in front of Father – you know what he thinks of you mixing with their sort. It'll just be our little secret,' she had said with a conspiratorial nod.

Sara was happy to leave it at that; she winced at the thought of confiding her attraction for Rosa's elder brother to her aunt. Anyway, the romance might come to nothing, she rationalised, so there was no need for the Cummingses to find out.

Rushing down the street, she heard someone call her name and looked back to see Colin ambling after her with his dogs. He had been bleary eyed and sullen at lunch and Sara had found it hard to speak to him now she knew of his part in Raymond's battering. She gave him a cold stare, not wanting to delay in talking to him.

'I can't stop,' she said.

'Going up the park?' he demanded.

'No,' she answered shortly and stepped past him. Gypsy followed, sniffing at her legs.

'Where you off to then?' he asked, keeping pace with her.

'Nowhere special,' she increased her step, uneasy at his lumbering presence.

'You're in a hurry for nowhere special.' He caught her up.

Sara cringed to think she had sought the friend-ship of someone who had made a vicious attack on a defenceless lad. He sickened her, yet at the same time she was unnerved by his powerful bulk and the way he stared at her continually.

'Stop following me!' Sara said tersely. 'It's none of your business where I'm going – you'll only go blabbing to your father, anyway.'

'Don't say that!' Colin scowled, plodding doggedly by her side.

Sara quickened her pace again.

'You meetin' someone?' he goaded her when it became clear she wasn't going to respond. 'Got a fancy man from the dance, eh? It can't be that little runt, Raymond Kirkup, surely?'

Sara stopped and turned on him angrily.

'Raymond Kirkup's a canny lad – ten times a better lad than you, Colin Cummings! Aye, you're nothing but a big lout – and to think I felt sorry for you being picked on by your father. But you're ten times worse – you're a bigger bully than he is.'

Colin took a pace back from her disdainful green eyes and Flash growled at her with menace. But Sara's temper made her go on recklessly.

'And I'll tell you this! Last night I had the best time I've ever had since coming to this dirty hole of a place. Some people know how to enjoy themselves dancing and being sociable without having a skinful of beer and picking on lads half their size.'

Colin gawped at her a moment, then, as she continued on her way, he ran after her, red-faced with fury. How dare she compare him to his father, the man he hated most in all the world, the man who humiliated him and made his life a misery every day of the week?

Finally, he gave up as she ran off down the street. 'You can gan to hell, Sara Pallister!' he shouted after her, almost incoherent with rage. 'I want nowt to do with you any road, *nowt!*'

A group of children playing in the street had stopped their game of marbles to stare. He turned and swore at the onlookers.

'Picking on a lass! Cowardy-cowardy-custard!' the cheeky-faced boys chanted and the others laughed to see the large youth colour with embarrassment.

Colin turned on them and drove his hefty boot into the middle of their marbles, scattering them into the drains. Cursing them foully, he took hold of the nearest boy by the hair and threw him to the ground, kicking his skinny rump. The boy yelped in pain and the mean-faced whippets yapped about his head. The rest of the children scattered in fear. Colin hurried away with his protective hounds about his heels, before his victim returned with his father or elder brothers to seek revenge.

Colin determined there and then, he would make Sara pay for rejecting him so publicly.

By the time Sara reached the dene, the church clock had already chimed the half hour. She searched for Joe anxiously, fuming at Colin for delaying her. Where would he wait for her? she worried. Was she too late? There were children splashing in the burn and fishing for tadpoles and several couples strolling down the over-grown pathways. The air was pungent with wild garlic and the spicy smell of elderberry flowers, but Sara could not enjoy the place for fear she had missed Joe. Ten minutes more elapsed before she emerged at the far end of the dene, where it petered out into a derelict railway siding. Beyond a broken-down fence proclaiming it as private lay the debris of a once-busy railway crossing.

About to retrace her steps, she saw Joe emerge from behind a rusty coal tub. 'Haway, Sara, the ice-cream'll be melted by the time we get to Durham.'

'Nice to see you, too,' she pouted, but allowed him to help her on to the motorbike. For a moment, she worried he might find her dull in the harsh light of day. She was clad in her own faded cotton dress and darned cardigan, ankle socks and sandals, though running through the dene, she had pulled her hair loose from its ribbon and

229

allowed it to fall around her face and she had splashed on some of her precious store of lavender water that her mother had given her before she left home.

Joe squeezed her bare knee as she settled behind him and she felt the familiar thrill at his touch. 'I waited, didn't I?' he answered dryly and kick-started the machine, pulling goggles down over his eyes.

They wound their way out of the siding on to the Durham Road and, picking up speed, soon left behind the last straggle of cottages that marked the edge of the village. The road was deserted and they sped along the winding lanes, through a patchwork of green wheatfields, yellow haystacks and poppy-filled meadows, disturbing showers of butterflies from the hedgerows as they passed.

Sara breathed in the smell of newly cut hay and felt a fleeting pang for home. But she had to admit that, for the first time in a month, she would rather be at Whitton Grange than at Stout House, and with the exciting Joe Dimarco than the quiet dependable Sid Gibson.

As they pulled up the final hill and descended into Durham, Sara was entranced by the sight of mellow brick houses and the tree-lined river coiled around the magnificent cathedral and stout Norman castle. The bike bumped over cobbles, winding through the narrow streets, almost brushing young men who strolled along in flannels or rowing shorts and disappeared into quiet college courtyards. Sara had only the vaguest memory of visiting Durham with her mother on a noisy and crowded miners' gala day. But today the banks were lush and green with willows trailing their branches into the river and a timeless air hung over the city's medieval stone bridges and cluttered streets.

'We'll stop here.' Joe brought the motorcycle to a halt by the river, near a boathouse that was doing a brisk trade in hiring punts and rowing boats. 'You can take the money.'

Soon Joe was calling out his wares and beckoning young children to buy his cones of Dimarco ice-cream. The day was breezy but pleasantly warm when the sun skipped out from behind the rushing clouds. In no time at all there was a willing crowd gathered around the drum of ice-cream, handing their pennies over to Sara, who gave them change from a pouch tied around her waist.

She felt a niggle of jealousy when Joe bantered with the young girls in their summer dresses and flattered them with his mix of Italian and Geordie.

'*Ciao, bella.* Try Dimarco's ices – the best in County Durham! Gan on and treat yoursel', bonny lass,' he coaxed a young girl with dark, wavy hair who was whispering about him with her friend.

The girl giggled flirtatiously and bought two cones. When she seemed in no hurry to pass on, Sara gave her a frosty look and demanded payment.

'Enjoy yourselves, girls.' Joe sent them on their way with a smile then he turned and winked at Sara. 'Nearly done,' he said. 'Stuff's going fast this afternoon.'

'So's the chatting up,' she answered dryly.

'The sooner we sell all this, the sooner we can have a bit time to ourselves,' Joe grinned at her, unrepentant. 'Gan on and have one yourself – I can see your mouth's watering.'

He dolloped an ice on a cone for her and she took it with a shy laugh.

Later, they abandoned the motorbike and its sidecar, empty of ice-cream, and took a punt out on the river.

'Do you know how to work these things?' Sara asked dubiously.

'Why-aye,' Joe said, helping her into the flat boat. 'You just sit back and relax.'

He discarded his jacket and rolled up his sleeves, taking hold of the pole and pushing them off from the landing. Sara watched his muscled arms work the punt round, plunging the pole into the water as he balanced on the edge of the boat. They glided away, Sara wondering how many other girls he had taken out on the River Wear to become so adept at handling a punt.

She leaned back and trailed her fingers in the cool water, listening to the dip of the pole as Joe manoeuvred them around the other creaking boats and drank in the sight of Durham's medieval skyline. Further up river, Joe ran the punt aground on a sandbank and jumped ashore. Helping Sara out of the boat, he spread his jacket on the bank.

She hesitated, unsure. There was no one else in sight. Joe flung himself down and patted the jacket beside him, loosening his tie. 'Want a toffee?' he asked, fishing a handful of sweets out of his pocket.

Sara sat down cautiously on the edge of his coat, pulling her dress well over her knees. She slid him a look and was disconcerted to see him amused by her modesty.

'Pity to cover them up,' he said, tracing a finger around the rim of her sock.

Sara shifted out of his reach, feeling suddenly vulnerable.

'I don't bite,' he chuckled. 'Here, have a sweet.'

Sara flushed and took the toffee from his open palm. 'I'm not used to going with lads,' she murmured, uncomfortable under his dark-eyed appraisal.

'I find that hard to believe,' he answered, popping a sweet in his mouth and edging closer. 'You came with me quick enough.'

'It's true,' she flashed him a look of annoyance. 'I've only ever been courted by one lad – and that can hardly be called courting. We only ever kissed twice...' Sara broke off, her face scalding with embarrassment, the toffee clutched tight in her moist hand.

'Well, I'm happy to kiss you as many times as you like, pet,' he replied, rolling over and placing his hand on her leg. 'When do we start?'

'That's not what I meant!' Sara flicked his hand away crossly.

'Come on, Sara,' he coaxed.

'Don't, Joe!' Sara rebuffed him, confused.

Joe just grinned and munched on toffee. 'I'm not used to rejection, Sara. Just one kiss, eh?'

His arrogance was infuriating! She had been rash coming to Durham with him and now he was making her look a fool. Others might have been content with a quick roll in the sand and nothing more, but she would not oblige so easily. How stupidly romantic she had been, filling her head with notions of love for this conceited lad! Sara jumped up, glaring down at him as he lay back lazily on his elbow, watching her.

'You're an arrogant pig, Joe Dimarco,' she shouted, 'and I'll not be taken for granted like this. I'll walk back from here,' she declared and plunged into the tall grasses and bushes that bordered their secluded cove.

For an instant Joe was too dumbfounded to move. Then, 'Sara!' he leapt up and caught her by the arm. 'Where do you think you're going?'

'Leave go!' she tried to shake him off, furious with herself for what she had done. Childish naivety had got her into this fix and she had no idea how she was supposed to behave with this dark and handsome youth who was so much more assured than she was. Then she chided herself for being so in awe of him; Joe Dimarco was just an ordinary lad with an inflated opinion of himself. Well, she was not going to be just one more conquest, she determined. She jabbed him in the ribs with her elbow and his hold slackened.

'You don't need me,' she said, flushed with anger, 'not when there are plenty other daft lasses who fall for all your fancy talk – *bella* this and *bella* that. Well, I didn't come here to get me'self into any trouble– I'm not that sort of lass. I just came 'cos I liked you – and I thought I meant more to you than– I thought...'

'Don't be daft!' He lunged forward and pulled

234

her back from the nettles that were stinging her bare legs. A briar caught her cheek and scratched it. 'Look, you're hurting yourself,' he said, 'and you'll get lost.'

'I won't!' She squirmed in his grasp. 'And if you don't let go I'll scream.'

Joe let go suddenly, raising his hands in the air and stepping back, 'I'll not touch you again. You bugger, I only gave you a toffee!'

She saw the baffled look on his face and wondered if she had misread the situation. Her leg throbbed with nettle stings and she was wretched for ruining the afternoon. He turned away from her, saying, 'I'll take you back now if that's what you want.'

The tears came easily, silent trickles at first, then accompanied by a great sob that made Joe look round in bewilderment. She stood and cried and shook and did not know why she felt so unhappy.

'Hey,' Joe stepped towards her and placed a tentative hand on her shoulder. 'Why you crying?'

'I d-don't know,' Sara shuddered and groped for a handkerchief.

'I've never made a lass cry before,' Joe said, peering at her scratched and tear-stained face. His self-assured demeanour slipped like a mask, leaving boyish incomprehension on his slim face. He seemed as wary of her now as she was of him, Sara thought dejectedly.

'Well, now you have,' she retorted with a sniff.

Joe stood mystified and unsure of this contrary country girl, whose moods flickered across her pretty face like the changing weather. He wanted to encircle her shaking body with protective arms, but dared not do so. Instead he patted her shoulder, feeling contrite at his casual behaviour. He had been too eager to show off in front of Sara and demonstrate that he was experienced with girls. With Olive Brown it had been easy.

He had viewed Sara's initial disinterest in him as a challenge, wanting the haughty green eyes to soften into liking for him. And at the Carnival dance he was certain he had recognised her attraction for him, the way he had felt stirred as he held her maturing body against his.

He had calculated that she would be willing to take risks and defy her guardians as he was prepared to incur the disapproval of his parents by going with local girls. Perhaps he was guilty of taking advantage of her, hoping that this trip up the river might lead to an afternoon of passion. Her rebuttal was sobering, he thought shame-facedly; Sara Pallister was as prim as the Italian girls with whom Domenica was always trying to match him.

Yet Joe hated to think he had upset Sara. She meant more to him, he realised as he touched her and smelt the scent on her skin, than the other girls he had courted so casually over the past two years. Sara was different. He thought about her when she was not near him and felt an uncomfortable longing when he looked into her green eyes and touched her honey-coloured hair. He brushed a strand away from her face in a tentative gesture and spoke.

'I'm sorry. I'm not trying to get me evil way, or

anything – least not unless you want it,' he added impudently.

They laughed, self-consciously.

'I just want us to be friends,' Sara mumbled, 'good friends.'

'Then that's what I want an' all,' Joe assured her, tracing her cheek with his fingers. 'Let's sit down and start again, eh?'

'And just chat?' Sara asked.

Joe nodded and plonked himself down. 'Can we eat toffees, too?' he asked wryly. Sara laughed and agreed.

For an hour they sucked sweets and talked about each other's families, sharing stories about their growing up. Sara relaxed and forgot her awkwardness with the young Italian, enjoying his tale-telling and amused by his descriptions of his many relations. He spoke of his friendship with Raymond and his family and his admiration for his boxing coach, Sam Ritson.

As the cathedral bells tolled drowsily for evensong, they left their sandbank with reluctance and returned to the boathouse. The air was chill as they sped away from Durham and Sara snuggled against Joe's back on the motorcycle as she shivered in the wind.

He dropped her once more at the disused siding.

'Better not to be seen together,' Joe told her. 'I don't want to cause you trouble with your uncle.'

'I don't care what he thinks,' Sara said boldly, but she knew he was right. Uncle Alfred thought nothing of the Dimarcos, and would be scandalised by her association with Joe.

'When can I see you again?' Joe took her hands

237

in his. 'Just for a friendly chat, of course.'

Sara could not prevent a smile. 'It's half day Thursday. Can you get away in the afternoon?'

'For you, *bellissima*, I will get away any time.' Joe lifted her hands, kissed them lightly, then dropped his hold.

'Can we go to Durham again?' she asked, excited at the thought.

'Aye,' Joe grinned, 'wherever you want.' As she turned to go he added quietly, 'Best not to tell Rosa about our little trips – or Domenica.'

'Why?' Sara asked in surprise.

Joe's slim face tightened as he replied, 'They might not understand. Italian lasses have different ideas about courting. We'll just keep our friendship secret for a bit, eh?'

'If you want,' Sara said, a touch disappointed. She had looked forward to confiding in Rosa about seeing her brother. At home she would have rushed down to see her friend Beth with such momentous news, but in Whitton Grange, Rosa was the nearest she had to a confidante.

'See you here Thursday,' he smiled, blowing her a kiss before remounting the motorcycle.

Sara skipped off into the dene, feeling ridiculously light-hearted at her new-found love. She wanted to shout it out to the world, but Joe's words of warning echoed in her head. For the moment, at least, their clandestine romance must remain secret. Then she remembered her diary. It was a relief to think she could pour out her feelings onto the pages of the battered exercise book. With that comforting thought she ran for her uncle's home.

Chapter Twelve

Sara began to call more frequently at the Dimarcos' parlour to see Rosa and felt a delicious thrill at the special looks and brief words that she managed to exchange with Joe. They met at the football matches on Saturday afternoons, but always there were other people around and no one but themselves knew that their careless comments were charged with meaning.

One Thursday a bashful Raymond passed on a message from Joe that Rosa wished to meet her that afternoon in Whitton Woods.

'Whereabouts?' Sara asked lightly.

Raymond eyed her. 'By the allotments.' Sara looked away quickly from his enquiring face.

'Rosa probably wants to pick some flowers for the cafe,' she flustered.

'Aye, when it is raining cats and dogs outside!' Raymond teased. 'I know it is Joe you are meeting – old Dimarco's not going to let Rosa go wandering off into the woods by herself, is he?'

'You won't tell, will you, Raymond?' Sara pleaded. 'Uncle Alfred would hit the roof if he found out. He's taken a dislike to the Dimarcos – just 'cos they haven't lived in Whitton Grange for as long as his people.'

'He wouldn't like them even if they had,' Raymond grunted.

'Why is he like that?' Sara asked with exasperation.

''Cos men like Cummings don't like seeing foreigners getting richer than them, that's all. It's the eleventh commandment; Thou shalt not have more stashed away under the mattress than me.'

Sara laughed. 'So you'll keep quiet about me and Joe?'

'You can do what you like, I'll not tell,' Raymond said with a blush and left with his deliveries.

Sara found Joe sheltering under a beech tree on the edge of the allotments that stood between the dene and Whitton Woods. His collar was turned up against the rain and his bedraggled appearance confirmed he had been there some time.

'I've got a couple of hours off – the bike's playing up and it's in the garage,' Joe explained. 'We can have the afternoon to ourselves at last.'

'Where are we going to go in this rain?' Sara's enthusiasm was dampened by the weather.

'I know where we can dry off,' he said at once and, taking her hand, led her to a dilapidated hut. It had long since been abandoned to fieldmice and the patch of surrounding ground to waist-high thistles and grass, a few broken canes showing where lines of runner beans and sweet peas had once been lovingly tended. Dusty seed boxes were piled against the door, but they clambered in through a gaping window and fell on to musty sacking.

'We can play cards,' Joe suggested with a wink.

Sara peered around the rotting shed. Pinned to the wall, dusty and faded with age, were drawings of birds and flowers and one of a handsome, gaunt-faced woman sitting reading a book. It was almost completely curled in on itself. Sara unrolled it and gazed at the haunting picture.

'She's got a nice face. I wonder who she was?' Sara mused.

'We'll never know,' Joe stood beside her, peering at the pencilled visage. He slipped an arm around Sara's shoulders. 'Not my type, mind. Too skinny.' He pinched Sara's waist.

'How did you know about this place?' she asked intrigued.

'Raymond mentioned it once,' Joe said casually. 'Used to belong to an uncle of his or something.'

'What if his uncle should come?' Sara said with concern.

'Stop worrying.' Joe was reassuring. 'You can see no one's been here for years. Both his Kirkup uncles moved away and his Uncle Sam's never been one for gardening – too busy with union meetings and the boxing club.' He put his head close to hers. 'So it's just our own little den – no one'll come looking for us here. It's been that hard getting you on your own,' Joe laughed, flicking wet hair out of his eyes.

Sara shivered, partly from the chill air and partly from excitement. 'Raymond knows I was meeting you not Rosa.'

'So?' Joe was unconcerned. 'Raymond's a marra of mine, he'll not tell anyone.'

'Don't suppose I'm the first lass you've brought here, then?' She pulled away from him a fraction.

He made no denial. 'You're the most beautiful,' Joe murmured, caressing her cheek.

'Let's play cards,' Sara turned from him and plonked herself down on a garden box, nervous of impending intimacy.

Joe did not protest but sat down, cross-legged, opposite her and drew out a well-thumbed pack of cards and a battered packet of cigarettes from his jacket.

'Want a smoke?' he offered. Sara shook her head and then changed her mind.

'All right, then,' she giggled. She watched him light up two cigarettes and toss the extinguished match out of the window. She took one from him and, holding it gingerly between thumb and forefinger, put it to her lips and puffed. Nothing happened. Joe drew on his and squinted with amusement through the spiral of smoke. His fingers bore the brown stains of frequent smoking.

'Suck,' he told her. 'Breathe it in.'

Sara drew in a huge breath and choked on a rush of smoke. She coughed violently and dropped the cigarette. Joe laughed and picked it up, pinching out the burning end with his fingers.

'It looks that easy on the films,' Sara spluttered and laughed. 'Here, I'll deal,' she said, reaching for the cards, thankful to have something to keep her hands from shaking. She and Tom and Chrissie had often filled in long winter evenings with games of Whist and Old Maid. Joe taught her an Italian game called *scopa*.

They played for half an hour and then the rain stopped and the sun broke out through the trees, sending a muted shaft of light into the damp-smelling hut.

'I want to take you somewhere,' Joe announced suddenly and got to his feet. He reached down and pulled Sara up. 'Haway, I'm sick of being beat at cards by a lass.'

She followed him back out of the window, her bare legs and skirt soon soaked from the wet undergrowth that hemmed in their hideaway. The heavy midsummer storm had chased away any would-be gardeners and the allotments appeared deserted. Joe grabbed her hand and led her out of the maze of pigeon lofts and shacks and cobbled fences towards the woods.

In silence, they climbed the path that burrowed through the trees, suddenly in awe of the moody, dripping quiet of the woods. At the top, the trees stopped abruptly and gave way to pasture. Beyond, Sara could glimpse the promise of moorland heather and a ribbon of old stone wall that reminded her of home. But she suppressed the thought, not wanting to dwell on the ties which tugged her memory to Stout House and Rillhope.

Joe had stopped by a narrow gate that allowed only one person to pass through it at a time.

'Do you know what this is?' he asked her.

'Aye, it's a wishing gate,' Sara answered, bemused.

'Step in and make a wish, then.' He held it open for her and she laughed, still uncertain, but stepped into the opening. Watched by Joe's dark, amused eyes, she made her wish. Sara reached forward to push the gate back to pass on to the Common and allow Joe to follow her, but he held the gate firm.

'Shall I tell you my wish?' he said quietly.

'You mustn't say, or it won't come true,' Sara answered, her voice husky.

He stepped towards her and slipped his free arm around her waist. 'I wish you'd give us a kiss,' he murmured, looking down at her full lips.

Sara began to giggle. She leaned back against the gate and met his enquiring look with shining green eyes. Out here in the open, with the smell of wet foliage and the distant bleat of sheep, she had no fear of him.

'What's so funny?' he asked, dropping his arm, his poise disturbed.

'Nothing,' Sara laughed and slipped her own arms around his neck. 'It's just I wished for the same thing.'

'You did?' Joe asked in astonishment. 'You mean – you want?– I thought–'

'Are you going to kiss me then?' she challenged.

Joe stooped towards her and they kissed tentatively. To Sara's surprise he seemed much more awkward about it than she had imagined. His lips were dry and at first he pecked her like an inquisitive hen. It did not seem half as romantic as in the occasional films she had seen in the old hall at Lilychapel, when stirring music brought tears to her eyes and her insides melted as the hero and heroine embraced and swore undying love.

Joe's hands fumbled around her waist, looking for somewhere to rest, and his brown eyes looked into hers for encouragement. Perhaps he had not kissed as many girls as he liked to make out, she thought wryly. Sara closed her eyes and searched for his mouth once more. This time it was better. Their lips touched and lingered over the kiss, exploring and moist. Sara felt a slow thud begin in her chest and Joe drew her closer to him, his confidence increasing.

They felt each other's faces, drew apart for a moment, laughed sheepishly and began kissing again. She ran exploratory fingers into his dark, cropped hair, while he stroked the long wavy strands away from her face.

Sara was unaware of how long they stood there, touching and kissing, oblivious to their surroundings, intent only on each other. Eventually the chug of a tractor disturbed their fondlings and they looked round guiltily. It was two fields away, but they drew apart and headed through the gate.

Hand-in-hand they skirted the top of the woods, out of sight of the farmer and continued walking across Whitton Common.

'We'll call it our kissing gate,' Joe grinned at her, his pulse still hammering at the experience. He had never been caught in such an exciting embrace in his life, not even with last year's Carnival Queen, whom he had enticed away from the pugnacious Normy Bell. Kissing Olive Brown had been satisfying only because Normy Bell had wanted her, whereas Sara's passion lit her green eyes and suffused her skin, making her quite beautiful. Sexuality pervaded her like a scent, he thought with admiration. He wanted more of it, but rain threatened again and the afternoon was nearly over. He knew he must get back to the parlour.

'You're bonny as they come!' He kissed Sara on the nose and took her hand. They walked slowly back down the path, Sara stopping to pick at wild garlic growing beneath the trees. She bit some and handed him a stalk. Joe chewed on it, releasing the pungent smell that reminded him of his mother's cooking. Joe grimaced at the thought of his parents and how they would disapprove of his growing interest in this penniless country girl. It was one thing for Rosa to have Sara as a friend, and quite another for him to court her. They might turn a blind eye to the situation, he thought, if they knew it was a summer flirtation, but he could never bring Sara to the house as his intended. Her ways were different, her family unknown. No Dimarco had married outside their own kind since his father and Uncle Davide had come to England before the Great War.

It was taken for granted that Joe would eventually find a girl from one of the Italian families here in Britain, or from their village back home as Paolo had done. His father had already talked about sending him on a trip to Italy, perhaps next year when he was eighteen, and Joe knew he would be expected to cast his eye over the unmarried girls. He was proud of his heritage, but he had never visited his parents' village and had no great desire to be stuck for weeks in an isolated mountain hamlet. After all, he hardly spoke a word of their dialect, Joe thought ruefully.

Shaking off such tiresome thoughts he consoled himself that there was no point in worrying about something that might never happen and at the moment he wanted nothing more than a summer romance, to divert him from the gloomy rumours of war. Looking at Sara, he felt gripped by a sweet, sweet longing.

June drifted into July and Sara and Joe's relationship blossomed as swiftly as the lush countryside about them. Sara saved up the measly allowance her uncle gave her from out of her earnings and spent it on bus fares into Durham to meet Joe on her free afternoons. They met in the back rows of darkened picture houses, at neighbouring village fetes where Joe was selling ice-cream, upon Highfell Common where the air was clear of coal smoke. They walked for miles across the low hills, Joe complaining at the enforced exercise, but Sara delighting in the gentle wooded countryside, awash with a sea of bluebells and wild irises, encircled by armies of purple and white trumpeted foxgloves. Sometimes they stopped at farm cottages and begged water from standpipes, or sat and talked to roving cyclists as they rested under the lacy cream flowers of hawthorn bushes.

Occasionally the conversation would turn to the prospect of war. To Sara's dismay, Joe had strong opinions on the matter.

'Bullies must be stood up to,' he said to a middle-aged veteran of the Great War, as they sat sharing a cigarette on the parapet of an isolated bridge.

'I signed the Peace Pledge five years ago.' The man's affable face had turned grim. 'Sanctions against an aggressor are the only moral answer.'

'They didn't stop Mussolini marching into

Abyssinia, did they?' Joe retorted. 'It wasn't right what he did to them Africans – and I'm from Italian stock me'sel'. I've argued with me Uncle Davide about it – nearly caused a family rift – but Musso should've been stopped. Look how he's mopping up in Albania now. And Hitler's the same. Bullies only take notice if they're kicked in the backside,' Joe said firmly, 'and in my mind, Adolf needs a good kickin'.'

The cyclist had shaken his head sadly and when Joe had looked set to argue, Sara had quickly changed the subject. She was amazed by Joe's knowledge of politics and the way he talked with familiarity about places of which she had barely heard. In contrast, she wanted to ignore such disquieting thoughts, but they would no more stay away than the rumblings of distant thunder that sent them hurrying off the hill and the cyclist on his way. How could war ever come to such a peaceful land as this? she wondered in perplexity, as they sheltered under a haystack and watched a couple of magpies swoop among the stooks. She wanted nothing to disturb the growing love between her and Joe, for she believed he cared for her. It showed in the tenderness of his dark eyes and the amused smiles he gave when she told him of her skirmishes with her uncle and aunt in order to win time away from the house to meet him.

For life at South Parade had become bearable, as long as she knew she could get away to see Joe. They had managed to keep their meetings secret, she was fairly sure, although sometimes she caught her aunt watching her suspiciously from the parlour window when she said she was off to meet Rosa in the park. Once, in Durham, they had nearly run straight into Aunt Ida coming out of a haberdashery, but Sara had pushed Joe into Woolworths and they had hidden until her aunt and Mrs Hodgson had gone past.

Furthermore she had had to smother her desire to tell Rosa of where she went when she made excuses not to meet her in the park. Fortunately, Rosa appeared too engrossed in arrangements for Domenica's July wedding to notice Sara's dreamy-eyed state or the flush of excitement on her face when Joe appeared in the Dimarcos' backshop where she and Rosa chatted over the washing up.

Three times she had treated Marina to fruit sundaes in the Dimarcos' parlour and her young cousin had been noticeably less hostile towards her, no longer threatening to tell her father if Sara arrived in late, because now they shared these secret trips to the cafe. Colin had not spoken to her since their public argument, but Sara was not troubled by his coldness, only relieved that he appeared to have stopped following her around.

Raymond, though, was party to her illicit courtship with Joe and it was he who suggested they could meet at his house in Hawthorn Street. To Sara's delight, Raymond's Auntie Louie gave her a warm welcome and Joe appeared quite at home among the Ritsons, who treated him like one of their own.

Sara would rush after work to the Ritsons' tiny colliery house with its dark mahogany furniture crowding the low-ceilinged kitchen and parlour. The floors were covered in a cheap linoleum, with multi-coloured clippy mats at the hearth and doorways and Mrs Ritson spent half the time wrestling with an old range, which she coaxed to the correct temperature for her baking and boiling water. There was no sign of any bathroom and Sara presumed they still used the tin bath hanging on a nail in the backyard. Once, needing to relieve herself, she was directed across the backlane to a primitive water closet.

'They're going to put in proper toilets soon,' Louie Ritson had apologised, 'Holly Street have them and we're next.'

But Sara loved her visits to Hawthorn Street and the shabby cosiness of Louie's kitchen on wet Thursday afternoons when they would sit round the kitchen table listening to the wireless and drinking tea, while Louie darned socks by the open fire and Joe discussed the situation in Europe with Sam. Sara soon learned that Sam had a great influence over Joe and that her boyfriend's opinions had been moulded by this gruff unemployed pitman who had taught him to box when only thirteen years old.

Sara was wary of Sam Ritson at first, having heard of his radical reputation, and his manner was often blunt and aggressive. But she saw how Joe and Raymond looked up to him and noticed the way his look softened when he watched his wife moving around the room. He was passionate and principled and staunchly loyal to his union, while Louie was kind and long-suffering to the youngsters who came and went and ate her precious store of food.

On one warm breezy Saturday afternoon, Sara

called round, knowing that Joe and Raymond would return to Hawthorn Street after the football match. She found the Ritsons' house full. Louie's father, the lay preacher Jacob Kirkup, sat in his chair by the fire reading a weighty volume as if none of the visitors or their chatter existed. Sara recognised Hilda Kirkup among the throng and her plump fiancé, Wilfred.

'Come in!' Louie called, catching sight of Sara hovering in the doorway. 'Our Sadie's back for her birthday. You haven't met cousin Sadie have you, pet?'

'No,' Sara smiled as she was pushed into the room. A small, dark-haired young woman in a smart worsted suit and cream blouse came forward and took her hand.

'How do you do?' she asked in a pleasant, cultured voice. 'I'm Sadie Kirkup, Louie's cousin.' Sara echoed the greeting, wondering how this grand woman fitted into a family of miners.

'Sadie's a teacher,' Hilda said with reverence, 'in a grammar school in Newcastle.'

Sadie smiled modestly. 'Louie and Hilda virtually brought me up – and Uncle Jacob,' she added quickly, glancing at the white-bearded preacher. 'It was thanks to them I had the chance of an education and becoming a teacher.'

'And thanks to our brother Eb, too,' Hilda added. 'He paid for your schooling after all.'

'Hush, Hildy,' Louie scolded her sister, with an anxious glance at her father. 'You know you shouldn't mention–'

'He's deaf – he can't hear us,' Hilda said dismissively.

'Family politics,' Sadie said to Sara with a rueful smile. 'Come and have some of Louie's sponge cake – it's delicious– and tell me about yourself. Louie says you're from up Weardale.'

Sara was surprised by how much this assured young woman knew about her and her family, and said so.

'You know Louie,' Sadie smiled. 'She takes an interest in everybody. Her house is always open to waifs and strays.' Sara blushed and Sadie said swiftly, 'Sorry, that was tactless. I was thinking of myself, really. Louie's parents took me in when I was orphaned at four years old and I can never repay this family for what they've given me.'

'Did you grow up in this house?' Sara asked.

Sadie nodded. 'There were never less than eight of us at any one time, I don't think! But most of the time it was a happy childhood – or perhaps we only remember the happy times the older we get.'

'Aye, I think that's true,' Sara mused. Already Stout House was bathed in fond memories of hot summers and games around the beck or dancing to the tunes on the gramophone in the huge beamed kitchen.

Louie pressed a cup of tea into her hand and introduced her to the others in the room; two middle-aged spinsters called Dobson and an elderly bespectacled woman with inquisitive eyes who turned out to be Wilfred Parkin's mother. There was a friend of Sadie's called Jane Pinkney and a friend of Louie's called Minnie Bell who had a bright-eyed daughter Nancy: somehow she looked familiar. Sara slid a cautious look at the

Bells, wondering if they were related to Normy. There had been no further threats to Raymond or Joe from Normy Bell and his mates since the dance and Sara pushed the incident to the back of her mind. But she was reassured to hear Minnie Bell was an aunt of Joe's friend Pat Slattery.

'You know Pat, then?' Minnie asked her with interest. She had straggling dark hair, but Sara thought she was still pretty for a woman in her thirties.

'Aye,' Sara was cautious. Something about the way Minnie Bell was looking at her, made her reticent.

'I've seen you before, I'm sure,' Minnie persisted. 'Have you been round to Mam's with Pat?'

'No,' Sara answered, feeling her cheeks begin to colour.

'Sara works at Sergeant's with Raymond,' Louie said quickly, 'that's where you'll have seen her.'

'Can't afford to shop at Sergeant's,' Minnie snorted. 'No, it was somewhere else.'

'Well, Sara's been in Whitton since the beginning of May,' added Louie. 'Want a refill, Minnie?'

Just then, Minnie's pretty daughter Nancy piped up. 'It was in Durham, Mam.'

'Durham, pet?' her mother queried. Sara felt her heart begin to beat rapidly.

'Down by the river. We had ice-creams by the river,' Nancy's voice was adamant. 'She was selling ice-cream with Joe Dimarco. Remember, I pointed them out to you?'

Minnie turned and scrutinised Sara. 'Aye, I

253

remember now – it was in Durham – about a month ago. We haven't been in Durham since.'

'Oh, yes,' Sara's voice came weakly. 'I sometimes help the Dimarcos when they're busy– I'm a friend of Rosa's.'

Minnie just looked at her with the knowing eyes of one woman confronting another. Sara knew she was not fooled by her innocent explanation and her burning cheeks were evidence enough that Sara was hiding the whole truth.

'You're courting, Sara, aren't you?' Minnie teased.

'Leave the lass be,' Louie tried to intervene.

Minnie smiled, triumphant at having guessed the truth. 'No need to be so shy. Joe Dimarco's a bonny-looking lad. Why should you want to keep it secret?'

'There's nothing to keep secret,' Sara bluffed. 'It's just me uncle doesn't like me associating with Catholics, so I'd rather you didn't say anything...'

Minnie laughed. 'Better not tell him you've been speaking to a Slattery, either! Who does Alfred Cummings think he is anyway, the Archbishop of ruddy Canterbury?'

'Minnie! Now don't you go causing any bother for Sara with that wagging tongue of yours,' Louie warned.

'I wouldn't speak to Cummings if I tripped over him in the street,' Minnie declared. 'You've nothing to fear from me, pet.'

All the same, Sara was unhappy that knowledge about her and Joe's relationship should be spreading. When she told Joe they had been seen together in Durham, he shrugged it off.

'We can't go round with sacks over our heads,' he teased. 'If we want to see each other, Sara, we have to take risks.'

It was true, Sara thought, and deep down she knew that, for both of them, the secrecy added a tinge of excitement to their courting. Still, there were times when she longed to shout out her secret to the whole world. At least at work she could confide in Raymond when Mrs Sergeant was out of earshot.

At first he had been teasing about Sara's infatuation with the tall Italian boy.

'Lasses are right soppy,' he had said disparagingly as Sara told him for the third time how wonderful the film of *Wuthering Heights* had been. They were making up a parcel for Mrs Naylor. Raymond's leg was healed and he had swiftly reasserted his right to the deliveries.

'It's my favourite story,' Sara sighed, 'and Laurence Olivier was so handsome...'

Raymond clutched his heart in mock agony. 'But not as handsome as my darling Joe,' he mimicked. Sara gave him a swipe.

'Shh, yousel', the dragon'll hear you,' she protested, glancing anxiously towards the storeroom door.

'So are you courtin' seriously?' Raymond asked.

'Maybe's,' Sara pouted. 'As long as Uncle Alfred doesn't get to hear about us – you know what he's like.'

'Aye, a narrow-minded vindictive old bugger. Pass me the string.'

'And Joe still doesn't want his family to know either – just yet,' Sara added, concentrating hard on the parcel. 'He says after Domenica's wedding when things calm down a bit, he'll tell his parents we're courting.'

'Oh, aye?' Raymond's look was sceptical. 'He's certainly got all the patter, has Joe Dimarco.'

'What do you mean by that?' Sara sparked back.

'I told you what the Italians are like – they stick with their own. Don't expect it to last.'

Sara was riled by the worldly-wise expression on Raymond's pale face, as if he were far her senior.

'Joe's different,' she replied stoutly. 'And he loves me – he told me so.'

'As I said,' Raymond nodded sagely, 'he's canny with words.' He caught her thunderous look. 'Don't get me wrong,' he added hastily. 'Joe's a canny lad and a good marra of mine. I don't doubt he's fond of you, but in the end he'll have to do what his people say and marry one of them – like Domenica's doing. They've probably got one lined up for Rosa an' all.'

'Ah, Rosa!' Sara cried, seizing on his weakness. 'That's why you're against me and Joe, 'cos she hasn't shown you any interest since the Carnival dance.'

'Get lost!' Raymond retaliated, his thin face flushing. It was true he had been hurt by Rosa's reticence to his clumsy attempts to ask her out. She had not even accepted his present of the cheap necklace, saying he should give it to Sara. But he was not going to show that he minded. 'I divvn't care about the lass – or any lasses for that matter. They cause nowt but strife.'

'You'll change your tune when you're older,' Sara said with a patronising air. 'Wait till you fall in love, like me and Joe.'

'Don't talk so soppy,' Raymond said with disgust and hurried off with his parcel.

After that, they avoided the subject of Joe or Rosa Dimarco and Sara noticed a growing reserve between herself and Raymond. They continued to lark around and joke together when Mrs Sergeant was absent or out of earshot, but if Rosa came in the shop, Raymond disappeared on some imaginary errand and he no longer accompanied Sara on outings to the Dimarcos' parlour. Rather than linger to chat to her at the end of the day, Raymond would be off to play football or meet his other friends as soon as Mrs Sergeant gave permission. In the middle of July, Raymond went off on a week's holiday to Redcar with a group of lads from the pit, who were enjoying their first-ever paid holiday, granted, however grudgingly by the Seward-Scotts, in the face of new laws.

When he returned, Raymond seemed different, more offhand and less inclined to pass the time of day with her. His talk was only of football or how he was thinking of going down the pit if war were to come. It saddened Sara that he spent less time at the Dimarcos' and showed no interest in her courtship with Joe, for she had no one else in whom to confide. He no longer helped out at the parlour and was seldom about when she and Joe went round to Sam and Louie's. As he settled into a new group of friends who worked at the Eleanor, his hero-worship of Joe appeared to be on the wane.

Increasingly, Joe spent less time with his other friends and Sara avoided Rosa for fear of her guessing her secret. They were so wrapped up in each other that they grew careless, thinking nothing could spoil their happiness. As her confidence grew, Sara made another bid for freedom and began attending the Methodist chapel in North Street which the Ritsons attended, instead of accompanying Aunt Ida to St Cuthbert's. She outmanoeuvred her uncle by producing a letter from her mother giving her permission to do so and, after a short tirade, he accepted the situation with bad grace.

Joe, on his part, did not see why their clandestine courtship should not continue like this forever, while Sara told herself, optimistically, that some day soon Joe would tell his family about them and make their courtship official before rumours about them reached her uncle and aunt. Then it would not matter what they thought. If they turfed her out of the house, she would find lodgings elsewhere in the village until she and Joe…

Sara forced herself to end the daydream. She must not look too far ahead. July was nearly over, and the prophets of war were increasing in number. It had been announced on the wireless that a Ministry of Supply had been set up to prevent shortages should war with the Germans be declared. Increasing numbers were being taken on at the Beatrice and Eleanor pits and extra production was demanded. Everyone had been issued with a gas mask and shown how to use it, but Sara kept hers in its canvas box, out of sight under her bed like a genie of ill omen that she did not want to let escape.

Then, a week before Domenica's wedding, the storm that Sara had been trying to avoid blew up at South Parade.

Chapter Thirteen

That Sunday Sara came in late. She had been to the Ritsons' after attending chapel and a rousing service led from the pulpit by Jacob Kirkup.

As soon as she entered the dining-room she was aware of a strange tension, like that among sheep huddling against imminent bad weather. Marina complained of a sudden tummy ache and a nervous Aunt Ida ushered her swiftly from the room.

'Where have you been?' Alfred demanded, his tone acid, as Sara took her seat. The lunch lay untouched and cooling on the plates.

'Chapel,' Sara said breathlessly. 'Sorry I'm late.'

'You bloody well will be by the time I've got to the bottom of this!' Her uncle banged the table, making her jump. She glanced across at Colin in alarm, but his look was sullen. Whatever was about to happen she had no allies among the fearful Cummingses.

'I've just come from The Durham Ox. I had to listen to that bugger Bomber Bell telling me how my niece goes regularly to visit the Ritsons – that Communist bastard I told you to keep clear of!'

'L-Louie Ritson's a friend of mine,' Sara stammered.

'Don't lie to me, girl,' Alfred snapped, 'it's not Louie Ritson you go to see – it's your fancy boy. Oh, aye, it's the talk of the village according to Bomber Bell – and he should know – he's married

260

to the village gossip, Minnie Slattery.'

Sara blanched. She was speechless. Minnie had *not* held her tongue.

'You've shamed me.' His face grew red with mounting rage.

'Uncle Alfred–'

'Don't try to deny it,' he spat out the words. 'I've got the evidence of your deceit!'

Sara's throat went dry. He was waving a battered exercise book at her. It was the diary she kept hidden under her mattress.

'By God you've got some explaining to do, Sara Pallister,' he swore, his face a mask of disgust.

'Where did you get that?' she croaked.

'That's no concern of yours.'

Sara shot Colin an accusing look but his eyes were downcast.

Her uncle was merciless as he began to rant. 'Aye, you little madam, it's all in here for the readin' – all your galavantin' around with that good-for-nothin' Italian lad when you should've been stopping in helping Ida like any other respectable lass. And the things you've written about your own relations – you deserve to be thrown out on your ear, you ungrateful little bitch!'

'You'd no right to go reading me diary,' Sara spluttered, puce in the face. She felt naked, knowing that he had read her innermost thoughts. Waves of shame and anger flooded her to think what lay written there; her bereavement for her father, her homesickness, resentment of the Cummingses, her love for Joe, the places they had been, anecdotes about his family, the guest list for Domenica's wedding... She felt the panic

261

rise in her throat like bile.

'I've every right to know what you've been up to,' her uncle said, crimson with fury. 'And it makes sorry readin'. You're that thick with these foreigners – you're a disgrace to the family. And don't pretend you made it all up, 'cos I've had it out with Colin and he's seen you on the back of that Italian lad's cycle. You've been seeing this Joe what's-his-name behind my back and now I'm the laughing stock of the village!'

Sara glared across at Colin, who finally met her look. His flabby face was puckered in a defensive scowl, but he tinged pink around the jaw at her hostility. Well it served her right, he thought, unrepentant. She had rebuffed him in favour of the arrogant, swaggering Dimarco who thought himself above the likes of the Cummingses just because his father was prosperous and he owned a motorbike and he was the star of the boxing club. Yes, he had followed Sara and seen her sneaking around with Joe Dimarco, but he had not thought he would get his revenge so swiftly.

'Aye, I've been seeing him,' Sara confessed with a jut of her chin, 'but I only kept it from you because I knew you'd have a closed mind on the matter. And I was right. You know nothing about Joe, so why are you against him?'

'I know enough about Catholics and foreigners to know they're not suitable company for my family. You think you're above us with your fancy friends and their fancy parlour and fancy van, but it's the likes of the Italians who are the cause of all our problems. They never suffered in the depression like us pitmen – they've grown fat off

262

our wages while there's lads like our Colin can't find work. It's the same with Catholics – they move in and take what's ours by right.'

'The Dimarcos have worked hard for what they've got!' Sara defended them, flabbergasted by his hypocrisy in now championing the unemployed he once dismissed as idle scroungers. 'And you've hardly suffered from the depression like others have – or from the '26 strike.' Sara accused.

That touched a raw nerve. 'And what's that supposed to mean?' he almost choked. 'You've been listening to Ritson's damned lies about me, I suppose? Well, you'll not be going there again – or to chapel. From now on the only place you'll go is to St Cuthbert's with Ida where she can keep an eye on you.'

'You can't stop–'

'Oh yes I can,' he thumped the table again. 'And I'll tell you this, I'll not have my daughter under the influence of Catholics – how dare you take Marina to the parlour without my consent? Filling her head full of nonsense about Popish weddings and fancy dresses – well you'll not be going to that, either!'

So Marina had blabbed, too, Sara realised. Their trips to the parlour when the Dimarcos had treated her to ices and Rosa had taken her upstairs to see the wedding gowns was to have been their secret. Her unreceptive cousin had shown a genuine interest in the preparations and in Dominica's soft satin dress with its lacy flowers. No wonder Marina had fled from the room. But she could hardly blame the girl, if she had given

263

under pressure from her father to tell. She could not have known what a hornets' nest of trouble it would stir up.

'And you're not to see this Italian lad again,' Alfred continued, ablaze with indignation. 'To think of you flaunting yourself about the place on his motorcycle and meeting him at dances like some cheap whore! Well, from now on you stop in the house after work and you only go out if Ida's with you. Do I make mesel' clear?'

Sara felt battered by his tirade, yet indignation flared within her. Why should she be dictated to by this man who drank away most of her wages at his precious club? Her own father had trusted her to go where she pleased and make friends with whom she liked, so who was Alfred Cummings to denigrate the kindly Dimarcos or Ritsons?

'At least let me go to the wedding, Uncle Alfred,' Sara continued her resistance. 'Mrs Sergeant's given me the day off.' It was true, but only because it coincided with the Miners' Gala Day, when all the pit villages in the county gathered together to march through Durham and enjoy a rare holiday. There was little point keeping the shop open as the whole village would decamp to the city for the day. 'And I've been invited – it would be rude not to go.' Sara's cheeks were flaming at her own defiance.

Her uncle's reddened eyes bulged at her mutinous reply. 'Don't you answer back! I can see your mother's let you become a spoilt little madam. Well, Pallister may have let you do as you like, but in my house you're going to get a spot of discipline. You'll stay away from those Italians, do you hear? You're not going to that wedding and you're not going to see that lad again while you're under my roof. I'm going round to have words with Dimarco after dinner. Now get yourself up to your room and stay there till I say you can come out!' He thumped the table so hard, even Colin was startled.

Sara sat fuming, but she bit back the rebellious words she wished to hurl at her uncle. In his present, drink-induced anger, she knew she would only make matters worse for herself and Joe by arguing with him.

She knew he was enjoying his sense of power over her, as he always enjoyed the sight of his family cowering around his table, mute and un-resisting. She despised their docility and her eyes smarted from her own humiliation. Pushing back her chair, she walked to the door without a word, trying to control her trembling. She glanced at Colin as she went, but his look slid away from hers and she could not guess what he thought of her defeat. Once she had escaped upstairs, she sat on her low bed and gave way to tears of frus-tration.

The Cummingses were all hateful! Not even Ida had stayed to protect her; none of them had the guts to stand up to her bullying uncle. She blew her nose and wiped her eyes, and vowed that she would not sit there impotently while her uncle went to cause bad feeling among her friends. She must somehow warn Joe, Sara decided.

Below she heard the sound of Ida clearing dishes and the low rumble of her uncle's voice. Presently she heard the front door bang and

265

knew he must be on his way to the Dimarcos'. Going to the window she watched Colin unchain the dogs and take them out of the yard just as a spatter of rain hit them. Over the back wall, Sara could see across to Dimarcos' cafe and the happy customers taking shelter from the rain. She was filled with dread at the thought of the trouble looming for Joe.

She could not bear to be cooped up for the rest of the day like some disobedient child. She would make her escape and go and find Joe. Only he could comfort and reassure her that all would be well whatever her uncle decreed. Waiting impatiently for sounds that her aunt had gone into the parlour, Sara finally opened the bedroom window. She judged that Ida would be settled by the parlour fire sewing and Marina playing with her dolls by the hearth. Neither would risk coming up to see her until her uncle returned and he probably intended leaving her there for the rest of the afternoon. She guessed she would be safe for the next hour.

Climbing out of the window, she reached for the drainpipe descending from the bathroom and clung on to it as she found a foothold on the bracket that held it to the brick. From here it was a short way down to the flat roof of the shed which housed the dogs. Sara prayed there was no one in the kitchen watching her descent as she scrambled and jumped into the yard. But all was quiet. The rain was heavy now, soaking her before she was halfway down the backlane, but nothing was going to stop her in her search for Joe.

The atmosphere in the Dimarco household was feverish with excitement for the long-awaited wedding. Joe had had enough of talk of dresses and processions and who should sit next to whom and should Uncle Gino in Glasgow be invited at the last minute?

'Perhaps he should,' his father was saying, undecided. 'Nonna would like to see him.'

'It will only cause complications, Arturo,' Anna argued in rapid patois, 'you know your brother Davide won't speak to him – they will fight – it will spoil everything! Please don't ask Gino, Arturo.'

Joe hardly remembered his Uncle Gino who had fallen out with his father and Uncle Davide over money years ago and had taken his share of the infant ice-cream business and retreated to Glasgow where he was now a less-than prosperous assistant in another man's shop. Uncle Davide, the most successful of them all, had never spoken to him since, declaring Gino a thief who deserved to struggle after trying to cheat his brothers out of their hard-earned cash. Joe's father was more forgiving and had invited Gino to his son Roberto's christening thirteen years ago. But there had been a huge family row and the bullish, forthright elder brother Davide had stormed back to Sunderland and not spoken to Arturo for six months.

'Mamma's right,' Domenica added her opinion. 'We don't want any fighting among the family. Please, Papa, it's my special day.'

Arturo sighed and shrugged with regret. 'Perhaps you are right.' He glanced at the armchair where his elderly mother dozed. 'If your Nonna wishes to see Gino, I'll arrange for her to visit him after the wedding.'

Domenica and her mother smiled with relief and lapsed into more conversation about the table arrangements. Arturo clapped a hand on Joe's shoulder and grunted, 'Come, let's leave the women to their plans. We're like fish without the water, yes?' he joked in English.

They were about to depart when the sound of heavy steps on the steep shadowed stairway stopped them. Paolo appeared with a short, blunt-faced man with hard unfriendly eyes. He wore a trilby which he did not remove. The room fell silent.

'Mr Cummings wishes to speak with you, Papa,' Paolo explained with a warning glance at Joe.

Arturo was at once polite. 'Please sit down, Mr Cummings. Domenica, fetch the gentleman a cup of coffee. Or do you prefer tea?'

'I won't have anything,' Alfred replied stiffly. 'I've just come about one thing and that won't take long.'

He switched looks between Arturo and Joe and Joe flinched at his hostility. Arturo smiled in a baffled way.

'It's about my niece, Sara,' Cummings was direct.

'*Si*, Sara!' Arturo encouraged. 'Such a nice girl – and so helpful. She and Rosa, they are like sisters to each other.'

The words seemed to inflame the surly visitor. 'Aye, well, did you know she's been acting more than just a sister to your son here?' he snapped, pointing accusingly at Joe. Joe felt his throat go dry.

'Joseph?' Arturo looked nonplussed. 'How you mean?'

'I mean he's been sneaking around seeing my niece without my permission and I won't have it. I don't suppose you know about it, cither – all this going to dances and the pictures together. Did you know they were courting?'

Joe heard his mother draw in her breath. Arturo turned to his son in perplexity. 'Is this true, Joseph? Have you been – how you say? – courting with Rosa's friend?'

'Aye, we're friendly,' Joe said defiantly. 'What's wrong with that?'

Arturo shrugged. 'He is right. What harm is there in a little friendship?' Arturo tried to be reasonable.

'Friendship!' Cummings shouted in disgust. 'How do we know what they've been up to in the backlanes?' he added crudely. Anna clucked her tongue on her teeth in shock, but Cummings continued regardless. 'We're different people, you and I, Dimarco, and we can get along fine if we keep to our own ways. But I don't want your son leading my niece up the garden path – there's no future in such a friendship, I hope you'll agree. So I've come to tell you to keep your son away from Sara, is that clear?'

Arturo flushed at such blatant rudeness. He struggled to maintain his courteous manner. 'You make yourself quite clear, Signor Cummings,' he replied.

'No!' Joe was stung into speech, furious at the

269

way his father was being humiliated. 'What right do you have to come barging into our home and tell us what to do? You're not Sara's father – let her decide for herself who she wants to see.'

'Listen to me, lad,' Cummings took a step towards him and narrowed his brown button eyes. 'I don't like your sort and I don't want you anywhere near my niece – in fact I don't want her coming here at all. I'm responsible for her while she's here and she does as I say. I can make things awkward for your family if I have to – so just watch your windows at night, if I catch you sniffing around Sara again.'

Anna and Domenica gasped together and Nonna Maria woke up with the noise. 'What is going on?' she asked in confusion.

Arturo stepped between Cummings and Joe. 'I think you better go, Signor Cummings. I'm sure Joe has understood your message.'

'Aye, well he better have,' Alfred answered and pulled at his hat. 'I'll see myself out.' He turned and pushed past Paolo, disappearing down the steps.

For a long moment there was complete silence, then everyone began to talk at once.

'How could you, Joe?' Domenica accused. 'You have brought shame to Papa and Mamma with this affair.'

'Oh, Joseph,' his mother trembled. 'Promise you will not see her again? That terrible man – with his wicked threats!'

'What is wrong?' Nonna asked fretfully. 'Tell me what is going on?' Paulo gave Joe a sad look and, with a shake of his head, descended to the

270

shop, where Sylvia and Rosa worked, oblivious of the row.

'Tell Rosa she cannot bring Sara here again,' Domenica decreed.

'Joseph, you will make your mamma white-haired–'

'Please, be quiet all of you!' Arturo ordered. He turned and looked sternly at Joe. 'Joseph Arturo, come downstairs with me, please. We will discuss this alone.'

Reluctantly, Joe followed him down to the backshop where Arturo pulled out a stool by the table and sat, indicating for his son to join him. Joe hesitated, unnerved by his father's silent disapproval, resentful of his family's frightened reaction.

'Paolo needs help in the shop,' Joe countered.

'Paolo can manage five minutes more. Please, sit with your father.' He was adamant, so Joe straddled the stool opposite, drumming his fingers impatiently on the seat. His father drew out a packet of Woodbines and, to Joe's surprise, offered one to him. They both knew he smoked, but never in the house. Joe took one and leaned forward for his father to light it.

'We've never had much chance to chat, you and I.' Arturo leaned his heavy frame on the table between them, clasping his cigarette between hairy fingers. 'That is my fault, I admit. We should have talked more, you and I.'

'You've always been busy, Papa,' Joe shrugged, beginning to calm down, 'working too hard.'

His father opened his hands in a fatalistic gesture. 'It's necessary to work hard – we are a

271

big family,' Arturo replied, studying him, 'but I should have found the time for you, Joseph, you've always been more – independent – than the others.'

Joe blew smoke. When his father said independent he meant unruly.

Arturo continued gravely, 'You've never told me about your friends – where you go – what you do – always rushing about on that motorcycle – vroom, vroom! It makes your mother worry. And now this business with Sara...'

'There's no need for Mamma to worry,' Joe flicked ash on the floor and took another deep drag on his cigarette.

'Isn't there?' Arturo asked softly. Joe shifted uncomfortably. He preferred it when his father was just plain angry with him and they could get their disagreement over with quickly and be done with it. Rosa dashed in with a tray of dirty glasses and caught sight of her brother and father sitting tensely opposite each other. Her face registered surprise and then concern.

'Leave those, Rosa,' her father waved her back into the shop, 'you can do them in a minute.' Rosa scurried back to the parlour and closed the door. Joe felt the heat of his burning cigarette nearing his fingers. He could hear the muffled rattle of plates and the hiss and gurgle of the coffee machine from the next room and the faint chatter from the women upstairs. But the humdrum sounds only heightened the hush in the backshop and his own disquiet.

'I worry for you, too,' Arturo continued at last. 'And for Sara.'

Joe reddened with guilt. 'So what if I have been seeing a bit of Rosa's friend?' he answered defensively. 'She's a canny lass – you and Mamma like her. And Sara's been a good friend to us – helping around the place when we're busy – you've said so yourself a dozen times. What harm is there in being friends?'

His father nodded. 'It's true what you say – Sara is a kind girl – and Rosa is a happier daughter since they became friends. As far as I'm concerned, there's no harm in a little *friendship*,' he stressed the word, 'but her uncle is not a good man– he has made threats against us. I might have turned the blind eye if Signor Cummings had not made his objections so plain, but he has. I cannot risk his damaging our business or threatening the family.'

Joe stood up in annoyance. 'And you're going to let him insult us and frighten us into turning our backs on Sara? She lost her father just a few months ago – she is far from *her* family – are you saying I can't see her, either?'

'I think it would be best if you did not,' Arturo remained calm. 'Sara is a nice girl, *si*. I can understand your attraction, but there are other girls – more suitable girls, Joseph. Cummings is right about one thing – Sara is not one of us, she does not understand our ways. Your mother – she would never accept her as anything more than Rosa's friend, you must see that?'

'No, I don't! Sara is just as good as any of your Italian girls!' Joe answered angrily, stung into defending Sara by his father's veiled attack. 'I'm a working man – I can see who I like, can't I?'

His father stood up slowly, his expression stern. 'I can't stop you seeing her if that's what you wish,' he admitted, 'I can't watch you every minute of the day. But for the sake of the family, Joe, remember what Cummings has said–'

'For the sake of your precious business, you mean!' Joe exploded.

'No, not just for that!' his father's voice rose too. 'Think of the trouble you make for Sara, too. Signor Cummings is an important man in Whitton Grange – I've heard people talk of him – Sergeant Turnbull is his friend. He could make life difficult for us, Joe. With all this talk of war – it makes me nervous – we are not as safe here as perhaps we thought...' Joe looked at his father in astonishment.

'What has war got to do with me and Sara, Papa?' Joe said in exasperation.

'Nothing I hope,' Arturo sighed. 'Listen, Joseph,' he was quietly grim, 'be careful. And just remember, when the time comes, you will marry a good Italian girl like Paolo has done. Don't cut yourself off from your family, Joe – or the business.'

The threat was so veiled Joe wondered if he had misunderstood, but the look of censure in his father's face confirmed it. He could play around if he did not get caught, but they would cast him into the cold if he brought disgrace on the family again. For a moment they glowered at each other across the table and then Joe kicked his stool away and marched out of the backshop into the unrelenting July rain.

Chapter Fourteen

Sara found Joe crouched on the steps of the deserted Palace Picture House, looking morose in the rain with a soggy cigarette stuck to his bottom lip. He seemed oblivious to the straggle of villagers hurrying by.

'Joe!' Sara sat down beside him on the cold step, 'I've been looking for you everywhere. I've got some terrible news – it's Uncle Alfred – he knows all about us – I'm not to see you – and Domenica's wedding – he says I can't go! He's gone round to tell your father about us. What shall we do, Joe?' she gabbled out her story, wanting him to reassure her that all was not really as bad as she imagined.

Joe dropped his cigarette and ground it out under his boot. He stood up. 'Come on, we can't talk here,' he said shortly, glancing around.

'Then where?' Sara grabbed his arm. 'I don't care if we *are* seen together.'

'Round the back.' Joe nodded down the back-lane and Sara followed, too unnerved by his sullen appearance to argue. Joe leaned against the wet drab brick of the cinema building and hunched into his jacket.

'He's told me to stay away from the parlour,' Sara said morosely, trying to make out the expression on Joe's half-hidden face. His jaw and nose looked angular and uncompromising, his

275

warm mouth expressionless. 'We had a terrible row over dinner. I'm supposed to be up in my room, but I climbed out the window.'

For the first time Joe turned his face towards her and smiled.

'You're a plucky lass,' he said, seeking out her hand and squeezing it briefly. 'I was there when your uncle came round. He insulted my father and me in front of my family.' Joe's voice was hard. 'He even threatened to smash our windows if I saw you again. What sort of man is that?'

'Oh, Joe, I'm sorry!' Sara answered. 'I *hate* him for what he's done. But can't your father do anything to persuade him to let us carry on seeing each other? At least we don't have to pretend to your family anymore.'

Joe sighed. The mention of his father plunged him into gloom again. He felt torn between his loyalty to his family and his affection for the girl beside him. Why should he have to choose between them? he thought with annoyance. He admitted, reluctantly, that it would be so much easier to court a girl from another Italian family and have the approval of his relations, instead of all this sneaking around trying to meet Sara. No one wanted them to be friends – his own father had made that quite clear and now Alfred Cummings was determined his niece should have nothing to do with the Dimarcos. Joe was offended. Yet it was not Sara's fault; she was risking further punishment by being with him at that very moment.

'Cummings has given my father a scare,' Joe's voice was low. 'He's worried about what might happen to the business – and to the family – and he doesn't want any trouble.'

Sara's heart plummeted. Joe's glum face told her that Mr Dimarco was not pleased at their courtship. 'Your father doesn't want us to see each other either, does he?'

'No,' Joe admitted.

'And your mother? Domenica?'

Joe shrugged. 'They're just old-fashioned – they want me to find a good Italian girl like Sylvia. But that's not what *I* want, so what does it matter?'

'Of course it matters what your family think!' Sara's eyes pricked with tears of disappointment. She felt sick as realisation dawned on her. 'They were never going to accept us seeing each other, were they?' Sara pressed him. 'That's why you put off telling your family, Joe, wasn't it?'

Joe let out a sigh. He felt an overwhelming guilt because her words were true; he had dismissed any thoughts of what might happen should his parents discover his relationship with Sara, content to indulge in a summer romance without a thought for the consequences.

'Hey, stop worrying,' he rallied, gripping her hand tighter, 'they can't stop me seeing you – my father said so himself. To hell with what they think!'

Sara pulled away. 'Joe! How can we see each other if both your father and my uncle are set on keeping us apart? How could I even look your father or mother in the face, knowing that they don't think I'm good enough for you!' She was indignant.

'They don't think that!' Joe's tone grew vexed.

'And I thought Domenica was my friend...' Sara said, full of hurt.

'She is,' Joe insisted, 'it's just...'

'Just what, Joe?' Sara demanded. 'That it's all right for you to play around with the likes of me – a common Durham lass – but don't get serious, because I'm not as good as the likes of your sisters? I'm not a spoilt, protected little Italian girl!' Sara's voice grew shrill.

'Don't ever speak about my sisters like that!' Joe was angry in turn. 'Rosa knows nothing about this – she doesn't deserve your insults.'

Sara turned from him, tight-lipped and resentful. Joe stood with arms folded and stared crossly at the ground.

Sara began to regret her hasty words, especially against her friend Rosa, but she still boiled with anger at the superior attitude of the Dimarcos. What was worse was that Joe did not take the matter seriously. Who were they but jumped-up shopkeepers anyway? she thought savagely. But no, that was unfair, Sara admitted; she was sinking to the petty level of her uncle and aunt.

The Dimarcos were generous and kind people, who had shown her great friendship and hospitality when her own relations had begrudged her a place in their home. She hated the thought of not seeing them again, of not being friends with Rosa. But what future was there for her and Joe? she wondered bleakly.

'Perhaps it's for the best if we don't see each other for a while – at least until things have calmed down,' he muttered without looking at her. 'You'll only get into trouble with your uncle – and I don't want him turning up again and causing problems for my family.'

Sara was bitterly wounded by his brusque words. For all his belief that he was a free spirit, Joe was not going to stick his neck out for her, in the way she was prepared to take risks for him.

'If that's what you want,' she answered stonily.

'Things will be easier after my sister is married.' Joe glanced at her, with a bleak smile. 'Domenica's always had this thing about me finding an Italian girl – once she's gone, I'm sure I can win my father round.'

But Sara did not believe him. Raymond's words of warning echoed in her mind, 'They stick with their own – don't expect it to last.' Joe was just trying to soothe her with empty promises, she thought. Perhaps he was even relieved to have this excuse to finish with her.

Sara turned from him and began to walk away down the dismal alleyway.

'Where you going?' Joe called after her.

'I'll see you around,' she told him coldly, trying to act with the unconcern of a screen heroine. But unlike a cinema hero he did not try to stop her going and as she tramped out of the lane on to the drizzly main street of grey Whitton Grange, Sara was filled with an overwhelming emptiness.

Rosa woke on the morning of Domenica's wedding day feeling sick with nerves. She and her younger brother Bobby went out early to watch the colliery band play down South Street and led a mass of villagers towards Whitton Station, where special trains had been laid on to take them to the Gala in Durham. Rosa had never attended the Big Meeting, but remembered her schoolfriends talking about the processions and banners and a huge fair, as the most exciting day of the year.

But today was Domenica's wedding day and the most exciting in *her* life! Rosa thought with a rumble of nerves. She had overcome her shock and disappointment over the revelation about Joe and Sara's deceitful romance, which had threatened to overshadow the wedding. Rosa was hurt that Sara had never confided in her, merely using their friendship as a way of seeing her brother, and she was upset at the way Cummings's visit had set her family bickering among themselves as to what should be done. With Joe and her father at loggerheads once more, she blamed herself for having introduced Sara into their home in the first place. And to think she had assumed Sara was being courted by Raymond! Rosa thought with annoyance, Raymond must have thought her so rude for the way she had avoided him since the carnival dance. How naive she had been!

So, on the one occasion she had visited Sergeant's, Rosa had been cold towards her former friend and ignored Sara's attempts to speak to her when the elderly grocer went into the storeroom. In future she would be content with the company of her own family and today nothing was going to spoil her enjoyment of Domenica's marriage, she decided, herding Bobby home to help with the final preparations. She had a beautiful dress to wear and an important part to play in the procession – and she was going to meet Emilio Fella, Pasquale's best man, for the first time.

The parlour was transformed for the occasion. The women had been up before daylight setting the trestle tables that Arturo had hired and which had been pushed together in the centre of the shop to provide a long banqueting table around which all the thirty guests would be squeezed. Starched linen cloths hid the rough surfaces and on them cutlery and glasses gleamed, white napkins were shaped into fans and a forest of freshly cut flowers filled the polished room with vibrant colours and scents. Rosa had helped her sister-in-law Sylvia make garlands of paper flowers which they suspended from the ceiling and anchored to the top table to create a colourful bower behind which the newlyweds would sit, while her mother's magnificent wedding cake stood in three tiers on the middle of the table.

Her father was flustering over what wine to bring out first, while Paolo quietly and efficiently saw to the problem. Her mother and Sylvia and Granny Maria had spent many hours preparing the wedding feast, but two girls from the church had been hired for the day to help serve out the food and wash up in the backshop during the feast.

Then Bobby shouted that Uncle Davide and Aunt Elvira were arriving in their new car and they dashed out to watch the family draw up in a gleaming black Humber saloon. Their student son, Benito, and two of their three daughters were going to be present. Rosa hardly remembered her eldest cousin who had returned to Italy to enter a convent. However, the youngest, Albina, was her own age and unmarried and was also to be a bridesmaid. There was an explosion of greetings and shouts and kisses as the two families reunited, the booming-voiced Uncle Davide clasping his brother Arturo to his solid paunch.

'Elvira!' Anna Dimarco embraced her bird-like sister-in-law. 'How was the journey? You are looking so well.'

'Mam, look at Uncle Davide's new car!' Bobby interrupted, hopping with excitement around the well-polished motorcar.

'I feel sick in it, if the truth be known,' Aunt Elvira admitted, 'but don't tell Davide.'

Rosa's cousin Val who had shocked everyone by insisting on training as a nurse, came over and embraced Domenica.

'I'm glad you could come,' Domenica said happily, linking arms with her slight, bespectacled cousin.

'So am I,' Val smiled, 'but I've got to get the train back this afternoon – I'm on nights.'

'But you must stay for the whole day!' Domenica protested.

'Sorry,' Val gave an apologetic shrug.

'How can you do it, Val?' Domenica shuddered. 'All that illness and mess. Give me a shop to run any day!'

Rosa eyed plump cousin Albina with caution. 'Would you like to try on your dress now,' Rosa urged, 'in case Sylvia has to alter anything?'

'I hope you don't mean I've put on weight?' Albina sounded offended.

'Oh, no!' Rosa replied hastily.

'Are you just going to leave your hair like that?' Albina said, with a critical look at Rosa's straight locks and fringe, patting her own thick, wavy hair with pride. Rosa felt dashed.

'I'll be wearing a flowered headband,' she defended her appearance, feeling at a disadvantage against her more sophisticated cousin.

They were diverted by the handing over of presents, while cousin Benito went out to admire Joe's motorcycle and Uncle Davide allowed his youngest nephew, Bobby, to sit in the driver's seat of his expensive and cherished car.

'Come, girls!' Rosa's mother put a stop to the gossiping and present opening. 'It's time to put on your dresses.'

The next half hour was frantic with activity as Rosa and Albina fumbled with Domenica's dress and veil and giggled with tension, under the scrutiny and direction of the older women. Eventually they were satisfied and Domenica did indeed look stunning in her dress of white satin and lace flowers and the elaborate headdress that trailed beyond her feet. Rosa felt pretty, too, in a dress of primrose yellow with a band of yellow and white flowers in her straight dark hair – no matter that Albina obviously thought herself the more attractive. Anna and Sylvia left to change into their outfits, bought specially for the occasion.

'Aren't you going to wear any lipstick, Rosa?' Albina asked, glancing up from a small mirror she carried in her handbag, her large mouth smeared with pink. 'Your face is very pale without it.'

'Here, try some of mine,' Domenica smiled at

her sister.

'But Mamma...' Rosa was reluctant.

'She'll not object today,' her sister dismissed her fears. 'Go on.'

'I've been wearing lipstick since I was your age,' Albina told Rosa with a condescending smile. 'But then we have more social get togethers in Sunderland than you do here, I expect.'

'I suppose you do,' Rosa agreed, quite in awe of her cousin.

'Rubbish!' Domenica contradicted. 'We have plenty dances and suppers in Whitton Grange. The Carnival dance this year was the best one I've been to in my life.' Rosa gawped at her sister for the blatant lie.

'Not better than the dances at the *fascio*, surely?' Albina's tone was disbelieving.

'Better than at the *fascio*,' Domenica declared, stung into such an admission by her cousin's patronizing manner. She turned from Albina's plump pout and winked at Rosa as she carefully applied the red lipstick to the younger girl's lips.

'Lend Rosa your mirror, Albina,' Domenica commanded.

Rosa looked with trepidation at her reflection. Albina was right, she thought, the deep colour of her lips gave warmth to her whole face. Rosa believed she could pass for seventeen or eighteen dressed as she was now. Tears of emotion pricked her eyes as she looked at Domenica in her finery.

'I'm going to miss you so much,' she said candidly. Domenica turned and threw her arms about her young sister.

'Me, too, Rosa.'

Rosa found herself crying in spite of Albina's presence, joy and sadness tugging her insides.

'Hey, it's supposed to be me who cries!' Domenica teased her. 'You're behaving like the bride – now stop stealing the limelight.'

Rosa laughed and wiped her eyes with a lace handkerchief. 'Sorry.'

'Listen,' Domenica smoothed her hair like a child's, 'you can come and stay with us in Sunderland as soon as you want. It'd be nice for me to have the company while Pasquale's working in the shop.'

'Won't you be helping your husband?' Albina interrupted.

Domenica winked. 'I'll be too busy having babies!' she said with a wicked smile. 'You'll understand when someone eventually asks you to marry him.' Albina flushed crimson at the snub.

'Domenica!' Rosa spluttered with shocked giggles.

At this point Anna Dimarco hurried in to their bedroom. 'What's all this laughter? You should be ready – oh, Santa Teresa!' she exclaimed, catching sight of her daughters, overcome once again by their beauty. *'Bellissima!'* she cried and pushed away a treacherous tear.

'Domenica says I can go and stay with her when she's married,' Rosa said cheerfully.

'We'll see,' answered her mother, in the infuriating way she always side-stepped requests from her youngest daughter. Soon, Rosa thought stubbornly, I shall be the eldest daughter at home and she will have to take more notice of what I want. Somehow she would make sure she got to

285

stay with Domenica and Pasquale. Her father would agree, Rosa was sure, and the best way to persuade her mother was through her father. But Albina opened her mouth and aided Rosa's cause unintentionally.

'Rosa, you should think of your mother,' she chastised. 'You'll be needed here more than ever once Domenica goes. Won't she, Aunt Anna?' she preened, smoothing the yellow satin over her full bosom. 'It's different for us, of course, with Papa having help in the shops. I've *never* had to work like you, cousin Rosa.'

'Oh I think we can spare Rosa for a week or two, if she wants to stay with Domenica,' Anna was brusque. 'My girls are very close you see, Albina,' she replied proudly, 'and we manage very well as we are without any outside help in our shop.' As a parting shot, Rosa's mother added, 'I always think it's a pity if a family has to depend on outsiders and can't manage for themselves.'

Domenica and Rosa tried to maintain straight faces as they followed their mother into the living-room where Aunt Elvira and Granny Maria were waiting for them. After that, there was no more time for rivalry. Rosa accompanied her parents and sister in the gleaming blue Austin that her father had hired to take them to the church, while behind came Paolo and his young family in the Dimarco van with Uncle Davide's huge car at the rear. Bobby and Joe elected to walk down to the church, accompanied by cousin Benito who was regaling them with stories of Manchester where he was studying law. For once, Rosa thought, as she glanced out of the window, Joe was looking smart in a suit and white shirt, his hair combed and shiningly clean. Thankfully he seemed to be his lively self again, laughing at something Benito was saying and Rosa gripped her bouquet of roses in happy expectation.

Sara watched the Dimarcos and Perellas disgorge in great numbers down the church steps, to a peal of bells and a blast of music behind them. The disruption of noise was even more deafening in contrast to the unaccustomed quiet of the Durham Road on Big Meeting Day. With talk of war on everyone's lips, all but the most elderly or infirm had gone into Durham to enjoy themselves on what might be the last Gala before conflict put a stop to frivolity. Only the ancient, the incontinent and the sandwich makers had stayed, Sara thought resentfully, having spent the morning at the Memorial Hall preparing a cold tea for when the pitfolk returned.

Yet she had succeeded in slipping away from the watchful eye of Mrs Sergeant, who had been detailed to look after her until Ida came back from Durham on the early afternoon train in time to supervise tea for the returning villagers. Sara and Mrs Sergeant had been preparing sandwiches when Sara, declaring she was feeling faint and needing some fresh air, made a dash from the hall. She half suspected Mrs Sergeant saw it for the excuse it was and that the older woman had allowed her to go and watch the wedding procession. The surly grocer did not share Uncle Alfred's aversion to foreigners or

Catholics, especially good paying ones, and had herself sent Domenica a present of a tea caddy, albeit an unsold one left over from the Royal Jubilee of 1935, depicting the late King George V and Queen Mary.

The sky was gun-metal, and ominous with rain as Sara peered out from behind a large chestnut tree. She sighed at the fairytale sight of the pretty dark-eyed bride in swathes of white satin and lace on the arm of a well-dressed, full-faced young man with thick dark eyebrows and a peak of black hair on his square brow. Sara was struck by how happy Domenica and Pasquale looked. Following them came Domenica's bridesmaids in fresh yellow, Rosa looking flushed and attractive beside a rather dumpy girl whom she took to be cousin Albina from Sunderland. A tall, good-looking young man with wavy hair and a thin moustache stood beside the girls and Sara wondered if this was the best man, Emilio, about whom Domenica had teased Rosa. A flock of neatly dressed young children hampered the photographer who was trying to catch the joyous moment and Sara tried to work out who all the relations might be.

She experienced a stab of jealousy to see Joe looking handsome in a suit she had never seen him wear before, talking animatedly with a slim, poised girl in spectacles who looked elegant in a simple blue dress and straw hat. Sara felt her loneliness and isolation compounded by the transparent joy of these close-knit families coming together to give the young couple their blessing. She was envious of Domenica's radiance, envious of Rosa's appearance, envious of the Dimarcos' protectiveness and the warmth that surrounded them while shutting her out.

Sara's throat flooded with emotion, unable to allow her bitterness to completely swamp her delight at the romantic sight before her. Grudgingly, she wished them well. Several minutes elapsed and huge slow drops of rain began to plop onto the roadway before Arturo took charge and ordered the chattering guests into their cars and back to Pit Street. She was surprised to see Sergeant Turnbull hovering awkwardly on the edge of the group with a prim-looking woman in green whom she took to be Mrs Turnbull. She had not realised they were such close friends of the Dimarcos.

As Domenica stepped into the waiting car with Pasquale, Sara could no longer contain her desire to be among them. Impulsively, she ran from the cover of the trees just as the heavens opened in a barrage of rain and rushed up to the bride and groom, pulling a bag of rice from her gaberdine pocket and throwing its contents over them.

'Good luck, Domenica!' she called at the astonished girl.

'Thank you,' she replied uncertainly, and waved as Pasquale pulled the car door shut.

Sara turned to see Rosa staring at her from the window of a blue car. They exchanged embarrassed looks and Rosa half raised her hand in farewell. The engine of the car was revving but Arturo Dimarco wound down his window and called to her.

'Sara, you will come for a piece of the cake

later, yes?'

She was filled with gratitude that he should ask, in spite of the trouble it might cause with her uncle. 'Thank you but I'll not get away again, we'll be that busy with the pitmen and their families,' she said sadly as the rain pelted her bare head.

He waved and she stood back as the procession of cars and vans chugged past. She turned to see Joe watching her, with a foot already inside the Dimarco van. His expression was strained, as if he were angered by her abrupt appearance. The driver, Paolo, started the engine and Joe scrambled into the van, followed by a square-faced young man shaking a wet umbrella. He had made no attempt to speak or even acknowledge her, Sara thought dismally. The sight of her in sodden coat and tousled hair was obviously an embarrassment to him among all his well-dressed relations.

As swiftly as they had appeared, the tide of wedding guests swept out of sight and the strange stillness that gripped the village descended again with the vertical rain. Sara pulled her coat up over her head and began to run for cover.

For Rosa, the day sped by far too quickly, yet she made an effort to remember every detail of the enormous wedding feast, with its speeches, conversation, music and dancing. To her delight, not only did she sit next to the attractive Emilio Fella but he showered her with attention, despite the watchful eyes and ears of her mother on one side and her brother Paolo on the other. With her stomach knotted in excitement, Rosa struggled through the eight courses of soup and salami and pastas, potatoes fried in garlic and olive oil, red peppers grilled until crispy black on top and a myriad of other vegetables which accompanied the strongly flavoured roast mutton. It was all liberally washed down with a succession of wines and then finished off with a selection of rich, creamy puddings and ices and cup after cup of her father's coffee.

Various Perella children, led by her brother Bobby, left the boredom of adult conversation and disappeared to explore the yard and its out-houses. Uncle Davide produced some bottles of his homemade wine with a proud flourish and, while he and Arturo fell to arguing over who made the superior wine, Rosa gave her full attention to Emilio's amusing chatter.

His English was poor, but his gesticulations and expressive face were mesmerizing to watch. Rosa blushed and giggled at her attempts to answer him in their mother tongue and he set about teaching her some Italian with exaggerated mannerisms, which made her laugh all the more.

'You laugh at poor Emilio, *si?*' he clutched his heart and gave her a soulful look. Rosa gazed into his hazel eyes and noticed they were flecked with gold, echoing the fair tint in his wavy brown hair. He was altogether fairer skinned than the other Italians she knew and his thin moustache was almost golden. She was quite overwhelmed that he should want to talk to her instead of the voluptuous Albina who was making eyes at him from across the table.

'No, I'm not laughing,' Rosa giggled, 'it's just you're so funny – and I think Papa's wine is going to my head!' She glanced at her mother, but she was in conversation with the balding, dignified Mr Perella.

'Lucky wine,' Emilio leaned closer, 'you have such a pretty head.'

Rosa blushed and felt him slip a hand on to her knee under cover of the tablecloth. She let it stay there, her heart beginning to thud with unimaginable excitement. She thought she had been fond of the bashful Raymond, but his boyish good looks did not set her heart hammering like the manly Emilio's did. This was altogether a different experience.

So when the lively wedding party grew more raucous and the tables and chairs were pushed back to allow for a small band of musicians to play, including an inebriated Uncle Davide on the accordion, Rosa did not hesitate in accepting Emilio as her first dancing partner. Domenica and Pasquale began the dancing and then her parents and the Perellas took to the floor, followed swiftly by Paolo and Sylvia, and Aunt Elvira with cousin Benito. More of the Perellas joined in as the dancing grew lively and Rosa noticed Joe lead cousin Val in a polka.

'Your cousin is giving black looks, yes?' Emilio spoke in Rosa's ear as they whirled in the tarantella. Rosa glanced round to see Albina scowling at them, munching on a chunk of bread.

'Albina doesn't like me very much,' Rosa grimaced.

'*Madonna!*' Emilio protested. 'She is jealous.'

'Of me?' Rosa laughed. 'She is much prettier than I am,' Rosa said without guile.

'No,' Emilio dropped his voice to a rumble, 'you are the pretty one. When God made your face – he take stars from the sky for your eyes!'

Rosa's insides melted at his flattery; she had never before experienced such attention and it made her thirst for more. Emilio Fella was the most exciting person she had ever known and, as the afternoon wore on, she felt she would do anything and go anywhere with him. She ignored her mother's warning looks and Albina's spiteful asides and gave herself up to the complete enjoyment of Emilio's company. If he was Pasquale Perella's best man, then it was quite circumspect for her to accept his attentions. And everything might have gone quite differently if an argument had not broken out when it did.

Rosa became aware of raised voices above the general hubbub and her father's untrained bass voice which had broken into song. She turned in her chair, where Emilio was daringly holding her hand under the table, to see Joe in confrontation with Uncle Davide. Cousin Val was standing to the side looking troubled and Benito was interjecting but being ignored by both his father and cousin Joe.

'*Il Duce* is a great leader,' Uncle Davide declared. 'How dare you dismiss what he has done for us Italians abroad as well as at home. Don't forget why we had to leave home, your father and I – because we were too poor to eat. Mussolini has given our country prosperity – there are roads and water running through our villages now. He has given us back our pride.'

'Pride in what?' Joe scoffed. 'That Italians massacred Abyssinians and Albanians? That Italy is now in league with bully-boy Hitler?'

'Pah!' Uncle Davide waved him away with a dismissive hand. 'You read too much of the English newspapers – where is your Italian heart, Joseph Arturo? Italy has a right to an empire as much as the English or French. No one complains about *them* slicing up the world like a cake!'

'But Joe is right when he says Mussolini is Hitler's man now,' Benito nodded gravely. 'What happens to us Italians if Britain goes to war with Germany – we will be seen as the enemy, too.'

'Don't talk such rubbish!' his father declared. 'Benito, you are my son and I love you, but you make worries for yourself. How can we be enemies of the English? We have lived and worked here all our lives – one day you will be a lawyer of English. The English are our friends – they like us – they like our ice-cream and our fish and chips, isn't that so, Signor Turnbull?'

The police officer was alert to their arguing, but maintained a cool distance. 'Very good ice-cream,' he nodded. Joe gave him a withering look, angry that this man who was continually getting him into trouble should be a guest at his sister's wedding.

'Some people treat us like the enemy already,' Joe was scathing.

Pasquale's father was drawn into the argument.

'That is not what I have found,' he contradicted quietly, 'yet the thought of war is worrying for our business...'

'War, war! Why does everyone talk of war?' Uncle Davide asked with exasperation. His wrinkled brow was sweating from the heat and labour of his accordion playing. He mopped his face with a large handkerchief.

'Because lads like me and Benito will get called up to fight for Britain if there's a war,' Joe answered aggressively. Rosa could tell from across the room that he was fired up with wine and not ready to be silenced. 'Val here might have to go, too, as an army nurse. Have you thought about that?'

'Valentina will stay at home with me and her mother!' Uncle Davide was frightened by such a suggestion. 'Or find a young doctor for a husband, eh, Valentina?'

'No, Father,' Val answered with quiet determination. 'I'm serious about my nursing. I want it to be my career.'

Uncle Davide's mouth dropped open, then he decided to ignore the challenge to his authority and returned to hector Joe.

'Listen, Joseph! If you are called up you will go like a good soldier – like your father and me. Don't forget we fought in the Great War alongside the British – but as loyal Italians. *Merda!* We fought and died with them – we are all ex *combattenti* together. How can the British see us as the enemy, Arturo?' he appealed to his brother. 'You boys are mad in the head!'

'Please, this is my daughter's wedding!' Arturo protested. 'Joseph, have a little respect for your uncle, say you are sorry for the pain you give him.'

Joe looked angrily between the men, unable to bring himself to apologise.

'No, see how he is silent?' Uncle Davide bristled at the offence. 'He is a bad Italian – he has no respect for his *compare*.'

Joe was stung by the reproof. It was true, Uncle Davide was his godfather and the man to whom he should look up to above all others and yet he had done nothing but argue with him since the wedding feast began. He loved his uncle and had idolised him as a small boy, yet now he represented the authority and *Italianata* that imprisoned him and prevented him from seeing his Sara. He could not be a good Italian and continue to love a girl from outside their community.

This past week he had felt increasing annoyance that he missed Sara as much as he did. He could settle to nothing, not even football, without thinking about the Pallister lass. Today Joe had determined to think no more about her and force himself to take an interest in his unmarried female relations or perhaps one of Pasquale Perella's sisters. But seeing Sara rush like some water nymph from out of the dene at the church, sprinkling rice and grinning at Domenica with her wide, impish mouth, he knew it was futile to try and banish her from his mind. His resentment at being denied her company boiled over now at his uncle and father.

'Perhaps I *am* a bad Italian,' Joe shouted, subduing the whole room, 'but then it's you who have brought me up in this country and encouraged me to be a good English lad. How can I be a loyal Italian if I don't speak the language or if I never visit our homeland? I don't sound like you and I don't think like you – so how am I supposed to feel the way you do? Tell me that, Papa – Uncle Davide!'

His father and uncle stared at him with a mixture of bafflement and anger. Unexpectedly, Val backed him up. 'I know what Joe means,' she said with a controlled passion. 'We are caught between two ways of doing things – the one we are taught at home and the one we learn at school and outside our family. It's not that we aren't proud of our *Italianata*, Father, we are. It's just we can never be as Italian as you want us to be. Yet we can never be as English as the English want us to be, either!' She turned her serious dark eyes on Joe's father. 'You shouldn't blame Joe for being the mix that he is, Uncle Arturo. It isn't easy living with divided loyalties pulling you this way and that.'

There was a moment of stunned silence and then Uncle Davide declared, 'I've never heard you say such things before, Valentina! Where do you get such notions? What divided loyalties? The choice is easy - you are Italians!'

'That's easy for you to say, Father,' Valentina grew more heated, 'but not for our generation.'

'Joe, is this how you feel?' Arturo asked his son, puzzled.

'I suppose so,' Joe replied, never having analysed it in the way his cousin had.

'It's my wedding!' shrieked Domenica, furious at the way she and her new husband were taking second place to the discussion. 'Joe, can't you behave yourself for one day?'

Granny Maria began to bluster with dis-approval in Italian and Anna Dimarco burst into tears at the tension. Aunt Elvira rushed to comfort her, while the gaunt-faced Mrs Perella maintained a distant, embarrassed look.

Soon the room was in an uproar of argument and recriminations once more. Two of the musicians decided to begin playing again in spite of the din and the Turnbulls left hurriedly with Arturo in pursuit, pressing them to stay longer. Emilio chose that moment to squeeze Rosa's hand.

'Let's leave them to the fighting,' he smiled, 'I think it would be nice to walk, *si?*'

Rosa glanced about her, but nobody seemed to notice them in their tranquil corner. Even Albina had gathered around the conflicting parties and was adding her voice.

'We could walk in the dene now the rain's stopped...' she smiled nervously.

'Anywhere,' Emilio said, squeezing her hand again. It felt so warm nestled inside his possessive hold, Rosa thought with a curious thud in her chest.

Quietly, they got up from the table and left by the back door.

Chapter Fifteen

The late afternoon sun that broke through the clouds was warm on her face and neck as Rosa strolled down South Street with the handsome Emilio. Still dressed in her yellow satin frock and headband of flowers, the tall Italian beside her in his formal suit, they made a becoming sight to the trickle of villagers who were returning wearily from their day out in Durham. People smiled at them and nodded in greeting.

They wandered arm in arm down the main street, turning past the Catholic church on Durham Road and into the dene. At this point, Emilio slipped an arm about Rosa's petite waist.

'The way is too tight,' he explained. 'We must walk close together.'

Rosa laughed. 'Too *narrow*,' she corrected.

'Narrow?' Emilio puzzled over the word.

'The path is too narrow,' Rosa repeated.

'You teach me good Inglese,' he announced, 'I teaching you Italiano, yes?'

'Yes,' Rosa agreed, pleased. She began to point things out as they walked and Emilio copied her, pulling comic faces at his attempts and making her laugh.

Presently they reached the end of the dene, where the path skirted the allotments and snaked into Whitton Woods. Rosa hesitated.

'It goes up to the Common,' she told him. He

looked nonplussed. 'The hill. You can look right over Whitton Grange. I've only ever been twice before. When it's clear you can just see the top of Durham Cathedral.'

'Ah, cathedral,' Emilio pounced on a word he understood. 'I like to see.'

They carried on walking, climbing the steep path through the trees, slithering on the muddy track and catching each other from falling. But before they emerged on to Whitton Common, Emilio pulled her to a halt and encircled her with his arms.

'Now I teach you some Italian, yes?' he murmured.

'Yes?' Rosa echoed, her heart hammering.

Emilio began to kiss his way gently across her face, speaking the words for forehead, nose, eyes and cheeks in his soft, seductive tongue. At her mouth he lingered for longer and Rosa closed her eyes and gave in to the delightful sensation of their lips touching. He pulled her closer and kissed her more firmly, his hands beginning to explore. Rosa gasped as he brushed her tiny breasts beneath the satin, but was too surprised to pull away.

'*Bella* Rosa,' he whispered, covering her face with exquisite kisses like butterflies brushing her skin. Rosa trembled. 'I can see why your papa call you a rose.'

At the mention of her father, Rosa's paralysed arms stirred and she brought her hands up between them.

'We shall be missed,' she croaked. 'I think we should go back now.'

'Oh, Rosa, Rosa,' Emilio buried his face into her slender neck. 'You have stolen my heart. How can I leave you?'

'Domenica has invited me to stay in Sunderland,' Rosa told him, equally reluctant to move from his hold. 'Perhaps we could see each other if I do?' she asked, holding her breath in anticipation.

'*Si!*' Emilio cried. 'You *must* come. I will come to Pasquale's house and ask to see you. If he says no, I sing in your window till he says yes.'

Rosa stifled a laugh. '*Under* my window.'

'Under, in, on, out – what you say! I come, Rosa,' he declared.

'Good, I would like that,' she answered with a flush of pleasure. 'But now I really think we should go back to the wedding before my sister and Pasquale leave.'

Hand-in-hand, they turned back along the muddy path, Rosa uncaring about the tell-tale stains spoiling the hem of her gown or the sorry state of her once-white shoes. She was in love with Emilio Fella and even the thought of her mother's scolding could not blight such a wonderful feeling.

Joe sat straddling his motionless motorcycle, brooding over the events of the afternoon. He still wore his suit trousers and polished shoes, but his jacket and tie had long been discarded and he shivered in his shirt sleeves as a chill breeze cooled the weakening shafts of evening sun.

His argument with Uncle Davide and his father had climaxed with Domenica slapping him across the cheek. Paolo, hating any family feuding, had stepped in and calmed tempers down by apologising to Uncle Davide on his brother's behalf and flattering him into playing another tune on his accordion. Uncle Davide had been mollified and Paolo, requesting a soothing waltz, had led Domenica in the dance, quickly followed by the relieved Perellas.

Joe, now ignored by the rest of his family – even the faithful Rosa seemed to have disappeared from sight – had offered to drive cousin Val to the station where she was catching the five-thirty-five back to Sunderland. Domenica said a frosty farewell to her self-composed cousin who she saw as having aggravated the situation, so Joe and Val had left swiftly.

'Don't worry,' Val had said to Joe as they waited for the train, 'they'll look back and remember today with nostalgia in a month or two. Father won't stay angry with you forever.'

'Not like he has with Uncle Gino, you mean?' Joe asked dryly.

Val allowed herself a wry smile. 'Well, give him twenty years or so and he'll come round to our point of view.'

Joe laughed; he liked his quiet cousin and her detached, dry humour. A pity he did not find her attractive, he thought, as he waved her away, it might have solved a lot of problems. Then he chided himself for his arrogance. Cousin Val would probably have turned him down anyway, he laughed to himself, she appeared firmly wedded to her nursing.

Unable to return to the merriment of the wedding party in Pit Street, Joe had motored around the streets aimlessly for half an hour before setting up vigil outside the Memorial Hall. He knew Sara was in there serving teas to the pitfolk and he would sit there until she emerged, not caring who saw him.

He chain-smoked and picked over the troubling words that Benito had said. 'If Britain goes to war with Germany, won't the English see us as the enemy?' Joe had never thought of such an outcome. He would be an enemy in his own country, the place of his birth, here in Whitton Grange among the people with whom he had grown up, played football, fought and loved... Impossible! he banished such gloomy thoughts, flicking his fourth cigarette into the gutter and watching it spit as it died.

'Wedding over, is it?' a voice behind shook him back to the present. Raymond was passing him, hands deep in his pockets, his large cap facing the wrong way on his auburn hair.

'It is for me,' Joe admitted. 'Had a canny day in Durham?'

'Aye, I've been celebratin'. I start at the Eleanor on Monday.' Raymond grinned foolishly. 'No more slave labour for the Sergeant-Major.' Joe caught a faint whiff of stale beer on the boy's breath. 'What you doing hanging around here for?' Raymond focused on Joe more closely.

'Sara's in there.' Joe nodded towards the hall.

Raymond whistled. 'You've got a nerve! The lass's life's been a misery since Cummings found out about you two.'

'Do us a favour, will you, Raymond?' Joe seized his chance before his friend's good humour waned. 'Gan into the hall and tell Sara I want a word.'

'Tell her yourself,' his friend answered, suddenly riled at being used as Joe's messenger boy. His new mates thought Joe Dimarco a show-off on his motorbike and Raymond had distanced himself from his old friend. It upset him, too, to think how miserable Sara had been since Joe had cooled relations with her.

'Haway, Raymond,' Joe coaxed, 'you know she's not allowed to see me.'

'Why don't you leave the poor lass alone? The rest of your family want nothing to do with her – even Rosa's turning up her nose now.' Raymond was suddenly aggressive.

'Well, I'm different. I need to see her.' Joe curbed his impatience. 'I'll do you a favour in return. We're still marras aren't we, Raymond?'

Raymond hesitated, feeling a twinge of guilt. 'Have you got any smokes?' Joe nodded and pulled out a packet of Woodbines. He knocked one out and handed it to the youth. 'The whole packet,' Raymond bargained, guessing his position of strength.

'Gan on then,' Joe sighed, tossing him the packet.

''By, you must be keen on the lass,' Raymond grinned, 'and on your sister's weddin' day, too.' He set off up the steps to the Memorial Hall.

'Don't let her Aunt Ida hear you,' Joe called after his friend as he wobbled unsteadily on the top step.

Joe waited an age, watching the faces which appeared from the double doorway, searching in

304

vain for any sign of Raymond or Sara and wondering at his foolhardiness in trying to contact her. He was about to give up when he recognised Sara's figure emerging out of the shadowy hallway. Her face was hot and flushed, with tendrils of hair stuck to her forehead and cheeks. She wore a faded apron that pinchcd her at the waist.

'Well?' she demanded at once. 'What's this all about, Joe Dimarco? Why are you bothering me on your sister's wedding day – I thought it was family only?'

Joe's spirits roused at her attack; to argue with her was ten times better than not to see her at all.

'I'm risking my neck waiting here for you,' he retaliated, 'so the least you can do is listen to what I've got to say.'

'Why should I?' Sara said crossly, gripping her arms in front like a barrier, determined to remain cold towards him.

'Because–' Joe paused, then swallowing his pride, ''cos I need to see you again, Sara.'

She gave him a disbelieving look and said nothing.

'I don't care what my family say,' Joe ploughed on, 'they can't keep us apart – and neither can yours!'

Sara glanced round nervously, half expecting to see her aunt fussing after her. 'But they *have*, Joe,' she said resignedly. 'Listen, I said I'd just gone to wash so I can't stay out here any longer – it's too risky with half the village about.'

'Sara, I miss you,' Joe spoke with desperation. 'Say you'll see me again.'

She was helpless with indecision, fearing the trouble they might bring upon themselves. Yet, seeing his handsome face so close and knowing she could not touch him made her ache with longing...

'It's not that I don't want to...' she wavered.

'Can you get away next Saturday?' Joe grabbed at an idea, seeing her weakening resolve. 'We're doing the refreshments at a dance in Durham. I'll go instead of Paolo – it'll be easy for me to get away.'

'But not for me!' Sara felt hopeless.

'Try,' Joe challenged her. 'Climb out of your window if you have to – anything, just be in the dene at our usual place by seven.'

'Oh, Joe,' Sara half laughed, half remonstrated, 'how can I?'

He lunged for her hand and kissed it impulsively. 'I want to dance with you again, *bellissima*. I'm going daft thinking about you.'

Sara felt a familiar thrill, his words warming the bleak emptiness she had nursed inside this past week.

'I'll try,' she promised and then snatched her hand away. She turned and ran back up the steps, with only a swift glance back at him betraying the longing she felt.

By the time Joe returned to the parlour, Domenica and Pasquale had left, as had the other Perellas and most of the other guests. The musicians had disbanded and Sylvia was helping the hired girls clear the tables, while Paolo and his father, Uncle Davide and Benito were staunchly drinking their way through the remainder of the wine.

'Ah, here is my worthless son. Where have you been hiding?' Arturo waved a hand at Joe as he slunk through the doorway. 'Domenica is gone,' he added with emotion.

'Valentina is gone!' Uncle Davide took up the mournful chorus.

'Our daughters – our jewels!' Arturo raised his glass once more and they drank to their offspring.

'Only Albina is left to me...' Uncle Davide became morose.

'And Rosa to me,' Arturo sighed. 'What would I do without my little Rosa?'

'Or me without my *pussetta* Linda,' Paolo joined in, with tears in his eyes.

At that moment Rosa appeared from the backshop cradling a drowsy Peter in her arms.

'I found him in Gelato's stable – the children built a camp in there,' she told Sylvia. 'Shall I put him to bed?'

'Ah, *bambino*,' Sylvia hurried over and took the sleepy child from his aunt's hold. 'I'll take him.'

Joe guessed that the rest of the women were upstairs and he hung about, reluctant to face their disapproval. As the men continued to ignore him, he began to help clear the debris.

'Leave that to the girls,' Arturo ordered, unable to keep up the hostility towards his wayward son. 'You can sit with us – if you can bear to be in the company of your family for a few minutes,' he jibed.

'As long as you talk no politics,' Uncle Davide growled.

Joe acceded and pulled up a chair. He drank a glass of wine and listened to their reminiscences of people and places he only knew by name. Even Paolo was joining in, confirming his earliest memories of life in the village outside Cassino where he had been born, his father having returned and married just before the Great War. Paolo had come into a bright sunny world in 1914 and Arturo had returned to England to prepare a home for his new family, only to be severed from them for nearly five years by war. While Arturo served in a British regiment Paolo had grown up with the village children in their close-knit community and he had a strong memory of the sea voyage at the age of nearly six that brought him and his mother to England.

Joe envied him his roots in that Italian past. He was the son to be proud of, Joe thought glumly, the one who never gave his father any trouble, who worked hard and had married a pretty Italian girl from a respectable family who gave him healthy children. If Paolo was not so mild natured and easy to like, Joe thought, he would enjoy fighting with him more. Eventually, Aunt Elvira and Joe's mother managed to coax the men apart and, after much embracing and tears and laughter, Uncle Davide was prised out of the parlour and into his large car between Aunt Elvira and an ill-looking Albina, who was still munching biscuits. Benito fished the car key out of his father's jacket and started up the car. With hooting and waving and calls of farewell, the Sunderland Dimarcos lurched off down the street.

A tired and emotional Arturo allowed his wife

308

to steer him upstairs to bed, where Granny Maria and the children were soundly asleep, while the rest of the family straightened out the tables and chairs for the following morning when business would resume as usual. Only Rosa seemed to have any energy left and was chattering ten to the dozen.

'I'm going to stay with Domenica in Sunderland in a week or so's time,' she told Joe. 'Isn't that wonderful?'

'Aye,' Joe grunted, feeling stirrings of remorse that he had not been present to wave his sister off to her new life. But Domenica would forgive him, he thought with optimism.

'I saw you disappear with Emilio Fella.' Sylvia gave her young sister-in-law a sharp look. 'Where did you go?'

'Just for a walk,' Rosa replied, colouring deeply.

'He seemed canny,' Joe said, coming to his sister's rescue.

'He is,' Rosa replied with a grateful smile. 'And he's kind and funny and I think a bit homesick. He told me about his village back home – said he liked the mountains better than the big city. Emilio said I reminded him of home,' Rosa added coyly.

'And he's good looking?' Paolo added with a wink. Rosa giggled and did not deny it.

Joe scrutinised his young sister. He could not remember seeing her so skittish and coy before. She's in love, he thought in amazement. It came as a revelation. He still thought of her as half a child – they all did. But the Rosa who blushed and gazed dreamily through the darkened window with secret smiles, was no longer a child, Joe realised. Perhaps, he thought wryly, it would not be long before there was another wedding in the family!

Sara's plans to escape the following Saturday came to nothing. Her aunt watched her like a hawk and kept her busy in the house, baking and making pastry. She had no way of getting a message to Joe and that evening she sat frustrated, watching her aunt sewing as the array of clocks ticked their way past seven and on into the evening.

The days passed and she saw nothing of Joe, unable to escape the watchful Cummingses or Mrs Sergeant who was told to report if Joe tried to contact Sara at the shop. Since Raymond had left to work at the pit, Mrs Sergeant had hired another boy, Eric, to do the deliveries and Sara was kept busy in the store and the backshop. Her narrow existence consisted of shopwork or housework with a once-weekly outing to St Cuthbert's with Aunt Ida and Marina. She became listless and dejected, and finally gave up attempts to slip out and find Joe. After a hard day's work, she did not even have the energy to risk starting another diary. What was there to write about anyway? Sara thought bleakly, now that she went nowhere and saw none of her friends. Louie Ritson had called in at the shop to see her on two occasions, but Sara was unable to say much under the watchful eye of her employer. It appeared Joe had accepted his parents' wishes and was staying away from her and, as for Rosa, she had not seen her around the village for several weeks. 'How's Raymond getting on?' Sara had asked Louie Ritson.

'Canny,' Louie had said, 'though I still don't like the idea of him down the pit.'

'Does he see much of his old friends?' Sara had asked pointedly, hoping for some coded message about Joe.

'No,' Louie Ritson had answered carefully, 'he goes around with a new crowd. But *we* do.' Her look was direct. When Dolly Sergeant glanced down at her books, Louie mouthed, 'And he's missing you.'

Sara felt a flicker of hope at Louie's words and smiled back gratefully, her spirits reviving.

But towards the end of August, war with Germany looked inevitable. There was a trial blackout which plunged the village into a sinister dark for one night and over the wireless came the fearful news that Germany had signed a non-aggression pact with Russia. Britain's isolation was increasing and Prime Minister Chamberlain finally bowed to pressure to recall Parliament. As the Fleet was ordered to its war stations, Sara gave an anxious thought for the cheerful sailor, Frank Robson, setting sail for sea. She and Marina stood outside the house and watched a rally on the green, drumming up air-raid protection volunteers and saw Hilda Kirkup fall in with scores of others and march away behind the colliery band.

On the final Sunday in August, Sara noticed that the red-headed Lady Seward-Scott, the coalowner's wife, did not attend communion. Reginald Seward-Scott sat alone and aloof in the gallery while below it was whispered that his wife had sailed to America and safety, leaving him to fend for himself. To Sara, living her restricted, humdrum life, these preparations for war seemed quite unreal, even Aunt Ida's endless meetings at the vicarage to plan for the arrival and billeting of dozens of evacuees from Tyneside did. Everyone continued to go about their everyday duties as if it would never come to war; crowds flocked to football games at the start of the new season and Bette Davis drew cinema-goers to The Palace. Yet the sight of children carrying their gas masks to school at the start of term, the shortening days and the first rusty tinges of autumn on the trees seemed to echo the dying hope of a reprieve.

Then a letter arrived unexpectedly from Stout House, in sister-in-law Mary's overlarge writing.

'...*it happened five days ago. Your mam slipped on the outside stairs in the rain. Dr Hall says it's broken and she's to rest. There's a big shooting party in the house for a month and your mam wants you back to help. I can't do everything as I'm in the family way - baby due in November. Bill and I are very pleased. Write and tell us when you are coming so Bill can meet you in Lowbeck. Regards to Uncle Alfred and Aunt Ida, Mary.*'

When she showed it to her uncle, his reaction was swift.

'That's it then, you'll have to go home. Not before time in my opinion!' Sara was angry that he expressed no concern for the health of his only sister.

'Of course I can't tell from this how bad Mam is.' Sara gave him a severe look. 'I may be gone for the whole month. I'll have a word with Mrs Sergeant about keeping me job for me.'

'Don't think you're coming back here, lass!' Uncle Alfred was indignant, 'I've done my bit to help Lily out – and precious little gratitude I've had from any of you Pallisters.'

Sara was dumbfounded. 'Gratitude?' she answered back. 'You've had better than gratitude. You've had me skivvying for you all summer, plus an extra wage which was supposed to be going to Mam!'

'You'll get what's owing to you,' Alfred snapped, red-faced, 'after a deduction for board and lodging, you ungrateful little bitch.'

Sara left the room, seething with anger and only later when her uncle had gone did she trust herself to be civil to the others.

'It's not that we don't want you,' Ida tried to make amends, 'but your bed'll be needed for one of the evacuees more than likely.'

'We're not having some scabby kid from the city in our house!' Colin made his objection plain. Up until then he had felt no regret that Sara was to leave, he wanted her out of his sight, constant reminder that she was of his own inadequacies.

Sara shot Colin a disdainful look; he was as mean-minded as his father and she doubted her uncle would permit an evacuee under his roof either.

'You don't have to make excuses, Aunt Ida,' Sara answered rapidly. 'Uncle Alfred's been wanting rid of me for weeks. I can look out for myself.'

As Sara considered this new turn of events she felt a mixture of relief that her time with the

Cummingses was to end and panic that she might not see Joe again. She had to get to see him, she thought desperately.

On the first of September, Rosa returned from Sunderland after three weeks with Domenica and Pasquale. Joe went to meet her at the station, hardly recognising the young woman who emerged through the clouds of steam from the sighing train.

'You've chopped your hair off!' he said in amazement, staring at her dark locks neatly turned in a wave on the nape of her neck under a red felt hat. His sister wore a new suit of soft blue tweed and blue court shoes with narrow heels that gave her extra height.

'Do you like it?' Rosa smiled in delight.

'Aye,' Joe approved. 'Have you and Domenica bought up half of Sunderland this past fortnight?'

'I've only got a couple of new things,' Rosa was defensive. He lifted her suitcase out of the train and they walked together along the crowded platform. Men in uniform sat on cases, their leave curtailed, anxious family standing around in edgy groups.

'So what was Sunderland like?' Joe asked.

'Wonderful...' Rosa answered with a wistful sigh. 'I didn't want to come back, but Domenica said I should. They're making preparations to evacuate the children.'

'How is Domenica?' Joe asked.

'She's very happy with Pasquale,' Rosa said guardedly, 'but...'

'But what?' Joe scrutinised her serious face.

'She's very worried – and Pasquale...'

'Everyone is worried about the thought of war,' Joe said with resignation. 'Even Papa is bad-tempered – and not just with me.'

'No, it's more than that,' Rosa said in distress. 'The Perellas are talking about shutting their shops and going back to Italy.'

'Pasquale too?' Joe asked in alarm. Rosa nodded, her eyes prickling. 'That means Domenica would go–'

'Yes, and Emilio,' Rosa gulped. Joe saw her dark eyes swimming with tears and suddenly realised what was really upsetting her.

'You've seen a lot of him, then?' he asked gently, swinging an arm about her narrow shoulders. Rosa nodded again, too choked to answer. Joe tried to look on the bright side. 'Even if the Perellas do return home, that doesn't mean Emilio can't stay. He could work for someone else, surely?'

'No!' Rosa's voice was anguished. 'Mr Perella holds his work permit – if the Perellas go, the permit is no longer valid – Emilio will have to go, too.'

They had reached Joe's motorcycle. He plonked the suitcase into the empty zinc barrel on the sidecar and sighed, wondering why falling in love had to be so painful. After Sara had failed to turn up for the dance in Durham, he had seen nothing of her, except to glimpse her in the distance on her way to or from church. Twice he had called into the grocery shop where she worked, but she had not been there. He had asked after her, but the frosty Mrs Sergeant had said, 'Keep away and stop bothering the lass – you've caused her enough trouble and I'll not have you using my shop as a courting place!' He wondered unhappily if Sara had finally bowed to pressure from her uncle and resigned herself to their relationship being over. He could not bear to admit that Sara's feelings for him had cooled because of his own family's rejection of her.

Joe helped his sister on to the pillion and Rosa regained her composure.

'We want to get married,' she told him with quiet determination. 'Emilio has proposed to me. If he goes, I want to go with him.'

Joe was startled. This was not the timid, home-loving girl who had left on holiday three weeks ago, he thought. He had not credited Rosa with such courage and he whistled in admiration.

'Good luck to you, Rosa.' He kissed the top of her head. 'It's time Mamma and Papa had someone else to worry about apart from me.'

Rosa gave him an anxious look. 'I know they won't like the idea. Will you stick up for me, Joe?'

'Aye,' he answered, 'for what it's worth.'

Rosa's announcement was met with shocked disbelief. The Dimarcos were gathered around the dining table, the small sash windows raised to release the steam from Nonna Maria's cooking.

'Go with Emilio Fella to Italy?' Anna Dimarco shrieked. 'Santa Teresa! How can you think of such a thing, Rosa Maria?'

'We would marry first,' Rosa whispered, her hands shaking in her lap.

'You are far too young,' Arturo was shaken. 'It's unthinkable!'

'It's too soon. We do not know his family,' her mother added. Granny Maria nodded in agreement.

'It would be very difficult for you, Rosa,' Sylvia interjected, 'Italy is different from here and you do not speak the language.'

'*You* managed to adapt to Whitton Grange,' Joe reminded her. 'If Rosa wants to marry Emilio, what's the harm in it? It's a bit of a rush, but there's not a lot of time left, is there?'

'That's right,' Rosa spoke louder, encouraged by her brother's support. 'He might have to leave in a matter of days. Please, Papa, let us marry? We could go to the registry office in Durham.'

Arturo was thrown by his daughter's request. How could his baby Rosa think of running off with a man she hardly knew? Yet Emilio was a trusted employee of the respected Perellas, so perhaps he was not such a bad choice for Rosa...

'Is it not bad enough that we will be losing Domenica?' Anna was close to tears. 'How can you do this to us, Rosa Maria? You are needed here, with your family. *We* are the ones who care for you. I can't bear the thought of you going far away with this man!'

'Emilio is Pasquale's *compare*, Mamma. He is a good man – and I love him.'

Her mother gave a shrill cry. 'How can you love him – you hardly know him! Arturo – tell her it is out of the question.'

'Perhaps later, when the future is more settled,' he tried to mediate.

'A fat lot of good that'll be to Rosa when Emilio's thousands of miles away,' Joe retorted.

'Did I ask for your opinion?' Arturo snapped at his son. He was suddenly angry at his children's rebelliousness. 'Where is Emilio Fella anyway? I do not see him here asking me permission for my daughter like a respectful boy.'

'He will come if you send for him, Papa,' Rosa insisted. 'There has been no time to do things properly – the way we would have wanted. I've seen the preparations for war in Sunderland, Papa – it's very frightening.'

'Aye,' Joe backed her up, 'there's no time for formalities–'

'Be quiet, Joseph!' Arturo silenced him. 'Paolo,' he turned to his eldest for support, 'you sit like a wise owl – what are you thinking?'

Paolo's solemn eyes looked pityingly at Rosa, he hated to see her upset and guessed her feelings for Emilio to be genuine. But his concerns went deeper than Rosa's lovesickness – he was plagued by the thought of war and the consequences for his young family whom he loved above all others. What would be the future for the chattering Peter or his smiling fat-cheeked baby, Linda, in a war-torn world? Where would they be safest? he agonised.

'I'm thinking that perhaps it might be best for the family if we *all* return to Italy,' he said quietly. 'None of us know what will happen should war come – but maybe it would be safer to go back home and be among our own people.'

Each one of them stared at him in astonishment.

'But this is our *home*,' Joe declared, appalled at the idea of being uprooted.

Arturo reached for his cigarettes and lit one in agitation. 'And the business,' he said, exhaling sharply. 'All we own is here – we do not have property in Cassino to fall back on like the Perellas do.'

Anna was alarmed at the prospect, too. 'We have worked so hard to have our own shop – it is everything to your father, Paolo – you are asking him to throw all this away?' She spread her hands wide.

But Rosa seized on the idea. 'What if Paolo is right? We should put the safety of Peter and Linda first. We can always return if it never comes to war.'

'This whole thing's a storm in a bloody teacup!' Joe said bluntly. 'What have we got to run away from? If war comes, we'll just have to fight alongside the British like Papa did in the Great War.'

'And risk fighting against our own people in Italy?' Paolo challenged him.

'If the fascists gang up against us, then aye,' Joe held his ground. *'I'd* fight.' The brothers glared at each other, aware for the first time of their deep-rooted differences.

'I could never do that!' Paolo answered, rattled by his brother's opposition.

'Well, you won't have to if you go scurrying back to Italy, will you?' Joe scorned. 'Me, I'm staying, whatever you do.'

'Boys, why are you fighting each other?' Anna cried in despair. 'Whatever we do, the family must stay together.'

'Your mother is right,' Arturo said, grinding out

his cigarette. 'We shall call the family together for a meeting – Uncle Davide shall be consulted. But we all stick together – are you hearing me?' he said grimly. 'And that goes for you, too, Rosa. You shall not leave on your own.'

Rosa was about to summon up the courage to say she would go with Emilio no matter what they chose to do, when her brother Bobby came clattering up the stairs in breathless excitement.

'Turn on the wireless!' he cried. 'Now!'

'Roberto, where are your manners?' Anna scolded him.

'It's the Jerry,' he was bursting with his news, 'they've invaded Poland. The lads at the cycle shop say we're going to war. Pow! Pow!' He aimed a playful finger at Joe. 'Will you go in the army like Dad? I will when I'm old enough.'

Then he stopped, nonplussed by their stony silence, wondering what he had said wrong.

'It does mean war, doesn't it?' Bobby asked, suddenly doubtful.

His mother put her face in her hands and burst into tears.

Chapter Sixteen

Sunshine warmed the back of Sara's head and shoulders as she walked back from church with Ida and Marina. Reverend Hodgson had prayed that war might be averted even at this late hour and Marina was talking about the practice air-raid precautions that had taken place at school.

'Nancy Bell forgot her gas mask,' Marina crowed. 'She got a right telling off from Mr Charles. Went home in tears.'

Sara saw people streaming out of St Teresa's and struggled to maintain an impassive face as she remembered Domenica among the throng as well as some of the faces she recognised from the wedding. She wondered what occasion had brought them back together again and whether Domenica was enjoying married life in Sunderland. There was no sign of Joe, but there was a short-haired Rosa in a becoming red hat. The Dimarcos stood close together, absorbed in conversation. Then they climbed into the family van and disappeared.

Aunt Ida switched on the wireless as she busied herself preparing for Sunday lunch. Sara automatically set to peeling vegetables. It would be the last time she did this mundane job for her aunt, as she would be leaving on Friday, Mrs Sergeant having insisted she work a week's notice. The yard was empty of dogs and Marina was attempting to cross-skip in the mellow sunshine. Catching her foot in the rope, she fell and grazed her knees, rushing into the kitchen with a wail of noise. As Ida fussed and placated, Sara realised Prime Minister Chamberlain's clipped voice was coming over the air waves.

'...at once to withdraw their troops from Poland, a state of war would exist between us.'

'Shush, Aunt Ida!' Sara ordered.

'...I have to tell you now that no such undertaking has been received – and that consequently this country is at war with Germany.'

Sara and her aunt looked at each other in awe. Then as the words sunk in, the doom-laden wail of an air-raid siren vibrated on the wireless. Ida grabbed Marina and hugged her fiercely.

'Stop it!' the young girl protested.

Sara, not waiting to ask permission, bolted out of the back door and rushed into the lane.

Children played, dogs barked, a wasp droned overhead. Running down the street she saw others come to their doors and look up as if they would see the spectre of German planes darkening the bright sky.

'Ack-ack-ack!' two children dashed past her imitating dive bombers. Sara did not know where she was going, she just kept running as if she could escape the dreadful foreboding that gripped her. Her brother Tom would have to fight now and she must see him again before... Sara ran on into the dene and up the steep bank on the far side to the allotments. An old pitman was working in his garden, wheezing between giant chrysanthemums. He pushed up his cap and called a greeting, but Sara could not stop. She did not want to spoil his peaceful world with the dreadful news.

Slowing to a walk, she entered the woods and tore at some unripe blackberries. They tasted bitter and she spat them out in disgust. When she reached the kissing gate, Sara stopped, leaned on its warm sun-blcachcd wood and waited.

A while later, footsteps approached, and Sara watched in hope that the same restlessness might have seized Joe and drawn him up here. But the steps were too light, the figure between the trees too slight.

'Rosa!' Sara cried in astonishment. The girl stopped in her tracks and looked up warily. 'You've heard...?'

'Yes,' Rosa's voice was dismal.

'Why are you out on your own?' Sara asked.

Rosa hesitated. This was the place she had come to with Emilio on the day they had first met and fallen in love, but she could not say so.

'They're all arguing at home,' she answered, 'Uncle Davide is here – and Domenica. Oh, Sara, I'm frightened,' she gave way to sudden tears. 'Domenica is leaving for Italy this week!'

Sara moved forward at once and put an arm around her friend, forgetting their estrangement at the sight of her distress and found herself listening to Rosa's story of Emilio, her visit to Sunderland and the family tearing itself apart over whether to leave with the Perellas or stay to face the uncertain future.

'Surely you won't all go?' Sara asked in dismay.

Rosa sniffed. 'Uncle Davide and Papa have decided to stay – but Pasquale and Domenica don't think it's safe – Pasquale's father is an important man in our community and he has been a supporter of Mussolini, a loyal Italian. They have chosen to go home. Emilio has no choice but to leave, too.' Rosa broke down again.

'And your parents won't let you go with him?' Sara stated the obvious.

Rosa nodded. 'Mamma is in a terrible state about Domenica and now Granny Maria says she wants to go home, too. Paolo has only agreed to stay because Papa was so insistent we should not run away.'

'What does Joe think?' Sara's voice was tentative. Rosa glanced up.

'Nothing will make him leave Whitton Grange,' she answered.

Sara sighed with relief and they exchanged awkward looks.

'Rosa,' Sara asked shyly, 'will you give Joe a message – tell him I need to see him?'

Rosa's resentment rekindled. It was Sara and Joe's illicit meetings that had started the family bickering and she was not sure that any good would come of acting as their messenger. 'Oh, Sara, why didn't you tell me about you and Joe?' Rosa reproved. 'It was such a shock – I thought you were going with Raymond, that's why I didn't–'

'Raymond!' Sara spluttered. 'He's far too young for me!' She saw Rosa flush and all at once remembered that Rosa and Raymond had been fond of each other. Without realising it she had spoilt their tentative friendship...

'I'm sorry, Rosa,' Sara was filled with regret. 'I

should have told you. I really wanted to – but Joe wouldn't let me – he said you wouldn't understand. And he was right – none of your family wanted me to see him.'

'I would have understood,' Rosa insisted, 'I know what it's like to be in love. But you used me, pretending to be my friend, yet all the time just wanting to see Joe. And you can't blame my parents – your uncle said such terrible things to them.'

'Do you really think I could have been so callous as to pretend to like you just for Joe's sake?' Sara demanded hotly, hands on hips. 'You were the best friend I had in Whitton, until you took your parents' side in all this. Don't you think that hurt me? Why is everyone so against Joe and me?'

Rosa capitulated. 'Don't let's argue any more,' she said wearily.

Sara's indignation subsided at the sight of her strained, unhappy face. After a pause she said, 'Haway, let's walk up on the Common and see if the Germans are coming.' She tried to make light of their fear and they linked arms and climbed the path together.

At the top Rosa asked, 'What will you do now?'

Sara sighed. 'I'm going back home on Friday to help out on the farm. Mam's had a fall and can't manage the farmhouse. The Cummingses want me out – pretending they're going to take in an evacuee. That's why I want to see Joe before I go.'

Rosa was dashed by the news. No sooner were they reconciled than this wretched war was going to finish their friendship once more.

'But you'll come back, won't you?' she asked.

325

Sara shrugged, asking herself if there was anything to come back for.

They gazed down at the tranquil village, lying in the dip of the valley veiled in smoke from coal fires. 'Uncle Alfred won't have me in the house again – he's been looking for an excuse to get rid of me since the bother over Joe. I'm a wicked influence on his angelic Marina,' Sara said ironically.

'We'll keep in touch?' Rosa looked for reassurance. 'You can write to me sometimes.'

'Aye, and you,' Sara squeezed her arm. 'I hope Emilio comes for you.'

'He will – we are promised to each other.' Rosa's face shone with a passionate hope. 'He *must* come.'

But no word came from Emilio. While Rosa fretted over his non-appearance, she delayed in giving Joe Sara's message, certain that if her parents knew she was attempting to bring them together again, they would deny her any last chance to leave with Emilio. On Tuesday, a telegram arrived from Pasquale bidding Domenica return to Sunderland; the Perellas had secured an earlier sailing and they must leave the next day. Rosa was distraught at the thought that Emilio might leave without her. The Dimarcos braced themselves for the parting with Domenica and Granny Maria. Anna Dimarco clung to her daughter in tears of distress.

'You will write, my *pussetta*, and tell us how you are getting on?'

'Of course, Mamma.' Domenica hugged her tearfully.

'And look after your *nonna*? She is becoming forgetful.' Domenica nodded. She turned to Rosa and they embraced.

'Tell Emilio I will wait for him,' Rosa croaked, 'no matter how long...'

'Yes,' Domenica agreed quickly, engulfed with guilt at having fostered the romance in the first place, 'I'll tell him.' She broke away and faced Joe.

'Ta-ra then,' he said awkwardly. 'But I'm sure you'll be back shortly to boss us all about.' Domenica stepped forward and gave him a hug.

'Look after the family, Joe, especially Mamma.' She wanted to say something about Sara, but did not know what, still believing such a match would be doomed.

'We'll be champion. Take care, pet.' He squeezed her briefly, then let go. Outside the parlour where a small crowd had gathered to watch the distressed leave-taking, Paolo was helping his grandmother into the van. Domenica left the parlour at Pit Street for the final time, glancing up at its familiar gold lettering and striped awning that flapped a farewell in the breeze. Her father was trying to persuade his mother to reconsider but the old woman was calmly fatalistic.

'When the time comes, I want to be buried in my mountains,' she told him in the old tongue, 'among my people. The saints keep you safe, my dear Arturo,' she smiled sadly and touched him on his leathery cheek.

Rosa saw her father gulp back his emotions as they kissed on each cheek. But when Domenica threw her arms around his neck, the tears flooded on to his face. Paolo revved the engine to cut short the agony of parting and a minute later the van was roaring down the street, with everyone waving and shouting encouragement. Joe turned to see Rosa running inside, unable to bear the thought of not going with them, puzzled that she had avoided him these past few days when he had spoken up for her and Emilio.

For the rest of the day she lay in the room she once shared with Domenica and Nonna Maria and sobbed inconsolably...

Sergeant's was busy all week, as villagers stocked up on tinned food and Mrs Sergeant did a brisk trade in pitch paper for blacking out windows. On Wednesday afternoon, Mrs Sergeant allowed Sara the rest of the day off to go with her aunt to the Memorial Hall to help with the arrival of over two hundred school children and their teachers from Tyneside. They swarmed off the special trains laid on to bring them to Whitton Station, some chattering and inquisitive, others pale and anxious at the alien surroundings, clutching pillowcases full of their meagre possessions and labelled like cargo.

To Sara's delight, Louie Ritson was among the helpers and, in the general confusion of noise and bustle, she was able to slip away from her aunt in the makeshift dining-room to help Louie in the kitchen.

'We're taking in a little laddie from Gateshead,' Louie told her excitedly.

'Lucky young fellow,' Sara smiled, knowing how Louie delighted in the company of young people and wondering why she had never had children of her own.

'Bright as buttons this lot,' Louie jerked her head at the din in the hall, 'singing "Down Mexico Way" when they came in on the trains!'

'Where will they all go?' Sara asked, overwhelmed by the numbers.

'We'll find room for them, poor little pets. Our lad'll share the upstairs with Raymond and me da. I'm sorry you haven't been to see us,' Louie said frankly and Sara gave a brief outline of her troubles, while stirring the hot soup and confirmed what Louie had gathered from Raymond and a tight-lipped Joe.

'I haven't seen that much of Joe, either,' Louie told her. 'He's had problems at home – young Rosa getting herself all upset over a lad and his other sister and nanna going back to Italy.'

'Aye,' Sara sighed, 'I heard.'

'And you, pet?' Louie asked.

'I'm off home Friday,' she said rather sadly, explaining about her mother.

Louie did not like to see the young girl so dejected. 'Come round and see us before you go – and to hell with what your aunt and uncle say!'

Sara was startled by the woman's vehemence. Then she laughed, 'Ta, Mrs Ritson, I will.'

Marina watched Sara pack her small suitcase. Now that the time had come to leave, Sara's relief was mingled with regret. She had even been touched by Mrs Sergeant's parting gift of a 1935 Jubilee tea caddy and the elderly woman's grumbling appreciation for her work. Tomorrow night she would not be able to look out of the small bedroom window and glimpse the entrance to Dimarco's parlour or hear the sounds of the street beyond. How quiet Rillhope would seem after these months in the town! Sara realised, suddenly, that she had grown fond of noise...

'Are you coming back?' Marina asked, her face moody.

'Your dad'll not have me,' Sara told her, 'so that should please you.'

'Who says it does?' Marina was petulant. 'I'll just have to share with some smelly girl from Gateshead instead – and it's all your fault!'

Sara could not help smiling. 'Well, that's a surprise.' She closed the drawer which had held her belongings, carefully slipping into her bag a photograph taken at a fair of her and Joe standing behind bawdy cardboard figures. How happy we looked, she thought with longing. Sniffing made her look up. Marina's head was bowed and her shoulders shaking.

She turned in surprise to see her cousin crying. 'What's wrong now?' she crossed to the bed.

'It's my fault you're going, isn't it?' Marina mumbled. 'And I don't want you to go.'

Sara put her arms around the young girl in bewilderment. 'It's not your fault – I just don't get along with your mam and dad.'

'No, it's because I found that book under your mattress and gave it to Dad and I didn't mean to get you into trouble – but you were going to go to the wedding without me and it didn't seem fair...' she blubbered.

Sara looked at her in shock. So it was Marina

who had caused the trouble and not Colin as she had assumed, and all because of Domenica's wedding! Yet she was the one who had encouraged Marina's interest in the Dimarcos, so how could she blame the silly girl?

Sara held her close and rocked her, half pitying, half vexed with the awkward child. 'That can't be helped now,' she told her. 'There's no need to cry like a baby.'

Gradually, as the sobbing subsided, Sara loosened her hold but Marina clung on to her. 'Will you sing me a song before you go, Sara?'

'Which one?'

'Bobby Shafto,' the girl said in a meek voice. 'Your sister's favourite.'

Aunt Ida was drawing the newly sewn blackout curtains when Sara slipped out of the house. Uncle Alfred was out and her aunt did not try to stop her, seeing little point in confrontation now that her niece was going. Sara scouted the streets for sight or sound of Joe and his motorbike, but it was eerily quiet, with the picture house closed and only ARP wardens about their business.

Growing desperate she approached Dimarco's and, peering in, saw Paolo serving in the almost deserted cafe. Sara took a deep breath and entered.

'I want to see Joe,' she told him directly.

Paolo showed little surprise though his look was cautious. 'To say goodbye,' she added. 'I'm going home tomorrow.'

His gaze softened and his slow smile lifted the trim moustache. 'You'll find him at the Ritsons.'

331

Sara retreated, not wanting to linger. As she left she heard him add softly, 'Good luck in the future, Sara.'

'Ta,' she smiled briefly, 'and to you.'

Joe had gone across the backlane to the water closet after an hour of drinking Louie Ritson's tea. Dusk was settling on the rows of terraces and evening birds called sleepily from the rooftops. The door of the Ritsons' kitchen was ajar because no one was yet used to the idea of shutting in the cracks of light. Joe lingered in the yard, thinking of Domenica setting sail for the Continent and feeling gloomy over Louie's news that Sara was leaving too. As the censorious Jacob Kirkup was inside, Joe had not dared light a cigarette. He lit one now and leaned against the brick wall in the shadows. Why had Sara not tried to contact him herself? he fretted. He had made it clear on the night of his sister's wedding that he cared for her in spite of what his family said. How he regretted the way they had argued and his own cowardly reaction to family pressure not to see her!

He would go round to the Cummingses' now, bang on their door and demand to talk to her, Joe thought with resolution. It would be his last chance and he had to know how she felt about him. But as he ground his cigarette out beneath his boot, Joe was suddenly aware that the Ritsons were talking about Sara again.

'It seems such a shame,' Louie was saying. 'What's there for a lass to do up Weardale?'

'Doesn't surprise me she wants to gan,'

Raymond was saying. 'What's there to stay for around here? Not working for the Sergeant-Major, that's for sure. She's never really liked Whitton – thinks it's a dirty old place.'

'But her and Joe...' Louie sighed. 'It's not right the way they've been kept apart, is it, Sam?'

Joe heard Sam grunt. 'Not the way it's put him off his boxing!'

'Be serious,' Louie chided. 'He's not a happy lad – he misses the lass – I told her so in the shop.'

Joe felt himself grow hot at the way they discussed him. He was about to re-enter swiftly when Raymond spoke again.

'Well, perhaps she's not so bothered now. She's got another lad up Weardale, you know.'

'Don't talk rubbish! What other lad?' his aunt asked in disbelief.

'It's not rubbish. Some lad wants to marry her – she told me once when she was missing home. Can't remember the name – Jim or Sid or something.'

'Well I never!' Louie clucked. 'Don't go telling Joe such tales, mind.'

Joe did not stay to hear any more. He turned and marched out of the yard, swinging on to his motorcycle, shaking with fury. How humiliated he felt! How much time had he wasted moping about missing Sara and feeling sorry for himself? he thought savagely. He had been prepared to rebel against his parents for her and all the time she had this lad waiting for her back home. Now she was choosing to leave Whitton and return home without attempting to see him or say goodbye. What a fool he had been over her!

Joe revved the bike and drove off recklessly down the lane, not caring where he went, just intent on escape, to put distance between him and the village. He did not use his light in the blackout and could hardly see where he went, but the bite of cold air on his face temporarily eased the hurt.

Sara hurried up Holly Street and turned into Hawthorn Street. It was almost dark now and the terrace was shrouded in blackout curtains and paper, making it difficult to find the Ritsons' back door. A figure in the gloom shouted out, 'You should be inside, lass, where it's safe!' Sara could just make out the dark uniform of an ARP warden. She waved at him and banged on the kitchen door.

Sam peered out. 'Oh it's you lass, come in.'

The kitchen was warm and fuggy, sealed from the outside world. Louie's old father snored in his upright chair and Raymond was polishing his football boots by the hearth. Louie ushered her into a seat, but there was a strange awkwardness about the Ritsons.

'I – I thought Joe might be here,' Sara broke the silence, trying to hide her overwhelming disappointment. 'Paolo said–'

'He was here,' Louie told her. 'You've just missed him.'

'Took off on his bike without saying goodbye,' Raymond added, head bent over his boots as he brushed with vigour. 'He's that moody these days.'

'So he might be coming back?' Sara asked hopefully.

'Not if Turnbull catches him flying around on that machine in the dark,' Sam commented.

'Oh dear.' Sara felt her throat tightening with tears. If Rosa had given Joe her message, there had been plenty of time for him to seek her out. But Joe had not tried to see her, she thought with bitter resignation.

'Was there something you wanted to tell him?' Louie asked gently, slipping a hand over hers.

'No,' Sara shook her head, then gulped. 'I just wanted to say ta-ra...'

It sounded so trivial in her ears, Sara thought, but how could she express her painful regret that events had not turned out as she had hoped?

'I'll tell him,' Louie Ritson said, squeezing her hand. Her pale, lined face was full of understanding.

Sara left soon after. Tramping back in the dark with the acrid smell of burnt coal in her clothes and hair, Sara wished there had been time to know the kindly Ritsons better.

Chapter Seventeen

Stepping off the bus at Lowbeck, Sara breathed in lungfuls of the sweet air. The hills around her, tinged with soft purple heather, were like old friends awaiting her return. The solid stone houses and the chapel stood mellow in the late summer sun and the muted sounds of bleating sheep and gurgling water were reassuringly familiar, yet part of her felt a stranger as if she was seeing it all for the first time.

It was so tranquil that she wondered if the news of war had just been a bad dream. But as she bade farewell to the bus driver, she turned to see a young man in uniform striding towards her.

'Tom!' Sara cried in delight and, dropping her small case, ran towards him. They hugged.

'By, you've put on weight,' he laughed, giving her the once over, 'Aunt Ida must be a canny cook.'

Sara ignored his comment. 'I never thought you'd be here – you don't look like you're wasting away yourself!' she retaliated. 'Oh, it's so grand to see you, Tom! How come you're home?'

He picked up her case and nodded across the road to where their brother Bill was waiting, perched on a mud-encrusted tractor.

'I'm on embarkation leave,' he told her. 'We're part of the British Expeditionary Force ganin' to France.'

Sara's stomach lurched at the stark words.

'How long have you got?' she asked.

'Three days,' Tom smiled ruefully. 'Three days to get Jane Metcalfe to say she'll marry me.'

Sara gaped at him. 'Are you serious?'

'Aye,' Tom grinned. 'Going to war concentrates the mind, Sara – and a lass can't resist a lad in uniform.'

Sara gave him a playful push, then Bill was helping her into the trailer behind his new machine, with an embarrassed peck on her cheek.

'This is smart, Bill,' she admired the tractor.

'Got it second-hand in the show at Lilychapel,' he said proudly. 'Should have had one years ago.'

'How's Mam?' Sara asked.

'A terrible patient,' Bill groaned, starting up the vehicle. 'She can hardly stand up, but she's chasing Mary round like a skivvy, fretting over these visitors.'

'Well, they'll be gone by the end of the month,' Tom shouted over the noise of the engine, lighting up a cigarette as they pulled away. 'There's a rumour we're going to get some of these land girls who're being trained up for farm work,' he grinned.

'And what about Jane Metcalfe?' Sara teased.

'She hasn't said yes, yet,' Tom replied, offering her a puff of his cigarette behind their elder brother's back. Sara glanced at Bill, but he was oblivious to the wickedness, happily driving his beloved machine. The smell of burning tobacco gave her a faint craving and reminded her nostalgically of Joe. She took a drag with a mischievous smile and handed it back.

'How's Mary?' she shouted to Bill. 'I'm pleased to hear she's expecting.'

Tom mimed a figure with an enormous belly.

'She's grand,' said Bill over his shoulder. 'But it's been a bit of a strain with all of us in the cottage. I'm glad you're back, Sara. It'll cheer Mam up and stop her going on at Mary all the time.'

There were changes at the farm. Stout House had a freshly painted green door and window frames and the yard in front had been cleared of hens and was occupied by a large black saloon car and a dashing blue open-topped sports car with large headlamps like frog's eyes. They belonged to the shooting party, Bill told her as he dropped her off and trundled away on the tractor.

Round the corner, she found her mother sitting outside the cottage, peeling carrots, and was fleetingly reminded of Granny Maria. It was a shock to see her mother looking older, her face drawn and grey strands in her brown hair, her once bustling body immobilised by a huge plaster-cast on her leg.

'Mam!' Sara flew at her, sloshing water from the tin bowl on to her mother's apron. But Lily did not protest, clinging on to her daughter and crowing with delight.

'Let's have a look at you. Did you not buy yourself something new to wear? I told you to go to the Store and get a couple of frocks,' her mother fussed. 'I hope you spent some of your wages on yourself.'

'I did,' Sara answered, deciding to leave until later the news that Uncle Alfred had only given her back a quarter of what she had saved, declaring the rest was for bed and board. She was still furious, too, at his refusal to hand back her diary.

'Doesn't she look well, our Tom?' Her mother's face lit with joy. 'I want to hear all about Whitton Grange – and Alfred's house – and who you met. You hardly wrote a word to us after the first month. Dolly Sergeant sounds just like the old battleaxe I remember.'

Tom brought some chairs out of the cottage and they sat together in the sun while Sara told them about the Ritsons and Kirkups, the chapel and St Cuthbert's, the Carnival and the village, now full of young evacuees with strange Geordie accents.

Mary appeared from Stout House with a mop and bucket in her hand, and Sara realised she had not thought to ask where her sister-in-law was. She looked vastly pregnant, and waddled down the steps, her chin a rash of spots, hair bound up in a cotton scarf.

'Come and say hello to our Sara,' Lily Pallister ordered. 'You can leave the cleaning till later.'

'It's done,' Mary said shortly. 'Hello, Sara.'

'Let me take that, Mary.' Sara sprung up, feeling suddenly guilty that the pregnant girl had been labouring alone in her uncomfortable condition. She looked exhausted and fretful. 'You have a seat.'

Mary gave her a suspicious look but plonked her weight down on the vacant chair as Sara relieved her of the bucket.

'I can do the tea tonight for the guests if you

like,' Sara offered, squeezing on to Tom's chair.

'They call it dinner,' Mary corrected, 'but I could do with the help.'

'Little Miss Domesticated now, eh?' Tom scoffed at his sister.

Sara groaned, 'I've done nothing else this past month – sweeping out the shop or helping Aunt Ida in the house – everything spotless. It's good to see a bit of honest farm muck around the place.'

'You'll not find any muck inside the house,' Mary bristled. 'We're giving them jugged hare tonight,' she went on, 'and summer pudding–'

'Quiet, Mary,' Lily flapped a hand at her. 'Sara was telling us about Whitton Grange.'

Mary would not be silenced. 'So what was all this trouble with the Italians?' she demanded.

Sara flushed. 'Trouble?'

Lily looked annoyed at her daughter-in-law, but answered. 'Alfred sent us a letter a few weeks back, telling us you'd fallen into bad company and that he was going to send you home. But as you didn't say you wanted to come home, I asked him to keep you on a bit longer – see if things settled down.'

'But once your mother had her fall,' Mary elaborated, 'it was obvious you'd be more use around here.'

'And keep you away from the wicked foreigners,' Tom laughed and nudged her.

'It wasn't my idea to bring you home,' her mother said, 'but I'm that pleased to see you, pet.'

'So *were* you seeing an Italian lad?' Mary persisted.

'Aye,' Sara answered, with a jut of her chin, 'until Uncle Alfred put the block on it. Not that he had any right to – the Dimarcos are a good family.'

'Never knew them,' her mother said. 'They came to the village after I'd married your father. Catholics, I suppose?'

Sara shot her mother a surprised look, but Mary interrupted again.

'I'm sure Uncle Alfred was right to be protective,' Mary said with a censorious look. 'He's a respectable man.'

'He's a pain in the neck!' Sara contradicted. Mary gasped with shock as Tom guffawed and Lily tittered.

'Yes, he can be,' her mother admitted.

'Anyway, it's all over now with Joe,' Sara said dismissively, as if she was trying to convince herself.

'Sid Gibson will be pleased to hear it,' Mary sniffed. 'Asks after you all the time, doesn't he, Mrs Pallister.'

Her mother nodded. 'We didn't tell him about the Italian – and he's not going to know, is he, Mary?' She gave a severe look.

Sara felt a flush of guilt at mention of Sid and the thought that he might have been waiting for her all this time.

'Well, it had nothing to do with Sid Gibson any road,' Sara said with a toss of her fair hair. 'I'm not courting him – or anyone – lads are just a nuisance.'

Tom laughed and stood up. 'I'll make myself scarce, then,' he said.

'Bill needs a hand in the top field,' Mary told him.

'I'm off to Thimble Hill,' Tom replied unconcerned. 'I'll be back in time for tea.'

'*Dinner,*' Sara corrected impishly.

'Let him go.' Lily put a stop to Mary's protest. 'He's got precious few days of freedom left.'

They watched him saunter off in his uniform, whistling his way down the hill in the sunshine.

Sara met her sister Chrissie off the school bus at Rillhope and, after they had helped Mary serve a four-course dinner to the guests at Stout House, they settled down to a family evening in the cottage. There was much chatter and teasing and laughter as Sara told them anecdotes about the pit village and the strange Cummings' household. When Bill and Mary and Chrissie had retired upstairs to bed and Tom gone down to Rillhope for a pint of John Lawson's home-brew, Sara and her mother sat on by the banked-up fire.

She wanted to tell her mother about her feelings for Joe Dimarco, but something about her mother's attitude made her reticent.

'Why should he hate the Dimarcos so much, Mam?' Sara asked.

'Alfred's always held strong views about things,' her mother mused. 'He's not broad-minded like your father was – but then, your dad had gone away to war and had seen a bit of the world. Alfred's known nothing else but Whitton Grange – he's suspicious of people from the next village, let alone Italy!'

'The next street more like,' Sara retorted. Her mother laughed and then the amusement faded.

'I'm sorry if he made life awkward for you, pet.' She stroked her hair as Sara sat at her feet on the hearth. 'And it's a pity about the money... He's not a bad man at heart – he just thinks that discipline and strictness arc what a father should hand out to his children. You see, our own father died when I was born and Alfred was just a bairn – we never had a father and Alfred's always been resentful of that. He used to be very protective towards me, too, to the point of being a pest.'

'I can imagine.'

'Aye, I sometimes think that's what made me run off with your father – just to get away from Alfred. But he always thought he was doing the best for me, I knew that.'

'He's a bully, Mam.' Sara would not be persuaded.

'Don't say that about your uncle!' Her mother grew defensive. 'And perhaps it's for the best you were kept away from that Italian lad.'

Sara pursed her lips together in annoyance.

Lily sighed. 'Anyway, you're safe home now,' she smiled. 'I can't tell you how much I've missed you, pet.'

'Me too, Mam,' Sara relented and laid her head on her mother's knee.

'And once the visitors have gone we can move back into Stout House,' Lily said with optimism. 'The bank'll not evict us now – farms are going to be important in fighting this war – food for the people. Bill says we're to start growing crops and things that weren't cost-effective before.'

343

'Tom says we might be getting land girls on the farm?'

'Yes,' Lily confirmed, 'Stout House will be full of working people again – a happy home – like the old times.'

Sara thought silently of the future. Whatever her mother said, with her father dead and Tom far away, they both knew it could never be the same again.

Tom left on the bus from Lowbeck, with a tearful Sara and Jane Metcalfe waving him away. Jane and Tom had become engaged on his final evening and the Metcalfes had said that Lily Pallister must visit them when she was able to travel once more. Sara went home to comfort her bereft mother and threw herself into the running of Stout House, even surprising Mary with her diligence. But it was only to ease the emptiness she felt inside, a niggling restlessness after the euphoria of the warm homecoming had evaporated.

With time to reflect, Sara realised how much she missed Joe and Rosa and Raymond and the Ritsons. With Mary constantly carping at her to do things, she almost admitted to missing Sergeant's where at least she could listen to the gossip of the villagers. The cottage was damp and primitive after the luxuries of South Parade, and she had to sleep on an old mattress on the floor of the parlour and tend to her mother on the truckle bed, as she was unable to climb the stairs.

When she was not needed around the house, Sara escaped for brief walks on the fell, watching the skylarks swooping over the moors and the creeping bronze on the birch trees. Apart from seeing Sid Gibson to nod to outside chapel, she had avoided meeting him and she was glad that Mr Gibson kept his son busy with the harvest and the taking of beasts to market for the autumn sales. She did not know what to say to him and the look of puzzled hurt on Sid's kind face only made her feel more wretched. Perhaps in time they could recapture their old affection...

By October, Stout House was vacant once more and Lily Pallister moved swiftly back into her home with Sara and Chrissie. After a couple of days, Bill said, 'No point wasting precious fuel keeping two stoves burning,' and so he and Mary took up quarters in the room he had once shared with Tom.

By the middle of the month, half a dozen young women arrived in the area, fresh from their training at Houghall Agricultural College in Durham. Three of them went to help with the harvest over at Thimble Hill, while the others were housed in the cottage and were detailed to help Bill and Mr Gibson with the ploughing and planting of fields that had hitherto been left as grazing.

'It's absolutely back-breaking,' a girl called Phoebe complained after the first week, as they all sat around the supper table together. She had been a debutante and 'come out' in the summer of 1938, but had rushed patriotically to help in the war effort.

'You'll get used to it,' Mary said with little sympathy. 'Some of us have had to work like this all our lives.'

'Well, bully for you,' Phoebe sounded equally

unimpressed and handed round her cigarettes to Mary's disapproval.

Sara soon realised she had gained a friend when Phoebe found her smoking up the beck one day and they stopped and shared the last of Tom's Capstans that he had left his sister.

'Bet you get bloody fed up around here,' Phoebe guessed, still managing to look poised in her working dungarees and headscarf. They sheltered under a copper-coloured rowan tree in the drizzle.

'Sometimes,' Sara admitted. 'I was working in a shop down in Whitton Grange until Mam had her fall.'

'That sounds more fun. What were you selling? Corsets or pipe tobacco?'

Sara laughed. 'Mainly pipe tobacco.'

'God, will my hands ever be smooth again?' Phoebe flexed her slim, grubby fingers and sighed over her broken nails.

'Tell me about your home,' Sara urged, 'the parties and dances and things.'

Phoebe needed little encouragement to describe a rich world of country houseparties, summer balls and winter hunts at her parents' estate in Northumberland and when the cold drizzle turned to relentless rain, they hurried for the farm.

'There's that boy again.' Phoebe pointed out a bedraggled figure on the lip of the hill. 'He's always skulking after you. Is he your boyfriend or something?'

Sara squinted through the rain and recognised Sid Gibson, drenched and looking forlornly after her.

'Used to be,' Sara answered briefly.

'Does he know he's in the past tense?' Phoebe asked bluntly.

'I'm not sure...' Sara felt uncomfortable at the thought. She had shirked meeting Sid on several occasions and had never allowed them to be alone.

'Well, I think you should tell the poor boy, it's game, set and match as far as he's concerned,' her friend was brisk. 'Stop him pining about the hills like a lost sheep dog.'

Sara blushed at the rebuke and hurried home.

Mary gave birth to a baby girl, Florence, the following month and Sara's mother went into hospital to have her plaster cast removed, so Sara found herself running the household. Her days were filled with catering for the hungry farm workers, rising early in the icy cold, while the nights were punctured by the wails of baby Florence.

In December, the christening brought a welcome relief from the daily drudgery and Phoebe helped her decorate the kitchen-cum-parlour with festive holly.

'Dip it in Epsom Salts,' the dark-haired girl instructed, 'makes the leaves sparkle – nanny taught me.' To Sara's surprise the solution dried like white frost and Mary was delighted with the cheerful sight.

The neighbours from several miles around were invited to celebrate at Stout House after the chapel service at Lowbeck. The Metcalfes and the Gibsons came and Mary's parents from Stanhope and Beth Lawson and baby Daniel from Rillhope. Beth crammed herself full of the homemade broth, game pie and winter vegetables and complained about her husband John who had run off and joined the navy.

'I blame Tom,' Beth told Sara, while Daniel explored the hearth and tumbled over Cath the dog. 'He turned his head about going to fight the Germans. When he's sober he's a coward – but three pints of home-brew and John's off to enlist.'

'Have you heard from him yet?' Sara asked.

'Got a postcard from Portsmouth – they've taken him, though he's never been on a boat in his life. Don't know when we'll see him again,' Beth sighed, 'and me with Daniel to feed.'

'I'm sure the Gibsons would give you a bit of milk for the bairn,' Sara reassured. 'I'll have a word with Sid about it if you like.'

Beth gave her a squint, considering look. 'So you are still courting?'

Sara did not answer.

'Tell him to his face,' Beth was brusque. 'It's the kindest way.'

After the party had dispersed and the clearing up was finished, Sara went out to find Sid. His father said he was tending a sickly newborn calf and she fumbled her way in the dark to the barn furthest from the Gibsons' large house at Highbeck. A storm lantern swung in the blast of cold air as she pushed her way in, sending weird shadows across the dimly lit byre. It was cosy inside with the smell of warm flesh and hay.

'Sid?' she called.

There was a rustling from one of the stalls and

he appeared with sleeves rolled up and straw stuck in his thick fair hair. He was startled when he realised who it was and Sara plunged into her request for milk for Daniel.

'Of course we can spare a bit,' he agreed. They stood exchanging embarrassed looks.

'I'm sorry I've been avoiding you, Sid,' Sara confessed, 'I've not known what to say. Things have changed while I've been away. I should have said something sooner–'

'You don't have to explain,' Sid's ruddy face was shadowed. 'I hear there's someone else.'

Sara flushed, cursing Mary for her interference. '*Was* someone else,' she said quietly with a forlorn shrug. Sid said nothing. 'Things are too uncertain with this war – I think it's best just to be single, don't you?'

Sid raised his eyebrows. 'You're different – you wouldn't have said that a few months ago with all your talk about Heathcliff and your romantic books.' With relief, Sara saw he was smiling. He seemed to be accepting the situation quite calmly so perhaps he had not missed her as much as everyone said.

'Still friends?' Sara asked shyly.

'Aye, friends,' he said with a note of mockery in his voice.

'I'll be off then,' Sara turned quickly for the door and, in her eagerness to be gone, dropped a glove. She was halfway across the yard before she realised her loss. At the risk of appearing foolish, she returned to claim it and heard laughter the minute she entered the byre.

Sid was standing under the lamplight, cuddling

a half-undressed girl whose dungaree braces trailed in the straw. Sara was too astonished to say a word, but Phoebe flicked her dark hair away and smiled.

'Bad timing, darling,' she said with unconcern.

'Aye, I – I dropped me glove,' Sara stuttered. 'I didn't realise...'

'No?' Phoebe sounded disbelieving. 'I thought you must have done. And, as your interests lie elsewhere, there didn't seem to be any harm done. Sid's too much of a man to waste being celibate, darling.'

Sara felt her cheeks burn. With one glance at the embarrassed Sid, she picked up her glove and fled, to the sound of Phoebe's laughter.

Only later, as she rubbed her frozen feet together under the cold sheets, did Sara's anger at Phoebe's behaviour subside. She had, in fact, done her a favour by telling Sid about Joe and ending any thought he still harboured about marriage. She had never been deserving of Sid's admiration and she knew that she had never loved him. If she could not have Joe Dimarco, she wanted no one.

The discovery of Sid and Phoebe's affair prompted Sara to write to Louie Ritson, asking about her friends in the village and confessing to the older woman how much she missed the place. She asked for news of Joe and Rosa and wrote again with Christmas wishes, begging for news, but heard nothing in return. Her card to Rosa went unanswered, too.

Christmas and New Year were spent quietly

thinking of Tom and his regiment far away in France and few people went first-footing in deference to those in the forces who were not with them. So when a letter came out of the blue from Louie Ritson, in childish copper-plate, telling her that Dolly Sergeant was looking for help in the shop again, Sara needed no further encouragement to return to Whitton Grange.

'...that lad Eric got a job at the pit. I said you would be pleased to have your old job back and Dolly asked me to write to you. You can stop with us if you like. Joe Dimarco sends his regards.'

Regards was better than nothing Sara thought, gripping the letter to her and feeling a prick of grateful tears. Dear, kind-hearted Louie, she thought excitedly, was offering her a way to return without being dependent on her uncle. Her mother agreed resignedly and quashed any complaints from Mary that Sara should not be allowed to go.

'We can manage fine now I'm back on my feet,' she declared. 'It's the first time Sara's had any spark in her eyes for months so you go, pet, and be a help where you can.'

Sara wrote to Louie and said she was coming, then severe weather set in and the farm was cut off by snow drifts for a week, while Sara fretted at the delay. Finally, at the end of the month, she got a lift with Dr Hall as far as Stanhope and boarded a crowded bus for Whitton Grange.

Clambering off outside The Palace cinema, she breathed in the delightful smell of coal fires and relished the bustle around her once more. Turning with her case, she caught sight of a motorcycle parked by the kerb and, with hammering heart, she saw Joe astride it, watching for someone.

He smiled straight at her. 'Louie told me you were coming. Want a lift?'

'Aye,' Sara gulped, her eyes smarting, 'please.'

'By heck, I've missed you, pet,' he said, slipping off the cycle and seizing her hands.

'Oh, me too, Joe! Me too...' Sara blinked back tears of relief and their arms went round each other in a joyful hug.

Chapter Eighteen

Sara was given a warm welcome at Hawthorn Street and Louie made up the pull-out bed from the old dresser in the kitchen corner for her use. Upstairs was shared by old Jacob and Raymond and a cheerful evacuee with a grating cough called Stan.

'Are you sure I won't be in the way? Once I'm earning I can find lodgings,' Sara suggested to Louie, aware of the extra strain she was placing on the household.

'You stop with us as long as you want, pet,' Louie insisted, as she fried up some potato scones. 'We've had more than this to feed in worse times, believe me. And if Sam gets called up shortly, I'll be glad of the company.'

Sara glanced up as she spread the tablecloth and saw a worried frown flit across Louie's face.

'They might take him on at the pit yet,' Sara tried to sound optimistic. Louie shook her head in disbelief and returned to her cooking while Sara busied herself setting the table for Raymond returning from the pit and Sam who was changing into his uniform to go on duty with the local defence volunteers.

'Give me that letter, pet, before me da comes in,' Louie instructed. Sara picked up an opened letter from the table and handed it to Louie who shoved it behind the tea caddy on the mantelpiece.

'It's from my brother Eb,' Louie told her, 'he's an artist – professional like.'

'The brother you're not allowed to mention in front of Mr Kirkup?' Sara asked.

'Aye,' Louie sighed. 'It seems daft now – but we were that upset when Eb went off with Eleanor Seward-Scott. She was still the boss's wife then and Mam and Dad thought it all very improper. They never got over the disgrace of the affair.'

'But Eb and Eleanor got married in the end?' Sara queried.

'Aye, once her divorce came through. And they've a lad not much younger than Raymond who Da's never seen, more's the pity.'

'Do you see him?' Sara paused over the table setting.

'Rupert? Hardly ever.' Louie's face was downcast. 'They can't come here and I get into Durham once in a blue moon. That's why Eb writes to us. Hildy visits now and then, though. Eb's anti-war paintings were right popular till a few months back, now Hildy says he might go to prison for being a conchie. It's a topsy-turvy world.'

How sad it was, Sara thought, that Louie should be denied the company of her brother and nephew because of stubborn family pride. Sara felt vexed at the futility of such prejudice. Had her own uncle not done his best to ruin her relationship with Joe with his bigotry? she thought angrily. But for Louie's intervention, they might have remained apart. She looked at the homely, compassionate woman making the tea and felt a rush of gratitude.

'Thanks for telling Joe I was coming back!'

'I've been around long enough to know when two people care for each other,' Louie said, matter-of-factly. 'I could tell from your letter you were missing the lad – and he's been moping around here getting under my feet for months.'

Sara laughed, 'Good! I'd hate to think he hadn't missed me.'

'Missed you! He's met every bus from Weardale this week,' Louie chuckled. 'Mind you,' her face grew troubled, 'I think the parlour's suffering – Joe says the blackout's killed the evening business stone dead. And it's going to be harder for everyone to get supplies now this rationing's coming in.'

'I'm going to see the Dimarcos on Saturday – Joe's taking me,' Sara's smile was triumphant. 'No more sneaking around the hillside.'

'I'm glad to hear it,' Louie smiled and shovelled the potato scones on to a plate with crisp bacon rinds just as Raymond clumped in the back door, grinning at them both with his coal-ingrained face.

The next day Sara started back at Dolly Sergeant's and the elderly grocer looked almost pleased to see her.

'You're in charge of deliveries now, lass,' she told her, 'and I know you'll make a better job of it than that useless lad Eric. Bobby Dimarco was round here every other day mending his punctures. Now off with you to Mrs Naylor's and take care.'

Sara was aghast at how the prices of goods had risen already and, riding around the village, she became aware of other changes. Half of the park had been dug up and prepared for the planting of extra vegetables that spring. Gleaming Anderson shelters had sprouted where people possessed gardens, while those without hurried to the large dug-out in the council schoolyard where hordes of children ran around in the crisp air with footballs and skipping ropes. Tynesiders like Stan, Louie's other lodger, tended to stick together, Sara noticed, while the local boys asserted their right to play around the block of outside toilets where a goal had been chalked on to the solid brick.

There was a bustling energy about Whitton Grange that raised the spirits. The two gaunt pits that loomed over the village at the top of the steep bank, no longer wheezed sleepily as before. Both were in full production, clanking and sighing with exertion to fuel the war effort.

That evening Sam Ritson came bursting into the kitchen like a run-away train.

'What in the wide world's happened?' Louie gasped in shock as her husband took her by the arms and shook her. Sara and Joe glanced at each other apprehensively, the teasing intimacy of moments before shattered.

'He's given in!' he shouted, almost incoherent with excitement.

'Who has?' Louie demanded. 'Hitler?'

'No, Seward-Scott! The management are taking me back. Louie, I start at the Eleanor the morra!' He lifted his wife into the air and spun her around.

'Eeh, Sam!' she screeched. 'Sam!' She smacked

him a kiss on his lips.

'And I'll be hewing at the bloody face!' he laughed. 'Oh aye and we'll get the wage rise we're after an' all. Us pitmen will work like the devil to beat Hitler and his fascists – give up our holidays and work all the hours God sends – but they'll pay us a decent wage for our toil.'

Joe and Sara grinned at each other to hear him so happy.

'Sam Ritson talking about God!' Louie teased. 'Whatever next?'

'Oh Louie!' Sam ignored the jibe and hugged her again. 'I'll be using these arms to graft again, not just parade around with a broomstick like a tinpot soldier. I'm a worker, Louie, a worker!'

Sara thought the hardened fighter before her would burst into tears with joy.

Joe nodded at Sara and she followed him to the door, grabbing a winter coat she had inherited from Mary.

'Just going for a walk,' she said, slipping out, but the Ritsons were hardly aware of their going.

Sara snuggled under Joe's arm as they stepped on to the frosty cobbles of the backlane. At first all was black as they blinked in the dark and slithered about on the icy path. Apart from going to fetch Sara from the bus, Joe had hardly used his motorcycle since the new year. Fuel was scarce, petrol about to be rationed.

They reached the fish and chip shop, lurid under dim blue lighting, and Joe paid for a bag of chips. As they shared out the steaming food, Sara told him, 'I can't wait to see Rosa again. How is she? She never wrote like she promised.'

Joe pulled a face. 'She took the Emilio thing very badly – blamed Mam and Dad for not allowing her to marry the lad. So it's their fault he went back to Italy without her.'

'She must have been very hurt,' Sara sympathised. 'Is she over him now?'

'Hard to say,' Joe shrugged. 'She never talks about him. In fact, she never talks about anything very much. Just sits around the house eating and snapping at anybody who speaks to her. She and Sylvia fight like cats when Paolo or Dad aren't around and Mam hardly notices – she's lost without Granny and Domenica for company. She always got on best with Domenica. And she works that hard in the shop she doesn't know the half of it.' Joe licked his fingers and smiled at Sara in the darkness. 'It'll do Rosa good to see you, cheer her up no end.'

But Sara's visit to the parlour that Saturday was a disappointment. She had thought about the place for so long that it appeared smaller and less exotic than she had remembered. The shelves in front of the long mirrors were depleted of sweets or cigarettes and the half-empty shop window was filled with cheap cardboard advertisements in place of fancy goods. The Dimarcos were still making ice-cream, but the over-riding smell was of potato and onion pies and fried food for which there appeared to be more demand.

Mr Dimarco, however, looked just as smart in his waistcoat and apron and greeted her courteously, as did Paolo. But Anna Dimarco gave her the briefest of nods and hurried into the backshop, her face drawn, her movements quick and tense.

'You are living with the Ritsons now, Joseph tells me,' Mr Dimarco smiled.

'Yes,' Sara answered, 'they've been very kind.'

Arturo carefully wiped a glass to a sparkle before voicing what concerned him. 'And your uncle...?'

'I wrote to say I was coming back,' Sara told him, 'but he hasn't been in touch. I'll pop round and see Aunt Ida before long. You mustn't worry about Uncle Alfred,' Sara said defiantly, 'he's not responsible for me anymore and he can't stop me seeing Joe.'

Arturo raised his eyebrows in perplexity but said no more. This girl of Joe's was too modern in her ways. Yet she was pretty and friendly and Joe's temper had improved since her reappearance, so he would content himself with that. By March, his son would be called up for military service and no doubt the friendship would fizzle out, so why spoil their happiness now? He hoped Alfred Cummings would be as philosophical.

Sara found Rosa upstairs, reading one of Bobby's comics and munching biscuits. Her face was fat and her girlish body had grown dumpy, Sara noticed at once. Rosa's once sleek hair was unkempt and unwashed and she wore a shapeless grey jumper and skirt, where once she had been proud of the way she dressed.

'Hello, Rosa,' Sara smiled, trying not to show her dismay, 'it's good to see you.'

Rosa looked up, her eyes betraying her embarrassment at the sight of her old friend looking radiant beside Joe, her cheeks glowing pink from the fresh winter air. She felt a swell of resentment to see them standing close together, which smothered the guilt she had harboured for months for not passing on Sara's message to Joe before Sara left. This is how it would have been for her and Emilio if only... She brushed crumbs off her soiled skirt wishing she could dismiss his handsome, sensuous face from her mind with as little concern.

'I hope you're going to clear up that mess,' Sylvia scolded in Italian, barely acknowledging Sara. Rosa gave her a resentful look.

'Well, say hello,' Joe reproved his young sister, annoyed by her rudeness.

'Hello,' Rosa muttered.

'I've brought you some boiled sweets from Sergeant's.' Sara handed over the paper bag she had been clutching.

'Don't you think I'm fat enough already?' Rosa said churlishly.

Sara persisted in a cheerful manner. 'Sergeant-Major's been asking after you, wondering why you've not been in the shop since Christmas.'

'I don't go anywhere now,' Rosa said in a dull voice, taking the packet without enthusiasm.

Sara wanted to shake her out of her lethargy, but restrained herself.

'How's Peter?' Sara controlled her annoyance, trying to think of something that might spark an interest in Rosa's lifeless brown eyes.

'He's got a cold,' Rosa said in a monotonous voice. 'He's asleep.'

'Rosa left him out playing in the yard for hours,' Sylvia said with disapproval.

'He's your child!' Rosa snapped.

'You were supposed to be looking after him, you lazy little madam,' Sylvia reprimanded in her native tongue. 'But you think of no one but yourself these days.'

'Leave me alone!' Rosa complained.

'Well, the saints have punished you for your wickedness,' Sylvia continued shrilly. 'Haven't they, Rosa?'

'Shut up!' Rosa screamed.

'That's enough, both of you,' Joe ordered, furious at their lack of courtesy in front of Sara. Sara looked at him in bewilderment. 'Come on, we don't have to listen to their bickering.' He took her by the elbow and steered her out of the gloomy living-room, before she could say goodbye.

After that Joe did not take her home to his house, but came every evening to see her at the Ritsons and on Saturday nights they went alone to the pictures.

One Sunday afternoon, Hilda and her fiancé Wilfred joined them for lunch and they gathered around the parlour table, tucking in to a piece of pork bought with Sam's first wages. Hilda was wearing a new flowery dress she had made from a chair cover at Greenbrae and was beaming with her news that she and Wilfred were at last to be married before he was shipped to France to join his regiment.

'We've decided to invite Eb and Eleanor,' Hilda said, stunning the family with her breezy pronouncement.

'What did you say?' Jacob Kirkup demanded,

361

cupping a hand to his ear.

'She says she's ganin' to invite Eb and Eleanor,' young Stan, the evacuee repeated loudly, used to shouting at the old man. Jacob Kirkup reminded him of his own deaf grandfather and he enjoyed acting as his ear-horn.

'Don't shout, boy, I'm not deaf!' Jacob thundered.

'It's time you spoke to each other, Da,' Hilda was unrepentant. 'Eb's willing.'

'He never came to your mother's funeral!'

'He wanted to,' Hilda argued.

'I'll not see him or–'

The old lay preacher's words were drowned by the urgent wail of the air-raid sirens.

'Everyone leave the table!' Louie stood up immediately and put her hand out to Stan. 'Get your coats and we'll be off to the shelter,' she instructed.

There was no time for further argument as the family trooped out of the house.

'Da won't leave the house,' Hilda said impatiently.

'Then I'll stay – he'll go under the stairs if I tell him,' Louie replied. 'You go with the others – no argument, Hildy.'

Sara hurried with Hilda and Raymond and Stan to the school shelter, while Sam rushed to his post. But twenty minutes later, panic subsided when the all-clear sounded and word went round it was only a practice.

'The Germans aren't daft enough to miss their Sunday dinner,' Raymond grumbled. 'Only our lot would think of having a practice when we're all stuffed to the eyeballs with the best dinner of the week!'

'Hush,' Hilda scolded, 'you mustn't say such unpatriotic things – you'll get reported.'

'Who to?' Raymond ridiculed. 'Uncle Sam?'

In the press of people in the school yard, Sara and Raymond became separated from the others and as they made for the gates she felt a tug on her arm. Looking round she saw a pasty-faced Rosa, her dark hair hidden in a knitted hat, her eyes puffy and blinking in the sunlight.

'Hello, Rosa,' Raymond said amiably, 'haven't seen you for ages.'

'No,' Rosa looked away from him, ashamed that he should see her so dowdy. 'Sara, I need to talk to you,' she pleaded. Sara hesitated. 'Please, Sara, can we go to the park?'

'Could you wait till after dinner? Hildy and Wilfred are having a bit celebration for their engagement,' Sara explained.

Rosa's flaccid face crumpled and she closed her eyes. *'Please.'* Her voice was almost inaudible. 'I have no one else I can talk to.'

Raymond put a hand on Sara's shoulder. 'I'll tell them you'll be back shortly – Auntie Louie'll keep something warm in the oven.'

'Thank you, Raymond,' Rosa whispered, sliding him a grateful look.

Raymond hurried on, while the girls turned up the hill to the park. Neither of them spoke until they were through the gates and heading for the bowling pavilion. The green was deserted in the raw February air and they sat on the bench where they had often met up the previous summer.

Sara turned to Rosa and asked, 'Why are you so unhappy? Is it Emilio?'

Rosa's young face looked desolate. 'It's everything – Domenica going and Emilio leaving me and being stuck here with my parents and that bossy Sylvia – it's terrible. I still love Emilio – it's like a pain inside every day.'

'Have you heard from him?' Sara asked gently.

Rosa shook her head. 'Nothing,' she admitted hoarsely, 'not a single word. I've written to Domenica asking her for news of him, but perhaps she never got my letter? If only we'd been allowed to marry – everything would have been so different. I know he loves me...' Rosa gave way to tears.

'The war may be over soon – Emilio will come back,' Sara comforted, placing an arm about her shoulders. She seemed suddenly so vulnerable and fragile, huddled in her coat, shaking with misery.

'It'll – be – too late,' Rosa sobbed.

'Not if you still love each other,' Sara reasoned.

Rosa gave out a great howl, disturbing a blackbird from the spindly bare tree behind them. 'Oh Sara, you don't understand – I'm so scared.' She began to sob hysterically. 'S-Sara, I'm – I'm carrying Emilio's baby.'

Sara was astounded. 'You're *pregnant?*'

'Yes.'

'Are you certain?' Sara looked at her in awe.

Rosa nodded. 'I didn't know what was wrong at first – feeling terrible. Then I began to get cravings for sweet things like Sylvia did when she was carrying Linda. Just after Christmas I felt the baby kick for the first time and now I feel him every day.' Talking about it at last seemed to calm her – she was no longer alone in her awful knowledge.

'But – but you must be well gone,' Sara blurted out, realising her friend had not seen Emilio since the end of August.

'Six months,' Rosa sniffed.

'And none of your family *know?* They must suspect – I mean, you've put on weight...'

Rosa shook her head. 'I think Sylvia knows – that's why she picks on me. But my parents are too worried about the shop to wonder why I've grown fat – they would never think of such a thing – it's too much of a disgrace. They'll hate me for what I have done, *hate* me!'

'No,' Sara protested, 'they would never hate you – but you must tell them, Rosa, give them time to get used to the idea of a baby.'

'A bastard baby,' Rosa cried. 'I wish I could tear it out for causing this shame!'

'You mustn't say that,' Sara was firm. 'It's your flesh and blood, Rosa – and it's Emilio's too. Don't blame the baby before it's born.'

Rosa pulled at the handkerchief in her lap. 'I was so ignorant about – you know. Emilio said it would prove to him how much I loved him – he said he would be careful.' Her voice was drained now of any emotion. 'I gave him everything and he left me. So why do I still love him like I do?'

Sara threw her arms about her friend. 'There's nothing commonsense about love,' she said ruefully. 'Come on, you shouldn't be sitting out freezing to death in your condition.'

'Will you come with me?' Rosa asked. 'While I tell my parents – I feel so much stronger with you around, Sara.'

Sara was nervous at the very idea – the Dimarcos were bound to think her interfering in family affairs. But she could not let Rosa down now.

'If you want me there, I'll come,' she agreed.

'Thank you!' Rosa smiled for the first time and they linked arms. As they passed the gates, Rosa asked shyly, 'Have you and Joe...?'

Sara flushed at such a personal question and shook her head.

Rosa sighed. 'I was so stupid, trusting Emilio. It's obvious that Joe loves you far more than Emilio ever loved me. So don't give each other up, Sara,' Rosa said passionately. 'No matter what my family think, don't give each other up!'

Chapter Nineteen

When they reached the parlour, they realised it would be impossible to break the news. The men were sitting in the backshop drinking tea with Sergeant Turnbull and Rosa's mother and Sylvia were busy in the shop with an unexpected influx of Tyneside children who were after what sweets they could buy.

Rosa looked terrified and Sara steered her swiftly away, telling Anna Dimarco she was invited for tea at the Ritsons.

'By, you look cold, lasses,' Louie made a fuss of them and sat Rosa by the fire. 'Have some bread-and-butter pudding, seeing as you missed most of your dinner.'

The men were sleeping off their lunch and Hilda had gone next door to Wilfred's home for tea with the Parkins.

'Where's Raymond?' Sara asked.

'Gone round to see a friend,' Louie said, 'so us women can have a chat to ourselves for a change.'

Her kindness reduced Rosa to tears once more and she found herself unburdening her troubles to the friendly Louie. At first the older woman looked taken aback, but she quickly recovered.

'Poor bairn – and that lad leaving you to face the music alone,' Louie tutted.

'He wanted to marry me,' Rosa defended Emilio.

'Well, he hasn't and now you've got to make the best of it,' Louie answered briskly. 'No doubt your parents will be angry, but they'll get over the shock – others have before them, so don't think you're the first lass to land yourself in trouble.'

'They might throw me out!'

'I'm sure it won't come to that,' Louie answered, 'but if it does, you can come here till you sort yourself out. The bairn must be born with a roof over its head, poor lamb.'

Sara got up and hugged her. 'You'd take in the bogeyman if he didn't have a home, wouldn't you Louie?' she laughed.

'Thank you, Mrs Ritson,' Rosa was quite overcome.

When the girls left after tea, Rosa was filled with a new resolve to face the wrath of her parents.

She found them all gathered upstairs, except for Paolo who worked below. The curtains were drawn and the room was cosy after the dark outside. Joe grinned with pleasure to see Sara appear with his sister, but he soon saw from their expressions that all was not well.

Rosa blurted out her news before her courage failed and the room went ominously quiet. Sylvia spoke first.

'I knew it! I knew all along you had been with that man.'

Arturo sank onto a chair in disbelief and Joe just gawped.

'My little Rosa,' her father grappled for words, 'not my Rosa. Pregnant? Impossible ... impossible! How dare you shame your family like this?' He stood up in agitation.

'I'm sorry, Papa!' Rosa crumpled at the sight of his pain. 'I'm so sorry.'

'She didn't know what was happening,' Sara tried to defend her. 'Emilio took advantage.'

'What do you know about it?' Anna Dimarco turned on Sara with venom. 'Why are you here? This is *family* business.' She came forward menacingly.

'Sara is Rosa's friend,' Joe said, stepping in her way.

'And this is why my daughter has brought such disgrace to us – because she makes friends with such girls!' Anna accused wildly. 'Did you put the ideas in Rosa's head, eh?'

'No!' Sara was insulted.

'Leave Sara out of this,' Joe said angrily. 'It's Emilio Fella who has brought disgrace on the family. And it's Domenica's fault for not keeping an eye on him.'

'No, not Domenica!' Anna shouted in fury.

'*Yes*, Domenica!' Rosa cried. 'It was your beloved Domenica who pushed me at Emilio in the first place! But in your eyes she could never do any wrong. Well, you're stuck with me now – and my bastard baby!' she yelled hysterically.

Anna pushed past Joe and slapped Rosa hard in the face. 'Shut up!'

'Enough!' Arturo shouted. 'Why are we all blaming someone else? We are *all* to blame. We've failed to teach Rosa how to be a good Italian girl and now she has done this terrible thing to us. We are *all* bad Italians.'

Sara felt a chill at the desolation in the man's voice and the haggard look of hurt on his face.

She felt her intrusion acutely at that moment. Then Joe moved towards his sister and put a tentative hand on her shoulder.

'Cheer up, bonny lass,' he said quietly. 'We'll stick by you.' Rosa turned to him and clung on, sobbing.

Sara backed out of the room, realising Anna Dimarco had been right; this was a family crisis and she was an outsider, no matter what Joe said.

'I'll come and see you in a few days, Rosa,' she mumbled as she withdrew, but no one called her back. Sara fled downstairs, nearly knocking Paolo over in the gloom of the backshop.

'Where is everyone?' he asked in surprise. 'Joe is supposed to be helping.'

Sara gulped. 'I think you should go up and see, Paolo – it's a family thing.'

'I can't leave the shop,' he shrugged, sensing trouble.

'Let me serve for a few minutes,' she offered. 'It's important for Rosa that you support her.'

Paolo accepted reluctantly and Sara grabbed an apron from the back of the door and hurried into the shop. For ten minutes she measured out sweets and made cups of tea and Bovril and served up small pies to the ravenous children hanging around the parlour.

Finally Joe appeared and said he would take over.

'Is Rosa all right?' Sara asked in concern.

'She's gone to lie down,' Joe replied. 'She's not feeling too well, but at least Mam is worrying about her now and not shouting at her.'

'They won't put her out, will they?'

Joe gave her a strange look. 'Of course not! She's family, no matter what she's done.'

Sara nodded and untied her apron. 'I'll be off, then. Tell Rosa if she needs anything...'

'Aye,' Joe said, 'and Sara – ta for helping out after the way Mam spoke to you.'

Sara smiled. 'It'll take more than harsh words to get rid of me this time!'

Joe grabbed her hand and kissed it quickly. Two boys eyeing them from the other side of the counter groaned in disgust. Joe flicked a teatowel at them and Sara laughed as she put on her coat and left.

Hilda and Wilfred were married two weeks later, at the end of February. Dolly Sergeant allowed Sara away for half an hour to see the ceremony and she noticed a tall couple with a dark-haired boy occupying a pew towards the back of the chapel and realised they must be Eb Kirkup and his wife, Eleanor.

After the service, Sara had to dash back to the shop, but arrived home just as Hilda and Wilfred were saying their farewells. In spite of Louie's great efforts to lay on a wedding feast with limited stores, and Sam's jocular comments, Sara was aware of the tension among the guests as she slipped into the parlour.

Louie's cousin Sadie at once introduced her to the elegant Eleanor Kirkup, smoking defiantly through a mother-of-pearl cigarette holder.

'You've left beautiful Weardale for Whitton Grange?' Eleanor asked with a smile of surprise. 'I must say I love to visit the Durham Dales.'

Sara blushed. 'Beautiful to visit, aye, but sheep farming's a tough life – and dull for a lass.'

Eleanor laughed. 'Good answer. Being married to an artist makes me far too romantic about the landscape.' She turned her slender, pale features to look at Hilda. 'Dear Hildy, it's such a shame she and Wilfred are to be separated so soon. I don't know why they didn't marry years ago.'

Across the room Hilda told Wilfred, 'It's time to go,' taking him firmly by the arm, believing they had taken long enough over their goodbyes.

'Ready when you are,' Eb Kirkup smiled at his sister. Sara thought what a gentle face the man had, with intense blue eyes that surveyed them all. His son Rupert had the same solemn wise look, though he was barely twelve.

A silence fell over the room, as Eb turned to his father, sitting aloof in the corner of the room.

'Goodbye, Father,' he said quietly, stooping to shake the old man's hand. 'I'm glad to have seen you again.' Jacob Kirkup ignored the gesture, chewing hard on an old pipe.

Hilda gave an impatient shrug and said to Eb, 'Come on, he'll not speak to you.'

From across the room, Louie pushed herself past the guests and stood before her father, her face severe.

'I'll not stand by and see you throw away this chance of making it up with our Ebenezer!' she scolded. 'Da – you might go to the grave without seeing Eb again.'

This galvanised the white-haired preacher. 'Like your mother did!' he almost choked. 'It finished your mother off, what he did.'

'That's not fair, Da!' Louie interjected. 'Mam had been poorly for years, it's *wicked* to blame Eb for her death.'

Jacob pushed himself to his feet and towered over his daughter.

'I *do* blame him,' he thundered, 'and her!' He jabbed a finger at Eleanor. 'You took my son away from me and for that I cannot forgive you.' Eleanor flushed and put a protective arm around her young son, but Jacob Kirkup stormed from the room without another word.

The wedding couple left swiftly in Eb and Eleanor's small Austin and the rest of the subdued guests departed soon afterwards. Sara and Sadie helped Louie clear up the debris, aware that she was trying to keep back tears at the way the day had been spoilt.

'He's a stubborn old fool!' she raged. 'He's lucky to have *any* family around him the way he carries on.'

'It's not worth getting bothered about, Louie,' Sam said, settling into a kitchen chair with the newspaper. 'He's too set in his ways to change now, so there's no point being upset.'

Hilda came back two days later and returned to her job at Greenbrae, with only her ring and the memory of a snatched honeymoon to remind her she was married at all.

'I'll not speak to Da after the way he ruined my wedding,' Hilda declared to Louie and, to Louie's disappointment, Hilda kept her word and called less frequently at the house.

Sara, taking a lesson from the futility of the Kirkups' estrangement, finally went round to

South Parade to visit the Cummingses after work. To her surprise, Marina appeared pleased to see her and questioned her closely on what it was like living at the Ritsons'. Aunt Ida fussed about nervously and made her tea, while Sara told her about taking over Sergeant's delivery round.

'I got a letter from home last week,' Sara changed the subject cautiously. 'Mam says your Colin has gone up there to work.'

'Yes,' Ida said stiffly, 'he's joined the land army. Against his father's wishes, of course. Father wanted him to go down the pit or join the forces – but not Colin – he wants a safe job on the land.'

'A very necessary job,' Sara answered with spirit. 'Uncle Alfred should be glad he's got one after being idle for so long. And it might make Colin happy for once.'

'Happy?' Ida answered, indignant, as if she had never considered such a thing. 'Why should he be happier working on a dirty farm than with us – with all the luxuries we've given him here? Just selfish to the last is Colin – and leaving us to feed his horrible dogs in the meantime.'

Sara decided to let the matter drop.

'Are you still friendly with the Dimarcos?' Aunt Ida asked.

'Aye,' Sara said with a jut of her chin. 'Me and Joe are courting.'

Her aunt looked away. 'Perhaps it's best you leave before Father gets back from the pit. He wouldn't understand...'

Sara went, feeling saddened, and Marina watched her go with sullen eyes.

Soon after that, Sara's contentment with life in Whitton Grange came to an abrupt end. She had been to see Rosa at Pit Street and as she left, Sergeant Turnbull, sitting downstairs with Arturo, eyed her as she made for the back door and the grey dismal afternoon outside.

'You'll be sad to see young Joseph leaving,' Turnbull said abruptly.

Sara looked at him uncomprehendingly and Arturo Dimarco shifted in his seat.

'Sara does not know, I think,' he said with an apologetic wave of his hands.

'Know what?' she asked with dread.

'I thought he would have told you.' Turnbull looked unrepentant. 'You two being sweet on each other.'

Sara grew hot. 'But he's not due to be called up until the end of the month!' she said. It was the moment she was dreading and had banished to the back of her mind for weeks.

'He's enlisted,' Arturo said, his large face tense, 'with the Durham Light Infantry. He's decided not to wait for the call-up.'

'I see...' Sara tried to hide her shock.

'Good for the lad, I say,' Turnbull said with an edge to his voice, 'knows where his loyalties lie. Well, I must be off. Thank you for the cuppa – I can see you're managing better than others despite this new rationing.'

'Signore,' Arturo stood up, too, 'we do not complain.'

Sara slipped out ahead of the police officer, shaking from his news and full of a nagging unease at his jibing towards Mr Dimarco.

Joe sought her out that evening in the chilly upstairs classroom of the council school, where she was on fire-watching duty with Hilda.

'I'll go and take a look around,' Hilda said and left them alone.

'Why didn't you tell me?' Sara reproached, clamping her cold hands between her knees.

'In case you tried to stop me,' Joe admitted, throwing a warm arm around her shoulders.

'We could have had another month,' Sara protested.

'We're not going to beat the fascists if fit lads like me hang around at home,' Joe replied. 'I want to be out there when the fighting really starts.'

Sara looked at him in dismay. 'You sound just like Sam Ritson.'

'And what's wrong with that? I hope when it comes to a scrap I have half his courage.'

Sara turned and clung on to Joe, desperate at the thought of him leaving.

'When will you go?' she whispered.

'Day after tomorrow,' Joe said quietly, kissing the top of her head. 'You'll look after Rosa, won't you? You're the only one who seems to understand how she feels.'

'Of course I will,' Sara promised hoarsely.

'Give us a kiss then, bonny lass,' Joe smiled, his dark eyes glinting with emotion. For a long moment they embraced, smothering their unhappiness at the imminent departure, and then Hilda returned and Joe slipped into the night.

Two days later, Joe got a lift with an army truck to the training depot at Brancepeth and Sara threw herself into long hours of work, ARP duty and helping entertain the evacuee school children at the weekends. The spring came, with growing rumours that the Allies were suffering setbacks in Norway and in the Atlantic. Joe wrote cheerfully from camp and Sara returned his letters with pages of correspondence, though keeping from him how hard his family were finding it to keep the shop running now that sugar was rationed. Neither did she tell him of the obscenities scrawled on the parlour wall after articles began to appear in national newspapers openly attacking the Italians in Britain as 'the enemy within' and 'little cells of potential betrayal'.

The Dimarcos kept their fears to themselves, but everywhere the tension of rumour and fear of spies infiltrated the village. One Friday in May two boys ran into Sergeant's shop shouting that the Germans had invaded Belgium and the following days brought news of the Nazis sweeping across Western Europe and heading for the Channel ports. Sara was desperately afraid for her brother Tom in France and saw the anxiety on Hilda's face for Wilfred. The miners redoubled their efforts to increase production and Raymond and Sam worked continuously, only returning to eat and fall into exhausted sleep before being called to work once more.

'Have you heard the news about The Grange?' Sam said one night. 'Seward-Scott is having to move into the lodge because the Big House is being commandeered as a hospital by the army.'

'About time it was put to some use,' Louie answered. 'To think that man's been rattling about in a huge empty house with a wife safe in America. He should have been made to take in evacuees.'

'Well, the army's got it now.'

Only Sara noticed Hilda's face crumple in fear. 'A hospital?' she repeated. 'They must be expecting a lot of wounded, then? I can't bear the thought of my Wilfred being hurt.'

Sam and Louie looked at her in silence and Sara knew what they were thinking: if Wilfred came home wounded, he might be one of the lucky ones...

Rosa's baby was late and the atmosphere in the house had worsened since news of the war in Europe had grown grim. She knew her mother worried for Domenica and Granny Maria and no news had come for over a month from Italy.

Her father and Paolo seldom spoke about the war, but Rosa could see the lines of anxiety on her father's face and knew they were not just caused by the thought of her illegitimate baby. There had been ugly scrawls on the outside of the shop, 'Wops are enemies' dribbling in black paint down the brick. Paolo had spent two hours scrubbing them from sight but ghostly letters remained to haunt them.

'It's come at last!' Her mother burst into the kitchen, waving an envelope. Sylvia turned from the stove where she was frying up some fresh green beans for her son Peter's lunch. Rosa roused herself out of her lethargy, knowing it could only be news from Domenica. Perhaps there would be some word of Emilio at last? she wondered forlornly. 'Someone has read it before us,' Anna Dimarco said with indignation as she opened out the letter and scanned the writing. Rosa knew her mother could not read and waited for her to hand it over.

'Quickly, Rosa, what does she say?' Anna asked impatiently.

It was written in English and Rosa began to read aloud. It was full of everyday concerns about the village and their neighbours and Anna Dimarco and Sylvia interjected with comments when someone they knew was mentioned. Nonna Maria had been unwell but was much better now and enjoying the summer sunshine. Rosa paused over the next sentence.

'Well, go on,' her mother ordered.

Rosa read on, 'I'm so happy to tell you that Pasquale and I are going to be parents. Isn't that wonderful? A third grandchild for you and Papa.'

Rosa glanced up and saw the delight on her mother's face.

'Another grandchild!' she cried, clapping her hands together. 'And Domenica a mother.' Rosa felt a stab of resentment for her absent sister who always got what she wanted. Domenica's baby would be cherished and loved by the family, while hers would be shunned as a constant reminder of her wickedness and shame.

'When are we going to tell Domenica about Rosa's baby?' Sylvia asked.

'There's no need to trouble her with that!' Anna replied brusquely, giving Rosa a sharp look. 'It would only cause Domenica embarrassment among our people at home.'

'You mean you're never going to tell *anybody?*' Rosa asked with incredulity. 'You can't just pretend the baby doesn't exist! It's still your grandchild as much as Domenica's – as much as Peter or Linda!'

'Don't compare it with my children!' Sylvia was indignant. '*They* have a good and honourable father.'

'Girls, stop arguing!' Anna cried. 'Always you are arguing like cats and dogs. Rosa, continue the letter.'

Rosa felt her heart pounding painfully. She was furious that Sylvia could upset her so easily. Her hands felt clammy and shook as she forced herself to read further. A twinge of pain knotted her belly.

There was a reference to the Perellas and how they were all managing on the family farm, then Rosa felt a sick lurch as her eyes alighted on Emilio's name. She stopped reading aloud and searched the page for news of him.

'What is it?' her mother demanded. 'Why have you stopped?'

'Pasquale has heard about Emilio from an old comrade. He's joined the army again,' Rosa said breathlessly, torn between relief at hearing news of him and anxiety that he had joined up.

'That's the last we'll hear of him, I bet,' Sylvia said brutally.

Rosa was about to protest when a spasm of pain gripped her and she gasped for air looking at her mother in fright. Anna jumped up and rushed over.

'Where does it hurt?' she asked, putting a hand on her daughter's distended belly. She felt the contraction herself without Rosa having to tell her. Rosa cried out at the sharpness of the pain and then it subsided.

'What's happening, Mamma?' Rosa asked terrified.

'It looks like the baby has decided to come at last,' Anna said with resignation in her voice. 'Come, Sylvia, help me get Rosa into bed.'

Rosa was engulfed in panic. 'Will it hurt? Will I die?'

Her mother became suddenly gentle. 'Of course you won't die – women are having babies all the time. I had five – am I a ghost, my little kitten?'

Rosa felt her eyes sting at the sudden endearment. 'Stay with me, Mamma,' she whispered.

When they had heaved her into bed, Rosa asked in a small voice, 'Can you get word to Sara? I want Sara to be with me.'

Her mother frowned. 'No, she is not family. We will manage this on our own.' Anna saw the tears in her daughter's dark eyes and relented a fraction. 'There is nothing to fear, Rosa. Sara can come once the baby is born.'

Chapter Twenty

Sara did not hear of the arrival of Rosa's baby until the following day. Paolo came into the shop and told her, with an embarrassed look at Mrs Sergeant, that Rosa had given birth to a baby girl.

'You will come and see her?' Paolo asked bashfully.

'Of course!' Sara answered. 'As soon as I finish.'

Mrs Sergeant was astounded by the news, for once quite at a loss for words. The Dimarcos had kept Rosa out of sight of the village but now there was no way of avoiding the scandal.

'Rosa Dimarco!' Dolly Sergeant blustered after Paolo had gone. 'The little madam! You never said a word, either,' she accused Sara.

But Sara ignored the grocer's censorious comments and rushed over to Pit Street as soon as the shop closed.

Anna Dimarco led Sara into Rosa's bedroom and swept the tiny bundle from her daughter's hold.

'We are calling her Maria – after Nonna Maria,' Anna announced, rearranging the shawl around the newborn baby.

'*Mary*,' Rosa corrected. She looked pale and tired but Sara could see the mixture of relief and triumph on her face.

'It's a bonny name,' Sara smiled.

'Look at her pretty face.' Anna rocked her new granddaughter. 'Isn't she like Rosa?'

Sara peered at the sleeping crinkled face with her shock of black hair and thought the comparison hardly flattering. But she was relieved Rosa's mother appeared so pleased with the unwanted baby.

'Let Sara hold her, Mamma,' Rosa encouraged, beaming with pride.

'You must be careful,' Anna ordered, handing over her charge with reluctance. Sara took hold of Mary gingerly.

Anna laughed. 'You have not held many babies, no?'

'No,' Sara admitted. 'Plenty of newborn lambs, though.'

'Then you make a good mother one day,' Anna declared, making Sara colour with embarrassment. She handed Mary back swiftly.

'I've got a present for Mary,' Sara said, producing a pair of pink booties she had bought at the store haberdashery department on her way over.

Rosa began to weep and Sara wondered what she had done. Anna indicated it was time she left.

'She needs to sleep. You can come another day, yes?'

'Aye, of course,' Sara smiled. 'And if there's anything I can get you, Rosa...'

'No, no,' Rosa's mother ushered Sara from the room. 'We can manage ourselves.'

Sara was in the middle of describing Rosa's new baby to Louie, when Raymond and Sam came in

383

from work, trailing black dust from their boots.

'What's all this excitement for?' Sam asked with a tired smile, his back aching from the punishing hours of hewing underground.

Louie took a deep breath. 'Rosa Dimarco's had a daughter,' she told her husband, placing bread and cheese and pickled beetroot and cabbage on the table for tea.

Louie and Sara had kept Rosa's secret even from Sam and he gawped at them in astonishment. 'So that's why she's been in hibernation,' he grunted.

Sara caught the stunned look on Raymond's face.

'What do you mean she's had a daughter?' he spluttered, unable to hide his shock. 'She's not even married.'

Louie and Sara exchanged looks. Sara had worried over how Raymond might take the news, knowing he had fancied Rosa, but that was nearly a year ago. Now Raymond had a new group of friends at the pit and was seldom about the house, only returning to sleep or eat and preferring to spend any snatched moments of free time with his friends on the football pitch. Just then, the young lodger Stan and a friend came charging in asking if tea was ready.

'No, five more minutes,' Louie jerked her head at the children, 'run outside now till I call you.' They looked about to protest that they were hungry, but a look from Sam sent them scrambling for the door.

'No, Rosa's not married,' Louie continued, giving her nephew a sympathetic look. 'She's been a foolish lass, but her bairn's not to blame and now she must do all she can to bring that baby up right.'

Raymond sagged onto a stool, his face red under the coal grime. Louie knew from Sara that Raymond had been sweet on the young Italian girl the previous summer. She had been disbelieving of the infatuation, thinking of her affectionate nephew as an immature boy whose voice still plunged and squeaked. But work at the pit had put muscle on his skinny frame, he had grown a head taller in the last year and his voice was now that of a young man. He was no longer the little lad she had delighted in bringing up for her absent sister-in-law, Iris Ramshaw, and she must not treat him like one. At times he reminded her achingly of her brother Davie, the father Raymond had been cruelly denied by that terrible pit accident that should never have happened, when Davie had died saving Wilfred Parkin's life.

'Who's the father?' Raymond asked in a small voice, full of embarrassment. 'Likely he'll stand by her?'

Louie nodded at Sara.

'He's called Emilio,' she said with an awkward glance, 'she met him at Domenica's wedding. The Dimarcos didn't approve of him and wouldn't let Rosa marry ... he disappeared back to Italy at the beginning of the war.'

'She knew him last summer then?' Raymond said in a tight voice. Sara met his look and nodded. His blue eyes in their grimy sockets were fierce.

385

'No doubt Joe would like to knock him to hell if he had half the chance,' Sam grunted, pulling off his boots.

'Well that's their business,' Raymond got up sharply, 'and Rosa's got no one to blame but herself. I don't know why you're making such a fuss over her.'

'It was Emilio's fault,' Sara corrected.

'Who cares?' Raymond answered savagely. 'These Italians are all the same – think they can have any lass they want.'

'Joe's not like that,' Sara protested.

'Isn't he?' Raymond glared.

'Tch, Raymond!' Louie tutted.

'Well, she's daft getting mixed up with I-ties.'

'That's enough,' Sam warned. 'Louie, get the water poured for our bath, will you?'

Louie bit back a remark and turned to the range. Sara gave Raymond a furious look and stormed out of the house.

Sara and Raymond did not speak to each other again for several days, Raymond's hurt at the discovery that Rosa was not worthy of his adoration preventing him from apologising to Sara for his bad-tempered words. But the deepening crisis of war soon overshadowed their personal lives as news filtered through of fierce battles in Belgium and Northern France and the Allies were pushed back to the sea. One day, as they listened anxiously around the wireless in Edie and Ernie Parkin's parlour, they learned of a huge battle to defend Arras. On the following day, a telegram was delivered to the Parkins for

386

Hilda. Wilfred was missing.

Hilda would not be consoled and Sara felt desperate to see her so wretched, imagining how she would feel if it were Joe or her brother Tom.

Four days later, on the 28th May, after Sam had come home fuming at the news of murdered Belgian trade unionists being tipped into mass graves, word spread through the village that Belgium had capitulated. For the next few days everyone gathered around wireless sets and seized what newspapers they could for news of the British withdrawal to Dunkirk and the astonishing rescue by the navy and a flotilla of small craft that plucked thousands of troops off the beaches and out of the clutches of the surrounding Germans.

The relief of escape for so many was soon overtaken by the dawning terror that invasion of Britain was imminent. Signposts were taken down to thwart the progress of an advancing army and volunteers flocked in increasing numbers for defence duties. Holidays at the pits were suspended and the miners spared no effort in the fight to produce as much coal as possible to support their French allies, still resisting the Germans on French soil.

Sara felt a wave of frustration that she was carrying on mundane shop duties while the war effort went on around her. So, after work one day, she took Louie's advice and went to volunteer at the WVS canteen in the Memorial Hall, set up to receive the influx of servicemen being temporarily billeted in the village on their return from France.

Sara found her Aunt Ida helping make tea in the hall kitchen.

'Just look at them.' Ida shook her head at Sara. 'They look quite done in.'

Sara went out to serve in the crowded hall, but it did not buzz to the sound of chattering voices as it had when the evacuated children had arrived. The men sat subdued and utterly weary, smoking reflectively over cups of tea and saying little. An air of defeat hung over them and, for the first time, Sara felt really afraid.

Ida was garrulous with nerves. 'It's a terrible thing, this war. And where's it going to end? As Mr Churchill says, we must all do our bit. When I think of the danger to our children – to Marina–'

'You mustn't get yourself upset, Aunt Ida,' Sara tried to calm her. She thought to change the subject. 'How's Colin getting on at the farm?'

'Oh, Colin!' her aunt screeched, and splashed scalding tea on to the floor.

Sara jumped out of the way. 'Aunt Ida!'

'Sorry. It's just my nerves. I hope he stays away. There'll be hell on if he comes back.'

Ida would say no more, so Sara busied herself clearing tables, before going on fire-watch duty with Hilda. She wished to fill each waking moment with activity and prevent herself dwelling on thoughts of her brother Tom, of whom there had been no word, and of Joe as he neared the end of his training. Hilda was the same. She could not talk of Wilfred without succumbing to tears and she spent her free time at the Parkins' house, waiting for news of her husband.

'Have you heard from Joe?' Hilda asked one evening, giving up trying to read her book in the gloom. They staved off the boredom of fire-watching by reading to each other and Hilda had astonished Sara with her knowledge of literature.

'A couple of weeks ago. He's in a camp outside Edinburgh, but he can't say much. I wonder where they'll send him? Do you think it'll be to France?'

Hilda gave her a strange look. 'Does it not bother you that he's an Italian – with all this talk of them being spies?'

'Joe a spy?' Sara laughed at such a suggestion. 'You read too many thrillers, Hildy! Joe's as British as we are. He's joined the DLI, hasn't he?'

Hilda persisted. 'But do you think he'd fight against his own people, though, if he had to?'

Sara was annoyed by the question. 'If you mean the Italians, I don't know. What does it matter? We're not at war with Italy.'

'We're as good as. Musso's just waiting for Hitler to do the dirty work, then he'll join in.'

'Well, it's got nothing to do with Joe,' Sara said indignantly. 'He'd defend this village and those he loves as much as W–' She bit back Wilfred's name. 'As much as *any* of the Durhams. Just like Churchill said last night – Joe'd fight in the streets and in the hills if he had to.'

They avoided talk of their men after that but, a few days later, Hilda came dashing in to Louie's kitchen and screamed, 'Our Wilfred's alive! Louie, he's alive! We've heard on the wireless.'

Louie hugged her sister in delight. 'What have you heard?'

'They read out a list of prisoners – the Germans did – we nearly didn't listen tonight – but we heard Wilfred's name.'

'So he's a prisoner of war?' Louie asked, her joy for her sister deflating.

'Aye,' Hilda nodded, undaunted by Louie's look of concern. 'But at least the bugger's alive.'

After finishing at the shop the next day, Sara went round to see Rosa and baby Mary, who was to be christened the following Sunday at St Teresa's. Mrs Dimarco was serving a handful of customers in the parlour, while Mr Dimarco and Paolo smoked and played cards in the backshop, the wireless crackling between them. They seemed preoccupied and Sara hurried into the courtyard where she heard voices. She found her friend sitting outside in the early evening sun, rocking her daughter in Linda's old pram. For once, Sylvia was sitting good-humouredly beside her, peeling vegetables and watching Linda staggering after her brother Peter and his spinning top. Bobby Dimarco was tinkering with a bicycle in a corner of the yard.

Sara, more confident now with the tiny baby, peered into the pram and stroked her cheek. 'Hello, bonny Mary. How are you today?'

'She's grand,' Rosa smiled, regretting that Sara could not be a godmother. She had tentatively suggested the idea, but her parents had dismissed the Protestant Sara as unsuitable.

Rosa went and fetched them lemonade and they sat chatting as an evening breeze picked up and the sun went behind the clouds. Even Sylvia seemed content just to linger in the quiet of the white-washed courtyard, the door to the ice-cream shed creaking gently on its hinges, punctuated by the soft snorting of the old pony Gelato. Linda crawled up on to her mother's knee and went to sleep, lulled by the soft voices and the somnolent sounds of evening.

Colin walked the final mile into Whitton Grange. He was fitter now than he ever had been in his life; farmwork had firmed his layers of bulk into muscle and he no longer felt embarrassed by his oversized frame. The farmer at Thimble Hill had praised his way with animals and one of the dairy girls, Beth Lawson, had blushed and smiled in a way that was flattering, whenever he had approached. Colin had found a satisfaction with outdoor work that he had never imagined existed and cursed himself for never having had the courage to leave home before. On the farm, no one called him ignorant, or treated him like the village fool and no one seemed to mind his occasional clumsiness. He joined in the local whist drives and Beth Lawson with her merry, squinting brown eyes danced with him at the monthly chapel hop.

'Sara never told me she had a handsome cousin,' Beth had said one evening, allowing Colin to walk her home. Colin had been speechless with delight at her coquettish manner and dared to kiss her goodnight.

Two weeks later, Beth had suggested he move into her cottage and share the rent.

'What if your husband should come back?'

Colin had asked, uncertainly.

'What husband?' Beth had answered bitterly. 'I've not heard from John since he went to sea – and I'm not likely to, either.'

So Colin had moved in and he was content and felt useful for the first time in his life.

Responding to Beth's cheerful, earthy humour, he found he could talk to her of his deeply unhappy boyhood with a resentful stepmother and a father who never attempted to hide his contempt and disappointment. Beth was the first person to whom he had admitted his fear of his bullying father and she was the first woman to give him the warmth of physical comfort. She made him feel less guilty at the way he had used his strength to bully younger boys in turn and for his aggressiveness toward Sara.

'You're not to blame,' Beth had said stoutly, 'your father made you what you were. But I know you're not a bad lad, Colin Cummings.' She had put her arms about him and kissed him and Colin had felt a wave of gratitude for her forgiveness.

Only one thing made Colin fret and that was being without his beloved hounds, so he had decided to fetch them and bring them back to his cosy new home at Rillhope with Beth and her son Daniel.

Yet, as Colin strode into the village in his dusty boots, the familiar fear of his father and his dread at returning to 13 South Parade, crept into his stomach. His head sank as he tramped nearer the green, where his home lay in the shadow of gathering clouds.

Rosa shivered now the yard was in shadow. 'Are you working at the canteen this evening?' she asked her friend.

'No. I'm on fire-watch,' Sara yawned, thinking it was time she made a move.

At once they were aware that the wireless in the backshop had been turned up to full volume. Sara glanced through the open doors and saw that Mrs Dimarco had drifted into the room, too.

The clipped voice of the announcer was reporting a speech delivered only hours ago by Mussolini. Italy had declared war on Britain and her allies.

Nobody spoke. Peter was laughing at something Bobby was doing with the bicycle and baby Mary whimpered in her sleep. Rosa stood up and, leaning into the pram, clutched the baby to her, making Mary wail. At once, all the Dimarcos began to talk.

'What does this mean for us?'

'I don't know!'

'We should have gone with Domenica–'

'Don't say that, this is our home!'

'Nothing will change–'

'Oh, *Madonna!*'

'Anna, calm yourself!'

Sara hung around on the edge of the arguing family, feeling useless and anxious. Eventually, she realised there was nothing she could say to put their minds at rest. No one really knew what such news would mean to Italian nationals in Britain. Sara had heard of German residents being sent to camps at the beginning of the war, but surely this would be different? These people had been here most of their lives.

'Don't worry, Rosa,' she tried to reassure as she left. 'This isn't Nazi Germany. The British won't mistreat you Italians – you're part of the community.'

But, as she hurried home, she realised she herself had referred to Rosa as an Italian for the first time. Had she, too, started to see the Dimarcos in a different light? Hilda's words about them being spies and the newspaper reports that warned of the 'enemy within' crept into her mind with their invidious message; can these people be trusted? Where do their loyalties really lie? Then Sara thought of Joe, training for danger and possible death with the Durham Faithfuls, her father's old regiment, and she felt ashamed of such suspicion.

Ida was taken completely by surprise when Colin banged the front door.

'You should've said you were coming home,' she said in agitation, appearing in the corridor to see who it was.

'I'm not stopping long,' he muttered as Marina darted out of the parlour.

'Your father's gone to the club to see if there's any more news.' Ida blocked his way. 'We heard it on the wireless. Italy's declared war on us,' Ida gabbled.

'Bloody I-ties!' Colin mumbled.

'Why don't you go in the parlour and I'll fetch you something to eat?'

'I'll see the dogs first.' He pushed past her.

'They're all I've come for.'

As he did so, Marina blurted out, 'They've gone.'

'What do you mean?' Colin jerked round. Marina cowered behind her mother.

'Father's got rid of them,' Ida croaked. 'The whippets...' Colin gave her such a look of scornful disbelief that Ida took a step back, but he spun round and marched through the kitchen, leaving a trail of dried mud.

The yard was ominously silent. No whippets sprang to greet him with licks and yelps of delight and the animal smell had gone – even their shed had been demolished. In its place stood a gleaming Anderson shelter.

Colin was outraged.

'Where are they?' he managed to ask, shaking with anger.

'We couldn't feed them any longer,' Ida stuttered. 'Not with rationing – the family comes first, Father said. And there's going to be bombing – we needed a proper shelter.'

'Where are Flash and Gypsy?' Colin shouted, grabbing Marina and shaking her. The girl screamed for him to let go.

'You're hurting me!'

Ida was galvanised into protecting her daughter. 'Take your hands off her! Your wretched dogs have been put down!'

Colin gasped, as if he had been winded. 'He did it, didn't he? He hates me that much, he'd do a thing like this?' He shouted something incoherent and fled across the yard, kicking the offending shelter with hatred as he ran out of the back gate. Ida clutched the crying Marina to her apron and closed her eyes in relief that her wild stepson had gone.

At Hawthorn Street, Sara bolted down a quick meal of cheese salad and bread pudding made from stale leftovers. There was a tension in the stuffy kitchen that made her nervous.

Sam looked across the table at Sara, who was rising to go. 'You're not going back to the parlour tonight?' he asked.

'No, I'm on duty,' Sara answered.

'Do you want me to walk you down?' he said self-consciously.

'No, I'm meeting Hilda, thanks.'

Sara left, quickening her pace as the evening clouds turned an ominous purple and the sky darkened early with the threat of a thunder storm. The air was heavy with moisture, but the rain held off while she and Hilda hurried to their post.

'What's wrong Sam?' Louie asked as her husband paced back from the door.

Sam shrugged. 'I don't know. It's just a feeling. Coming back from work – there was a mood among some of the lads.'

'What sort of mood?' Louie pressed him.

'People are afraid,' Sam said quietly.

'I know,' Louie whispered.

'And they're looking for someone to blame,' he added.

Sara was the first to notice something was amiss. Climbing on to the flat roof of the boiler house, she heard the distant call of voices in the oppressive gloom.

'There's a lot of people out in the streets tonight,' she commented to a puzzled Hilda. 'I can hear them.'

'Perhaps the Home Guard are on manoeuvres,' she suggested.

'They wouldn't be shouting like that. Listen.'

The young women peered into the half dark of the June night and strained to catch the discordant noises of the villagers abroad.

'I'm sure I can see torchlights. I'm going to take a look,' Sara determined, clambering off the roof. She was filled with an unease she could not define.

'Not on your own, you're not,' Hilda declared and scrambled down after her.

They made their way out of the school gates and walked closely together towards South Street and the centre of the village. Turning into Mill Terrace, they stopped in their tracks to see a wave of dark figures emerge at the top of the street, heading straight towards them with an uneven thud of boots.

'Scarper!' Hilda hissed to Sara. 'It's trouble.'

But the crowd was moving so rapidly, they had no time to turn and run. The first young men were around them in seconds, jeering aggressively, their faces blackened to hide identity. Someone shone a dim torch in Sara's face.

'It's Joe Dimarco's lass!' he shouted. Sara went rigid with fright as, through his disguise, she recognised the hostile face of Normy Bell thrusting close to hers. He spat in her face.

'Wop's whore!'

'Traitor!' another cried.

'Let's give her it!' Normy pushed Sara against the wall.

'Get off me!' she cried, trying to push him away.

Hilda grabbed at Norman Bell's arm. 'Leave her alone! She's got nothing to do with them Italians.'

A large man elbowed his way to the front. 'Don't waste time on her,' he argued. 'It's the Dimarcos we want.'

Sara gasped, 'Colin!' as she looked into her cousin's angry face.

'She's my cousin, leave her be,' Colin said, levering his way between Norman and Sara.

Norman shook him off, but fell back undecided.

'Haway, Normy,' his mate tugged his arm, 'we're wasting time. It's the I-ties we're after.'

Some of the crowd had already moved on and Norman Bell did not want to miss out on any fun.

'Stay away from Joe Dimarco if you've got any sense,' he threatened Sara, his eyes narrowing.

Seconds later the pack of men were passing on. It was easier now to see that most were young, some hardly more than boys. They strutted along shouting words of hatred, intoxicated with the excitement of violence. At the back of the crowd, Sara was certain she recognised a tall figure in an overlarge cap.

She began to shake violently and Hilda's arms went around her in comfort.

'R-Raymond,' Sara stammered. *'Raymond's*

with them.'

'Never!' Hilda disclaimed.

'There.' Sara pointed him out, but the semi-dark had already swallowed him up.

'Oh, Hildy, what can we do?'

'Don't you go near that parlour,' Hilda ordered. 'It's not your business.'

'What about the Dimarcos?' Sara was aghast. 'Rosa and her baby? We can't leave them to that mob. Imagine it was your family in there, Hildy.'

Hilda felt shamed. Italians they might be, but they did not deserve to be terrorised, she admitted. Overcoming her fear, Hilda spoke with decision. 'We'll go for Sam. He'll know what to do.'

Without further words, they turned and ran up Mill Terrace, the sound of savage chanting filling the night sky behind them.

Chapter Twenty-One

As soon as the news of Mussolini's declaration of war had been confirmed, Arturo closed the parlour. Paolo and Bobby helped him wind in the canopies, close the inner shutters and draw down the blind behind the door. Paolo, ever methodical, swept the floor and wiped down the tables before they bolted the door and retreated into the backshop.

'It's just a precaution,' Arturo assured his wife. 'And we don't get much business in the evening now, anyway.'

But the men had not lingered downstairs and, as the sky grew dark, the family gathered around the kitchen table for the evening meal. Arturo attempted to jolly them, but the conversation was muted as they listened for changes in the sounds of evening beyond the open windows. The thrum of the pits mixed reassuringly with the languid call of birds, settling to sleep.

Rosa pushed away her spaghetti without appetite and went to check on Mary. She slept peacefully. Returning, she saw young Peter standing fretfully in the doorway of his parents' bedroom.

'I can't sleep,' he grizzled.

'Come here.' Paolo smiled at his son and the boy ran forward and scrambled into his lap.

'Tell me the story of the magic donkey, Daddy,' the boy asked.

No one protested as Paolo began to indulge the boy with the old tales, as timeless as the mountain villages from which they came. Arturo smoked steadily. As dusk deepened, Anna drew the blackout curtains and switched on a cheery light.

The women were clearing the table when the jar of voices became noticeable. Anna stopped and cocked her head. The noise was growing louder, coming nearer.

'What's that?' she demanded.

Paolo's story-telling ceased. Arturo stood up and went to the window, peering through a chink in the blackout into the dark. He could see nothing, but the sound of people advancing was unmistakable. He pulled the window firmly shut.

'Arturo?' his wife whispered.

'It's nothing. Just the ARP patrolling. Time you were in bed, little Peter.'

Paolo swept up his son and gave him a kiss as he began to protest. He handed him over to Sylvia who coaxed him back in to the bedroom. She was still settling him down when noise erupted below in the street.

'Come out, you bastards!'

'Enemy scum!'

'Hang the traitors!'

'We know you're in there!'

'Catholic pigs!'

All at once the shouts were drowned in a deafening shatter of glass as a brick was hurled at one of the shop windows.

Rosa screamed and ran to her mother. Anna crossed herself and appealed to her husband, but he just stood in stunned disbelief at what he was hearing.

'My shop!' he said, incredulous.

'Arturo!' Anna beseeched.

Indignation seized him. 'I'll not let them smash up my shop!' He strode to the stairs.

'Don't go out there, Arturo!' Anna pleaded. 'Paolo – don't let him go out!'

Paolo pursued his father down to the backshop and seized his arm.

'No, Papa.'

'I will speak with them – it is a crime,' he protested.

'Think of the children upstairs,' Paolo was insistent. 'They must be protected first – not the shop.'

As he spoke, the sound of further missiles being hurled at Dimarco's shop door pierced the night and splintering glass skidded across the pristine tiles.

The seriousness of the attack struck Arturo at last. 'Barricade the doors!' he shouted.

Together they heaved sacks of foodstuffs and crates against the backshop door and, upending the solid table, pushed it against the bolted back door, wedging it with chairs.

'We must ring for the police, Papa,' Paolo urged his father.

'Yes,' Arturo agreed. He lurched for the telephone in the corner of the backshop, the noise of the mob turning his fury to fear.

It seemed an age before he got through to the police station and, in his relief, gabbled half his message in his native tongue.

'Let *me* speak.' Paolo took hold of the receiver, but the line was dead.

'They will come any minute,' his father assured him. 'Sergeant Turnbull is our friend. He will put a stop to this violence.'

Hurrying back upstairs they closed the door to the flat and pulled the heavy sideboard against it. Rosa sat rocking Mary in her arms, while Anna and Sylvia comforted a frightened Peter, and Linda slept on, oblivious to the commotion. Bobby crouched on the floor, trying to overcome his terror by reading a comic.

Tensely, they sat around the table listening to the destruction below. Five minutes later they heard the rabble break into the shop and begin to break up the furniture...

Sara was hardly coherent as she gabbled out her story to Sam and Louie who forced her to sit down and drink a cup of water, while Hilda explained more calmly what had happened.

'They were heading for the Dimarcos' shop,' Hilda said.

'We must stop them!' Sara cried. 'They looked ready to kill!'

'Oh, that poor lass and her new bairn,' Louie said, horrified.

'Are there no police or ARP around to calm them down?' Sam asked, grim faced.

'We didn't see any, but they've probably caught up with them now,' Hilda replied. 'We should be back on fire-watch an'all...'

'No!' Sara sprang up. 'This is more urgent – the Dimarcos are in *danger*.' She saw the cautious looks on their faces, a reluctance to get involved. 'It wasn't just louts like Normy Bell and my cousin Colin, there were dozens of them.' She looked at Louie directly. 'Raymond was there.'

Lottie gasped. 'Never!'

'I saw him,' Sara was adamant. 'He was hovering at the back, but he was with them.'

Louie turned in horror to her husband. Sam grabbed his jacket from the back of a chair and pulled it on. 'I'm going for the police.'

Sara made to follow him, but he stopped her at once.

'You stop inside with Louie and Hildy and don't you dare go out on the streets again tonight,' he told her severely. 'Louie, make sure everyone stays in.'

'Aye, Sam,' Louie agreed.

With part reluctance, part relief, Sara sank into a chair to wait for Sam's return, sending up a silent prayer for the safety of her friends.

On the way to the police station, Sam detoured by Pit Street just to see for himself if Sara's fears were founded. He heard the mayhem before he got to the end of Mill Terrace and, running into Pit Street, saw the rampaging crowd of villagers flinging stones and abuse and dragging furniture into the street. For a moment he watched in horror as three men demolished a cigarette machine and raided its contents; chairs and tables were hurled into the street and men ran into the night with stolen goods, their boots crunching on a sea of broken glass from the large parlour windows.

Sam had witnessed violence before; he had

taken part in running battles on picket lines during the bitter strike of '26. But never before had he seen wanton destruction or such naked hatred against a defenceless family. The ugliness of it filled him with an angry shame, compounded by the thought that his nephew was among them.

'If I get my hands on the beggar...' Sam shouted aloud, knowing he could do nothing alone against such a volatile crowd.

He turned and raced for the police station, but was astounded to find only a young constable on duty who seemed at a loss as to what to do.

'Where's Simpson or Turnbull?' Sam demanded.

'Constable Simpson's up at Eleanor pit answering a call and Sergeant Turnbull's been called to Durham for an urgent meeting,' the policeman said.

'Well, telephone for reinforcements. Get them out of bed if you have to,' Sam ordered. 'There's a battle going on out there.'

'I'll have to wait for Serg–'

Sam crashed his fist on the desk. 'Now! Half the village is smashing up Dimarco's shop and they'll tear the poor buggers apart if they get hold of them, too. Telephone!'

Rosa was sure they were all going to die. The shouting and violence seemed to go on for ever as they huddled in the dark of the kitchen, pretending not to be there and wishing that they were not. She was too terrified to speak, clinging on to her baby, attempting to nurse Mary and stay calm. Paolo had stopped Peter's crying by inventing a game of hiding under the table and keeping quiet as a mouse, but now the little boy was growing tired of it.

'When will the banging stop, Daddy?' he asked tiredly.

'Soon,' Paolo promised. 'Soon...'

Arturo said he would go down and telephone the police again, but Anna worried it would be too dangerous. Then, for a while, the crowd seemed to tire and the noise of vandalism diminished.

'Perhaps the police are here at last?' Arturo's haggard face brightened in hope. He got up from his cramped position and went to the window to look out.

'There he is!' a voice shouted. 'They're in there!'

Arturo cursed his lack of caution, as the attack began anew. Twenty minutes later the assailants broke in to the backshop and the sounds of destruction came terrifyingly close.

Arturo sat holding his wife as they listened to their life's work being destroyed. What had they done to deserve such hatred? Arturo wondered bitterly. He had thought they were liked in the village, respected as hardworking and for paying their own way and being generous when they could afford to be. Only boorish men like Cummings had shown them any ill feeling before and there were few of his kind.

Arturo could not understand the hostility. He had chosen to live in Whitton Grange most of his life, had fought alongside these Durham people in the Great War, had brought up his family among their families. He felt shaken with betrayal – and, most of all, he felt betrayed by his friend Signor Turnbull who did not come to his rescue...

For an age they remained in the flat, praying for deliverance. Finally, in the middle of the night, the attackers appeared to fall back and disperse, melting into the dark, as if sated by their destruction.

'They're going to spare us,' Anna whispered tearfully, hugging her husband in relief.

But hardly had they dared move from their protective circle when they heard subdued voices and steps on the stairs, followed by a sudden battering on the door to the flat that made Sylvia wail with terror.

'Mr Dimarco?' a man shouted. 'Are you all right?'

'Who is it?' Arturo demanded with suspicion.

'Sam,' the man replied. 'Sam Ritson. It's safe to unlock the door.'

The family gave a communal cry of joy.

'Help me move the sideboard,' Arturo said to Paolo. 'Switch on the light, Anna.'

A minute later they had the door open and, in the dim electric light, they saw Sam and a young constable appear, followed by Sergeant Turnbull.

'Signor Ritson!' Arturo gave Joe's boxing teacher a hug in his relief.

'As long as you're all unharmed,' Sam muttered with embarrassment.

'We are champions, as you say,' Arturo said with a bravado he did not feel. 'Signor Turnbull, I am so glad.'

But Turnbull stood aloof. 'I'm sorry you had to endure such an attack. We were quite taken by surprise by its ferocity.'

'You should have acted a bit sharper,' Sam accused bluntly. 'Got yourself back from Durham before midnight.'

Turnbull gave the pitman a disdainful look and Arturo intervened quickly.

'I'm sure you did your best, Signore. We are grateful to you both.'

'It was Sara gave the alarm, Mr Dimarco,' Sam said. 'Not me or the police, so thank the lass, not us.'

'Sara? Oh, I will!' Arturo nodded. 'Now, please, will you sit down with us?'

'No,' Turnbull said abruptly, 'I'm afraid this is not over.'

'What are you saying?' Anna asked anxiously. 'Are we still in danger? Have they not gone away?'

'Hush, Anna, let the Sergeant speak.'

'I'm afraid I have to ask the men to go to the police station for the rest of the night – and we must search the house.' As Turnbull spoke, two constables appeared from the dark of the stairwell.

'Why must you go, Arturo?' Anna asked in panic.

'Just a few questions...' Turnbull kept his voice even. 'If you could come along now, Mr Dimarco – you and Paolo.'

'For how long?' Anna persisted.

'A day at the most,' the police officer assured. 'No need for any big goodbyes.'

The room erupted in a barrage of questions as Turnbull instructed his men to search the flat.

'What are you looking for?'

'What is this all about?'

'Can we go with them?'

'I must pack a case for you, Arturo.'

Turnbull began to lose his patience. 'There's no need to pack anything. Just do as I say, please.'

Sam watched, appalled, as the constables scooped up letters and accounts and poked into the Dimarcos' private possessions. He knew what it meant – these people were now 'enemy aliens', a supposed threat to the nation's security and they would be shown no mercy by Turnbull whom Sam knew to be vindictive and calculating.

'Listen, Turnbull – what are you going to do to protect the women while you question the men?' Sam demanded.

'The crowds have gone – there won't be any more trouble,' Turnbull snapped. 'Anyway, they'll be safer once the men are locked up.'

'You bastard!' Sam seethed.

'Out the way, Ritson, or I'll take you in, too! Get them out of here now.' He jerked his head for Arturo and Paolo to be taken away.

Anna flung herself at her husband.

'Just a day, Anna,' Arturo said, trying to hide his agitation.

Sylvia thrust a hunk of bread into her husband's pocket and a bleary-eyed Peter grabbed at his father's hand.

'Daddy,' he sobbed, 'I want to go with Daddy!'

Paolo leant down and hugged the child. 'Daddy will be back soon, *bambino.*' He pressed his son into Sylvia's arms and kissed her briefly.

'Paolo!' she held on to his hand, but Turnbull pulled them apart.

'There's no need for all this fuss.'

Suddenly there was a squeal from the corner of the room, as a policeman spotted a cowering Bobby. 'Here's another one, sir.' He hauled him to his feet. 'Shall we have him, too?'

Bobby kicked and struggled and Anna screamed. Sam stepped over and shoved the policeman out of the way.

'He's just a lad!' Sam defended him.

'Yes, he's only thirteen, leave him,' Turnbull ordered with indifference. 'Where's your son Joe?' he turned to Anna.

'He's not here,' she said, bewildered.

'You know he's with the DLI,' Sam answered savagely. 'Not even a bastard like you would try to arrest a Dimarco in uniform, would you?'

Turnbull threw him a look of loathing and left without another word. Arturo was pushed after him, his face dignified and impassive, Paolo's supportive hand on his shoulder. Then they were gone.

Rosa looked at her mother and sister-in-law in disbelief trying to shake herself awake from the nightmare. But it was real; the people of Whitton Grange had run amok in their shop and her father and brother had been arrested.

'I'll stay until the morning,' Sam told them unhappily. 'I'll stop downstairs and make sure no one comes back.'

Rosa's mother merely nodded, past deciding what should be done and Sam left, not knowing how to comfort them.

At early light he went home, exhausted and grey-faced, to tell Louie and Sara what had happened, then left for his shift.

'Tell Raymond I'll have it out with him after work,' Sam said grimly, pulling on his pit clothes. 'You go and see what help you can be to Mrs Dimarco.'

Sara went at once to Pit Street. At first she did not recognise the devastated shop front. Wreckage was strewn everywhere; as she picked her way over the broken glass and Mr Dimarco's prized coffee machine which had been wrenched from the counter, she saw Mrs Dimarco and Rosa attempting to sweep up the mess in the backshop. Tea leaves and flour spewed from bags and a fine white dust lay over everything. In the backyard, Sara saw Bobby squatting beside Joe's damaged motorcycle, rubbing it ineffectually with a cloth.

'Our precious sugar,' Anna lamented.

'Oh, Sara!' Rosa caught sight of her friend. They hugged each other in sympathy. 'Thank you for trying to help us.'

'Sam says they've taken...'

Rosa nodded. 'Mam's going down to the police station to try and see them as soon as we've cleared some of this mess.'

'We shall be all right once Papa and Paolo come home again,' Anna Dimarco said stoically.

Sara looked at Rosa, but saw her face ridden with doubt.

'I wish Joe were here,' Rosa said.

'Well, he isn't,' her mother snapped, 'so we will have to manage on our own.'

'Not on your own,' Sara replied. '*I* want to help.'

Mrs Dimarco looked up from her sweeping, her handsome face ghostly and lined with fatigue. They looked at each other for a long moment, Sara wary, Anna suspicious.

At last, 'Thank you,' Mrs Dimarco said quietly and bent again to her sweeping.

Some time later Louie appeared, having seen Stan off to school.

'You get along to the police station and see what's what,' she told Mrs Dimarco. 'Sara and I can get on with the clearing up.'

Anna needed little persuasion to go, taking Sylvia with her, while Rosa stayed and looked after the children. But they returned disconsolate an hour later having been refused permission to see their husbands.

'They will tell us nothing,' Anna fretted. 'Why are they holding them? Are we all criminals now because of our Italian blood?'

Sara and Louie could say nothing that would ease their fear and shortly afterwards they had to leave for work.

'I'll get Sam to have a word once he's back off shift,' Louie promised as she left.

The day dragged on interminably as they piled the broken furniture in the shop hoping it could be salvaged, and made an inventory of all that had been destroyed. Sara returned at lunch time and took Bobby off to scrounge some boarding to nail up the gaping windows. She kept Dolly Sergeant's doleful warning to herself.

'Feelings are running very high towards them

Italians,' the grocer had told Sara, sucking in her cheeks. 'I don't think you should be seen with them, lass.'

'They're good customers of yours!' Sara had been indignant.

'Used to be,' Mrs Sergeant sniffed. 'But Mr Dimarco's been arrested and I don't suppose we'll be doing business again.'

'He's just being asked a few questions,' Sara had retorted. 'They'll not hold him for long. He hasn't done anything that'll keep him in prison.'

Mrs Sergeant shook her head. 'I don't have anything against Mr Dimarco personally, but he's an Italian and people see him as the enemy now. I'm just warning you, lass, for your own good. They'll not let Mr Dimarco or his son out until the war's finished, you mark my words.'

In the late afternoon, Anna and Sylvia returned to the police station with a parcel of clothes and toiletries for their men. For brief minutes they were allowed to see one another, but their strained exchanges left the women feeling more apprehensive than ever. The stocky Sam Ritson, of whom Anna was rather in awe, was there in his dirty pit clothes trying to pump the sergeant for information, but Turnbull had thrown him out and been barely courteous to them.

As the women emerged, a group of youths who had gathered outside the cells jostled around them with sneers and abusive language. They abandoned the idea of waiting for news and hurried for home.

'It's too dangerous to go again,' Sylvia had warned her mother-in-law. 'Those boys wish to harm us.'

'I'll go and wait,' Sara volunteered. 'I'll come as soon as there's any news.' No longer did Anna protest that it was family business, so Sara hurried away.

Arriving outside the police station, she saw a scene of confusion. A police van had driven up and was surrounded by shouting and jostling youths being pushed back by a line of constables. Sara, straining to see what was happening, caught a glimpse of Mr Dimarco's hatless greying head among the throng as he was forced into the van. As Paolo was pushed after him, the crowd surged at them like baying hounds but the police heaved them aside as the van revved into life and lurched past the protestors.

Sara ran up to a policeman. 'Where are they taking them?'

The man shrugged. 'Don't worry, they'll not be letting them out in a hurry. Collar the lot, Churchill's said, and he's right.'

Sara felt sick. She could not return with such dreadful tidings to the anxious women at Pit Street so, deciding to alert Sam and Louie first, she ran to Hawthorn Street, stumbling in the back door to find a furious row in progress. Sam, still in his filthy pit clothes and haggard from lack of sleep, was berating a resentful-looking Raymond who had just returned from work.

'I'm that ashamed of you! A lad of mine–'

'I'm not your lad!' Raymond struck back. 'You're just my uncle – I've never had a proper father.'

'Raymond!' Louie looked close to tears. 'Sam's

414

always done his best for you – we both have.'

'I've always had to share him with all the other lads,' Raymond said angrily. 'Pat Slattery and Joe Dimarco – aye, he thinks more of Joe than me. But the Dimarcos are traitors – that's what the lads say. I was just being patriotic.'

'Patriotic!' Sara choked with anger at his words. They all turned to stare. 'How does it help our country to attack innocent families and drag away their men?' she demanded. 'We're supposed to be fighting the fascists – not behaving like them.' She advanced on Raymond furiously. 'What you did last night was unforgivable – cowardly! How dare you criticise Joe as a traitor when he's away training to defend all of us – Joe, who stopped you being beaten up by Normy Bell's gang! Have you forgotten what Joe did for you, Raymond? Are you no better than louts like Normy Bell?'

Raymond felt a wave of shame at Sara's stinging rebuke. How had he become involved in such a dreadful attack? he wondered miserably. He had allowed himself to be led by the angry lads at the pit with their cries about patriotism and hatred of foreigners, and all because Rosa had made him feel foolish for caring for her while she slept with another man. But he had known the Dimarcos all his life, helped out in their shop and always been welcomed as Joe's friend. His was the greater betrayal.

He flinched under Sara's contemptuous stare, unable to bear her disapproval of him. 'I didn't smash the shop up,' Raymond defended himself weakly. 'I – I just went along to protest – I didn't know it would get out of hand.'

'Well, it did,' Sam growled, 'and now Arturo Dimarco's spending a second night in the cells wondering how he's going to feed his family now his business is gone.'

'No, he's not,' Sara said, still shaking from her furious outburst. 'They've taken them away – no one knows where. And there're lads out looking for trouble again – and no one to protect the family.'

Louie gasped but Sam was quick to answer.

'We'll have to protect them – you an' all Raymond,' he ordered sharply. 'Start knocking on the neighbours' doors – I'll not see women and children harmed, no matter what their race. I'll go for some of the lodge.'

Sara saw Raymond hesitate, fear on his slim face.

'You owe it to Joe,' she challenged.

'Yes, son,' Louie added, her eyes brimming. 'Show yourself you can be as brave as your father was. He lost his life saving another man.'

Raymond gulped back his fear, gripped by another wave of remorse at what he had done. Since the attack a year ago, he had been terrified of violence, of being at the receiving end of a beating. Last night he had felt safe as one of the pack, half intoxicated by their crude jingoism against the Italians. But as the attack had grown out of control, Raymond had run away in horror. He saw now how much he had hurt his own family and Sara, too. They watched him and Raymond knew he would be judged for the rest of his life on the way he acted now.

He swallowed. 'I'll go and get Mr Parkin,' he said and followed Sam out of the house.

Louie sent word to Hilda to come and look after Jacob and the young evacuee, Stan, while she went with Sara to be with the Dimarcos and break the news that their men had been taken away.

'Sam'll find out where they've taken them,' Louie tried to reassure Mrs Dimarco. 'I'm sure they'll be back soon.'

But nothing they said could erase the tense worry from the faces of the Italian women as they settled the children for another uncertain night.

As darkness came again, Sam set up a picket of union men and neighbours who had responded to the call to protect the Dimarcos from further attack. They gathered outside the Pit Street shop, a solid phalanx of miners, ready to fend off the rioters of the previous night.

The sky was lit by a bright moon that threw shadows across the street and illuminated the skeletal wheel of the Eleanor pithead at the top of the bank. Just as Sam thought the danger had passed over, figures appeared out of the shadows. Tonight they came softly and in less numbers, like a guerrilla army that wished to be un-detected. They stopped short at the sight of their elders amassed around the shop doorway.

'Be off with you!' the burly blacksmith Ernie Parkin shouted. 'We want no more trouble in this village.'

Normy Bell stepped forward. 'We're not making trouble – it's them I-ties in there. We

417

want the enemy out of Whitton.'

'The men have gone,' Sam answered sternly, squaring up to the youth. 'Leave the women and bairns alone or I'll break your bloody neck.'

Normy stepped back, only too well aware of Sam Ritson's reputation as a fighter.

Indecision infected the crowd as their leaders held back and Sam knew bullies like Bell were only brave when they were sure of outnumbering their opponents.

'What should we do?' Normy mumbled belligerently to a smaller man behind him. As he stepped aside, Sam recognised Alfred Cummings's jowly face in the moonlight.

'So you're behind all this, Cummings,' Sam said scornfully. 'Alfred Cummings, the biggest coward of them all!'

Alfred Cummings looked at Sam with venom. He hated him with a loathing that had grown like a cancer, year by year, since the dreadful strike of 1926 had killed his first wife through malnutrition. Radicals like Sam Ritson had been responsible for the months of misery; if they had given in sooner his first wife might still be alive.

'You're the biggest traitor of them all, Ritson, defending these foreign muck against your own kind!' he accused. 'Just like you betrayed your own kind back in '26.'

Sam stepped forward, outraged by the vindictive words. It was men like Alfred Cummings who had voted to return to work who had destroyed the strike and made the sacrifice of their people pointless. Seven gruelling months, during which he had gone to prison and Louie had lost the only bairn she had ever been able to carry, had all been for nothing because Cummings and his kind had thought only of themselves.

'Don't you talk to me about betrayal.' Sam shook as he spoke, the frustration and bitterness of years of unemployment fresh in his mind once more. He clenched his fists, thinking of how Cummings' toadying to the bosses had given him a comfortable prosperous life.

Ernie Parkin put a restraining hand on his friend. 'He's not worth the bother.'

'Yes, he is!' It was Raymond who suddenly sprang forward to Sam's side. 'My uncle's right – Cummings is the traitor – he killed my father!'

'Raymond Kirkup, you little runt!' Normy Bell shouted in surprise. But Raymond no longer cared what Norman Bell thought of him as he glared at Cummings.

'How dare you speak to me like that!' Cummings glowered at the tall youth.

Raymond jabbed a finger at him, furious. 'You were deputy the day my dad and the others died in that explosion – Sam told me. Everyone who survived said there was enough gas in it to blow them all to Germany, but you still made them work in it – just to impress the bosses. You're a bloody murderer!'

Raymond raised a wiry arm and landed a fist in the overman's astonished face. The gesture was like a match to explosives and the two sides fell on each other with punches and kicks. Louie and Sara, who had crept to the window to witness the confrontation, watched in horror at the confused brawling as old scores were settled. They saw

Raymond and Normy Bell hammering away at each other, while Sam blackened Cummings's eye before he ran off. To Sara's amazement, Colin's huge bulk detached itself from the shadowed chaos and threw Normy Bell off Raymond where he lay on the ground, kicking the belligerent Bell out of the way. He pulled Raymond up.

'I wish I'd hit the bastard myself years ago,' Colin panted and Raymond suddenly realised that Colin was referring to his own father!

The fight raged for nearly fifteen minutes, the original aggravation over the Dimarcos forgotten. Then they heard the blast of a constable's whistle and the troublemakers began to scatter. Constable Simpson arrived with three other policemen and told the pitmen to go home. Sam and a handful refused and Simpson thought better of challenging them.

Raymond, his nose broken, was taken inside where Louie fussed over him. Anna Dimarco insisted Sam and the other men came in for a hot drink before returning to their watch.

'What a carry-on,' Louie tutted, bathing Raymond's face, while Anna Dimarco and Sylvia made Bovril. 'Isn't there enough fighting in the world without you men having to settle old scores?' She gave Sam a severe look.

'Cummings had it coming to him for a long time,' he grunted.

'I understand now...' Sara said, her face sad.

'Understand what?' Louie asked.

'Why you all hate my uncle Alfred so much. I never heard anything about his part in the explosion that killed Raymond's father.'

'It was all a long time ago,' Louie sighed. 'It doesn't do any good to open up old wounds...'

But Sara could tell from the tender way she treated Raymond that Louie was secretly proud of the boy she'd adopted all those years before.

Sara became aware of Rosa hovering in the doorway of her bedroom, rocking Mary in her arms as she watched Raymond with timid eyes. Raymond glanced away embarrassed by her attention.

'We ought to be getting home,' Louie said with a gentle shake of Raymond's shoulder. 'Come on, Sara, we'll be more use to Mrs Dimarco once we've had a bit sleep.'

'Aye and I'll get downstairs again,' Sam said, slurping off his drink, preparing to follow the other men.

Reluctantly Sara gathered her jacket and beret. But, as they said their farewells and promised to return in the morning, they heard footsteps clumping up the staircase. Everyone turned and held their breath to see who the latecomer was. The door swung open.

'Joe!' Sara gasped.

Joe stood in his uniform, his chin unshaven and his dark eyes wide.

'*Merda!* What the hell's been going on here?'

Chapter Twenty-Two

Joe listened with increasing anger to the account of the previous night's riot and the arrest of his father and brother.

'But how did you know we were in trouble?' Anna asked her son, perplexed.

'I didn't. We were passing through Carlisle on our way to a new camp and I saw what they'd done to the Italian shops there, so I jumped the train and came home. I never expected it to be this bad...' Joe's handsome face looked harrowed.

'It would have been worse,' Rosa spoke up, 'if it hadn't been for Sara and the Ritsons – and Raymond – he stopped them harming any of us.'

'Aye...' Joe looked gratefully at them all and put a hand on Raymond's shoulder, saying 'Thanks, marra.'

Raymond dropped his gaze guiltily, but his uncle and aunt remained loyally silent. He did not like to admit that it was Sara's scorn that had made him take action and he had been gratified by her look of approval as she helped Louie bathe his cuts. But, glancing at her now, he saw her face full of tenderness for Joe.

Sara felt a sharp longing as Joe's dark eyes met hers, but she was inhibited in front of her elders. Joe, too, appeared reticent, betraying the guilt he felt at not having been there to protect his relations.

'Anyway, I'm here to take care of you now,' he said turning to Rosa.

'What about the army?' Louie interrupted. 'You'll get into all sorts of bother if you don't go back, surely?'

'They'll give me leave.' Joe stood up and put an arm around his mother's shoulders, 'My family must come first.'

'They'll give you court martial!' Sam retorted. 'You must go back tomorrow – *we'll* look after your mother and family.'

'No! I'm staying until me dad and Paolo come back,' Joe began to bluster.

'Listen, lad, first we have to find out where they've been taken,' Sam reasoned. 'Then we'll make a fuss until they're released – but that could take weeks, months. It should help, you being in the army – but you'll do your dad no favours if you're thrown in prison for desertion.'

Joe sighed with frustration.

'Signor Ritson is right,' Anna said, squeezing her son's hand. 'You *must* go back, Joseph. It's what your father would want. We will manage.'

Sara looked across at Mrs Dimarco and saw a look of stubbornness in her brown eyes. She's more resilient than I thought, Sara realised, and felt a flicker of hope for the shattered family.

Joe eventually bowed to the combined pressure of family and friends.

'All right, I'll go tomorrow,' he said grudgingly.

Just then, baby Mary began to cry where Rosa had lain her in Granny Maria's old clothes basket. Joe looked startled, then realisation dawned.

'My niece?' he queried. Rosa nodded. 'I forgot,' Joe smiled. 'Let me look at her.' He went over and plucked the squawking baby from the basket, unabashed by her protests. 'You're a little angel!' He grinned over the bundle and rocked her vigorously. 'As pretty as your mother, yes?'

Sara smiled ruefully to herself, admitting a fleeting envy for the crinkled, month-old-baby who held Joe's attention.

Rosa blushed with pleasure and made him relinquish her daughter. 'She needs feeding,' she said, and disappeared into the bedroom. Talk of food sent Anna bustling to the larder to see what she could give her son while the Ritsons said their farewells.

Sara and Joe looked at each other in frustration at such a tantalisingly brief reunion.

'I'll see you out,' Joe said quickly and took Sara's hand in the dark of the stairwell. Sam and Louie and Raymond walked ahead briskly, giving them a brief moment alone.

'I miss you,' Sara whispered as they kissed hungrily.

'I think of you all the time,' Joe sighed, nuzzling her neck.

'Good...' Sara smiled and they kissed again.

'You're a brave lass, sticking up for us – some people won't like you for it,' Joe became serious.

'The louts that did this to your family aren't worth the time of day, any road,' Sara answered stoutly. '*I'm* not afraid of helping your family.'

Joe pulled her to him and kissed her fiercely in reply. Sara managed to croak a goodbye and fled before Joe could see her cry. He watched her hurry after Louie and Raymond as the pale pink light of dawn caught the glint of gold in her hair and felt an aching emptiness.

A week later the Dimarcos received the briefest of notes from Arturo to say they were being held in an old cotton mill in Lancashire along with hundreds of other Italians. 'Davide is here and cousin Benito,' Rosa read out, 'and we are well. We do not know where we go next.'

She looked at her mother. 'That's all it says. At least Uncle Davide is with them too. It's not so bad if they're all together.'

Anna bit back the thousand questions that rushed into her head. What did they sleep on? Did they eat? Where would they take them? When, oh God, would they see them again? Instead, she led her family down the road to St Teresa's, holding her head high as some people ducked to avoid speaking and there they lit candles for their loved ones and prayed for their release.

They returned to find Bobby crying in the backyard, huddled on the bench where Granny Maria used to sun herself next to the pots of plants.

'Why are you not at school?' Anna asked her youngest son sharply.

'I – I h-hate it,' he sobbed and buried his head further between his knees.

'Nonsense.' She shook his shoulders. 'It's important you learn your lessons. What will Papa say when he comes home?'

'He's not coming home!' Bobby wailed, raising

a blotchy face. 'The lads at school say he's been shot by a firing squad as a tr-traitor!'

'What *have* they done to your face?' Anna exclaimed, her fingers reaching quickly to touch the puffy bruising around his left eye. 'Who did this?'

'The Gateshead lads,' Bobby mumbled, wincing at the contact. 'They all hate me and I'm not going back. I'm *never* going back!'

'Roberto, Roberto...' his mother hugged her youngest to her, stroking his hair to calm him. 'They are wicked to say such things. Of course your father has not been shot – we had a letter from him this morning. He's living in a big place with Paolo and Uncle Davide and cousin Benito and lots of other Italians. He's quite safe – the British are *not* going to hurt them.'

'Then why have they taken them away?' the boy asked her miserably.

'It's difficult to explain,' Anna sighed, wondering herself what the answer was. 'They are suspicious of us because we are Italians and Italy is at war with Britain. But when they discover that your papa and Paolo are good men, they will let them come home.'

'So they won't come back for us, then?' Bobby asked, sliding her a cautious look. 'The lads said we would be next.'

Anna curbed her anger at such childish cruelty. 'No, we will stay here, this is our home,' Anna reassured. 'And we must try and get the shop open again. You are the man of the house now, Bobby,' she encouraged, 'so you must be very brave and help us all you can.'

Anna did not force her son back to school and, when he stayed away for the rest of term, no one made a fuss as attention turned to the swiftness of Nazi victories abroad. France made an armistice with Germany and Britain braced itself for invasion. Hilda, resigned to not seeing her captured husband Wilfred indefinitely, volunteered for the anti-aircraft service and went off to train. Bombing raids on the east coast of England began and the local newspapers reported night attacks on Sunderland on the 18th and 21st of June.

Anna, wondering about the safety of her sister-in-law Elvira and her family in Sunderland, asked Rosa to write a letter. But on the day it was posted, Elvira and her plump daughter Albina arrived on an overcrowded bus, clutching what belongings they could carry.

Elvira was aghast at the wrecked parlour, the coloured glass gone from the wooden booths, the marble tables cracked and the windows still boarded up.

'Our shop is untouched,' Elvira told Anna, spreading her tiny hands in amazement. 'We had no trouble until they came for Davide and Benito.' She gulped back tears, worry lines creasing her bird-like face. 'The policeman was very polite – he had a cup of tea and a sandwich and said it was just a formality. Then he took them away and we haven't seen them since...'

Anna handed Elvira her handkerchief and she blew her nose.

'At least they are all safe,' Anna comforted. 'And Val?'

'She is still training. We managed to get word to her and she came before we left – collected some of her things.'

'Well, you must stay with us while this bombing continues,' Anna insisted, 'I'm glad you decided to come.'

Albina said petulantly, 'We had no choice. It wasn't because of the bombing we came – we were told to leave.'

Anna looked at her perplexed. 'What do you mean, Albina?'

Elvira held up her hand to silence her youngest daughter. 'It's for security reasons – the place we live – what they call it, Albina?'

'A restricted zone,' the girl replied, eyeing Rosa and her new baby with distaste.

'So we are not allowed to stay,' Elvira said, shrinking into her chair. 'We board up the shop and come here. What else can we do, Anna?'

Anna hid her dismay. Elvira and Albina might not be able to go back to Sunderland for months and in the meantime they had two extra mouths to feed. Somehow they must start selling food again, though she had little idea how to go about ordering supplies; that was something Arturo and Paolo had always done.

She stretched out a hand and patted her sister-in-law's arm. 'Of course you did the right thing. We will help each other, Elvira, and show our husbands we can be strong.'

The Fall of France brought production at the Eleanor and Beatrice pits grinding to a halt, as the demand for Durham coal in the French steel industry was severed by the occupying Germans and scores of men were laid off, confused and angry after their strenuous efforts of the past few months to dig out coal as fast as they could. Haunted by the spectre of the Great Depression, union men like Sam Ritson beseeched the other coalfields to share their production quotas with the Durham pitmen who seemed hardest hit, but the other mine owners would not help.

'The lads can't even go and work elsewhere,' Sam railed at home.

'Perhaps Raymond could get a job in munitions?' Louie suggested, worried that their nephew was hanging around the streets, idle.

'He can't, Louie!' Sam lost his patience. 'There's a law against pitmen going into other trades – they made it when the government couldn't get enough coal – now we're stuck with nothing to do!'

Sara was uneasy at the rising tension in the Ritson household. Young Stan was waking them all at night with nightmares that his home on Tyneside was on fire from falling bombs and Louie had allowed him to move into the parlour to sleep with her and Sam. Jacob was growing increasingly frail and, since the bitter row over Hilda's wedding, he had become a crotchety old man, awkward about his food. Uninterested in venturing from the house, he no longer went for his customary walks or even to read at the Institute. When the air-raid sirens went Jacob refused to leave his bed, declaring the Hun would not chase him into the cold in his nightshirt and, if his time had come, it was the Lord's will not the Germans'.

Sara worried about Louie trying to keep the peace among her fractious menfolk and feared that, with nothing to do, Raymond might fall in with bad company again. But she knew that her wages from Sergeant's were a welcome supplement to Louie's small income and suspected Louie was grateful for the company of another woman in her house of bad-tempered men, especially as she missed Hilda's cheerful visits. Yet her overriding concern was for the abandoned Dimarco women and their children.

Sara gathered from Rosa that the strain of not knowing the fate of their men was compounded by arguments between Albina and Sylvia who could not agree about anything.

'For once Sylvia is taking my side,' Rosa told her wryly. 'Albina is driving her *mad*. She gets up late and won't help around the house and she shouts at the children. It's terrible.'

'At least your mother's got the shop open again,' Sara said, trying to cheer her friend.

'But hardly anybody comes,' Rosa frowned. 'Just the bairns for sweets – and we're running out of them. Mam doesn't know where to get stuff from and none of the travellers have been here since...'

Sara realised that the morale of Rosa and the other women would only be lifted by positive news of the arrested men. Talking it over with Sam and Louie that evening after Jacob and Stan had gone to bed, Louie made a suggestion.

'Eb and Miss Eleanor might be able to do something.'

Sam gave Louie a critical look, not liking the way she still spoke of Eb's wife with the deference given to the upper classes. 'What could Eleanor do?' he asked pointedly.

'Miss Eleanor's our county councillor,' she said, 'and she's well connected. Perhaps she could make enquiries.'

'Anything's worth a try,' Sara said quickly. 'Could we go and see her?'

Sam and Louie looked at each other.

'She comes to Whitton a couple of times a week, doesn't she?' Sam queried.

'Aye,' Louie nodded. 'She still visits the mothers' clinic she started in South Street. We could call there tomorrow.'

Louie and Sara went to the baby clinic the following day in Sara's lunch hour but Eleanor Kirkup was not there. However, returning the day after, they found her in a small office above the main clinic at the top of a steep, dingy stairway. In contrast, the room was white-washed and brightly lit, with comfortable chairs covered in floral patterns. The councillor looked up as they entered, her slim, serious face breaking into a pleasant smile.

She rose. 'Louie, how wonderful to see you! Please sit down and I'll get us a cup of tea. And it's Sara, isn't it?' she asked. Sara nodded, pleased to have been remembered by this woman of importance.

'We don't need a cuppa,' Louie protested, uneasy at the fuss being made.

'There's always one on the go at your house, Louie,' Eleanor waved a pale bony hand, 'just sit

431

down and I won't be a minute.'

Sara watched her cross the room, her movements graceful and unhurried, her clothes plain but elegant. At Hilda's wedding, Sara had thought Eleanor Kirkup quite middle-aged and a bit severe, but here she seemed relaxed and her face younger under the page-boy hairstyle, especially when she smiled. Her face bore no trace of make-up and the way she looked with her dark eyes was direct and interested.

She helped them to tea from a china pot while Louie told her the family news.

'But it's Sara's Italian friends we've come about,' Louie cut short the pleasantries. 'We wondered if you'd be able to find out what's happening to them?'

Eleanor blew on to her black tea and considered. 'Give me what details you know about the men and I'll see what I can do,' she promised. 'I've seen what's been done to the shop – dreadful,' she shuddered. 'War brings out the worst in some of us.'

'And the best,' Louie countered. 'Look at our Hildy on an ack-ack gun, not knowing if she'll see Wilfred again but just getting on with it. And Eb, of course, getting his medal for bravery in the Great War.'

'That experience changed your brother's mind about the war, Louie,' Eleanor said adamantly. 'He's a registered conscientious objector now.'

'Well he's done his bit for his country,' Louie said, feeling uncomfortable. She stood up and Sara followed.

'Thank you very much, Mrs Kirkup,' Sara

smiled gratefully and took the thin hand Eleanor offered. It was warm in spite of the woman's pallid, fragile appearance.

'I'll do my best, Sara,' she smiled back. 'Come and visit us soon, Louie,' she urged, 'Eb and Rupert would so love to see you – and you can meet our Belgian refugees. They'll be with us till this ghastly war is over, I suspect.'

'Thanks.' Louie blushed as Eleanor kissed her on the cheek, but Sara doubted Louie would go to Durham. However much she yearned to see her brother and nephew, Sara knew that old Jacob Kirkup held too much sway over Louie. While he lived her loyalty lay to her father first.

Arturo rose stiffly from his straw palliasse, damp from the rain that had gusted in through the gaping windows opposite, and shivered. Paolo lay next to him, huddled in a childlike position, managing to sleep. He felt a wave of affection for his eldest son, uncomplaining throughout their ordeal. It was Paolo who raised his spirits when all seemed bleak and calmed his temper when they were taken for endless questioning.

Arturo looked around him at the scores of figures sighing in their sleep or sitting in hunched groups, unable to rest on the cold, pitted factory floor with its rank smell of machine grease and blocked drains. In his walks around the derelict mill, queuing for water at one of the few taps or trying to exchange possessions for a packet of cigarettes from the guards, he had met dozens of the incarcerated Italians; Northerners and Southerners, cafe owners and shop workers, musicians and artists, boys of seventeen and men in their sixties. Most were as confused and anxious as he was and their unease had not been lessened by the rumour that the Commandant had a list of dangerous fascists marked for deportation.

Arturo recalled his last interview with a stony-faced man in a smart suit, who reeled off his name, age, occupation and where he was born in Italy.

'You seem to know all about me already,' Arturo had quipped.

The man looked at him with hostility. 'You are a member of the *fascio* in Sunderland?'

'I am a member,' Arturo shrugged. 'I have a tiny piece of land near Cassino and so I pay my tax through the *fascio*, 2/6d a year–'

He was interrupted. 'Your brother Davide Dimarco is an active member of the fascist club, is he not?'

'Davide? Well yes, but it's not what you think – the *fascio* is – what you say? – a social club.'

'Your daughter Domenica married a Pasquale Perella in July of last year. The Perellas are known fascists. Where is your daughter now?'

Arturo gawped at the man. As far as he knew, the Perellas had no political leanings; apart from a natural patriotism towards Italy, they were prosperous business people who had returned home in order to keep the family together.

'She is in Italy,' Arturo replied nervously.

'Have you heard from her since her return?'

'A couple of times.'

'And your son-in-law? What is he doing now?'

The voice was hard, the eyes already held him guilty.

'I think he is in the army. Naturally he would have been called up on his return—'

'That will be all,' his interrogator dismissed him.

Afterwards Arturo had berated himself for not mentioning his part in the Great War when Italy and Britain had fought together. Unable to get home to join up, he had volunteered with the DLI and been offered naturalisation at the end of the war. Why had he not taken it? he cursed now. Because he had been proud of being Italian; they could strip him of his livelihood and rob him of possessions, but he still had his pride in his family and his people.

He thought of them now as he straightened out his crumpled clothes and went to wash. How would they manage without him and Paolo? he fretted. He agonised over the danger they might be in and how they would feed themselves. But at least the kindly Ritsons had offered to look after them and he must take comfort from that.

For the umpteenth time he went over the events of that last horrifying night in Whitton Grange, the rioting and looting and then the arrests. It came to him, suddenly, as he splashed the trickle of cold water from the ancient tap on to his unshaven face; Signor Turnbull must have supplied the information on his family. He was the only one in authority who knew such details about them all. Arturo gave a howl of anger to think how the policeman had infiltrated his family, been welcomed in with open arms, only to betray them. How could he trust any of them again?

The man queuing behind Arturo put a hand on his shoulder to see if he was all right. Arturo turned his haggard face and stared in disbelief at the familiar figure.

'Gino!' he gasped. 'Gino.'

'Arturo!' his brother cried. 'You old bastard!'

They threw their arms around each other in delight.

Sara came home from work to find a surprise visitor sitting in Louie's kitchen. Her mother rose to greet her with a hug of affection.

'Oh, Mam! It's so good to see you. But why didn't you say you were coming?' Sara reproached. 'I would have met you.' Her face shadowed. 'It's not bad news is it? Is Tom...?'

'Tom's here,' her mother broke the news. 'He got a message to Uncle Alfred to say he's at the army hospital – up at The Grange.'

Sara's hands flew to her face. 'Is he all right?'

'He's as well as can be expected,' Lily Pallister told her daughter, 'though his left leg's shattered and giving him pain. I've been to see him. He was one of the last to get out of France – they transferred him up here last week.'

'Oh, Mam, if only I'd known I'd have gone to see him,' Sara cried.

Her mother's face clouded. 'Well, if you'd bothered to keep in touch with your uncle, you might have heard. You've been getting yourself mixed up in this Italian business, I hear.'

Sara glanced at Louie, who was busying herself

at the kitchen range.

'Your mam's staying at your Uncle Alfred's,' Louie explained. 'He tells a different story from ours...'

'Uncle Alfred stirred up all the trouble,' Sara retorted. 'He would have had them all lynched, Mam.'

'I know you're keen on this lad Joe,' her mother sighed, 'but you can't go interfering with the law, Sara. These people are a danger to our security – like it or not, they're the enemy, else they wouldn't have rounded them up. I think Alfred's right on this one, pet.'

Louie lost her patience. 'They're not dangerous! They're just defenceless women trying to do their best for their bairns while their men are locked up. It's what we'd all do, isn't it, Mrs Pallister?'

Lily looked with dislike at the woman who had enticed Sara back to Whitton Grange and away from her. 'The best thing they could have done for their families was to have gone back to Italy when this war started, instead of causing all this bother!' Lily said heatedly, reaching for her hat.

'Don't go yet, Mam,' Sara protested.

'I'll be at Alfred and Ida's for the next two days,' Lily said briskly. 'And I hope you'll think of paying your own family some attention instead of running around after those foreigners. You haven't even asked after Bill and Mary or the bairn.' Lily gave Louie a look of accusation as she bustled to the door, as if Sara's disloyal behaviour was her fault.

Louie saw the shimmer of tears in the girl's eyes

as her mother banged the back door behind her and went to put an arm about her shoulders.

'Don't worry, pet,' she comforted. 'Your mam's just a bit upset at finding Tom in hospital – it was bound to be a shock. She didn't mean to be angry with you.'

'Yes she did,' Sara said sadly. 'She had the same look on her face as Uncle Alfred when she talked about the Dimarcos – she doesn't even *know* them but she hates them. What should I do, Louie?' She buried her head in to Louie's soft bosom.

'Don't let them bully you,' Louie said stoutly. 'You stand by your friends. And go and see Tom – you'll feel better once you've seen him, I'm sure.'

But Sara's joy at being reunited with Tom was short-lived. She found him nervy and full of bitterness at the injuries to his leg.

'I'll not run again,' he said morosely. 'Left leg's as useless as a piece of wood.'

'Give it time,' Sara urged, trying to keep cheerful in the face of his black mood. Where was the joking, carefree brother she had last seen off on the bus at Lowbeck? she wondered sadly.

'Time!' Tom bemoaned. 'I've got all the bloody time in the world.'

'Is Jane Metcalfe coming to see you? Now you're back you'll be able to get married.'

'She'll not want to marry me now,' Tom said, looking at his sister with bleak blue eyes. 'She'll not want to marry a cripple.'

Sara wanted to talk to her brother about Joe and his family, but she did not have the courage to ask what Tom thought. His mind only lighted on his own problems and she left, feeling discouraged.

But on the way home her attention was diverted by a passing car on the Durham Road. It was an unusual sight to see a motorcar on this road since petrol rationing had been introduced and Sara was wondering whose it was when it braked beside her. Eleanor Kirkup threw open the passenger door and beckoned Sara into its leather-smelling interior.

'I've got news of the Dimarcos,' she told her. Sara climbed in and Eleanor drove swiftly to Pit Street.

Anna clasped her hands nervously in her lap as they gathered about the well-dressed visitor to hear what she had to say.

'It's not very encouraging, I'm afraid.' Eleanor looked at them with compassionate eyes. 'Mr Dimarco–' she stopped, realising the confusion. 'Paolo and Benito Dimarco are to be interned in a camp on the Isle of Man – that is where the majority of the men are being sent, it appears.'

Anna grasped Sylvia's hand. 'Where is that?' Anna asked for them both.

'It's an island off the west coast – not so very far,' Eleanor tried to reassure them. 'And it's possible, that from there they might be released, if they agree to help in the war effort.'

'And the others?' Elvira asked in her high-pitched voice.

Eleanor took a deep breath, dreading their reaction. 'Your husbands have been selected for deportation.'

Elvira stifled a cry.

'Where?' Anna demanded. 'Back to Italy?'

Eleanor shook her head. 'Australia and Canada have agreed to take internees.' She omitted to add what her contact in the Foreign Office had said, 'They've grudgingly agreed to take the dangerous ones.'

'So far away!' Anna cried and reached for Rosa who flung her arms about her mother. 'Can we see them before they go?' she gulped.

Eleanor's heart ached for them in their distress. 'They may already be on their way. Your husbands have been allocated tickets on a ship from Liverpool – it sails in the next couple of days. It's called the *Arandora Star*.'

Chapter Twenty-Three

Arturo and Davide were locked in discussion about what should be done. Someone somewhere was playing a harmonica and they shared a cigarette to mask the stench of hundreds of unwashed bodies closeted together in their rusting prison.

'I want to go with you, Papa.' Paolo broke in to the dispute. 'They can't separate us. I'll swap papers with Uncle Davide.'

'No, Paolo.' Arturo refused. 'Gino says you and Benito have a better chance of getting home if you are taken to a British camp. The rumours are that our group will be deported.'

'What does Gino know!' Davide exclaimed, breaking into a fit of coughing.

Arturo looked at his elder brother in alarm. He looked ten years older since the ordeal of arrest and confinement, his face tinged with yellow and his eyes darkly ringed. Yet even in these wretched conditions Davide would not speak to his estranged brother Gino who lived among the Scottish faction and had not come to Domenica's wedding. Gino was to be deported with them and Arturo suspected that accounted for Davide's reluctance to sail. But it was a shock for Arturo to see his ebullient elder brother so subdued and indecisive, looking to his son Benito for guidance in everything. The brother he had once admired

441

and looked up to was now a sick and frightened old man...

Paolo took his father aside. 'See how ill Uncle Davide is? He'll not survive a long sea voyage, Papa. Let *me* take his place and Benito can look after him.'

Arturo considered his eldest son. From a small boy, Paolo had been like his shadow; quiet and sensible, loyal and loving. He had grown from an affectionate child into a cheerful youth and was now his best companion. Arturo was secretly thankful of Paolo's insistence that they should stay together; he had been miserable at the thought of their imminent separation.

So Arturo agreed to the plan to switch papers and the next day Benito and Davide were moved out with dozens of others. The selection had been haphazard and random for many of them and Gino had told Arturo that he had simply been picked from a line and told to stand on one side. Now, like Arturo and Paolo, he had a passage on a boat.

Word filtered back that the first group of men had been sent to the Isle of Man and, the next day, Arturo, Paolo and Gino were herded in to trucks along with hundreds of other compatriots and transported to Liverpool. When they saw the size of the ship they were to board, Gino laughed, 'We're no going on a wee ferry trip, here – more like a bliddy cruise.'

'She's flying a swastika,' Paolo noticed. 'There must be German prisoners on board too.'

'Aye, that'll really impress the Nazis,' Gino joked. 'Just Hitler out for a wee paddle they'll say.'

But even his humour was blunted by the hostility of the soldiers who pushed them up the gangplank of the *Arandora Star* with their rifle butts. A man in front of them carrying a small suitcase of possessions had it snatched away and opened. His clothes spilled out and a soldier picked up a pair of drawers with his bayonet and held them aloft. The suitcase was tossed on a huge pile on the deck and, when the man protested, he was struck in the face and pushed down below deck.

Arturo was searched and his watch and chain taken, while Paolo's pockets were emptied of the few coins he had left.

'You cannie find a bliddy penny on me, pal,' Gino pulled out his pocket linings. 'Royalty don't carry money.' But the guards did not like his insolence and hit him in the back with their rifle butts, swearing at him as he staggered against Paolo.

The Italians were thrust below to the bottom deck where there was chaotic confusion as men jostled for space for themselves and their relations. Gino disappeared for ages, eventually returning with a report on the ship.

'The ballroom's full of German Jews,' he panted, 'and they're trying to keep them away from some captured German sailors – bliddy punch up's worse than Ibrox. But if we move we can get a wee cabin on the mess deck – nice and cosy.'

Arturo looked at Paolo. His son was already looking green and they had not yet pulled anchor. Here in the bowels of the ship, with the claustrophobic press of bodies, he knew his son would suffer miserably.

'Come on,' urged Gino. 'We cannie hang about – they're putting up barbed wire.'

Paolo nodded quickly and, grabbing their jackets, they followed Gino along a warren of narrow corridors. He mollified a suspicious guard with a couple of cigarettes he had tucked in the lining of his cap and found them a cabin with two other Italians, Cesare and Lucca, who originated from Milan. They were political exiles who had been working for an anti-fascist organisation in London.

'That's bliddy bad luck,' Gino commiserated. 'And now you're stuck in the same boat as a bunch of Nazi sailors. Sante Guiseppe, what madness!'

'It's blind panic on the part of the government,' Cesare replied in a cultured voice. 'We've been in England since 1922 and we know who the Italian fascists are in Britain. Yet no one has asked us for information.' He regarded them dolefully through round spectacles. 'They just see a foreign face or hear a foreign name and decide to lock us all up – the snakes in with the lambs.'

'And have you seen many Italian snakes on board?' Gino asked, curious.

Cesare shook his head. 'Snakes have the habit of wriggling out of reach. All I see on this ship are a bunch of shopkeepers and waiters – you're about as politically aware as sheep,' he said with a touch of disdain.

The phrase 'lambs to the slaughter' came into Arturo's mind, but he kept the thought to himself. 'Where are we being taken, do you know?' he asked.

Cesare lifted his glasses and rubbed his eyes as he replied, 'Canada. We're lucky – some of the poor blighters are being shipped to Australia. Imagine being stuck on a ship like this for weeks.'

In the early hours of July 1st, the *Arandora Star* set sail into the North Atlantic, unescorted and flying the Nazi flag to denote to the enemy that they carried German prisoners. Paolo was sick before breakfast time, but as breakfast did not materialise he spent the rest of the day retching spittle as the ship rose and fell among the white spume.

Gino played cards with his Milanese cabin mates while Arturo attempted to sleep. But insomnia had plagued him since his arrest and he made them all edgy with his restlessness. Constantly his thoughts went back to Anna and Rosa and the grandchildren and wondered how they would cope without him for so long. Canada was another world away; how would he ever return home from there? Bobby was too young to take the responsibility of the family on his narrow shoulders and Joe...

Arturo felt a great stab of regret when he thought of his son Joseph and the times they had wasted quarrelling. Perhaps he had been too hard on Joe, expecting him to be as compliant and dutiful as Paolo, suppressing his extrovert nature and disapproving of his lively friends. And had he been right to discourage Joe's liaison with Sara? Arturo wondered. But then, how could he have known how little time for happiness had remained to them all before this hateful war had destroyed their lives? Soon Joe would be fighting for the Allies, possibly even against people of his own blood. Arturo turned to the wall to hide the tears of desolation that trickled down his leathery face and dampened his thick moustache.

Early next morning Arturo woke from a fitful doze to see Paolo gazing out of the porthole at the dawn. It shone pink on his square, open face, for a moment as vulnerable as a child's. Seeing his lips move noiselessly, Arturo suddenly realised his son was praying. He looked away quickly, not wanting to intrude on the intimate act, but Paolo sensed he was being watched and turned to see his father awake.

'Papa,' he smiled...

There followed an almighty boom which shook the whole ship. The others woke up instantly and Gino blasphemed as the vessel juddered like a wounded beast.

'We've been hit!' Cesare shouted, scrambling from his bunk fully dressed. Opening the door he saw the corridor was plunged in darkness, and others were spilling out of cabins in the rush to escape as the sirens wailed. The next minutes were ones of horrifying confusion as men groped and cried out one another's names. Arturo was paralysed with fright. He had no idea what they should do; there had been no boat drill in the event of an emergency and he did not know where to go.

'Bliddy hurry up, Arturo!' Gino swore at his brother.

'Haway, Papa,' Paolo coaxed him, his voice

betraying no alarm and Arturo marvelled at his coolness as he pushed him firmly after Gino.

They stumbled up the corridor looking for a door that would allow them onto the open deck. The ship was already listing, making them stagger as if drunk and knock into the other passengers. Someone found a door.

'The poor buggers below!' Gino shuddered as they felt the blast of fresh air on their faces and pushed their way outside. Arturo felt horror grip his stomach to think of the scores of men stuck beneath them on 'A' deck, locked in by barbed wire, trapped in the pitch black.

'This way, Papa!' Paolo urged, dragging him by the arm.

No one seemed to be in charge and no officers were coordinating an evacuation. Gino spotted a group of Italians attempting to loosen the ropes of a lifeboat with little success. He went to help. Precious minutes passed as they failed to release the boat, then two young German prisoners pushed their way to the fore, shouting instructions that no one could understand.

They managed to winch the lifeboat over the side and there followed a desperate scramble for places. The German sailors went onto the next boat, but there were now hundreds of men on deck hoping for rescue. Even Arturo could see the number of lifeboats was totally inadequate for the overcrowded ship. Some were already jumping into the choppy grey waters of the Atlantic, fifty feet below, while others were throwing things they thought might float into the water and jumping after them. A barrel went hurtling into the sea and

447

landed on a man below, a slipstream of blood oozing from the man's head as he sunk into the steel-grey water.

'Lifejackets!' Gino cried, grabbing at the cork ones he found stowed in a locker. 'Stick this on,' he told Arturo.

An officer near them was wielding a hatchet to cut the ropes of a raft that was strapped to the railings. Paolo rushed to help him and together they hurled it over the side of the sinking ship.

'Jump, Papa!' Paolo ordered.

'I can't swim,' Arturo argued. 'You go.'

'You've got a lifejacket on, you'll be all right.' Paolo pushed him to the railings.

'I'll jump with you,' Gino said and grabbed him. 'Close your eyes and pray like hell.'

'You too?' Arturo turned anxiously to his son.

'I'll follow,' Paolo assured him and helped Gino heave his father on to the railings.

Arturo closed his eyes and felt himself rushing through cold air, hitting the icy water with a smack that nearly knocked him out. He howled from the shock of the fall and the excruciating cold of the sea. All around him, figures bobbed and splashed in the half-light, crying for help. Only yards away he could see where the metal bow of the ship had been torn by the treacherous torpedo, the sea gushing into its gaping side. The flimsy swastika had not saved them from a deadly U-boat.

Straining around for Gino, Arturo could see no sign of his brother and he became aware that his saturated clothing was dragging him down. He clung to the cork jacket which bobbed around his neck, loosened in the drop, and called out Gino's name.

Steadily Arturo began to lose sensation in his legs as numbness gripped him and he became strangely calm as he realised he was going to die. He began to pray, then hands from behind grabbed his lifejacket and he found himself being hauled on to a raft. Arturo tumbled backwards and looked up in to the face of Cesare, the anti-fascist.

'Paddle like hell!' an officer commanded.

'Gino?' Arturo gasped. 'And Paolo?'

'I haven't seen them,' Cesare answered, heaving Arturo to a sitting position. The men on board began to paddle frantically with their bare hands.

Arturo looked back at the dying ship and searched for Paolo's stocky frame. They were still close enough to make out faces, but he could not see his son, so perhaps he had already jumped. Young German sailors were stripping off and plunging naked in to the sea; fully clothed men were swiftly drowned by their sodden clothes. He watched a packed lifeboat being lowered precariously, but it hit the ship's bow at an angle and lurched into the water, tumbling passengers on top of each other and tossing them into the sea like rag dolls.

Suddenly among the rows of older men still lined up at the railings, Arturo spotted Paolo. He was looking out on the mayhem, watching to see if his father and uncle were safe, his arm around a behatted old man.

'Stop!' Arturo choked. 'My son, *Madonna!* Wait for my son, please!'

Someone struck him on the head as he rose in panic.

'You'll have us all drowned, you bloody fool!' the officer shouted. 'Do that again and I'll throw you over myself.'

Cesare seized Arturo's shoulders to restrain him. Arturo looked back in desperation as the ship was consumed by the greedy Atlantic.

'Jump, Paolo!' he bawled, *'Sante Guiseppe,* jump!'

Put Paolo made no attempt to follow. It was then Arturo noticed that he no longer wore a lifejacket; he must have surrendered it to someone else and, without it, he had no chance of survival in the water. They were mountain people, they could not swim. Why had no one ever taught his boy to swim? Arturo wept.

Almost at the last moment, as silver light grew in the sky and lit up the doomed ship and the water round about, Arturo thought Paolo saw him. His son raised a hand in farewell, but whether to him or the flotsam of prisoners scattered on the sea, Arturo was uncertain.

A minute later the *Arandora Star* was sucked into the deep with a sigh of capitulation, taking with her the hundreds of stranded men who had stood in dignified acceptance of their fate.

The sea bubbled and gurgled for minutes, drowning the cries of those still attempting to reach the lifeboats. Arturo buried his face in his numb hands and wept uncontrollably, knowing that the sight of his first-born going to his death would haunt him forever...

'Please can you help them?' Sara asked Dolly Sergeant for the third time that day. 'Give them a few things on tick – just till the travellers come round again.'

'I've got a business to run too, lass,' Mrs Sergeant grumbled. 'You'd think I was made of money the way you go on.'

'Mrs Dimarco's got relations staying from Sunderland now – they can't go home,' Sara persisted. 'If you could just give them a bit of flour and margarine for baking and some sugar–'

'Sugar!' Dolly Sergeant nearly exploded. 'I can't spare any *sugar* – I get my allocation and that's that.'

But Sara knew that somehow her employer was managing to get a larger allocation of goods than other shops and she wondered if it had anything to do with her Uncle Alfred who appeared to be favoured when sought-after commodities came in, such as cigarettes and fresh fruit. She knew her uncle had contacts everywhere and would not be above helping Mrs Sergeant in a spot of black marketeering if he got something out of it, too.

Sara got nowhere with her pleading and the rest of the day was spent in frosty silence, except for the occasional barked command from the ill-tempered grocer. The next morning, Dolly Sergeant was on the attack.

'I'm going to offer Raymond Kirkup his old job back,' she announced, before Sara had tied on her overall, 'You said he's hanging around with nothing to do – well, he can be a help to me.'

'And what am I going to do?' Sara asked,

451

completely taken by surprise. The deliveries were now her preserve and she resented the thought of having to give them up, even to Raymond.

'You can do what you did before – helping in the storeroom and stacking the shelves,' Dolly Sergeant said, her breathing laboured as she moved around the shop.

'But I like going out on the bike!' Sara protested. 'You can't just take me job off me.'

'I'll run my business how I like, young lady,' Dolly snapped, her puffy face growing red.

Sara's eyes narrowed. 'Has my uncle been on at you to get rid of me or something?' she asked in suspicion.

Dolly Sergeant sought refuge in her account books. 'It's my decision and I'm not getting rid of you – I just don't want you doing the deliveries any more.'

Suddenly the truth dawned on Sara. 'Has this anything to do with me being friendly with the Dimarcos?' she asked.

Dolly Sergeant's look was defensive. 'Your association with them foreigners isn't helping business,' she admitted. 'I've had complaints and I'd rather not have you out doing deliveries. Now, if you were to stop spending your time with the Italians, I might reconsider...'

Sara was stunned by the woman's heartlessness; she obviously cared nothing for the distress of the Dimarcos who were once her valued customers.

'You selfish old woman!' Sara accused hotly. 'These people have had their husbands interned and don't know how they'll survive – and all you

452

think about is your precious business!'

Dolly Sergeant's down-covered face turned purple with indignation.

'How dare you talk to me like that, you wicked lass!' she thundered. 'Get out of my shop – I'll not have you in it a minute longer. You're sacked!'

'And I wouldn't stay for all the tea in China!' Sara retaliated, tearing off her overall and throwing it on the floor. 'I'll not be threatened by you or any of your small-minded customers. The Dimarcos are worth ten of your kind.'

With that, Sara stormed from the shop, grabbing her string bag and cardigan from the storeroom as she went. But by the time she reached Hawthorn Street, her fury had subsided and she wondered whether she had spoken too hastily. Not only was she out of a job, but there was now no chance of Dolly Sergeant supplying the Dimarcos with anything. She ran in to tell Louie what she had done and found the pitman's wife straining over the tub in the washhouse. Sara felt a stab of guilt at the thought that she had just forgone her meagre wages, but Louie was more philosophical about Sara's rash words.

'It's Dolly Sergeant who's in the wrong, not you, pet,' Louie said, thumping the poss stick up and down. 'You'll find something else. Anyways, if she's offering Raymond some work we'll have some wages coming in, so don't you worry.'

But Sara *did* worry about being a burden to the long-suffering Louie. If she found nothing else, she thought gloomily, she might have to return home to Weardale, but she had parted on frosty terms with her mother after her visit to Tom at

The Grange and knew that her family also hated her involvement with the Italians. Above all, it was the thought of not being able to help the Dimarcos if she were miles away at Stout House that made Sara the more determined to find employment. Even if it was voluntary war work that might provide her with the odd meal away from Louie's she would be glad to take it and she wanted to be more useful than she had been lining the pockets of Dolly Sergeant.

That afternoon, deciding to visit Tom, an idea came to her as she made towards The Grange. Passing servicemen hosing down military ambulances and the row of tents pitched on the tennis courts, Sara entered the vast mansion by the front steps.

'Yes?' a clerk at the reception desk in the hall demanded, glancing at her over wire-rimmed spectacles.

'I want to help,' Sara said, feeling foolish.

'Help?' He gave her an impatient look.

'I want to volunteer for something,' she smiled.

'Look, we're not the Girl Guides,' he said and waved her away. 'And we're expecting another lot of wounded in the next few hours. Be a good girl and hop it.'

Sara reddened at the man's officious attitude, all the more determined not to be dismissed as a nuisance.

'Perhaps there's something I could do in the kitchens? I'm a canny cook.'

The clerk gave a short sigh. 'We have our own personnel. Go back home and help your mother in her kitchen like a girl should, eh?'

454

'Listen, I'm not just out of nappies, I'm seventeen,' Sara raised her voice. 'I've got a wounded brother lying upstairs in this hospital and the lad I'm courting's in the DLI and might be one of the next to come here – that's if he's lucky! They're doing their bit for their country and I want to do mine – so don't treat me like a bairn! I heard you were taking lasses on in the kitchens last month. Have you got something for me or not?'

The clerk gawped at her then rustled the paper in front of him.

'Orderly!' he called at a passing soldier. 'Take this girl round to the tradesman's entrance and see if there's anything she can do.'

The bald-headed orderly nodded and smiled and Sara fell in beside him. He led her down a warren of corridors, the strong smells of disinfectant and steaming cabbage advancing in waves to greet them.

But to Sara's disappointment there was no work to be had in the kitchens. She was about to give up when the orderly suggested they could do with another hand in the laundry as one of the local girls hired had suddenly left to get married.

'It's damn hard work,' Miles, the orderly, grinned.

'I'll start tomorrow,' Sara said, undaunted, and went to tell Tom of her new situation and her delight in securing paid work. She found him in better humour than the last, strained visit when her mother had pleaded with Sara to have nothing to do with her Italian friends.

Tom was teasing a nurse and showing a flicker

of his old spirit and Sara was pleased to see him attempting to walk with crutches.

'So they're trusting you to keep my sheets clean? What's the army coming to?' he joked.

'I'll be able to see you more often,' Sara smiled.

'I only speak to nurses – not washerwomen,' Tom said, winking at the nurse.

'Dirty sheets for Private Pallister, then,' Sara laughed. She left without either of them mentioning the Italians.

That evening the Ritsons sat around the kitchen table discussing what the could do to help the Dimarcos.

'They should start growing their own vegetables,' Raymond suggested.

Sam nodded. 'Aye, we could help them dig up some of their back yard – it's big enough.'

'Perhaps Eb would come over and help,' Louie said, thinking of how gifted a gardener her eldest brother had been when he had lived with them.

'Ssh!' Jacob suddenly hushed them. 'Listen to the news.' He turned the wireless up as loud as he could to catch the day's events, the one gloomy occupation he still seemed to enjoy.

Their attention was riveted by the announcement of the sinking of the *Arandora Star*. She was carrying prisoners-of-war ... some Italian enemies ... torpedoed by a German U-boat ... not known how many on board ... some survivors have been picked up by a Canadian destroyer.

'Dear God!' Sara gasped. 'Joe's father and Uncle Davide were on board.'

'Oh heaven's above!' Louie's hand reached to

grab Sara's. 'Those poor women.'

'I must go to them,' Sara said, jumping up from the table. Without hesitation, Louie pulled off her apron and seized her hat from the back of the door, following Sara out of the house.

They found Anna Dimarco, pale with shock at the news and Sylvia trying to comfort a distraught Aunt Elvira and Albina.

'They may have been picked up,' Sara tried to comfort them.

'Oh, *Madonna! Santa Teresa!* Help us!' Elvira sobbed.

'How can we know?' Anna asked in distress. 'There are no names... We know nothing!'

'Papa is dead!' Albina was hysterical. 'And Uncle Arturo.'

'Shut up! Shut up!' Rosa cried at her cousin. 'Sara's right – we must wait–'

'Wait?' Elvira looked on the verge of fainting. 'How can we bear to wait? I wish I was dead, too.'

Sara and Louie felt quite helpless, but stayed with the distraught family. Later that evening Eleanor Kirkup arrived in her car from Durham, having heard of the tragedy.

'I'll try and get news of the survivors,' she promised. 'I'm so sorry – it's all I can do.'

The next day, Sara had to start work at the hospital laundry and it was late in the afternoon before she got away. Rosa's small, anxious face told her that they had heard nothing and it was not until nearly a week later that Eleanor returned with news that Arturo was among the survivors and was recovering in a Scottish hospital. Anna gripped the counter of the empty shop as she listened beside Rosa and Bobby.

'It's likely he'll be sent to the Isle of Man once he's well enough to travel,' Eleanor told Anna.

'Oh, *Santa Teresa* be praised!' The woman's drawn face relaxed in relief. 'Your papa's alive!'

Rosa and Bobby embraced their mother tearfully.

'But Davide?' Anna asked, suddenly concerned. 'Is there good news for his family, too?'

Eleanor shook her head. 'I'm sorry – I've not been able to find out what happened to Davide Dimarco. There were no proper lists of passengers – it was all done in such haste...'

Anna's eyes flickered to the flat above where Elvira and Albina were making soup.

'What am I going to tell them?' she whispered.

For two weeks Elvira pulled the curtains closed and did not leave the flat, already mourning her lost husband. Nothing the others could say would change her mind. Anna, rallied by the news of Arturo's lucky escape, found a new determination to get their shattered business running once more. They no longer had enough sugar or butter to make their famous ice-cream, but with a recipe from Louie Ritson, using arrowroot flavouring and dried milk, they experimented with making a mock cream. Bobby and Rosa, who laboured in the shed stirring and scraping the concoction, thought it tasteless, but Anna was optimistic and opened the shop door for business. With Sara's help they erected a large sign outside advertising, 'Tasty New Cream – British made', and before long, inquisitive and sweet-toothed children were coming in to try it.

'If you covered over the family name above the shop,' Sara suggested tentatively, 'you might get more custom.'

'Dimarco is our name!' Anna protested. 'I'm not ashamed of who we are. What would Arturo say?'

'Perhaps we should, Mamma,' Rosa added pressure. 'Just for a while.'

'People will forget the bad feeling soon enough,' Sara coaxed, 'but it doesn't do to remind them. I'm sure Mr Dimarco will understand.'

So Anna gave reluctant consent and Sam and Raymond came to paint over the golden letters of Dimarco and replace them with the anglicised 'Arthur's Cafe' instead and that weekend, the trickle of customers grew, Anna ran out of new cream and, with the takings, she and Rosa went to the Co-operative Store to buy more ingredients.

The next week Eb Kirkup, Eleanor's artist husband, turned up to help Sam and Raymond create an allotment in the Dimarcos' back yard.

'He was the best gardener in Whitton before he took to painting,' Sam told Rosa as she watched them heave up the old cobbles.

Rosa was fascinated to see a real artist and could not take her eyes from the bald man with the gingerish beard and startlingly blue eyes. He said little and Rosa wondered how this mild-mannered man had ever had the temerity to cause such a scandal in the village by eloping with the wife of the local coalowner.

Rosa knew the story of Eb and Eleanor's

romance from Sara and wished she had had the courage to leave with Emilio at the end of that sunny summer. For what kind of life was she able to give her daughter Mary, an outcast in her own village, with no man to protect or provide for her, carrying the added shame of her illegitimacy? At times her yearning for the handsome Emilio Fella still engulfed Rosa and left her feeling resentful towards her family.

Then Rosa chided herself for her self-pity. How could she think such disloyal thoughts at a time when her family needed her more than ever? She had never felt closer to her mother than during those last few weeks – and they could not complain when they had friends like Sara and the Ritsons and the Kirkups who were standing by them.

She turned to see Sara coming through the back gate, waving a letter.

'The postman's just handed me this,' Sara called to her, her fair face flushed. 'The postmark's the Isle of Man.'

Rosa seized it and went rushing into the house. 'It's Papa's writing, I know it is!' Sam and Eb stopped and looked up as Sara hurried inside after her friend.

The news caused consternation among the women as they gathered around Rosa in the upstairs kitchen, leaving Bobby to man the downstairs shop.

'Read it, Rosa,' Anna urged, yanking back the curtain to let light into the darkened room where Elvira and Albina spent their days brooding.

Rosa tore at the envelope and scanned the page

of shaky script.

'I can't read Papa's writing,' she said in frustration.

Anna grabbed the letter and thrust it at Sara. 'Please,' she begged, 'read it to me.'

Sara looked at them all shyly; Elvira and Albina were suspicious but Rosa and her mother regarded her with eager faces. Sylvia was trying to hush an excited Peter who was demanding to know what the fuss was about.

'Dearest Anna,' Sara began, 'I am in a camp on the Isle of Man. I was on the ship that sank but God chose to save me. Benito and Davide are in the same camp–'

'Davide?' Elvira whispered. 'Did you say *Davide?*'

Sara repeated the line and went on, 'We are all well. If you hear from Elvira, tell her. Davide has had no reply to his letters.'

Elvira looked at the letter as if it came from beyond the grave, unable to comprehend its message.

'Papa's alive?' Albina shrieked and smothered her fragile mother in a hug. 'He thinks we are still in Sunderland, that's why we haven't heard from him. Oh, Mamma!'

'Davide didn't drown,' Elvira said in disbelief. 'He didn't drown!' Then she burst into tears. Anna went to her and hugged her in relief and excited chattering broke out in the kitchen. It was then that Sara glanced at the rest of the letter.

Her mouth went dry at what she read and she found herself unable to speak. It was Sylvia who

461

noticed first. She had kept quiet as the others celebrated, for there had been no news of her Paolo.

'What is it?' Sylvia asked Sara. 'What else does Papa say?'

Sara began to shake.

Anna's face paled. 'Tell us Sara.'

Sara forced herself to read on, 'I wish I could be with you to tell you this. Our beloved Paolo and my brother Gino were drowned when the ship went down. They saved my life. I saw Paolo go under. Now our good son is with the saints. I pray for Sylvia and the children.'

Sylvia let out a soft moan. 'But he wasn't on the ship! How can he be dead?'

They all turned to look at Paolo's young wife as she clutched Peter to her side and screwed her eyes tight against her tears.

'Not Paolo, *please* not Paolo,' she said in supplication.

'Mammy, are you all right?' Peter asked in confusion as his mother doubled up in grief.

Rosa skirted the table quickly and put her arms around her sister-in-law and Paolo's small son.

'Oh, Rosa...' Sylvia whispered, clutching at her for comfort. 'How can I tell the bairns?'

Chapter Twenty-Four

Sara stood on a chair and fixed the end of the silver tinsel to one of Louie's picture hooks. She had treated them to a few gaudy strands and a handful of painted wooden decorations to adorn the parlour mantelpiece and to bring some cheer to the second sombre Christmas of the war. Sara knew Louie was missing young Stan, who had gone home to Tyneside for the holidays and she was also worried about her father, Jacob, who had not risen from his bed upstairs for two weeks.

Sam had been taken on at the Eleanor again, after a flood of young miners had been released for military service in October, among them the cantankerous Norman Bell who had gone off to join the navy. Raymond, however, swayed by a Christmas bonus and the arrival of the green-eyed Nancy Bell as Dolly Sergeant's assistant, had decided to stay on at the grocery store. Louie was discussing her nephew now.

'Does he talk to you about young Nancy?' Louie asked with a frown.

Sara pushed back her long hair and considered Louie. 'Not much. She seems canny enough, though – full of beans.'

'Aye,' Louie grimaced, 'too full I reckon – just like her mother.'

'I thought Minnie Bell was an old friend of

yours, Louie?' Sara asked in surprise.

'We were very close once,' Louie sighed. 'Then things came between us – Sam fell out with her husband Bomber over the strike – and there were other things...'

Sara did not want to hear any more about the wretched strike that had happened so long ago and yet still seemed to hold such a grip on them all. Neither did she care if Minnie Bell were out of favour in the Ritson household, for it still rankled to think that Minnie's gossiping had started all the trouble between Uncle Alfred and the Dimarcos. But that was hardly the dark-haired Nancy's fault, Sara admitted.

'Nancy's barely fourteen – she'll not be interested in lads yet,' Sara smiled. 'And I wouldn't worry about Raymond – all he thinks about is football.'

'Aye. I'm just a born worrier,' Louie confessed with a shake of her head. 'Now that looks bonny!' She stood back and admired Sara's handiwork. 'Hildy will be pleased to see we've made an effort – to think it should've been her first Christmas with Wilfred...'

Louie broke off and looked at Sara, knowing how concerned she was for the bereaved Dimarcos.

'How is Sylvia Dimarco?' Louie asked.

Sara shrugged. 'She doesn't say much – not when I'm there. And she's so thin. Rosa says she only keeps going for the children.'

'Poor lass,' Louie tutted. 'I wish there was more we could do.'

Sara climbed off the chair. 'You've been grand,

Louie – all your family have,' Sara assured her. 'And Eleanor Kirkup's being doing all she can to get the men released,' Sara said, 'not to mention your brother Eb chasing up his old contacts in the DLI.'

'Aye, I know Eb tries, but they'll not listen to him now – not since he signed the Peace Pledge,' Louie answered.

'It seems so unfair,' Sara said in annoyance. 'There's Joe in the army and his father treated like a spy... Oh, Louie, when will I see Joe again?'

Louie gave Sara a hug. 'Perhaps they'll give him some leave soon, pet.' She pulled back and looked into Sara's dejected face. 'How about us inviting the Dimarcos for Christmas dinner? With Da in bed and Stan away home, we'll be rattling around the parlour. That's if you're going to stop too?' Louie scrutinised.

'Aye I'm stopping,' Sara said at once. 'Especially since Tom's still here. Oh, Louie, that would be champion! Do you think we could manage them all?'

'Why-aye,' Louie laughed. 'Mam used to feed just as many when I was a lass. What about Tom?'

Sara's face fell. Tom had been convalescing at the Cummingses' since his release from hospital in November, the doctors having been satisfied with his gradual recovery. With Colin away on the farm, there was more room for Tom at Uncle Alfred's than at Stout House where Bill and Mary were occupying his bedroom. 'I doubt he'd come,' Sara answered. 'Uncle Alfred's turned him against the Dimarcos and he won't listen to me when I try to talk about Joe or his family. Tom

465

doesn't see why Joe's father shouldn't spend the rest of the war locked up when the Italians are fighting us in Africa!'

'I suppose his comrades *are* out there in the thick of it...' Louie was philosophical. 'You can see how he feels.'

'Well, he should have a bit more feeling for Joe,' Sara sparked. *'He's* lost his brother.'

'You don't have to tell me, pet,' Louie's voice trembled. 'I know just how he must feel.'

'Sorry, Louie.' Sara squeezed her arm remembering how Louie had lost her brother Davie. 'I say things without thinking sometimes.'

After work the next day, Sara hurried down to Pit Street to issue Louie's invitation. The afternoon air was raw and Anna Dimarco was closing up the chilly shop and pulling the blackout blinds. In the gloom her face was wan as a ghost's, her tightly bound hair lined with silver like snails' trails that glinted in the dim light.

She ushered Sara upstairs with her usual politeness, but still with that touch of reserve that reminded Sara she was just a visitor, whatever they had experienced together.

'I'm sorry I haven't been for a while – what with working at The Grange and doing ARP duty–'

'No need for sorry.' Anna waved aside her apology. 'Rosa is glad to see you when you can come.'

Sylvia's children were romping on the small sofa and Rosa was changing Mary's nappy on the floor while Elvira and Sylvia cooked at the stove and Albina sat wrapped in a coat and blanket, sneezing into a handkerchief.

466

Linda fell off the sofa with a wail, sending Peter scurrying to Sara and demanding to play leapfrog.

'Not in here, Peter,' Anna said in exasperation. 'And be gentle with your sister.'

Sara diverted an impending tantrum with her Christmas invitation. The older women looked at each other doubtfully.

'It's very kind of Mrs Ritson,' Anna began, 'but we cannot–'

'Oh, yes Mamma,' Rosa interrupted, 'it would be fun to have Christmas with Sara. The children would love it and it would do us all good. Say yes, Mamma!'

A discussion broke out in Italian in which they all gave vent to their opinions. Finally Anna had the last word.

'Please tell Mrs Ritson we are happy to have the dinner with her family. She is a good woman. Thank you.'

Sara left, heartened to see how their spirits were lifted by the prospect of Christmas in another home, away from the house at Pit Street, so full of painful reminders of the past. Hilda came home two days before Christmas from her anti-aircraft battery in Newcastle and helped Sara and Louie make stuffed toys for the Dimarco children from old scraps of material and Sam's pipe cleaners.

Christmas Eve was Sara's eighteenth birthday and, just as she was leaving the hospital laundry, she ran in to a gaggle of young carol singers gathered on the steps outside The Grange and listened entranced to the wavering, high-pitched voices of St Cuthbert's Sunday School as they sang in the dark to the blacked-out mansion. The moon had not yet risen, but a flicker of screened torches wavered among them like fairy lights. Moving closer, Sara made out the muffled figure of her cousin Marina. Beside her stood Tom in an army coat.

An officer came out and invited the children in to the house.

'Splendid singing – perhaps you could repeat a couple of carols in some of the wards?' he requested.

As the choir scrambled eagerly for the stairs, Sara dashed towards Tom and Marina and greeted them.

'Will you call and see us tomorrow?' Sara asked her brother, knowing she was not welcome at her uncle's home.

'I'll try,' he said, looking embarrassed, 'but you know what Uncle thinks about the Ritsons.' Sara had heard from Louie how Alfred Cummings was making life difficult for Sam at the pit because of his friendship with the Dimarcos and it annoyed Sara that her brother would not put himself out to see her on such a special day.

'Tom, I'm family!' Sara chided.

Marina regarded the two of them. 'Tom's more fun than you are,' she told Sara spitefully. 'And Mam and Dad like him better than you. We *never* have arguments like when you lived with us.'

Sara gave her cousin a look of exasperation and, turning to her brother, said accusingly, 'Happy families, eh? You've changed your tune about Uncle Alfred quick enough.'

'He's not as bad as you think, once you get to know him,' Tom said defensively. 'Treats me like a son.'

At first Tom had been suspicious and awkward about the attention Alfred heaped upon him, praising his bravery in France while bemoaning his disappointment in Colin as a son. But Tom had come to enjoy the cosiness and attention at South Parade and the adoration from his Aunt Ida and cousin Marina.

Sara humphed in disgust at Tom's siding with the Cummingses.

'Come on, Tom,' Marina said and pulled him after her. 'We'll miss the mince pies.'

Tom hesitated, not wanting to part on bad terms with his sister.

'I could have a word with Aunt Ida – see if she'll have you round for tea – she does a grand tea,' Tom grinned.

Sara decided to be frank. 'The Dimarcos are coming to us for Christmas – I'll be helping Mrs Ritson.'

Tom scowled and dropped his hand from her shoulder. 'I don't understand you, Sara,' he complained, 'choosing to be with strangers rather than your own family at Christmas – it's not natural.'

'If I'm closer to the Ritsons and Dimarcos than to most of my own family,' Sara was indignant, 'then it's only because they've shown me more friendship and love than my own kin!'

For a moment Sara thought her brother would hit her in his fury – and for the first time she saw the look of disgust on his face which was so like

Uncle Alfred's.

'Uncle's right – you're wayward and ungrateful!' he snapped and, turning on his weak leg, hobbled away from her without a backward glance. He had not even wished her a happy birthday, Sara thought bitterly. Spinning round, Sara sprinted across the gravel drive away from the hurtful scene, determined not to let the argument upset her or spoil her Christmas.

The last train to heave into Whitton Station that evening was overflowing with servicemen and civilians attempting to reach their families for the brief holiday. Throwing his kit bag out of the moving train and jumping after it, Joe landed on the crowded platform and flicked his Woodbine on to the track. Pat Slattery fell out after him and the two friends marched shoulder to shoulder, joking as they went, Pat trying to keep Joe's mind from the thought of an emotional reunion with his depleted family.

'Fancy a pint at the Durham Ox on the way home?' Pat suggested. 'Lad on the train said they've just had a beer ration.'

'No, better go straight to Pit Street,' Joe said with reluctance.

'Haway, just a half to wet the whistle...' Pat jostled his friend.

'Typical Slattery,' Joe teased, 'not happy till you're pissed.'

Pat grabbed him round the neck and laughed, 'And all you can think about is lasses and how to–'

Joe clamped a hand over Pat's obscenity and

they broke in to a friendly tussle, attracting the attention of two members of the Home Guard who came to intervene. One turned out to be Bomber Bell, Pat's brother-in-law, who gave them a lift in to Whitton Grange and deposited them outside the Durham Ox, offering to buy them a pint.

'Take advantage,' Pat told Joe. 'Bomber's only nice to his Slattery relations once a year – before Mam's Christmas dinner.'

The bar was unusually crowded, but a fuss was made of the servicemen as pitmen bought them watered-down beer and shared precious cigarettes, demanding to be told what they knew of the war. Pat and Joe had been training in Wales and had no idea where they would go next, but spun a yarn about a top secret mission which brought a flurry of extra drinks.

Joe was about to wish Pat a merry Christmas and leave when a drunken Norman Bell fell through the door in his able seaman's uniform with Dick Scott and his former workmates in support.

'There's that bastar' Dimarco,' Normy slurred. 'Haven't locked you up yet like the rest of 'em?'

Joe bristled and Pat put a restraining hand on his arm. 'Steady.'

'Pint,' Normy ordered. The barman ignored him. 'I said a pint!'

'Looks like you've had plenty, son,' Bomber Bell said to his cousin. 'We don't want any trouble in here.'

'No trouble – want to buy this hero a drink.' Normy pushed his way to Joe. 'Hey, don't turn your back on me, Dimarco!'

Joe felt anger rising inside, ready to choke him. Here was the lad who had led the attack on his parents' shop, who had terrorised his family. If it had not been for narrow-minded men like Normy Bell, his brother Paolo would still be alive today.

'Leave him alone,' Pat Slattery ordered.

'Not doing any harm,' Normy sneered. 'Just want to ask Dimarco if he's pleased the British have kicked the I-ties out of Libya. That must please you, eh? Dimarco the wop!'

Joe turned and struck Norman Bell with a well-aimed right punch that felled the sailor in an instant. He was sprawling on the floor before he saw the punch coming. Scotty retaliated by kicking Pat Slattery in the groin and a fight erupted in the crowded bar.

It took ten minutes for the police to arrive and the fighters to be ejected into the street, by which time Joe had a black eye and grazed temple, Pat's cheekbone was broken and Norman Bell was carried out unconscious.

Sara, on ARP duty, came rushing from Hawthorn Street with Sam to find out what was causing the commotion. When Sam saw it was brawling he told Sara to go home, but in the moonlight she recognised Joe's tall figure.

'Joe!' she cried and rushed towards him. He turned from the groaning Pat, his face breaking into a grin of delight at seeing her. Throwing his arms wide he enveloped her in a beery embrace.

'When did you get here?' Sara demanded, breathless.

'A couple of hours ago.' Joe hugged her again.

'Just long enough to cause some bother,' the portly Constable Simpson butted in. 'Why don't you get along home, lad?' The policeman was content to shrug off the disturbance as holiday high spirits, unhappy at the thought of arresting Joe after what had happened to his family. He ordered everyone else home to their beds.

'I'll see Pat home to his mam's,' Sam told the young couple, embarrassed by their public embracing.

Joe walked Sara back to Hawthorn Street, their arms linked around each other possessively as she told him the plans for Christmas day.

In the backlane Joe pulled Sara to him again. 'I've thought of you every day, bonny lass,' he whispered. 'Happy birthday, pet.' He kissed her enthusiastically and Sara was delighted he had remembered.

For several minutes they stood shivering and kissing, then Joe finally asked, 'Can I come in?'

'I think you should get home,' Sara said gently. 'They'll be that pleased to see you.' Sara saw the hesitation in his face. 'It'll be all right. Your mam's been very brave – she's kept them all strong – I wouldn't have believed it.'

'And Sylvia?' Joe asked.

Sara thought of the skeletal, withdrawn young woman shrouded in black, who found it hard to smile at her children.

'I think Sylvia needs loving back to life...' Sara answered and kissed Joe on the lips.

'Till tomorrow then, *bellissima.*' He kissed her hand and walked off in the moonlight. Five minutes later he was in his own backyard throwing stones up at Rosa's window and his sister's shrieks of delight at discovering who the intruder was banished all his anxiety at what he might find.

They lit candles and brought out cold sausage and bread and a bottle of Arturo's homemade wine to celebrate Joe's return and sat up half the night. They talked and wept and listened and occasionally laughed at Joe's tales of army life, until finally Anna sent them all to bed.

'Tomorrow we go to mass and give thanks that Joseph is with us for Christmas,' she decreed.

'And light candles for our loved ones who are not with us,' Elvira added sombrely, thinking of her own scattered family.

Sylvia sniffed and then let out a howl of grief. Rosa rushed to her, never having heard her sob so openly before, but Sylvia shook her off. Joe stepped round the table and put his arms about his sister-in-law, resisting her attempts to push him away.

'Cry all you want, pet,' he told her gently, 'it's time you did,' and he felt her lean against him as she shook with sorrow.

The chapel was packed on Christmas morning and Sara sat with the Ritsons and Hilda and Raymond and joined in the lusty carol singing, wondering if her mother and family were doing the same at Lowbeck. She felt a new surge of goodwill towards them and vowed to herself that she would go and see them soon, even contemplating a visit to Tom and the Cummingses over

474

the holidays.

Afterwards, Sam escaped to the pub and Raymond disappeared on some ploy of his own, leaving the women to return and make ready the lunch for their numerous guests. The kitchen and parlour tables were pushed together and covered with linen tablecloths and set with the extra cutlery and crockery that Hilda had borrowed from her mother-in-law, Edie Parkin. Louie had invited the Parkins, too, so they would not spend Christmas alone, brooding over their captured son Wilfred, and Edie had made a large Christmas pudding – without eggs – from a recipe in the local newspaper.

Hilda had brought two chickens from Eb and Eleanor in Durham – they'd turned part of their garden into a chicken run – and Louie's stove was crammed with simmering vegetables; runner beans preserved in salt since the summer and dried peas and broad beans from the family allotment which Sam had rescued from wilderness. Sara brought out Louie's homemade rowan jelly from under the stairs and the walnuts and chestnuts they had picked in the autumn and stored in sand for a Christmas treat and would roast on the fire after lunch.

At one o'clock the Dimarcos arrived with small cakes and the last two bottles of Arturo's homemade wine.

Louie looked doubtfully at Sam, but he opened them without hesitation saying, 'Your father can't see us drinking through the floorboards, Louie.'

Joe gave a toast, 'To the Ritsons!'

'To the Dimarcos,' Sam returned.

'To the lads overseas...' The stout Ernie Parkin raised his empty glass and Sam refilled it.

'To absent friends,' Louie added swiftly and smiled sympathetically at Anna.

There was a momentary silence, then Joe turned to Raymond and began to talk of football. Ernie Parkin immediately leapt in and soon the stilted exchanges relaxed into laughter and conversation. Peter and Linda tore open the toys Hilda had wrapped for them and started a game of jumping on and off Sam and Louie's creaking bed in the corner of the parlour.

In the fug of the small room they all squeezed around the table and tucked into the special food, Linda balanced on Sylvia's knee and Peter clambering between Rosa and his grandmother. Sara noticed Rosa's shy looks towards Raymond as he chatted with Joe.

'Your mam not coming home this Christmas?' Joe asked.

Raymond shook his head. 'She's doing a panto in London.'

'I thought all the bairns had left London,' Hilda said, coming round with more potatoes.

'She is a brave lady to stay in London, yes?' Anna commented.

'Iris has plenty spirit, I'll give her that,' Sam grunted.

'Is she an actress?' Albina asked with interest, eyeing the fresh-faced Raymond in a new light.

'Aye,' he answered proudly, 'a famous one – she's been on the wireless.'

'How wonderful!' Albina marvelled and fixed her attention on Raymond for the rest of the meal. To Sara's amusement he was happy to show off and boast about his exotic mother to an admiring audience. Only Sara seemed to notice Rosa withdraw frostily from the table and disappear to feed Mary in the kitchen.

Later, when the tables were cleared and the men sat smoking in the parlour while Louie and Hilda and Edie Parkin prepared the tea and the others helped Peter play tiddlywinks, Joe and Sara slipped out for a walk in the cold dusk. They made straight for the dene and took the path through the bare, blackened trees to their kissing gate. It was too cold to linger, so they crossed the Common and circled the village, invisible now in the dark, wrapped in a pungent blanket of coal smoke. Fire flickered from the spoil heap, betraying the location of the Eleanor pit.

'They're going to employ men to dampen the heap – it's a target for air attack,' Sara said, her breath clouding as she spoke.

'Proper little fire spotter, aren't you?' Joe chuckled and kissed her head.

'I wish you could meet me brother Tom,' Sara said, suddenly struck by how similar their humour was. 'You'd get on so well.'

'Like a house on fire?' Joe teased.

'You wouldn't consider calling at Uncle Alfred's?'

'After what he did to my father's shop? To my family?' Joe was at once indignant. 'I can't believe you'd want to see him either, after the way he's treated you.'

'It's Tom I want to see,' Sara tried to explain. 'I've always been closest to Tom.'

Joe stared out across the valley, the outline of the village plunged in unnatural darkness by the blackout. He longed for Whitton Grange to return to the cheerful, grubby town he loved with its gas lamps and bustling traffic, the shops full of goods and his family accepted once more. He longed for the day when there would be petrol for his rusting motorcycle and the only uniform he had to wear would be Whitton's football strip. But that day might never come; they had to live with the dangerous, uncertain present.

Joe came to a decision about the one thing that had preyed on his mind for weeks. 'You can take me to see your brother,' Joe turned and encircled Sara, 'on one condition.'

Sara looked up in to his serious face. 'What's that?'

'You marry me first.'

Sara's mouth fell open in astonishment at the abrupt proposal. Although she had sometimes daydreamed about marrying Joe, the problems that had bedevilled their courtship and the attitude of their families had made such hopes seem futile. Yet she had heard him quite clearly; he wanted her the way she wanted him, despite the obstacles.

'Joe?' she queried. 'You want to get married?'

'Aye, don't you?' he grinned. 'Don't tell me I'm going to get turned down – no one says no to a Dimarco.'

Sara laughed.

Joe added, less confidently, 'I've never asked a lass before, mind.'

'And I hope you don't go asking anyone again

– 'cos the answer's yes.' Sara kissed him.

Joe laughed in relief. 'That's settled then! We'll do it before my leave ends.'

'But that's in five days' time,' Sara gasped. 'What about our families – it'll be a bit of a shock. My mam won't have time to come down from Weardale and–'

'We won't tell them,' Joe replied. 'We'll go to the registry office in Durham.'

'No, Joe,' Sara said in disappointment. 'I want to get wed in the chapel.'

'My parents wouldn't agree to that and your family would cut you off if we got married in a Catholic church, wouldn't they?' Joe argued.

'They might cut me off for marrying you anyway...' Sara was suddenly full of doubts.

Joe lifted her chin. 'Let's face it – neither your family or mine are going to approve of us marrying. Having Christmas together is not the same as accepting you as family. I know my mam still wants me to choose an Italian girl, even after the way we've been treated – perhaps even more so. Let's not take the risk of anyone saying no.'

'All right,' Sara agreed excitedly, seeing the force of his argument. 'What do we do?'

'We'll go into Durham and get a special licence,' Joe said, 'and we'll need a couple of witnesses, that's all.'

Sara had a thought. 'Let's ask Eb and Eleanor Kirkup – they've been trying to get your father released. And they know all about families who disapprove of a love-match.'

Under the shadow of the Eleanor pithead, Joe and Sara sealed their engagement with a kiss and returned to the others at Hawthorn Street where Raymond was entertaining them on the piano. He played badly but had an ear for a tune and, with hearty singing from his aunts and the Parkins, his wrong fingering was drowned. Sara found it hard not to let her excitement show and wished she could shout out her news to the roomful of people. But the Dimarcos were so enjoying the music that nobody rebuked or questioned Joe for slipping away with Sara.

'My Davide plays the accordion,' Elvira clapped in appreciation. 'We love to sing and dance.'

'Let's push the furniture back and dance, then,' Joe suggested.

Three days later as Sam was washing in the tin tub in front of the fire, and Raymond was eating his tea, Louie found a note written in Sara's sprawling writing tucked behind the tea caddy on the mantelpiece. Louie realised the girl must have put it there after breakfast, knowing she would find it later that day.

'I've gone to Durham to marry Joe at the registry office. Sorry we could not tell you, but then no one can blame you later for knowing. We'll be back tomorrow before Joe's leave finishes. My love, Sara.'

Louie gawped at the message and re-read it in disbelief. 'Well I'll never!' she cried and burst out laughing.

'What's tickled you?' Sam looked up, coal grime still clinging to his neck and ears.

'Sara and Joe have run off to get wed!' Louie waved the note at her husband.

Raymond gawped in shock, a piece of pie halfway to his open mouth.

'Daft buggers,' Sam grunted, 'what they want to do that for?'

Louie snorted. 'Why do you think?' For the first time in ages she saw Sam blush.

Raymond felt a deep flush rise up from his neck too, until his cheeks burned. He'd never imagined Joe would ever really marry Sara, despite their obvious attraction for each other. But he had and Sara had chosen Joe and would be leaving their home for good. It struck him how much he would miss her, and he felt a stab of envy for his Italian friend.

'Well, they've got no sense,' Sam blustered. 'What a time to pick with Joe about to leave for God knows how long and them without a home...'

'They've always got a home here if Joe's mam won't have them,' Louie said stoutly. 'And there's never a good time to get married – we know that – you just have to get on and do it. I think it's *grand* they're getting wed.'

'Since when have you become the great romantic, Louie Ritson?' Sam teased. 'I thought you were the sensible one.'

Raymond pushed away his plate, his appetite gone, and grabbed his jacket, mumbling that he was off for a game of billiards. Louie looked at him in surprise, but was too preoccupied by Sara's news to stop him.

The door banged behind her nephew as Louie took the flannel and began to rub her husband's hairy chest and knotted arms. 'I've seen how too

481

much pride and misunderstanding can stand in the way of people's happiness,' she said thoughtfully. 'Look how my da tortures himself with not seeing Eb, when he could have been enjoying the company of his grandson Rupert. And I was just as much to blame for taking Da's side, I see that now. Well, I'm glad Sara and Joe aren't going to let their families meddle in *their* lives. I'm that fond of them both, I want to see them happy – and they've got such a short time...'

Sam took hold of Louie's hand and held it firmly to his chest. 'Louie Ritson, how did I ever deserve such a wife?' he smiled with affection. 'And you would have made such a canny mother, too,' he added almost inaudibly.

Louie was moved by the unexpected words and, looking with tenderness at Sam's once-handsome, channelled face, leaned over the tub to kiss him.

'We've been blessed with each other, Sam,' Louie answered and let him put his wet arms about her as he kissed away her tears...

Chapter Twenty-Five

After the brief marriage ceremony, Eb and Eleanor Kirkup insisted on treating Sara and Joe at the British Restaurant behind Silver Street. They celebrated with a filling meal of onion soup, mince and leek dumplings and milk pudding and then went back to the Kirkups' small house in the Bailey and sat round a roaring fire drinking punch and listening to Eleanor's Jack Buchanan records, while the rain battered the curtained window. They filled the cosy sitting-room with pungent smoke from Eleanor's Turkish cigarettes and Joe taught card tricks to the Kirkups' serious, bespectacled son Rupert. Sara warmed to Eleanor in her old-fashioned fringed dress talking of German politics and obscure poets and Eb, in a threadbare green Paisley tie, sketching his son who sat cross-legged on the floor. Sara felt grateful that they should be accepted so easily by the unorthodox couple and not criticised for their rash behaviour and Eleanor made her feel knowledgeable about literature by encouraging her to discuss *Wuthering Heights* and *Jane Eyre*.

'I wish you would stay,' Eleanor urged the young couple, enjoying their lively chatter. 'Our Belgian friends are away until New Year – you could have their room.'

'Thanks, Mrs Kirkup, but I've booked us into a place – it's already paid for,' Joe grinned and Sara blushed. In a short while they would be alone together at last, she thought with a pang of trepidation.

'Well, come back here for breakfast, then,' Eleanor insisted. 'It seems so dismal to think of you both in a cold guest house.'

Joe and Sara exchanged looks, finding it hard not to smile. Suddenly Sara was eager for them to leave, to have Joe to herself, away from the elegant Eleanor and her engaging conversation. It was the quiet, bearded Eb who saved them from embarrassment.

'Eleanor, pet,' he interrupted in his strong Durham voice, his face amused, 'the cold'll not bother them.'

He turned his startlingly blue eyes on the newlyweds, sitting close together on the sofa and remembered how once he had yearned to be left alone with his lover. His relationship with Eleanor was now deep-rooted, comfortable and familiar, but he recognised in Joe and Sara the sweet intensity of first love that had driven him and Eleanor together to the disapproval of all.

Eb said wryly, 'My wife is a terrible one for organising folk. If you'd like breakfast tomorrow come any time – but don't feel you have to. We'll say our goodbyes now, just in case.'

Joe and Sara rose quickly to meet the artist's outstretched hand and Sara was astonished by the firm clasp from such a gentle man.

'Ta for all you've done for us.' Sara smiled at her hosts.

'Aye – and for what you're doing for my father,' Joe added.

'It's precious little,' Eleanor said, closing her bony hands about Joe's warm ones. 'I wish we could do more.'

'Let's hope your father's released by the time you're next on leave,' Eb said with a smile of optimism, but Sara felt a twinge of anxiety at the words, for none of them knew when Joe would be back again.

They left the Bailey, eerily quiet without the tolling Cathedral bells, and, lurching across the wet cobbles in the dark of early evening, found their way to the square where Joe had paid for a room above the Market Inn. The portly, perspiring publican, Ramshaw, turned out to be the father of actress Iris Ramshaw and grandfather of Raymond Kirkup, so he bought them drinks on the house for news of his grandson.

'He's a canny lad, Raymond,' Mr Ramshaw wheezed and spat. 'The Ritsons have brought him up well – poor as church mice – but Raymond's not suffered.' Sara was fascinated to hear more about the itinerant Iris. 'My Iris?' Ramshaw mopped his brow. 'Swopped at birth by the gypsies if you ask me. All she ever wanted to do since she was a young lass was sing – and, by heck, she can sing.' Ramshaw dropped his voice, 'Her mother thinks she's wayward, leaving her own bairn the way she did – but I think she did right leaving him with the Ritsons. Raymond would have been a right tearaway if he'd been dragged around the country with his mam and her strange friends.'

Tiring of talk of Iris Ramshaw, Joe asked to be shown their room and the publican called for his small wife. Turning out the light, she led them outside again and through a separate entrance to the flat above, chattering all the while.

'...But our Tom and our Percy are in the forces – RAF and Navy – and Jean's a nurse in Newcastle. That just leaves Nora at home – she's a telephonist at Shire Hall. So we've plenty room. Get a few servicemen staying – not so many travellers now. Fancy you knowing Raymond! I'll send a pie back with you for Louie.' She stepped round a dish that was catching drips in the passageway and opened a bedroom door. 'Is this all right?'

'Champion,' Joe assured her, and held the door for her to leave.

'Just shout if you want anything,' Mrs Ramshaw winked. 'Always happy to oblige one of our brave lads. It's a shame you hadn't time for a proper wedding – cried buckets at our Iris's. Been a widow fourteen years now, though, poor lass.'

As Joe closed the door on her chatter, Sara glanced round the tiny boxroom with its three-quarter size bed and a chest of drawers with a hairbrush and empty scent spray and a framed newspaper cutting of a slim-faced woman dressed as Prince Charming in a local pantomime.

'This must be Iris.' Sara picked it up. 'She's bonny, don't you think?'

'You're the only bonny lass I'm bothered about,' Joe grinned and grabbed her round the waist.

Sara laughed and twisted to kiss him. They went to bed at once, undressing hurriedly in the chill room under the flickering electric light and burrowing down under the bedclothes.

'Come here, Mrs Dimarco...' Joe pulled her

486

against him and covered her in kisses. At the sound of the alien name Sara had a moment of doubt that she had done the right thing, but she banished all thoughts of the world beyond as they began to make love...

The daydreaming Sara Pallister of two years ago would have been appalled at the prospect of spending the first night of married life in a shabby pub bedroom, listening to the drips from a leaky roof plop into a metal pail, with a hand-me-down coat and woollen Sunday dress as discarded wedding garments piled on top of her husband's army uniform to give them extra warmth. But she had learned a lot about life since leaving the security of Stout House and Sara knew she must make the most of this brief gift of time with Joe before they were parted. So they laughed bashfully at their unromantic surroundings as they spent a first joyful night of intimacy.

The light went out inexplicably in the late evening and they dozed, then Joe roused Sara again in the early hours, whispering tender words that she would remember long after, as they took each other again.

When Mrs Ramshaw banged on the door the following morning and shouted that breakfast was ready, they ignored her and stayed in bed for a final snatched hour. Then Joe said, 'I suppose we should go home and face the music, Mrs Dimarco.'

Sara stretched and yawned on his chest, 'Can't we just stay another day?'

Joe kissed her soft hair. 'I leave tomorrow, *bellissima*. We must get you settled at Pit Street before I go.'

Sara was instantly nervous at the suggestion. She had imagined she would stay on at the Ritsons while Joe was away and the thought of moving in with the Dimarcos filled her with dread.

'But what if your mother doesn't want me there?' Sara asked.

'There's no going back now, Sara,' Joe dismissed her fears. 'Mam will have to accept you.'

'But there's so little room,' Sara protested lamely.

'Sara...' Joe took hold of her. 'I want you to live at Pit Street – you're my wife and it's where you belong now. You're part of my family and I want you there where I can look after you.'

'But you won't be there to look after me!' Sara bridled.

Joe looked cross. 'My family will while I'm away.'

They dressed in a frosty silence, which Sara could not bear.

'When you come back, Joe,' Sara asked quietly, 'can we find a place of our own?'

Joe saw the unhappiness marring her face and relented. 'If that's what you want, bonny lass.'

Sara was cheered by the thought and reached up to kiss him on the lips.

'That day won't come soon enough,' she whispered with tears in her eyes.

On the train journey back to Whitton Grange they discovered they were ravenous and shared the pie Mrs Ramshaw had sent back for the Ritsons, already reminiscing about their wedding and laughing at their boldness. But their high spirits were soon shattered by the reaction of the Dimarco women.

'How could you do such a disgraceful thing?' Anna exclaimed after she had swallowed her astonishment. 'Without the blessing of your parents...'

'You aren't properly married unless a priest marries you!' Elvira flustered. 'No, it just won't do.'

'What will your father say?' Anna worried.

'And your godfather,' Elvira added, faint at the thought of her husband's reaction. 'Anna, you've always been too soft with your Joseph.'

'Fancy getting wed in a registry office,' Albina said with disgust. 'I'd *never* do such a thing.'

'Saint Teresa! What have I done to deserve such children? First Rosa and a baby with no father, now you two running off together!' Anna fumed. 'How will I tell your father you have married the niece of that devil, Cummings?'

'Stop it!' Joe ordered, infuriated by his mother's condemnation. 'We're married now and you'll just have to get used to the idea. Sara's stood by us when half the village would have strung us up, so you'll treat her with a bit more respect. I don't give a damn if she's Cummings's niece – she's my wife and this is her home!' Joe seized Sara's hand and waved the cheap wedding ring at them.

Sara cringed with humiliation at the bickering she was causing. Joe's mother was just as bigoted as her uncle Alfred; it would be impossible for her to live here, she thought miserably. She looked around the room for help, but even Rosa stood frozen in disbelief.

'We have nothing against Sara,' Anna answered stiffly, 'but you had no right to go behind our backs like that. It's *shameful*. And do you think Sara's family will ever agree to her living here? No, of course not. It will mean more bricks through our windows from the Cummingses!'

'I knew it would be like this,' Sara nearly choked with anger as she spoke. 'Don't use my family as an excuse, Mrs Dimarco – you're just as narrow-minded as the Cummingses! After all that's happened, you should be happy for Joe and me – we love each other. But you'll never accept me whatever I do, just because I'm not Italian.' Sara turned from Anna Dimarco's appalled face and said to Joe, 'I'll go back to the Ritsons'.'

For a long moment they stared at each other, wondering if their fledgling marriage was doomed. Joe knew that he had to make a choice that might effect the rest of his life and, as he hesitated, the image of Eb Kirkup defying his family for the one he loved, came in to Joe's mind.

Joe took Sara's hand and said fiercely, 'I'm coming with you.'

Sara smiled back, almost sick with relief.

'No!' It was Rosa who stepped forward, recovering from the shock of her brother's announcement. 'You mustn't go, Sara – this is your home. I'm ashamed of our lack of courtesy – Papa would never have allowed it.' There was a sharp intake of breath from behind, but Rosa, braving her mother's wrath, went up to Sara, kissing her on the cheek and smiled, 'I'm really pleased for you and Joe – and I can't think of anyone I'd rather have for a sister-in-law.'

Sara hugged her for her kindness and then Rosa embraced Joe.

'Thank you, Rosa...' Joe kissed his younger sister with affection.

There was an awkward silence in the unlit sitting-room, even the children had stopped their playing, confused by the tension. Unexpectedly, the gaunt-faced Sylvia turned from the stove where she had appeared to be taking no notice of the row and a wintry smile crossed her face.

'You can have my room tonight,' she told Joe. 'The bairns and me can sleep with Rosa. I'm sure your father won't be angry at what you've done – not after all the bad things that have happened to us – and I know my Paolo would have understood,' she added hoarsely.

Sara felt a rush of gratitude towards the bleak-faced woman in black who still bared her grief to the world, yet had the generosity to wish them well.

'Thank you, Sylvia,' Sara answered, holding her head up with dignity.

She left with Joe to collect her few possessions from Hawthorn Street and, an hour later, Sara moved in to the flat above the Pit Street shop, as the wife of Joe Dimarco.

Once Joe had left, Sara shared a room with Rosa and baby Mary and resumed her job at the hospital laundry. Her modest wages proved welcome to the Dimarco household who struggled on with little to sell in the shop. Elvira and Anna sold jelly pies for a halfpenny and Sara helped Sylvia

491

concoct a mock fruit salad by boiling turnip until it was tasteless and disguising it with pineapple essence. Relations with her new mother-in-law were cool, but Sara spent as much time as possible out of the house, working or helping at the WVS canteen where her Aunt Ida studiously avoided her.

At the beginning of February, Sara cornered her aunt in the kitchen. 'How's Tom?' she asked pointedly. It still rankled that her Uncle Alfred had refused to let Joe inside the house when they had tried to see Tom before Joe went back off leave. Tom had been out at the pub, but had not attempted to see Sara since.

'He's going home at the end of the week,' Ida told her, without looking into her eyes, 'to make preparations for the wedding.'

'Wedding?' Sara queried.

'Hasn't your mother told you?' Ida glanced around, as if nervous to be seen speaking to her. 'Tom's getting wed to Jane Metcalfe at the end of the month. He's been passed fit – wants to marry before rejoining the regiment.'

'Why has nobody told me?' Sara asked in annoyance.

Ida gave her a strange look with her close-set eyes. 'You've only yourself to blame for cutting yourself off like you have. Going off and marrying that Italian!' Ida flustered, going puce in the face. 'It's no wonder your mother's upset. At least Tom's giving her something to be proud about – marrying a good local lass – your mam's lucky to have him. Alfred and I are as fond of Tom as if he were our own – I'll be sad to see him go.'

'When is the wedding?' Sara demanded, trying to control her temper.

'Last Saturday in February,' Ida said, clattering the dishes to cover their conversation. 'We're invited, of course, but I doubt you'll be welcome.'

Sara was furious. 'I'll go to my own brother's wedding whether you like it or not,' she declared, throwing down her tea-towel and storming out of the kitchen.

As it turned out, none of the Whitton Grange family attended Tom's wedding, as heavy falls of snow enveloped the valley and made travel impossible. Sara was wretched at the thought of not being able to see Tom married, but worse was her deep hurt that she had not been invited.

The schools closed for a week and Sara lived in at the hospital rather than risk falling into the yard-high drifts that hid the roads, trying to keep herself busy so as not to dwell on her disappointment. The daily clatter of coal trucks from the pits stopped and coal shortages bedevilled the country once more. Snow drifted into the eaves of the Pit Street house and, when it thawed, it ran in torrents down Sara's bedroom walls and she and Rosa moved in to the sitting-room to sleep. Baby Mary caught croup and Rosa fretted her daughter would not see her first birthday, until the Ritsons scraped together enough money for her to see the doctor.

Some time later, Sara's sister Chrissie wrote to her telling of how they had sledged down to the chapel at Lowbeck for Tom's wedding and Sid Gibson had been best man. Sara felt again the deep hurt that she had been excluded from the family occasion.

'*Tom looked grand in his uniform,*' Chrissie wrote, '*and Sid looked handsome, too. He was sad for a bit after that land girl, Phoebe, left, but he's better now. Phoebe went off to marry some officer, by the way. I think Sid's better off without her. Phoebe was too posh. Mam made my bridesmaid's dress out of old net curtains. Jane Metcalfe wore her mother's old wedding dress, but she looked pretty. What did you wear when you got married? Is Joe really one of the enemy like Tom says? Jane and Tom are living in one of the cottages, but Tom's gone now. I wish you would come and see us – I want to see what you look like now you're an Italian. I miss you. Love from Chrissie.*'

Sara swallowed her bitterness, grateful for contact from her sister, and wrote back to Chrissie, telling her about her own wedding day and she wrote to her mother and her new sister-in-law Jane but got no reply. Spring came, and with it renewed heavy bombing over the coastal towns of Wearside and Tyneside, making Elvira fear nightly for her daughter Val in a Sunderland hospital. A stray German plane, returning from a raid, off-loaded incendiary bombs close to Whitton Grange, causing a fire in the dene and killing Constable Simpson who was patrolling on his bicycle. Then, with the coming of June, the raids ceased as the Luftwaffe turned its full attention eastwards on the Soviet Union and opened up the Eastern Front.

On the anniversary of the Dimarco men's arrest, Eleanor Kirkup appeared with news of the internees.

'Benito is to be released,' she told a delighted

Elvira. 'He's volunteered for the Pioneer Corps.'

'What is that, please?' Elvira's drawn face furrowed again.

'It's made up of men who've been classed as aliens,' Eleanor explained. 'They will help in the war effort – but not engage in direct armed combat. He could be sent abroad, though.'

'At least he is free,' Anna bolstered her sister-in-law, 'and you will see him again soon. Thank the saints for that.'

A fortnight later, Benito was briefly reunited with his mother and sister Albina before travelling on to join his new outfit. The women pooled their coupons to buy extra provisions for a celebratory meal of freshly made pasta and roast mutton and Anna took the bold step of going to Dolly Sergeant and bartering for black market cigarettes and sugar to make real ice-cream and homemade rhubarb wine, pawning a family necklace to do so.

Benito was given a joyous reception and Sara was grateful that he did not show disapproval at her presence, going out of his way to include her in the conversations by speaking only in English. Sara was beginning to pick up odd words and expressions in the Dimarcos' native tongue, but was quite lost when they all began to talk at once across the table.

'Papa has gone in front of two tribunals now,' Benito told the women, 'but they will not release him. Uncle Arturo is the same.'

'But what harm can they do?' Elvira protested. 'All they want is be allowed to come back to their families.'

Benito shook his head and drew heavily on his cigarette. 'It's not that simple. They have to agree to collaborate with the authorities. Even if they were released they would not be allowed to simply return and run their businesses like before – they would be sent off to do war work.'

'So why don't Papa and Uncle Davide agree to do that?' Rosa asked, perplexed. 'Surely that's better than being locked up?'

Benito studied his young cousin. 'For the old men it is a difficult choice – their loyalties are split. The British officers ask them if they will work against Italy to win the war and some, like Papa, see it as asking them to betray who they are. He cannot bring himself to disown Italy. And there is pressure in the camp for them to remain "good Italians" and that means to stay inside with the others.'

'But you've agreed to fight with the British after what they've done to you?' Rosa pressed him.

Benito crushed out his cigarette. 'For me this war is a fight against fascism – not against our people in Italy. Many of them are just caught up on the wrong side as happens in any war – and that I regret. But for the sake of your Mary and Sylvia's children – all our children – the dictators *must* be beaten. I know we've been treated badly by some of the British – but not by all – and I'm prepared to fight with them against the fascists.'

Elvira clicked her teeth. 'You must do what you feel is right, Benito,' his mother said with resignation. 'But your father would not want to be seen as a bad Italian – that I can understand.'

'Well, I don't,' Anna answered sharply. 'Davide

and Arturo's first loyalty should be to us – their wives and families. We are the ones who are suffering most while they remain in the camps. God forbid we have to survive another year like this last one. We need our husbands *here*.'

'I've already tried to persuade Papa,' Benito shrugged. 'And Uncle Arturo will not go against my father's wishes. You will have to manage without them, I'm afraid.'

'We shall see about that,' Anna said with determination.

'What can you do, Mam?' Rosa asked, feeling the situation was hopeless.

'I will go and see your father on this Island of Man – talk sense into him,' she replied.

'But you've never travelled anywhere without Arturo!' Elvira was dismissive, 'You would never manage such a journey.'

'I could go with you,' Sara volunteered quietly, wary of being brushed aside as interfering. 'It would be easier to go with someone who could understand...' She flushed awkwardly as tactful words eluded her.

Anna gave her a long, hard look, wondering why it was that she so resented Sara's presence in her home. Was it just because Sara reminded her of the humiliation and terror heaped on her family by the evil Cummingses – or was she jealous of her son's love for this bright, attractive girl? Joe had always been her favourite child, but he had shown, on that awful day in January, that he would choose Sara rather than his mother and family if they pushed him too far. She had been deeply hurt at losing him to someone else, she

497

now realised, especially this girl from outside their community whose ways were so different from theirs. Yet, here she was, offering to help once again and Anna felt a wave of guilt that she treated Sara so coldly.

'Thank you, Sara,' Anna found herself saying, 'we shall go together.'

Having borrowed money from Eleanor Kirkup to pay for the train fares, Anna and Sara set out one warm July morning, Bobby taking them to the station on the old cart pulled by their ancient pony Gelato. Rosa's brother was impatient to see them away and return to the cycle shop where he had been taken on part-time that spring. With petrol rationed, cycling was having a renaissance and Bobby was busily employed fixing up the stream of ancient machines that were brought to the shop for repair.

'Don't be late for work,' Anna reminded her youngest needlessly. 'And remember you are in charge while we're away.' She kissed the shy youth affectionately, hoping to please him with the responsibility.

'Does that mean I can tell Albina what to do?' Bobby asked timidly.

'If you dare,' his mother smiled. Sara winked at the cautious boy, beginning to relish the thought of escaping the confines of Pit Street and Albina's petty bitching for a few days.

Even the overcrowded trains, the delays and the cramped waiting rooms where they dozed did not dampen Sara's enthusiasm for travel. She found herself taking charge of their journey as a

498

bewildered and anxious Anna Dimarco increasingly relied on her to buy tickets and food. But when they tried to find accommodation in Carlisle for the night, Sara was aghast at their reception. Some landladies took one look at the sallow-faced Anna in her old-fashioned coat and tightly bound hair and would not let them through the door. Another woman was quite friendly towards Sara, while Anna stood outside, until she handed over her ration book.

'Dimarco?' the woman said with suspicion. 'Foreign are you?'

'I'm from Durham way,' Sara answered, her stomach knotting.

'Married an I-tie, have you?' the landlady's look grew hostile.

'My husband's British.' Sara felt her indignation rise. 'He's in the army.'

The woman peered out at the dark-haired Anna standing patiently on the pavement. 'Who's she?'

'My mother-in-law,' Sara said tensely. 'Look, all we want is a bed for the night and a bit of supper...'

'Get out of here!' the woman said with contempt. 'I'll not have any enemy I-ties under my roof. You should be ashamed of yourself getting mixed up with dirty traitors. Be off!' She pushed Sara out of the door before she had time to retaliate.

Anna did not ask what had happened as they tramped out of the town, but Sara was mortified by the episode. For the first time she felt frightened to be Joe's wife. Up until now she had

499

thought herself protected by being English, but now she realised she was as vulnerable as the other Dimarcos. To the people of Carlisle there was no difference; she was one of them.

'I never really knew what it was like for you before,' Sara said, walking beside her silent mother-in-law, engulfed by guilt that her fellow British should treat them so shamefully. 'That woman knew nothing about me – yet she hated me just because of my name.'

'We can sleep in this field,' Anna said without emotion, 'and thank the saints it's a clear evening.'

She did not wait for Sara to agree, but hitched up her skirt and climbed the gate. Spreading out her coat to sit on, Anna divided up the bread and apples they had intended to keep for the following day.

'Come, let's eat,' she encouraged a subdued Sara, who was still feeling responsible for failing to find them shelter for the night.

Around them birds sang in the hedgerows and a musky smell of wild roses permeated the still evening. Sara was reassured by the peacefulness of the countryside and the uninterested munching of the grazing sheep. She watched her mother-in-law sitting gracefully on the rough ground, peeling an apple with a small knife, a few stray wisps of hair the only sign of their exhausting day and marvelled at her calm acceptance of their situation.

'Do you ever feel frightened like I did back there?' Sara blurted out.

Anna looked up and regarded her with dark

eyes like Joe's. 'Sometimes, of course.'

'You never show it,' Sara said with admiration. 'You just seem to take what comes to you – like when the shop was smashed up and your husband taken away – now this, sleeping in a field like a vagrant. I wouldn't have thought...'

Anna gave a slow smile. 'I've slept in fields before. My father was a shepherd.'

'Just like my dad!' Sara exclaimed. 'I've never thought of you as a country person,' Sara said, tilting her head to one side in thought, finding it hard to imagine Anna Dimarco doing anything outside her shop. The older woman seemed to read her mind.

'We haven't always had the business,' she explained. 'We were very poor people in Italy. Arturo and Davide walked halfway across Europe to find work before they came to Durham. They had *nothing*. It has never been an easy life like some people think – they see our shop and our van – but we worked night and day to have our own business, to have something to pass on to our children...'

Anna broke off, her eyes smarting at the memory that Paolo, who had been groomed to inherit the shop, was dead.

'Do you ever wish you had never come to England?' Sara dared to ask.

Anna struggled for a moment to compose herself. 'There have been times in the last year when I have thought such a thing. And sometimes I think it would have been wiser to have gone back with Domenica and Nonna Maria.' Anna shrugged. 'But it is useless to wish. God leads us

501

where he will and we must accept the lives we are given.'

'I'm glad you and Mr Dimarco came to Whitton Grange,' Sara said quietly, 'else I would never have met Joe.' Anna did not answer. A sheep bleated nearby.

'We should try and sleep,' Anna said, shaking crumbs from her skirt.

Impulsively Sara reached out and touched her arm. 'One day, Mrs Dimarco, I'll take you up to my family's farm. It'll make you feel at home, you being a country lass.'

Anna was startled by the sudden gesture, once again taken aback by the girl's warmth towards her. Fleetingly, she covered Sara's hand with her own.

'I'd like that. One day we go. Now we sleep.'

They lay back-to-back for warmth as the sun dipped and the stars appeared in a heliotrope sky, each grateful for the companionship of the other.

The following day they walked back to the railway station and continued their journey. Two days later they were on the Isle of Man, at Ramsey camp where Arturo was held. The camp was a terraced row of former boarding houses, now shabby from neglect and surrounded by barbed-wire fences. Washing hung limply from open windows and bored men peered with interest at the visitors, waving through the perimeter fence. The women's first reaction was one of relief to see that conditions were not too squalid.

But when they were allowed to see Arturo

under the eye of a guard, Sara was shocked by his lacklustre appearance. Joe's father had lost weight, his face was sagging and haggard like an old man's and his dark hair had turned quite grey. She looked for a sign of his old ebullience, but his attempts to be cheerful were shadowed with fatigue and Sara found herself quite tongue-tied.

'We've brought you some homemade sausage,' Anna fumbled with her parcel. 'And a bottle of rhubarb wine. It's not as good as your own, but it's drinkable. Benito had some.'

'Ah, Benito,' Arturo said, latching on to the name. 'He's left us. Davide is sad – and his health is bad.' He lapsed into thought.

Anna tried again to kindle his interest with talk of the family. 'Linda is becoming a little chatterbox and Mary is sweet-natured like Rosa – she's taken her first steps.'

'Rosa.' Arturo's sad eyes sparked. 'Why has Rosa not come?'

'She has Mary to look after,' Anna explained patiently, as if to a child. 'Sara offered to travel with me.' The women exchanged looks and Anna steeled herself to add, 'She's one of the family now.'

Arturo looked at them both blankly and Sara wondered if the news of her marriage to Joe would prove too much of a shock to the disheartened Arturo. No one had written to tell him of the marriage, Anna insisting that it would be better to tell her husband in person.

Sara cleared her throat. 'Joe and I got married,' she told him, her heart beating nervously, 'when

503

he was on leave at Christmas.'

'Joseph – and you?' Arturo queried, finding it hard to grasp this latest piece of news. His life had been so turned upside down that nothing seemed to make sense anymore. He no longer had control over anything that happened and he was overwhelmed by his impotence. It was Anna who held the family together and it was little Bobby who was the breadwinner. He had not been able to prevent Paolo from dying or Domenica from returning to Italy or Rosa from bearing an illegitimate baby – and now Joseph had defied him in his absence and married this Durham girl.

Arturo gave a sigh of frustration and to the consternation of them all, began to weep.

'Please, Arturo,' Anna gasped, as the guard looked on with derision.

'Forgive me!' he sobbed. 'I am not worthy of the name Dimarco.'

Anna was dismayed at the broken man before her. She had come to beg him to renounce his nationality and return home to look after them, but the feeble man before her was not the brave and considerate husband who had fought in the Great War and battled to give his family a good home against all the odds. A part of her despised him for his show of weakness and yet she wanted to fling her arms around him and protect him from any more trouble. Whatever happened, Arturo Dimarco was her husband whom she loved and now it was her turn to take care of him.

'Come home, Arturo,' she begged softly, clasping his hands in hers. 'We *need* you with us. Your first duty is to us, not the men here.'

'But Davide...' Arturo sniffed, trying to pull himself together.

'Make your own decision,' Anna challenged. 'You don't have to do everything that your brother says.'

Arturo's head drooped at the thought of what she was asking him to do, to deny his *Italianata*. But was his pride more important than his own family? he asked himself.

'The girls and the children,' Anna persisted, 'they wait for you. Do you want me to go home and tell them you would rather sit here in this dump than help them? They have no shoes to wear, we go hungry half the week, children spit at us when they walk past.'

Arturo was jolted out of his indecision by her words. 'Anna, I'm sorry,' he squeezed her hands. 'I will do what you want,' he forced out the words.

The women left with spirits raised at the success of their visit, yet Sara could tell her mother-in-law was shaken by the state in which they had found Arturo.

'He will recover once he is home again,' Anna said with fortitude and they spoke no more about it. And although Arturo had been so obviously upset about her marriage to Joe, Sara took heart from Anna's words that she was now part of the family.

When they arrived back at Whitton Grange, Bobby came speeding down Pit Street on a bicycle to greet them. Their news of the trip was cut short by Bobby's cry. 'You've missed him, he went this morning!'

'Who went?' Anna asked as the boy dismounted and took his mother's small bag.

'Joe,' Bobby said, glancing shyly at Sara under his thick black lashes.

'He's gone?' Sara cried in dismay.

'Aye,' Bobby nodded. 'Came the day after you left, but he couldn't stay any longer. He's going abroad.'

'Where?' Sara asked, feeling sick as they approached the shop.

'He didn't know. But somewhere hot, I reckon, 'cos he's got a special cotton uniform,' Bobby announced, feeling knowledgeable.

Rosa rushed down the stairs having spotted them at the window and gave Sara a hug.

'Joe left a letter for you,' she told her disappointed friend. 'He was that upset at missing you.'

Sara took the letter and hurried off to read it alone. She sat on a charred tree stump in the dene, close to where the German bomb had dropped and set fire to the budding trees in April.

Joe's letter was short and cheerful and intimate. He was sick at missing her and teased her that she would go anywhere to have a few days off work. He told her he loved her and missed her like hell and he'd make it up with a month in bed when he next came home.

Sara smiled and kissed the letter. Dragging herself up, she turned for Pit Street, realising, as she did so, that she thought of it as home for the first time.

Chapter Twenty-Six

Arturo came home in the late summer, when the leaves were beginning to tinge with yellow and fade. He was sent to work in a munitions factory outside Durham and was away for long hours, cycling to work on Paolo's old bicycle.

'They've taken my driving licence off me,' he complained to Anna.

'Well, we have no petrol for the van anyway,' she answered briskly. 'We've been using Gelato for the past year.'

But they talked little of the past; it only fed Arturo's moroseness to think how they had suffered in his absence. To Anna's relief, her husband's health improved and it was a leaner and fitter Arturo who cycled fifteen miles every day to and from the factory and, when the winter set in, was sometimes seen riding the icy roads on Gelato. Yet at home he remained subdued, preferring to sit in the corner brooding behind a veil of cigarette smoke, rather than join in the family chatter.

He seemed happiest when Rosa sat at his feet and played with Mary, who was turning into an enchanting child with light brown hair and eyes like her father Emilio's and an infectious giggle that brought a smile to Arturo's weathered face. Anna saw how Elvira and Albina's presence in the cramped flat irritated her husband and served to remind him of his brother Davide still interned with the other Italians. But as Davide remained a prisoner, the women had nowhere else to go and Anna did her best to try and smooth over the petty arguments and aggravations that arose during the winter months which saw them all hemmed in by the blackout for long evenings.

She set Albina to unravelling old jumpers to reknit into outfits for the children, while Sylvia and Sara played endless games of Ludo with Peter. It was Sara, however, who saved Anna from insanity that winter by teaching her to read. The tuition started accidentally when a letter arrived from Joe.

'What does he say?' Anna asked Sara eagerly.

Sara skimmed over the more intimate messages and read, 'The weather's canny during the day, but it gets parky at night. Don't know how the locals can stand it, just dressed in long nighties. At night all the stars come out, much clearer than at home with all the smoke from the houses. The only other lights are from our cigarette ends, all glowing in the dark. There's nowt else to do out here. I wish I was at home with you...' Sara broke off and blushed.

Anna humphed over her mending. 'If he has nothing to do, why doesn't he write letters to me too, eh?'

Albina laughed disparagingly, 'Because you can't read like we can, Aunt Anna.'

Sara saw her mother-in-law flush with embarrassment. 'I – I never had the opportunity like you girls – and I manage well enough.'

'I could teach you, Mrs Dimarco,' Sara suggested tentatively. 'Then you could surprise Joe and write him a letter.'

Anna was flustered by the idea. 'No! I'm too old to learn. You can write for me.'

'I think it would be grand if you learned a bit of reading and writing,' Rosa piped up. 'Think how pleased Joe would be to get a letter from you, Mam.'

At first Anna had refused and the subject was dropped, but one evening, when all but she and Arturo had gone to bed and Sara came in late from visiting the Ritsons, Anna approached her with a recipe.

'What does this say?' she asked, avoiding Sara's eyes. 'Rosa cut it out from an old newspaper.'

Sara took the scrap of paper without showing her surprise. 'It's a recipe for using up stale bread. And there's another one here for carrot jam. Sounds disgusting.'

Arturo grunted in agreement, but Anna persisted. 'Which word says carrot?' Sara pointed it out. 'And that says bread?' Anna asked.

'Aye,' Sara nodded. 'How did you know?'

'I've seen it written in shop windows,' Anna replied defensively. 'I can read some words. I'm not the village fool.'

'You're anything but a fool, Mrs Dimarco,' Sara agreed. 'I don't think it would take you long to learn to read all of this,' she waved the cutting. 'It's just you've always worked so hard, you've never had time for reading and writing.'

Anna appeared pleased at her words of encouragement. 'And when would I have time now?' she said, only half resisting.

Arturo spoke unexpectedly. 'Sara could teach you in the evenings – Albina can do your sewing, seeing as she has the brains for two!'

The women laughed at his sudden flash of humour and Anna looked at him with fondness for his support.

'*Bene,*' Anna smiled. 'Tomorrow I go to school, yes?'

With the spring weather of 1942, unrest sprouted at the Eleanor pit over low wages and bad morale. News abroad was grim, with India threatened and U-boat attacks on merchant ships in the Atlantic slowly strangling the life-blood of supplies. Annual holidays for the pitmen were suspended once more and at Easter the government appealed for people to stay at home.

'As if we ever go anywhere at Easter!' Sam Ritson was scornful. 'It's not holidays that are causing loss of production – it's lack of fit men. We've got old men working down there, 'cos none of the young 'uns want to work for a pittance. And the conditions!' he complained to Louie and Sara as they sat working over a hooky mat. 'We've had more accidents this year already than for the whole of last year. There was another fall of ground on the flat this morning and it's a miracle no one was hurt.'

'Aye, even the lasses at the munitions factory are getting more than lads at the face,' Raymond said, adding his discontent. He had returned reluctantly to the pit that winter, not relishing the thought of being underground for long hours once more. But Dolly Sergeant had 'sent him

510

home with a flea in his ear', as Louie had put it. Raymond would not tell them why he had been sacked, but he suspected Sara had guessed the martinet Mrs Sergeant had found him carrying on with Nancy Bell in the storeroom. She had teased him about Nancy on several occasions, but he did not tell her that Nancy was keener on him than he was on her. Louie, however, had appeared strangely relieved that he was no longer working at Sergeant's and to his surprise did not protest at him taking a putter's job underground.

'Even Seward-Scott agrees with us that the price of Durham coal should be raised to give us better wages,' Sam continued. 'And there's a turn-up for the books.'

'And if the government doesn't agree?' Louie asked, prodding a scrap of material in to the hessian stretched on the frame.

'We'll withdraw our labour,' Sam said firmly.

Sara saw Louie's face sag with worry and decided to argue. 'It doesn't seem right to strike when our lads are out in the desert fighting for us and our ships are being sunk every week – and people in this street are saving every spare penny to buy a Bren gun.'

'That's the excuse the government makes to keep our wages low!' Sam said sharply. 'But it's just short-sighted. Us pitmen don't do a glamorous job like the lads in fancy uniforms, but we're just as important when it comes to winning this war.'

'Joe and Tom didn't join the army just to wear fancy uniforms!' Sara sparked.

Sam saw he had upset the girl and lowered his

511

voice. 'Listen, pet, I'm sorry. Joe and your brother are doing a grand job. All I'm saying is that we're trying to do our bit, too, but our efforts are wasted if they won't spend money on improving the conditions underground and if we can't earn enough money to buy the extra rations we need to keep us strong. It's bloody hard work digging for coal, believe me.'

'What you need is a pit canteen,' Louie suggested calmly. 'Some lads have to walk miles in wet clothes before they get home for something to eat. It's no wonder they're done in. An extra meal in their stomachs would make all the difference,'

'Seward-Scott would never agree to it,' Sam was sceptical.

'He will if he thinks it's in his own interests to keep his workforce fed,' Louie countered.

Sam fell into thought as Raymond bolted down his cheese pie and grabbed his cap. He was smelling of hair oil and his face was well scrubbed and mischievous. At seventeen, Louie's nephew was a handsome sight, taller than Sam, his thick auburn hair short-cropped and his chin darkening with a man's bristle.

'Where you off to?' Louie demanded.

'Pictures,' Raymond said lightly.

'She must be special for you to miss football practice,' Sara teased.

'I remember when *you* were never out of The Palace,' he joked back, sliding her a look with impish blue eyes. Sara laughed, but Louie looked anxious.

'Who are you going with?'

'The Queen of Sheba,' Raymond laughed and left.

'I thought he would have come and watched the Home Guard play tonight,' Sam said aggrieved. 'It's our charity match for Warship Week.'

Sara could not hide her amusement. 'It must be love.'

'He's seeing that Nancy Bell, I'm sure of it.' Louie's face was set with worry. 'How else would he know what the lasses at the factory are getting paid? Nancy's working there now, Minnie said. You'll have to speak to him, Sam.'

Sam looked uncomfortable. 'Best to leave the lad be, Louie. If we make a fuss he'll only see her behind our backs. He's not that interested in lasses – it'll blow over.'

Sara wondered what all the fuss was about. Raymond was a good-looking young man now and it was not surprising if he was courting someone.

'I know you're not that friendly with the Bells,' Sara said, 'but why shouldn't Raymond be allowed to go out with Nancy?'

Louie and Sam exchanged looks. Sam coughed and began to clean his pipe.

'It's a family thing,' Louie answered vaguely and got up to clear Raymond's dirty plate. Sara wondered if they disapproved of Nancy because she was a cousin of Normy Bell and feared Raymond might get into trouble again by too much contact with the Bells. But it was obvious Louie did not want to discuss the matter and Sara let the subject drop.

Sara forgot about the concern over Raymond as the summer brought alarming news of the allied defeat in the Egyptian desert and Rommel's capture of Tobruk. She knew from hints in Joe's letters and rumours in the village that his battalion had been moved from the Middle East to Africa and that he would be amongst the fiercest fighting. In the last letter before the battles of May and June, he had surprised her by referring to her brother Tom.

'We're in the same company,' Joe had written. *'He ignored me at first, but I was teaching some of the lads* scopa *and he joined in. We play for cigarettes. Tom's a right miserable bugger when he's got no smokes, so I let him win a bit.'*

Then the letters had stopped and Sara and the Dimarcos waited anxiously for news of Joe, as telegrams arrived in the village reporting the deaths or imprisonment of other people's sons and husbands. Only much later did they hear the full extent of the carnage in the desert that decimated the DLI battalions, but by then a letter had arrived from Tom, reporting them both alive.

'I'm sorry I haven't written to you before,' her brother's tone was contrite, *'and I regret the way I spoke to you about Joe. I could blame Uncle Alfred for the thoughts he put in my head about you two, but that wouldn't be fair. It was me. I couldn't see why you wanted to go and marry an Italian when they were against us and I was still that angry about Dunkirk and seeing my mates killed. But your Joe's a canny lad, keeps us all laughing here. Mind, he's terrible for scrounging smokes. I was wrong about Joe.*

I thought he'd be windy when it came to fighting –
like we expect foreigners to be. But he's got some
bottle. Reckon he saved my life in one attack – but I
can't write about that with the censors.

'When I come home, Sara, I'll make it up to you, I
promise. Take care. Love Tom.'

Scrawled at the bottom Tom had added, 'Go
and see Mam. She misses you.'

Sara thought of home and how remote Stout
House seemed to her now. She had only been
home once to help with the hay-making since
returning to live in Whitton Grange two and a
half years ago and she had not seen or heard
from her mother since she had married Joe. Her
only source of news was from her sister Chrissie,
who wrote long and interesting letters about life
on the farm.

From Chrissie she had heard the extraordinary
news that cousin Colin was living with her old
schoolfriend Beth and her boy Daniel at Rillhope,
Beth's husband John having disappeared to sea at
the beginning of the war and never been heard of
since. Sara wondered at the scandal her cousin
must be causing, but from what Chrissie said,
their country neighbours seemed to have
accepted the situation as a consequence of war.

Bill and Mary were expecting their second
child that autumn and there was much chat of
Sid Gibson helping around the farm. Her
mother, however, was seldom mentioned and
Sara determined she would make an effort to
travel home before the end of the summer.

At the end of August, Sara took an unpaid week
off work in the laundry and arranged a lift as far

as Stanhope, prepared to walk the rest of the way if necessary. She went round to say goodbye to Louie and found her in a state of distress; Jacob had had a stroke.

'The doctor's been. He's paralysed down one side – can't speak,' Louie said tearfully. 'Doctor's trying to get an ambulance, but there was a raid on Sunderland last night, he says, and the services are stretched.'

'Perhaps I could get one from The Grange?' Sara suggested. Louie shook her head.

'He doesn't want to leave here, Sara, I can see it in his eyes. This has been his home since he married,' Louie said forlornly.

Louie sent Sara into the parlour where Jacob had been moved the previous winter when he had become housebound. 'It might cheer him to see you,' Louie said in hope.

Sara found the old man lying in bed, with young Stan sitting beside him reading to him from a tattered *Boys' Own* annual. His grey, expressionless face looked like a death mask, then the old preacher's fierce blue eyes opened and watched her approach. His useless mouth tried to form coherent words as Sara took hold of his large, veined hand lying immobile on the sheet, and she tried to interpret what he said. She gave up and chatted to him about a letter she had received from Joe, saying he was on local leave while the regiment was in refit.

When she stood up to go the old man appeared agitated, as if he were trying to tell her something.

'Is it Louie you want?' Sara guessed. Jacob

moved his head on the pillow. 'Hildy, then?' This time he sighed with weak frustration. Sara looked helplessly at the faithful Stan, whose freckled face peered anxiously at his adopted grandfather.

'He wants to see his son,' Stan told Sara. 'He wants to see Ebenezer.'

It was Sara who went and telephoned Eb from the backshop in Pit Street and asked that he come to see his father.

'I'm so sorry, but he's not here.' Eleanor's cultured voice was apologetic. 'He's taken Rupert camping for a few days before he returns to school.'

Sara let out a gasp of frustration. 'Where have they gone? Can you contact them? Old Mr Kirkup's very weak.'

'They're somewhere up the valley from Whitton,' Eleanor answered. 'I'd drive out and see if I could find them, but I'm on ambulance duty tonight.'

'That's all right, we'll find them.' Sara rang off.

When Raymond came off shift, Sara and he set out to comb the surrounding Common and the hills beyond the pit village, before the light went. It was a still night, fragrant dust lifting from the heather as they tramped across the moor towards an angry sunset in the west. A blood red sky, Sara thought uneasily, and wondered what Joe was doing in far-off Africa under his sky of bright stars. If his regiment was being replenished and revived in bustling Alexandria, it must only be a matter of time before they were sent back to the front line.

'Don't worry, we're bound to find them.'

517

Raymond squeezed her hand, misunderstanding her silence. 'It's good of you, Sara, to stay and help Auntie Louie out. I know you should have been off home for a holiday.'

Sara smiled. 'I care about your family, Raymond – you've all been good to me. And Mr Kirkup's a great old man, for all his stubbornness. It'd be so sad if...'

'Aye, it would,' Raymond agreed, thinking of Eb, too.

The hillside dipped down towards a sheltered stream screened by gorse bushes and the pair followed a sheep track into the gloom.

'Your aunt's worried you might be seeing young Nancy.' Sara spoke to the shimmer of flies suspended in the last shafts of evening light. 'Why's that?'

Raymond seemed taken aback by her directness, then shrugged. 'Nancy's mam and my mam never got on. I think Auntie Louie's worried my mam will find out I'm seeing Minnie Bell's daughter.'

'So you *are* seeing her?' Sara queried.

'Aye, but there's no need to bother Auntie Louie about it, mind,' Raymond mumbled.

'Are you serious about the lass?' Sara persisted.

Raymond flushed, wondering why he was so embarrassed talking about such things with Sara. He could not possibly tell her that he courted the giggling Nancy to take his mind off thoughts of her. Sara was Joe's wife and he must push the daydreams he had about her from his mind for good. 'You're as bad as my aunties with all your questions,' he laughed.

Sara got no proper answer as, a moment later, Raymond spotted a tiny canvas tent pitched by the side of the burn. Hurrying nearer, they heard Eb's strong voice and found the artist and his son Rupert squatting over a small fire, toasting bread and, as far as Sara could gather, talking about poetry.

It took only minutes for Eb to dismantle the tent and pack it into his old rucksack, while Raymond helped Rupert extinguish the fire. They tramped back across the hills, Eb setting an urgent pace and the others struggling to keep up with him. Sara noticed Rupert's moodiness at his precious camping holiday being abandoned so abruptly.

'What were you reading back there?' she asked, attempting to make conversation.

'A poem,' he mumbled, his dark head bent. 'A war poem, but it never mentions the war.' Rupert's frostiness thawed as he spoke.

'Oh.' Sara was nonplussed.

'My Uncle Rupert wrote it during the Great War. It's called "The Hungry Hills" and Mama got it published – but Uncle Rupert was dead by then, killed at the Somme. I'm called after him, Dad says.' The boy's studious face looked proud in the moonlight.

'That's grand,' Sara replied and changed the subject, not wanting to talk of war.

Eb entered the parlour with Louie. It was shrouded by blackout paper and Louie was aware of the smell of the old man's incontinence and Sam's stale pipe tobacco. A paraffin lamp hissed on the table and threw shadows into the corners, and Louie wondered if Eb was reminded of his childhood when his job had been to trim the lamp wicks before school. The family piano which he had often played on happy family Saturday nights, stood hunched and silent next to the iron-framed bed that held the waxlike figure of their father.

As Eb drew close the rasping wheeze in the old man's throat grew louder and Louie saw how Eb was aghast to see the shrunken state of Jacob's once-muscled body, victim to decades of stone dust which had settled on his lungs. The same slow death would have been her brother's, Louie thought morbidly, had he remained at the Eleanor pit, so ironically named after his wife. She silently worried about Raymond working down the pit but for the moment that couldn't be helped. The alternative was worse...

'Father?' Eb spoke gently, pulling a chair near the bed. Quietly, Louie withdrew.

His father's eyes opened in their deep hollows, taking a moment to focus. For an instant they registered alarm and then recognition at the tall, bearded man who hovered over him, looking the image of himself as a younger man. Jacob held out one trembling hand, the other lying useless on the bedspread, and tried to speak.

Eb could make out nothing. 'Oh, Da, why did we leave it so long?' he cried in remorse. 'It's been as much my fault as yours for this daft quarrel. Many a time I've nearly come, in the hope you might see me – and Eleanor and Rupert. But I was always frightened for their sake that you might be hostile towards them.'

Eb gripped his father's hand, seeing how the old man's throat worked to form words in reply. Jacob gave up, tears welling in his faded blue eyes.

'I know you're as sorry as I am, Da,' Eb said softly, 'so don't try and tire yourself. There'll be time for words when you regain some strength.'

For a while, Eb sat with the dying Jacob and told him of his life in Durham, of Eleanor's work as a councillor and Rupert's prowess at English and cricket.

'He wants to be a writer,' Eb laughed. 'Who would've thought we'd have a budding poet in the family, eh?'

Half of Jacob's face seemed to lift in a smile. His hand moved from under Eb's and pointed with exhaustion at the door as he grunted a name.

'Rupert?' Eb queried. The old pitman sighed in affirmation. 'Aye, he's out-by, waiting with our Louie and Raymond. Would you like to see him?'

Eb took the rattling noise in his father's throat to mean yes, and he retreated into the subdued kitchen to fetch his son. Rupert's dark, bespectacled eyes looked wary, but he did not flinch from his father's request, following him into the gloomy parlour to meet his censorious grandfather.

Sara sat with Louie, helping her make a pair of shorts for Stan. Louie had made the young boy abandon his vigil and had sent him off to bed when Eb arrived to make his peace with his parent.

'What do you think they're saying?' Sara asked, curious at the reconciliation. Louie shrugged.

'It'll be all one-sided,' she sighed, 'but better late than never, as they say.'

Twenty minutes later, Eb and Rupert re-appeared and Louie could tell her brother had been weeping. Perhaps one day she could ask what had been said after these years of separation, but now was not the time.

'He's sleeping,' Eb said hoarsely and went out into the yard to be alone.

Jacob hung on for two more days, drifting in and out of consciousness. Louie sensed the peacefulness that had settled on her father's battered spirit after Eb's visit and was not surprised when he slipped into death early one September morning, while she was stoking up the kitchen fire and preparing him an infusion of mint picked from Sam's allotment.

Word was sent round to the neighbours and family that the funeral would be held the following Saturday. Cousin Sadie came to help and Hildy arrived from Newcastle the day before, but their brother John and family sent word from Derbyshire that travelling was too difficult. He would come and pay his respects when he could.

Sara stayed to help Louie with preparations for the wake, half relieved at the excuse not to visit her own family. She felt cowardly, but justified her decision by telling herself the Ritsons needed her more at that moment than her own family did.

Unexpectedly, Raymond's mother Iris Ramshaw blew in on the day of the funeral. Louie had sent word to the last address they had for her in London and it had been forwarded to the theatre where she was just finishing the summer run of a Noel Coward musical. Fond of her old father-in-law, and thankful of the excuse to escape the bomb-battered capital, Iris rushed north to see her family.

'By you've grown, young man!' she exclaimed on seeing her son Raymond. 'As handsome as his father, too,' Iris kept telling everyone that day. Raymond revelled in her admiration and Sara saw it reflected in his blue eyes as he watched his vivacious mother take centre stage in the crowded cottage after the funeral.

Sara gawped at the actress, slim and long-legged in a gaudy pink dress with black spots which clashed with her reddened hair under her neat, veiled black hat. Sara was mesmerised by her incessant chatter and attractive, heavily made-up face. She was so different from the village women, Sara was not surprised she had never settled among them. Iris had Raymond's quirky humour, but there was a tough brittleness about her too, that was unlike anything in her son. Iris apologised to Louie that she had nothing more suitable for a funeral.

'Still,' Iris patted Louie, speaking in the semi-southern accent she had acquired, 'your da isn't here to tick me off, bless him. Wish I'd seen him before...' She waved a hand and, popping another biscuit in her mouth, edged round the table to speak to Eb and Eleanor.

Raymond hovered at her side and fetched her cups of the precious rationed tea that Louie had provided with contributions from the Parkins next door.

'How long can you stay, Mam?' Raymond asked eagerly.

'I'll have to go Monday, pet,' she told him, running a slim hand over his cropped hair. 'But I promise I'll be home for Christmas this year – or you can come to me – I'll show you London town.'

'Not while the Jerries are still bombing it you won't,' Sam butted in.

'Still Mr Sensible, aren't you, Sam?' Iris teased, winking at Raymond. 'Well, I'll just have to come up here and liven you all up a bit. Whitton's like a morgue these days – oops, sorry, Louie.' Iris's pretty slim face blushed as she glanced across at her sad sister-in-law.

'Whitton's canny,' Raymond defended his home town. 'There's always some'at good on at the pictures.'

'And who are you taking to the pictures, then?' Iris smiled, swinging an arm about her son, who now towered over her. Raymond flushed and Sara waited to see if he would confide in his mother. But he obviously did not want to risk incurring her disapproval and diverted the conversation to Sara.

That evening, Sara invited Iris round to the Dimarcos' parlour, sensing her restlessness in the Ritson household and the relief on Louie's mournful face at a respite from the talkative Iris. Sadie left and Louie and Hilda settled to a quiet evening of reminiscence while the Dimarcos gave Iris the attentive audience on which she thrived.

It was after eleven when Iris said her goodbyes and Sara went out into the cool darkness, to see her safely away. The whitened doorsteps and kerbstones gleamed in the blackout, like ghostly trails showing the way home.

'Take care, Sara pet.' Iris kissed her as if they were old friends, 'Joe'll be back safely, you wait and see.'

As she turned to grope her way home, a couple came past them in the shadows.

'Hey, is that you, Raymond?' Iris shouted in recognition of the tall figure, arm-in-arm with his girlfriend. The pair stopped but kept their distance.

'Mam,' Raymond muttered.

His furtiveness only increased Iris's curiosity. 'Introduce us, then,' she laughed.

There was a pause and a muffled whispering, then Raymond said, 'You know her, Mam. It's Nancy Bell.'

'Hello, Mrs Kirkup,' Nancy chirped.

Sara saw Iris visibly flinch at the girl's greeting. 'Are you all right, Iris?' she asked in concern as the older woman grabbed her arm for support.

'Let me see you...' Iris whispered.

Nancy and Raymond stepped forward together and Iris shone her dimmed torch into the girl's round face, framed by black curls. She looked nervous and very young.

'Nancy Bell,' Iris gulped.

'We're courtin',' Raymond announced stubbornly, 'so you might as well know. Auntie Louie and Uncle Sam think they've stopped us seeing each other, but I knew you'd understand better. You don't mind do you, Mam? Nancy's got nothing to do with you and her mam falling out.'

All at once Iris found her voice and her famous temper ignited.

'She's got everything to do with our falling out!' she cried and, lunging at the girl, pushed her from Raymond's side.

Nancy, caught off balance, fell to the ground with a howl of surprise. Iris turned to Raymond and slapped him hard across his astonished face.

'Don't you go near her again, do you hear? Never again!'

'Mam!' Raymond protested, reaching to rescue Nancy.

Iris let out a stream of abuse at the two of them, consumed by rage.

'And your mother's nothing but a slut!' she yelled. 'By, I'll have words with Louie about this – it's her fault for allowing the two of you together.'

'Belt up!' Raymond was finally goaded into opposing his mother. 'And don't you go blaming Auntie Louie for anything. She's the best in the world – cares more about me than you've ever done.'

'And what about all the clothes I buy for you and the money I send home?' Iris choked with anger. 'Haven't you ever thought how hard it was for me to leave you with Louie – how hard it is every time I leave you behind?'

'No,' Raymond was hurtful in return, ''cos it's not true. All you've ever cared about is your singin' and dancing'.'

Sara, quite mystified by Iris's outburst and distressed by the harsh exchange, intervened. 'Don't fight each other, please.' She put a hand on Iris's arm. 'You'll only regret it when you're gone. Old Mr Kirkup's just been buried...'

Iris turned pained green eyes on Sara and her aggression evaporated. She burst into tears and flung her thin arms around her son.

'Sorry, pet,' she sobbed.

'So am I,' Raymond mumbled, while Nancy stood sulkily, ignored by them all.

'What about me?' she complained. 'And all those things you've said about my mam – what about saying sorry to me?'

They turned to peer at Nancy in the dark and Raymond loosened his mother's hold, feeling torn between the two.

To Sara's surprise, Iris answered her quietly. 'I am sorry for you and Raymond – but it's your mam's fault that you mustn't go on seeing each other.'

'How can it be?' Nancy asked in annoyance. 'She isn't stopping me.'

'Well, she should be,' Iris replied more sharply. 'But she's obviously too frightened to tell you in case that bad-tempered husband of hers beats her up.'

'Don't speak about my father–'

'*Not* your father,' Iris interrupted, glaring at the girl. 'Your father was Davie Kirkup – my husband.'

'What in the wide world do you mean by that?' Nancy retorted.

'I mean you are Davie Kirkup's daughter – just as Raymond is Davie's son.' Iris's voice was dull. 'Your mam and Davie had a fling on Stand High Farm during the strike. It has to have been Davie who's your father 'cos your dad was in prison at the time.'

That bitter strike, Sara thought again, is still poisoning the lives of these pit people a generation later. She saw Raymond's stunned figure turn and vomit into the road.

An ARP warden advanced down the street, shouting at them to get home. Nancy began to cry.

'Do you want to come inside to talk?' Sara asked, feeling deep pity for them all. Raymond and Nancy were half-brother and sister! It was no wonder Louie had been so anxious about their friendship.

'There's nothing more I want to hear,' Raymond said, his face ghastly. Without another word to any of them, he turned and ran down the street into the night.

'I never wanted him to find out,' Iris said mournfully and, turning to Nancy, put a hand on her shoulder. 'Nor you, pet. You're not to blame for what Minnie and my Davie did, but you had to know.'

Sara felt a stab of pity for the sad-faced Iris having to admit her husband's infidelity after all these years, and marvelled at her sudden compassion towards Nancy. Sara left Iris comforting the girl her faithless husband had conceived.

Chapter Twenty-Seven

By the time Sara saw Raymond again a week after Jacob's funeral, Iris was gone and he had immersed himself once more in work and football, his dedication getting him picked for Whitton's first team. He determined to waste no more time over lasses, for they had brought him nothing but heartache. From the autumn, Nancy Bell was never mentioned in the Ritson household and Raymond never went near the Bells' house in Oswald Street or bothered what films were showing at The Palace. Sara learned from Louie that Bomber Bell had thrown Minnie and Nancy out of the house when news of the scandal spread and they had sought refuge once more with Minnie's long-suffering mother, Mrs Slattery.

Just before Christmas, Sara heard that Nancy had left Whitton Grange to work as a maid in a big house in Sunderland and wondered if the unfortunate girl would ever get over the shock of discovering that the lad she had courted had turned out to be her half-brother.

But by then, the village gossip about Nancy and Raymond had been eclipsed by momentous news at the pit and abroad. The persistence of union men like Sam Ritson had resulted in an enquiry and the Greene Award of a national minimum wage.

'£4.3s underground and 6d a shift extra for "wet work",' Sam told Louie. 'It's taken a bloody world war to get us back some of the rights we had before the '26 lockout!' Sam shook his head, but Louie could tell he was encouraged by their success.

Then news came of Allied counter offensives in the African desert, as the Battle of Egypt began and days of gruelling combat ended in the German Afrika Korps retreating west, pursued for a thousand miles by the British Eighth Army who captured hundreds of Italian Infantry on the way.

For the first time since the threat of invasion had shadowed the country, church bells were allowed to be rung once more in celebration and people went to stand at their doors in the crisp November air to listen to the joyful peal from St Cuthbert's belfry.

Sara walked up onto Whitton Common, restless at the thought of Joe and thankful she had had no dreaded telegram to spoil her feeling of optimism. Returning by the kissing gate and the allotments, she spotted Raymond digging in Sam's plot.

'I thought you'd be out drinking a toast to the lads with all the others,' Sara teased him.

'Thought I'd lift the last potatoes for Sam,' Raymond grunted, unbending from his task and pushing back his cap to look at her. He felt a familiar tightening in his chest at the sight of Sara's rosy face and tangled fair hair licking around her temples.

'Hardly see you these days,' Sara said, leaning

on the battered fence. 'You never call round to see us at Pit Street any more.'

Raymond blushed. 'Prefer to keep to myself.' He glanced away, feeling guilt towards his friend Joe for the nagging want he felt inside for the Weardale girl. When was it, he wondered, that his friendly affection towards Sara had fanned into desire? Ever since that terrible summer of 1940 when the Dimarcos had become scapegoats of the war and Sara had given him the courage to stand by Joe's family she had been special to him. Her contempt for his part in the attack on the Dimarcos' shop had shamed him deeply and he had been desperate for her approval. But when Sara had chosen Joe for good and he knew that his love for her was futile he had filled his emptiness by courting the pretty but juvenile Nancy.

Sara sensed Raymond's reticence and wondered whether Rosa and Albina, vying for his attention when he and Sam had come to do jobs for the Dimarcos, had frightened Raymond away. Since the incident over Nancy, Louie had told her, Raymond showed no interest in courting anyone else.

'Is Iris coming for Christmas?' Sara asked.

'No, I'm going to stay with Mam in Manchester for the holiday – she's in a pantomime.'

'That's grand,' Sara smiled, 'it'll do you good...'

'To get away from all the wagging tongues, you mean?' Raymond's voice was suddenly bitter.

'Nancy's gone now. Can't you try and put that business behind you?' Sara asked him gently.

'How can I?' he scowled. 'They should have

531

told me long ago I had a sister – why didn't they?'

'To protect Minnie, I suppose, and your mam,' Sara sighed. 'And not to spoil your memory of your dad too.'

'I don't have any memory of me dad,' Raymond answered, spitting savagely onto the black earth. 'All I know is that he's done nothing but harm. It's because of him that Mam had to leave me – and it's his fault I got me head kicked in by Normy Bell – and that I nearly had incest with me half-sister. I *hate* the bastard!'

'Don't say that about your own father,' Sara said, shocked. 'He can't have been a bad man – your Auntie Louie thought the world of him.'

'Well, I can't forgive him for ruining my life.' Raymond was uncompromising.

'Iris did,' Sara replied gently. 'So can't you?'

Raymond's handsome, sullen face looked suddenly vulnerable as he met Sara's concerned look. He was wretched that he had ended by arguing with Sara and would never be able to tell her how he felt about her. He hardly cared about breaking up with Nancy, it was the knowledge of yet another betrayal by his father that really hurt him. So he turned back to his gardening, thrusting his spade into the soil and said no more. Sara left him and did not see Raymond again until after Christmas and his visit to his mother, by which time he had recovered much of his old humour.

The arrival of 1943 brought renewed resolution at the pit to increase production in support of the Durham Light Infantry campaigning in Africa. After insistent demands from the pitmen a makeshift canteen was erected in the pit yard and Louie went to work there in February, happily giving in her notice at the Naylors', where she had cleaned for years.

'Doing my bit for the war effort,' she told Mrs Naylor, the under-manager's wife, hardly suppressing her glee.

'Surely you can manage here as well?' The formidable Mrs Naylor was dismayed.

'Not with my two workers to wash and cook for – and Stan our evacuee,' Louie added pointedly. It had always rankled with her that the Naylors had somehow managed to avoid taking in any displaced children, yet they had four empty bedrooms.

'Well, I do think this is rather ungrateful of you, Louie,' Mrs Naylor sniffed, 'after the good money we've paid you and the hamper every Christmas.'

Louie nearly struck the woman in her anger and might have done so had Sara not been with her, on her way to work at The Grange.

'You're the one who should be grateful,' Louie trembled as she spoke. 'Grateful that I've worked so hard for you all these years, after the way Mr Naylor evicted Sam and me after the strike.'

Sara steered Louie away before Mrs Naylor recovered from her astonishment. When they had marched down the drive, Louie burst into tears and told Sara how she had lost her only baby when Naylor had attempted to evict her the first time, during that dreadful year of 1926. Sara had never seen Louie cry before.

'I never carried a bairn again after losing Louisa,' Louie said in deep sadness. 'And I still think of her all these years later and what might have been...'

'I'm sorry,' Sara said, feeling quite inadequate and struck once more by the fortitude of Louie and the Whitton women like her who rarely complained of the hardships they endured. How the generous-hearted Louie must have suffered over the years at her childlessness! No wonder she was so devoted to Raymond.

'Haway, flower,' Louie recovered her composure and gave Sara a hug as if she needed comforting. 'Let's get ourselves to work.'

That spring, Sara was kept busy at The Grange hospital as battle-ravaged men returned from North Africa for operations and recuperation. Some brought grim stories of bloody hand-to-hand combat with bayonets and of heroism against a tenacious enemy. Others could only remember the tedium and dysentery.

At home, the Dimarcos eked out an existence, opening the shop as a matter of pride, even if there was nothing to sell. Yet Arturo's wages from the factory, Bobby's small payment from the cycle shop and Sara's meagre pay packet kept their large family from going hungry and Rosa and Sylvia became adept at refashioning old clothes to fit their growing children. Sylvia's son Peter was now at school and had a ferocious appetite, often bringing small friends home to the parlour with promises of jelly and custard, which could not always be honoured.

From what Sara could gather, Joe and Tom's battalion was somewhere in the Middle East being reinforced or retrained once more, for where, no one seemed to know. After a visit to see her husband Davide on the Isle of Man, Elvira returned resigned to her husband's imprisonment and threw herself with more vigour into helping Anna run the household.

With initial instruction from Sam Ritson, the tending of their yard allotment became Elvira's preserve, and, no matter the weather, she would be seen flitting about her crowded garden like a sparrow, busily planting and weeding, raking and harvesting her crops of potatoes, onions and carrots, runner beans, peas and marrows. Anna's old pots of flowers became home to cascades of parsley and fragrant herbs which the women used to enliven their pasta and vegetable soups.

In the early summer, when Albina and Rosa turned twenty, Albina was shaken out of her lazy existence by a direction from the Ministry of Labour and National Service to go and train with the ATS.

'Why haven't you been summoned?' Albina accused Rosa with petulance.

'Because I have a daughter to look after,' Rosa defended herself.

'It's not fair!' Albina protested.

'No, it's war,' Sara answered dryly.

Albina shot her a hostile look. She had never kept her dislike for Joe's Durham wife a secret. Sara had taken over the family with her English lessons and her chatter and her over-anxiety to please and, Albina thought with resentment, she always sided with Rosa against her. Albina was filled with jealousy for the pretty, blunt-talking girl who had even won the approval of her cautious and conservative mother, Elvira.

'And what are you doing to help?' Albina turned her vicious tongue on Sara. 'Washing dirty pyjamas, that's all.'

'Aye, washing dirty pyjamas,' Sara replied with spirit, 'and sheets covered in soldiers' blood and surgeons' overalls covered in guts. I clear up the mess of lads who've lost half their bowels. Imagine, Albina, what would happen if nobody did. There are plenty different ways of fighting this war – and doing the army's washing is one of them.'

The Dimarco women gaped at Sara's outburst and Albina turned puce at the raw language. But for once she was silenced and shortly afterwards took the train south, to the relief of all but Elvira. Rosa, although not obliged to work, volunteered at the pit canteen and, after the first terrifying days of serving soup and cheese to the blackened pitmen, began to revel in her new-found independence. It was after Rosa had started working at the Eleanor pit, that Sara noticed Raymond beginning to call at Pit Street once again.

He would saunter round with his second-hand bicycle, bought by Iris on his eighteenth birthday, and chat to Bobby while the younger boy looked it over with a critical eye. Raymond brought fruit from Sam's apple tree for Anna to bake and took Peter out for football practice in the park. It cheered Sara to see more of him again, and she speculated as to his reasons for calling. She noticed how Raymond was kind to the children and friendly to Rosa, yet never attempted to get Rosa alone.

In July, the war-jaded village decided to put on a field day as the pitmen's Big Meeting was cancelled for the fourth year running.

Rosa and Sylvia dressed the children up in fancy dress and took them along to see Raymond and Sam play in a charity match, in which the Home Guard challenged the WVS and female ARP wardens to a game of football.

Raymond persuaded Sara to join in and Rosa and Sylvia whooped with delight as Sara rushed on dressed in galoshes and a pair of flowery shorts she had made out of cushion covers. Peter and Linda screamed with mirth to see their aunt cavorting around the field and Rosa had to restrain an inquisitive Mary from straying into the middle of the pitch. Dozens of goals were scored on either side and no one was quite sure who won in the end.

After sack races for the children and a tea of indigestible cakes made from dried egg, the people of Whitton Grange took their tired but jubilant families home.

'Come back for a drink of lemonade,' Sara invited a hot-faced Raymond. 'Mrs Dimarco's managed to get some specially for the field day.'

'Aye, I'd like that,' Raymond answered with a bashful glance.

It was while they were sitting in the backshop with the door open to Elvira's fragrant yard that the sound of her humming was disturbed by the announcement on the wireless that the Allies had invaded Sicily. Arturo and Anna came in from the shop and stood listening to the report of the

British success in overpowering Italian divisions and the prisoners taken.

'It will be the Italian mainland next,' Arturo said dully, his face furrowing into familiar lines of anxiety.

Sara thought of Joe fighting in the heat against his father's countrymen and kept quiet.

But Raymond did not. 'Perhaps Italy will come over to our side now, if they see it's no use putting up a fight against our lads,' he said optimistically.

The silence around him was awkward.

'But Italy is full of German soldiers who do not want to lose.' Arturo gave a dispirited shrug. 'They do not care if Italy is destroyed under the jackboots.'

Raymond left in a hurry, uncomfortable in the sudden atmosphere of worry, taking refuge among villagers who were rejoicing at the news.

As July wore on, there were reports from Italy of fierce German resistance and heavy casualties. Then the startling news of Mussolini's resignation and the fascist party being banned boosted the morale of the country. Despite a gleeful obscenity about Mussolini and cowardly Italians daubed on the shop window that night, the Dimarcos felt a certain relief at the news.

'King Victor Emmanuel will make peace with the British,' Arturo was confident, 'and then perhaps Davide and the others will be allowed to come home.'

August arrived and, after heavy fighting, the British finally marched into Catania, then Taormina to secure Sicily under Allied control.

One Saturday afternoon, late in the month, Sara and Rosa took the children up to the Common for a picnic and a romp around in the fresh air. The sky was hazy from the warm day and they looked down on the shimmering village, its dirty brick muted and indistinct. Around them, the yellow cornfields were newly shorn and speckled with scavenging blackbirds.

'Someone's coming up the path,' Rosa pointed at a lone figure, making determinedly towards them.

'Probably a rambler,' Sara said, uninterested, chewing a strand of grass and languid from the heat.

But Rosa appeared more interested. 'He's in uniform.'

Sara sat up, tumbling Mary off her stomach to peer at the dark-headed figure. She scrambled to her feet.

'It's— I think. Is it, Rosa?' she gasped.

'Go and see!' Rosa pushed her friend forward.

Sara began to walk towards the soldier and then, as certainty dawned, she broke into a run.

Joe climbed the wall and threw his arms open as he caught sight of Sara dashing across the stubbled field. His deeply bronzed face broke into a beaming smile of delight.

'*Bellissima!*' he laughed at Sara's dishevelled appearance and she fell against his body in a joyful embrace.

Keeping a tight hold of each other, they climbed back towards Rosa and the children.

'It's been so long!' Sara clung to her husband happily. 'Has it been terrible out there? You look grand, mind.'

'And so do you,' Joe kissed her again, almost sick with longing for his honey-haired wife. In the two and a half years of absence the girlish Sara had matured into an attractive woman.

Joe hardly contained his impatience to be alone with Sara, while Rosa and the children fussed over him and he gave Linda a piggy-back home, with Peter diving at his feet pretending to be a fighter pilot. But there was no privacy in the crowded flat as Anna and Elvira bustled around Joe, pressing him to eat their precious rations whilst the children begged him for stories of the war. Joe's relief at being home for this longed-for leave was only marred by the change he saw in his father. Arturo looked so old and forlorn, as if he had lost his way in life. He showed little interest in the young grandchildren playing around his feet and asked few questions about Joe's months of combat. When he returned from work he slumped in his corner chair and went to sleep.

'He works hard, your papa,' Anna made excuses for her husband's disinterest, 'and in that awful factory – telling him what he must do all day long.' Joe's mother made a dismissive gesture. 'He is not used to that.'

Joe took comfort from his mother's resilience and saw, with increasing admiration, how she coped with her motley household on their meagre resources. After a welcoming supper of pasta and home-baked bread, Joe shook off the fatigue that gripped him and took Sara out for a walk.

'I thought I'd never get you alone!' he laughed as they hurried up to the woods, unashamed in their desire for each other. Joe pulled her in to the battered allotment shed that belonged to the Kirkups and where they had played cards out of the rain so long ago.

'What if Sam or Raymond were to come?' Sara said bashfully.

'They won't,' Joe replied, not caring and pulled the ill-fitting door shut behind them.

They made frantic love on a pile of old sacking and straw, ignoring the discomfort, then shared a cigarette and talked quietly of the past. Sara told him of her work at the hospital, of old Jacob dying and the fuss over Raymond and Nancy's courtship.

'Poor lad,' Joe sighed. 'He's had some knocks in life.'

'He'll bounce back,' Sara was sanguine. 'Raymond always does.'

'I hope so,' Joe smiled. 'He's been a good friend to my family – Rosa told me how much he's done while I've been away – little jobs here and there.'

'I think he still likes Rosa,' Sara mused. 'He's often round at the shop of an evening. But enough of Raymond,' Sara said, snuggling against Joe, 'tell me about the army.'

Joe was reticent about the war in the desert and Sicily, not wanting to tell her of the carnage he had witnessed, but gave her news of Tom and their growing friendship.

'He's gone home, too,' Joe told her, 'and he's hoping to see you.'

'I haven't been home for such a long time,' Sara admitted. 'I've put it off that many times.' She felt a new surge of guilt at the way she had allowed the gulf to widen between herself and her family. She could have gone before now, but had avoided doing so.

'Because of being married to me?' Joe asked, squinting at her through smoke.

'They're that narrow-minded about Italians,' Sara tried to explain, 'I've been frightened they'd turn me away. I know Mam was mad at me going off and getting wed without telling anyone – and then to a Dimarco.'

'Tom was like that until he got to see I was just like the next lad,' Joe reminded her. 'I think you should go and see your mam. The longer you leave it, the harder it'll be.' He handed her the cigarette.

'It's not that I don't want to see them...' Sara faltered. Then, 'Will you come with me?' she asked quietly.

'Aye, of course,' Joe said, undaunted. 'You don't think I'd let you out of my sight for a minute of my leave do you?' he grinned.

Sara pressed against him and kissed his face. 'I love you so much, Joe Dimarco – and if Mam doesn't too, I'll not go home again.'

For the next few days, Rosa and Mary moved out of the bedroom they shared with Sara, allowing the young couple a degree of privacy. Sara took time off work and they spent a happy week of picnics on Whitton Common in the mellow September sunshine, visiting the Ritsons and Pat Slattery's family, going to the pictures and travelling into Durham for the day to see Eb and Eleanor Kirkup and take a boat out on the river. A dance was organised at the Memorial Hall for the servicemen on leave and Joe persuaded Raymond to take Rosa, with the consent of a more tolerant Anna and an acquiescent Arturo.

The foursome were full of a happy nostalgia as they recalled the Carnival dance of four years ago.

'My one and only big dance,' Rosa said ruefully.

'And I had me leg bandaged up,' Raymond laughed.

'I was mad because Joe was ignoring me!' Sara nudged her husband.

'It was you who was ignoring me!' Joe protested.

'Well, are you dancing now?' Sara laughed and led him onto the dance floor.

Rosa watched them go with a stab of envy, thinking what a striking couple they made with Joe's dark good looks and Sara's long, shining hair. And they are so in love, Rosa thought, wondering for the hundredth time what might have been if she had followed Emilio Fella back to Italy...

Raymond, too, found it hard to watch Joe hold Sara so close on the dance floor, wishing it could be him. But Joe was one of his most generous friends and Raymond was flooded with guilt at the disloyal thought. He would never do anything to betray Joe or hurt Sara, so he forced himself to be attentive to the sad-eyed Rosa.

'My dancing's improved since the last time,' Raymond broke into her thoughts, 'if you want to risk it.'

Rosa turned and smiled gratefully at Raymond.

He was funny and kind and over the past year had matured more quickly than the other lads his age who came into the pit canteen with their ribald remarks at the girls. A pity she had not fallen in love with Raymond four years ago instead of Emilio, she thought sadly, for she could see it was only out of kindness that he asked her to dance now. Rosa knew no respectable lad would be interested in a penniless fallen woman with an illegitimate daughter.

'Of course I'll risk it,' Rosa smiled and took the arm Raymond offered.

The dance was one of the happiest evenings of Joe's leave, their spirits lifted by the music and dancing and no ugly scenes with Normy Bell or his former gang to spoil the occasion. The WVS served up soup and spam sandwiches in the interval.

'You can tell the Yanks are here,' Joe muttered. 'All this spam.'

'Me mam's got an American friend,' Raymond announced as he waded through the crowds, balancing the pink, pressed meat on a plate. 'Met him at a party in London.'

'Will she bring him here do you think?' Sara asked excitedly.

'Not likely,' Raymond snorted. 'Probably told him she's from somewhere posh. She said he's from near Hollywood, so she'll be out to impress.'

'Shouldn't be ashamed of where you come from,' Sara answered.

'I don't think she is,' Raymond defended his mother. 'She just likes to make life sound more exciting than it really is.'

The four left, pink-cheeked, from the hot hall, singing popular songs and finished with a Bovril at the parlour before Raymond said his good-byes.

'I'll see you when we get back from Sara's mam's,' Joe told him.

'Aye,' Raymond nodded, hovering in the doorway. 'Good luck with seeing your mam again, Sara,' he added.

'Thanks,' Sara smiled at him gratefully. She was nervous at the prospect of meeting her family again, anxious at the reception she and Joe might receive.

'Goodnight, Raymond,' Rosa said with a shy smile. 'I did enjoy the dancing.'

Raymond flushed. 'Ta-ra then, I'll be off.'

As Raymond opened the door quickly Joe clapped a hand on his friend's shoulder. 'You're a canny lad, Raymond Kirkup – I wouldn't mind you in the family,' he winked.

Raymond dived away with an embarrassed grunt and Joe shut up shop, following Sara eagerly upstairs to bed.

The next day they took the bus to Stanhope early and from there to Lowbeck on a dilapidated bus crammed with school children coming to help with harvesting. After three years away Sara thought how shabby the houses in Lowbeck looked, with their peeling doors and window frames and how forlorn the rusting vans aban-doned by the lower fields. They saw an antiquated threshing machine being pulled by horses and several carts and traps drawn by ponies, a sight uncommon since Sara's early childhood.

Sara's nervousness mounted as they walked up the valley to Rillhope and took the rough track up the steep mountainside to Highbeck and Stout House. She had decided to surprise them with the visit, but wondered now if the idea had been foolish. It had been so long since she had seen any of them, would she know what to say? Then she reminded herself she was a married woman of twenty and should not behave like a timid girl. She quickened her pace.

The first person to spot them tramping up the hill with their parcels of gifts was a tall girl with bobbed fair hair whom Sara took to be one of the land girls. She gawped at them a moment and then, dropping her pail with a clatter, raced over to greet them.

'Sara!' she screamed. 'You've come home at last.' And Sara found herself being enveloped by her younger sister.

'Chrissie, you're as tall as a beanpole,' she cried, hugging the girl back.

'You look grand,' Chrissie said with admiration. 'Tom said you might come. He's over at the Metcalfes' with Jane.' She stopped, suddenly aware of Joe's amused regard.

'This is Joe,' Sara introduced her husband, 'and this is Chrissie.'

Joe took the girl's rough hand and kissed it swiftly before she could protest. 'Pleased to meet you,' he grinned. Chrissie giggled and went pink as she snatched her hand back.

'Don't try that with Mam,' Sara warned him sharply, nervous at the thought. 'Where is she?'

'In the kitchen as always,' Chrissie answered. 'She's looking after the bairns while Mary's away at her mam's – her dad's poorly bad.'

Sara felt a guilty flush of relief that her critical sister-in-law Mary would not be around to make things more difficult for her or Joe.

'Haway, then.' She linked a possessive arm through Joe's and led him up the uneven stone steps into her former home.

Her mother nearly dropped the cast-iron pan she was wielding at the black range when Sara walked in with Joe. Her mouth opened, shut and opened again in astonishment at the sight of her grown-up daughter on the arm of the tall, swarthy man in uniform. She put down the pan, her knees giving way, and crumpled into the battered armchair beside the fire.

'Mam?' Sara rushed forward, alarmed by the colour draining from her mother's tired face.

'Sara?' she clutched at her daughter as if needing proof she was no illusion.

'Aye, Mam, it's me,' Sara said, kissing her mother's greying hair. 'And this is Joe...'

To her dismay her mother burst into tears and Joe halted in his advance towards her. Sara stood up but Lily Pallister grasped her on the arm.

'I'm not crying 'cos of your Italian husband,' she managed to say, 'I'm just so happy to see you, pet!'

Sara put her arms around her mother and they hugged each other in relief.

Later when Lily had recovered from her shock, she sat them both down at the large kitchen table and gave them a meal of bacon and egg pie made

547

with real eggs and gooseberry fool that had been made for Tom and scones with some of Mary's scarce, homemade blackberry jam. At first they ate in silence as Lily watched over them and Sara cringed at the awkwardness between her mother and Joe. But when he presented her with a present of bananas he had bought in the charity auction at the dance, her frostiness thawed a fraction.

'I can't remember what they taste like!' Lily cried. 'And they used to be my favourite fruit.'

'Sara told me,' Joe smiled. 'And here's something from my mam for you.' He handed over a bottle of rhubarb wine and a handkerchief embroidered with delicate lace. 'And Aunt Elvira wanted you to have some leeks from her garden.' Joe pulled a face. 'You've probably got plenty, but she's that proud of them.'

Lily looked with embarrassment at her handsome son-in-law, uncomfortable at his family's generosity. 'Nice of her to bother – I'll make some leek dumplings. You can't beat leeks grown in Whitton soil.'

When Sara attempted to help her mother clear the table, she was shooed away. 'You'll be wanting to visit Beth down Rillhope, no doubt. You show your lad around the farm and make yourselves scarce until tea-time.'

They went quickly, relieved that the first encounter was over and that Sara's mother had at least been civil to Joe. They walked up the beck and onto the moors, Sara pointing out all the landmarks for miles around. Circling the farms of Highbeck they descended to Rillhope and knocked at Beth Lawson's door as an early autumn squall hit the row of stone cottages. Beth gave them a cheery welcome and pulled them in beside her small fire.

'You never write,' Sara admonished her friend.

'Can't get paper,' Beth answered unconcerned, stoking the smouldering fire. 'You've got yourself a bonny lad, mind,' Beth said, giving Joe a saucy look.

'And you've taken up with my cousin Colin, so they say,' Sara was equally blunt.

Beth straightened up and gave Sara one of her considering squints. 'You're not fond of Colin are you?' she asked. Sara did not answer. 'I can understand why from the tales Colin's told me. But he was that unhappy in Whitton – he's different here. And he's been canny to me and the bairn. Does everything around the house – not like John Lawson.' Beth spoke of her husband as if he were a stranger.

'Well, you must have reformed him,' Sara retorted, still sceptical.

'Perhaps all he needed was to get away from your uncle,' Joe commented, lighting a cigarette.

'Aye,' Beth laughed, 'he doesn't have a good word to say about his father or stepmother. And they don't want anything to do with him, either, from what I can see. Not since he took up with a married woman.' Beth chuckled.

They stayed an hour, by which time Beth's son Daniel had come staggering in with a pile of firewood he had been collecting with Colin. There was an awkward exchange of nods and forced greetings when Colin discovered who their visitors were. Sara could sense Joe's tension as he faced his old adversary and she could not reconcile Beth's glowing picture of Colin with her memory of the surly cousin who had beaten up Raymond Kirkup and joined a vigilante mob against the Dimarcos. He had certainly changed physically, looking brawny and weathered as if he had farmed all his life, but Sara found it hard to forgive him his past faults.

'We'll be off then.' She rose quickly. 'I want to see Tom.'

'Call before you leave, won't you?' Beth encouraged.

'Aye, if there's time,' Sara promised.

Colin and Joe exchanged looks then, quite unexpectedly, Colin held out his hand in a gesture of reconciliation. Joe's bronzed face deepened in colour as he hesitated, then shook Colin's hand.

Colin, unable to form the words of apology that he knew he ought to say, muttered tactlessly, 'There's a bunch of POWs working up at Thimble Hill – Italians.'

Joe stiffened at the words. 'So?'

'I've been working with some of them,' Colin added. 'They're canny lads – always wanting to show you photos of their families. Just thought you'd be interested,' Colin mumbled.

Joe did not reply, still suspicious that some offence had been meant. He doubted he would ever be able to fully trust a Cummings.

As they made their way home, Sara mused. 'Fancy Colin ending up working with Italian prisoners and finding he likes them. You might have captured them in Africa.'

Joe was silent as they trudged back up the slope, a curlew crying mournfully in the wind.

'They're just like us,' he said softly, 'probably homesick and missing the wife like I was.' He kissed the top of her head.

Sara slipped her arm around his waist and shivered in the wind. 'I wish you didn't have to go back so soon.'

Their three days at Stout House were made easier by Tom's cheerful banter and Lily Pallister warmed towards her unwelcome son-in-law when she saw how friendly Joe and Tom had become. She began to forget his alien origin and his foreign appearance and allowed herself to smile at his jokes and flattery at her cooking. When the time came for Sara and Joe to leave, she found herself strangely emotional.

'You'll bring him again, won't you?' Lily asked her daughter on their final evening. They were in the pantry washing up.

'You like him don't you, Mam?' Sara said, pleased.

Lily sniffed. 'I can see why you married him, though it would have been easier if he wasn't...'

'He's Whitton born and bred, just like you,' Sara reminded her mother sternly.

'Aye,' Lily sighed. 'Anyway, I'm glad you're happy, pet.' She kissed her daughter affectionately on the head.

'And you'll come and visit Joe's family sometime, too?' Sara urged.

'Aye, maybe's,' Lily said, unable to commit herself that far. 'You'll take that box of eggs and the jam for them in return for their presents.' Sara had to content herself with this half-hearted approval.

The next day, Tom took them down in the trap to Lowbeck and said an emotional farewell to Sara.

'Take care of each other, won't you?' she told her brother. 'You're my two favourite lads.'

Tom gave her a thumping hug. 'You'll not get rid of us that easily,' he teased. 'We've been through the worst,' he joked.

As they awaited the bus, a truckload of men came trundling into the hamlet. The vehicle juddered to a stop and three men piled out the back, coughing in the exhaust fumes.

'POWs,' Tom told them casually, watching the men troop past the disused slaughterhouse, closed down at the beginning of the war when the government took control of the food supply. 'They'll be going to Dr Hall's garden to pick fruit. These lot were captured after El Alamein.'

Sara glanced at Joe. 'What's wrong?' she asked, seeing the look of shock on his face.

He did not seem to hear her as he shouted after the men in Italian dialect. One of them turned at the familiar words, his unshaven face startled.

'Joe?' Sara asked in concern.

'I know him,' Joe said, 'I know that lad.'

'Who is it?' Sara asked as the bus rumbled round the corner into view.

'Emilio Fella,' he answered, 'the lad that got Rosa into trouble. I'm *sure* it's him.'

Chapter Twenty-Eight

The day Joe and Sara returned to Whitton Grange, the surrender of the Italian forces was announced and the household was thrown into such turmoil that they delayed telling Rosa of Joe's sighting of Emilio.

'What does this mean for us?' Elvira demanded. 'Will Davide come home now?'

'What about Domenica and Pasquale?' Anna asked anxiously. 'Will their village be occupied?'

'They are already occupied,' Joe reminded his mother, as news came through of the German takeover of Rome and a puppet fascist government under Mussolini being set up by Hitler in the north.

On the day Joe left, the invasion of Italy by the Allies was already under way.

'At least I will not have to fight my Italian cousins any more,' he joked with his father, who did not find it amusing.

'God go with you, Joseph, my son,' Arturo croaked and nearly broke down as he embraced him.

Bobby took Sara to the station to see Joe off on the crowded train and stayed at a respectful distance while they said their goodbyes.

'Should I tell Rosa about Emilio?' Sara asked, trying to think of things to say to delay their parting.

'It might bring out all the anger in the family again,' Joe was doubtful, 'and maybe it wasn't Emilio I saw.'

'He recognised you!' Sara was adamant. 'You could see the shock on his face, too.'

'You must decide for the best, Sara pet,' Joe said with resignation and pulled her close against him. 'Oh, *bellissima*, I'll miss you like hell.'

Sara felt the tears sting her eyes as she clung to him.

'I'll not be happy till I see you again, Joe,' she choked.

He smiled down at her. 'You mustn't be sad, pet, 'cos I know you keep the others going with your happy nature. Now give us a kiss and I'll be off.'

They kissed with desperation and longing and with deep tenderness, both engulfed by the intensity of their love for each other. When they pulled away, neither could speak and Sara saw the tears on Joe's face.

He grabbed her hands and kissed them, then turned and threw his kit bag onto the train, climbing after it and fighting for a place at the window to keep Sara in view.

'Write to me!' Sara cried as the train lurched along the platform in a blast of steam.

'I love you!' Joe shouted and blew her a kiss. The last glimpse he had of Whitton Station was of a tearful Sara running along the platform, waving, her long hair shining golden in the soft September sun. Then they were rattling past a row of dismal terraced cottages and she was gone from sight...

When Sara broke the news that Emilio Fella was a prisoner of war up Weardale, the family temporarily forgot their sadness at Joe's departure. The questions rained down on the bereft Sara and she wished she had kept quiet.

'I must see him!' Rosa cried, almost hysterical at the news. 'Poor Emilio a prisoner. Take me to see him, Sara, please. He must see his child too.'

'I'm the one who should have words with Emilio Fella.' Arturo was provoked out of his apathy. 'He has shamed my family, I will take a gun to his head and blow his pretty face away!'

'Arturo!' Anna was shocked at his vehemence.

'Papa, don't say such a thing,' Rosa said in distress, 'he's Mary's father and I'm going to see him.'

'Then I will come, too,' Arturo barked. 'You shall not face him on your own.'

'Arturo, you cannot go – you're not supposed to travel – you might get into trouble,' Anna fretted. 'No, it would not be a good thing. Let Sara go with Rosa if she has set her heart on seeing this man. Perhaps he will do the honest thing by her.'

It was a month before Sara could arrange to travel back up the valley and Rosa drove them all to distraction with her impatience and excitement. Sara had never seen her so full of purpose, filling her time sewing new outfits for Mary for the journey.

Raymond, who had been paying Rosa visits since the charity dance in a half-hearted attempt to rid himself of thoughts of Sara gave up in despair. 'She's never got over this Italian, has she?' he asked Sara, as she walked back with him to visit Louie.

'It doesn't seem like it,' Sara sighed. 'I wish I'd never told her – it's dividing the family already. And what if it's not Emilio?'

Raymond grunted. 'You'll just have to hope it is – for your sake *and* Rosa's.'

Sara looked at the tall Raymond, loping along at her side. 'You're a good'un. You'd rather lose Rosa to Emilio than see her unhappy, wouldn't you?'

Raymond felt a stab of pain as he looked into Sara's warm green eyes. It means nothing, he said inwardly, it's you I hurt over, Sara Dimarco, but you must never know.

'Have you heard from Joe yet?' he changed the subject.

'Just a postcard,' Sara smiled wistfully, 'before sailing.' She felt better talking to Raymond about Joe, knowing they were old friends and that Raymond missed him too.

'Send him my best when you write,' Raymond mumbled and fell into silence, as Sara spoke of Joe all the way back to Hawthorn Street.

The day they left for Lowbeck, Sara felt unwell and the motion of the bus made her queasiness worse, but Rosa did not notice her quietness. She chattered like a child at the sights from the bus window and held Mary up to see the bustling villagers of Stanhope. At Lowbeck, Sara's brother Bill came to collect them having got her message, and the family were waiting in expectation of meeting Joe's sister.

To Sara's relief, her mother took at once to the bubbling Rosa and her pretty daughter Mary and accepted them into the busy household. The next day Sara went to seek out Colin Cummings to discover where the POWs were working and whether it would be possible to see them.

'It's all pretty lax now that Italy's given in,' Colin told her. 'They're allowed to visit around Lowbeck – some folk have had them in for meals after chapel. They've built themselves a makeshift Catholic church up at Thimble Hill, but some of them come down to the chapel.'

'So you go to the chapel now?' Sara asked in surprise.

'Aye,' Colin flushed, 'I gan with Beth and Daniel. And I'm made to feel welcome,' he added defensively.

'I'm glad,' Sara said swiftly. 'So where can I find the Italians?'

Sara returned with the news that most of them were working over at Thimble Hill and so they set off that afternoon in search of Emilio. They were permitted to talk to the prisoners, but Rosa scanned their unfamiliar faces in vain. The Italians only spoke the most rudimentary English, but they all gathered round to make a fuss of Mary.

'Can't you ask them in Italian?' Sara urged. But when Rosa tried a few halting phrases, the men looked blankly back.

'Emilio Fella?' Rosa repeated the name.

Just on the point of giving up, one of the men understood and jabbered a reply, pointing towards the farm outhouses. Rosa thanked them and grabbed Mary as they waved goodbye.

Entering the stables, Rosa knew instinctively that the man bending over and mucking out the stalls was Emilio. She called his name and he jerked up in astonishment. He was unshaven and older looking, but the soft brown hair and pale hazel eyes were unmistakably his. Rosa stumbled forward, sick with nervousness at seeing him again, while Sara scooped Mary into her arms.

'Rosa?' he questioned in disbelief and yet there was a flicker behind his eyes, as if he had half expected her.

'Emilio,' Rosa gulped and smiled. 'My brother said he'd seen you. I can't believe it's you!'

'Me too, Rosa!' Emilio wiped his hands on his trousers and stepped towards her. They hugged each other and laughed self-consciously. 'You are a beautiful woman now, not my little Rosa.'

Rosa thrilled to hear his words and Sara hung back in embarrassment as they fumbled with pleasantries.

'I've brought you some pasta and bread,' Rosa gabbled. 'Do they feed you enough?'

'Yes, but pasta! – that is good,' Emilio smiled.

Rosa burst out, 'Oh why did you never write, Emilio? Why did you never come for me before you left for Italy?'

Sara coaxed Mary out of the byre to let them be alone and took Mary to see the sheep. A while later Rosa and Emilio emerged from the stables and Rosa beckoned them over.

'This is Joe's wife,' she told Emilio, 'my friend Sara. Oh, Sara, Emilio's explained all about how he was coming to get me when his passage was brought forward and he had to leave. Now the saints have brought us together again.'

Emilio appeared embarrassed by Sara's presence and made straight for Mary.

'And this is my little *bambina?*' he stooped down to smile at Mary and held out his arms. The girl shied away and ran to her mother. Emilio laughed.

'She will get used to me, yes?'

'Of course she will,' Rosa beamed. 'Say hello to your papa,' she coaxed her scowling daughter.

'It doesn't matter,' Emilio said pleasantly. 'Next time you come, I make her a dolly, from corn.'

Sara looked at Rosa and saw the delight in her face. She could hardly believe fate had been so kind in delivering Emilio to Rosa unharmed and here in County Durham.

'We'll come again tomorrow before we leave,' Rosa promised as Emilio was detailed to join the other prisoners.

'Then I am happy,' Emilio smiled, hiding his bewilderment at their sudden appearance out of the bleak landscape.

As they left, Sara caught sight of her cousin Colin among the other workers. He was looking after them, his long face impassive. Still that unnerving stare, Sara thought and looked away. But that night, Colin came up to Stout House and asked to see her.

'I'll not come in, Aunt Lily,' he was stubborn. 'I just want a word with Sara.'

Sara went out nervously to meet him and they stood several feet apart, shivering in the courtyard. The yellow harvest moon threw light on to her cousin's jowled face.

'That Italian you went to see,' he said, clearing his throat. 'I gather he's the father of Rosa's bairn.'

'Aye,' Sara said coolly, 'but that's no concern of yours.'

Colin flinched at her rebuff. 'No, you're right,' he was surly in return, deciding he would bother no further, 'they can do what they like.'

He turned from her and strode across the yard. Sara almost let him go, then the thought of how he had made Beth happy prompted her to act.

'Wait, Colin,' Sara went after him, putting a hand on his arm. 'I'm sorry. You had something to say.'

Colin turned and said awkwardly. 'I think he was boasting about the bairn to the others after you went. I don't understand them, of course, but I got the general message.'

'Well, that's not surprising.' Sara was relieved that this was all there was to worry about. 'He's just discovered he's a father.'

'Aye, well that's not all he is,' Colin muttered, 'he's married an' all.'

Sara gawped at him in the moonlight. 'He's not?'

Colin nodded.

'How in the wide world do you know that?' Sara asked in dismay.

'He's shown me photos of his wife – a bonny lass with fair hair. And he's got one of a kiddie an' all. Right proud of them he is.'

'Oh, Colin,' Sara groaned, 'how am I going to

tell Rosa?'

Rosa's shock gave way to a white rage Sara had never before witnessed in the young woman. She pleaded with Rosa to forget Emilio and not to return to see him, but Rosa wanted her own proof. Leaving Mary with Sara waiting for a bus in Lowbeck, Rosa found him picking turnips in the raw, dank October air. His pleasure at seeing her soon turned to bewilderment at the ranting, furious woman before him, causing everyone in the field to stop and watch.

'Rosa, the other woman means nothing to me. It was for comfort, nothing else,' he protested. 'I forget her and marry you.'

Rosa was almost speechless at his lack of feeling. 'I wouldn't have you now, Emilio, not if you paid me. I've waited four years for you – four years! I've looked at no one else. I've brought up your child in the hope one day you would return and make up for all the shame – prove my family wrong. But you don't give a damn about me or the bairn.'

'I do,' Emilio tried to salvage the situation. 'I give a big damn!'

Rosa's look was contemptuous. 'Oh, you'd string me along while the war's on, wouldn't you? Happy for me to bring you treats and think you'd marry me when you're free. But you'd just disappear back to Italy again, wouldn't you? Just like the last time!'

'Rosa, how can you say such things?' Emilio put on a wounded expression, more for the benefit of his comrades than for her. 'I love my little rose.'

561

He tried to think back to that time in England before the war and how, briefly, he had fallen in love with the sweet, innocent Rosa Dimarco. But he could hardly remember his desire for her. Better for her to storm off now with the unwanted child and not trouble his life again, Emilio thought.

Rosa saw the relief in his soft eyes. She stepped towards him and struck him hard on the face. Before he could recover she hit him again, 'And that's from my father.'

She fled from that bitter field and the sound of ribald laughter from the other men. He would not see her cry, Rosa determined, holding her head high as she went – and never again would she be humiliated by another man. She would keep to herself and her family, trusting no man and bring Mary up to despise Emilio's callous behaviour.

Travelling home with Sara, Rosa refused to mention her lover's name again, stoical in her misery. At Stanhope Sara was sick and it was Rosa who took charge and helped her onto the next bus.

As they made their way wearily through the village to Pit Street, Rosa said with quiet authority, 'We shan't tell them about Emilio being married or having a son. We'll pretend we never found him – that Joe was mistaken, it wasn't him at all.'

'But, Rosa,' Sara argued, 'won't it be worse for you keeping it to yourself?'

'I have my pride,' Rosa said with a jut of her small chin. 'At least my parents will never know how little Emilio thought of me – or thinks of

Mary. I can save them *that* shame.'

Sara put an arm around Rosa's narrow shoulders and gave them a squeeze. 'Oh, Rosa, you've grown up such a lot since I've known you. I'm so glad you're my friend.'

Together they kept their secret and went to rejoin the family.

It was Anna who diagnosed the cause of Sara's sickness and fatigue.

'You're going to have a baby,' she smiled in delight. 'Isn't that right, Sylvia?'

'Yes, Mamma,' Sylvia nodded over her knitting. 'We've both thought so since you came back from that wild-goose chase after Emilio,' she told her sister-in-law.

'Joseph will be so pleased,' Anna said, patting Sara's pale face.

'He will, won't he?' Sara smiled back. And perhaps I will be accepted as a true Dimarco, Sara thought to herself, once I have a young Dimarco to cradle, for at times she still sensed a reserve towards her from her parents-in-law and Sylvia. She decided that she'd agree to have her baby christened at St Teresa's, knowing how it would please Joe's family.

On her way back from work she stopped to tell Louie Ritson the news of the baby.

'That's grand, flower,' Louie gave her a hug. 'Isn't it, Sam?'

'Aye, I'm chuffed for the pair of you,' Sam said, pausing over the polishing of his boots. 'It'll be something to keep Joe going while he's out there in the thick of it.'

'Aye,' Louie sighed, 'you must be proud of your lad.'

Suddenly Raymond pushed back his chair without finishing his tea and grabbed his jacket. 'Well, some of us are in the thick of it here,' he snapped, 'and facing danger underground every day. How many people think of that?'

Sara looked at him in astonishment, puzzled over his anger which seemed to be directed at her.

'I'll be late for me shift,' he muttered, marching out and banging the door.

Outside, he at once regretted his surliness. Why did it matter so much that Sara was carrying Joe's child? he wondered. He was ashamed of his jealousy towards his old friend and he had not meant to demean Joe's courage in the battlefield. But he couldn't help resenting the fact that the army lads would all get medals for their bravery when this rotten war was over, whilst the pitmen's efforts would soon be forgotten.

As he tramped unhappily through the frosty evening, boots crunching in the dark, Raymond was aware of someone hurrying after him.

'Haway, Raymond, what's got into you?' Sam complained. 'No need to take off like a runaway train, eh?'

'Sorry,' Raymond muttered. 'I forgot you were on the same shift.'

'That's not what I meant – and that's not what's bothering you, is it?' his uncle guessed, falling into step with Raymond's long stride. His nephew did not answer. 'It's no good fretting after something you can't have,' Sam continued bluntly.

'What do you mean?' Raymond was defensive.

'I mean, stop wasting your time over Sara.' Sam was brutal in his frankness, 'It's Joe she's chosen, not you. But you don't have to let that spoil your friendship with either of them – and they've both been good friends to you, Raymond, don't forget that.'

Raymond stopped in his tracks, shocked that Sam should have guessed his feelings. He gulped. 'I know they have,' Raymond was contrite, 'and I don't mean to...' He carried on walking.

The gates of the pit yard loomed ahead. 'You haven't had much luck with lasses yet,' Sam said more gently, 'but one day you'll find the right one – like I found your Auntie Louie.'

'How did you know I felt that way about Sara?' Raymond mumbled, his face burning.

'Louie notices these things,' Sam said wryly. 'There's not much gets past your aunt.' Raymond grunted in agreement.

Reaching the pit perimeter fence they saw others ahead and Sam added quickly, 'Perhaps it'd be best if you didn't call round to Pit Street so often, eh? No point giving yourself extra strife. You could come down to the boxing club if you like. I know you're not keen on fighting, but it'd be somewhere else to go.'

Raymond was grateful for his uncle's concern and, not for the first time, wished that Sam had been his real father. He and Louie had been all that a lad could have wished for in parents.

'Ta, I might do that,' Raymond smiled as they caught up with their marras in front.

In the New Year of 1944, an influx of young men came to the pit, directed there by the government to help meet the voracious demand of the war for extra coal. They were nicknamed 'Bevin Boys' after the Minister of Labour and the ones in Whitton Grange were housed in primitive hostel accommodation in a disused church hall. Rosa came home from the canteen with stories of how there were fights at the hostel every weekend among the locals and the Bevin Boys. One new-comer, the son of a wealthy industrialist who had made no bones about his distaste for the job he was forced to do and his rough surroundings, had been attacked walking home from the pub.

'His left eye was all closed up,' Rosa grimaced on her return from the canteen, 'and he could hardly walk.'

After that, attempts were made to lodge the new workers among the villagers and it was no surprise to Sara to find one living at Louie and Sam's home when she called in February.

'Malcolm's a grand lad,' Louie told Sara. 'He's from Edinburgh. Raymond's been friendly to him and suggested we took him as a lodger, now Stan's gone back to Gateshead to start work.'

'The day this house has no lodgers'll be the day they pull it down,' Sara teased the older woman.

Louie chuckled. 'I do like the company,' she admitted. 'And the house is that quiet with Stan gone.'

'And how's Raymond?' Sara asked. 'I never see him these days. Is he courting at last?'

Louie shrugged evasively. 'He's always out and about – you know Raymond. Now, tell me about

yourself,' she changed the subject. 'You're looking bonny and you'd hardly know you were
carrying a bairn of seven months, you're that
trim.'

'I feel fine,' Sara smiled, enjoying the fuss that
was made over her by the older women. Anna
and Elvira had wanted her to stop working
straight away, but Sara had insisted she was
needed at the hospital. 'This bairn's a lively one,'
she covered her stomach under the tight skirt
with protective hands, 'a footballer like Joe, I
reckon.'

'Have you heard from him recently?' Louie
asked, making some hot barley water for her
visitor.

'Aye, I got a letter two days ago. He's that
excited about the baby,' Sara grinned. 'If it's a
boy he wants it called after his brother Paolo –
but anglicised as Paul. And if it's a girl he wants
to call it Louise.'

'Why's that?' Louie looked surprised. 'Is it a
family name?'

'No,' Sara said, taking the mug of hot juice, 'it's
after you, Louie – because you've been such a
good friend to the two of us.'

Sara saw tears spring immediately to Louie's
blue eyes and the pitman's wife turned away
quickly to pick up a pile of ironing. A minute
passed while Louie sorted the clothes and kept
her back to the girl.

'You don't mind do you?' Sara asked at last.

Louie cleared her throat. 'Mind?' she whispered. 'I'm touched to the heart, pet, so I am.'

Sara wrote to Joe of Louie's delight at his idea.

She spent the lengthening spring evenings as she had spent the long winter ones, pouring out her thoughts and feelings to her husband in tiny writing on scraps of cheap quality paper. In return she got short, tender notes, telling her to rest and keep healthy for their baby's sake, full of how much he missed her. In only one letter did he refer to being in Italy directly.

'*The mountains are massive and it's bluer at night,*' Joe wrote in his slightly scrawling handwriting. '*But they're not like anything else I've ever seen. They're barren and beautiful and little flowers grow in no soil at all. When this is all over, Sara pet, I'm going to bring you here to see them – the hills of my forefathers.*'

But in the middle of the month the Dimarcos were appalled to hear of the bombing and destruction of the ancient mountain monastery of Monte Cassino in their home region.

'Surely that was not necessary?' the white-haired Arturo exploded, scandalised by the attack. 'It's a place of God. *Santa Teresa!* – my cousin Guiseppe is a monk there.'

'Don't upset yourself, Arturo,' Anna tried to calm him, knowing how his moods could swing from listlessness to rage in seconds.

'I will be upset!' he stormed around the sitting-room.

Sara kept quiet, thinking only of where Joe might be in all the destruction of the futile attack.

But Anna knew her husband's outrage was tinged with real fear for the safety of their remaining family in Italy, for Domenica and Pasquale and Arturo's mother who were in the path of the advancing war. They heard nothing to lessen their anxiety and by mid March their worst fears were realised when the wireless announced the bombing of Cassino itself, the nearest town to their family village. Later they learned it had been reduced to a city of rubble.

Sara did not know how to comfort her parents-in-law who had relations scattered around the countryside of Cassino, and Sylvia became as withdrawn and subdued as when Paolo had died, worrying over her own parents and family. Only when the spring turned to early summer did news finally reach them from Italy that Domenica was alive and her two children safe, as well as Elvira's eldest daughter, whose nunnery had miraculously escaped destruction. But the letter brought a sad footnote that Nonna Maria had died of a heart attack when they had fled for refuge to a neighbouring valley.

Arturo was plunged into a deep gloom at his mother's death and became further withdrawn. Sara went with Anna and Rosa to light a candle for the old grandmother in St Teresa's and Sara recalled the sharp-eyed matron who had chaperoned them at the Carnival dance and told her that the green dress suited her. Sara would never know whether Nonna Maria would have approved her marriage to Joe. Probably not, Sara thought, yet she would always remember Granny Maria's kind crinkled face and bright dark eyes smiling in greeting as she sat in the sunny backyard and peeled potatoes.

Away from the Dimarcos' private grief for what was happening in Italy, there was a mood of excitement and optimism in the bustling village. The Eleanor pit was at full production and rumours were rife of an imminent invasion of France. Slogans appeared on walls, exclaiming 'Second Front Now!' and Hilda came home for some leave after a spell in the south full of high morale.

'London's bursting!' she told Louie and Sara. 'I met that many foreign folk – Poles and Frenchies and Norwegian sailors – and Yanks of course. Eeh, I've never had so much fun.'

Neither Louie nor Sara questioned Hilda closer. She had been four long, dreary years without Wilfred and working away from home had given Hilda a taste for independence that she appeared to relish. Louie wondered briefly how her sister would settle to married life in Whitton Grange with the plodding Wilfred, should he return safely one day, but she kept her doubts to herself.

In early May, work at The Grange hospital slackened as half the army staff packed up and moved off south to become part of the Expeditionary Force making ready for France, and Sara finished work, her girth suddenly spreading in the final month of pregnancy. She borrowed looser fitting clothes from the taller Louie and took short walks with Rosa down to the dene to pick bluebells, impatient for her baby to be born.

Then the momentous day of June 6th arrived and the news that the invasion was on. Everyone gathered around their wireless sets, eager for information, and, although work went on as normal at the pit, all talk was of the invasion of France. As far as Sara knew, Joe and her brother Tom were still in Italy where the Allies were making grim progress north in order to engage German forces away from the Second Front.

That evening, Sara met Raymond walking down from the allotment as she sat on a tree stump overlooking the burn, watching children play close to the disused railway siding. Raymond looked at her warily in the evening light, shivering at the memory of that place where Joe had saved him from a savage beating five years ago. Norman Bell would think twice about taking him on these days, Raymond thought. Now he was a head taller than Normy and twice as agile. He pushed the bad memory away.

'Heard the good news?' he asked cheerily, as if anyone in the whole country could be in ignorance of the events of the day.

'Aye,' Sara smiled, chewing on a strand of wild garlic and looking plumply content. Raymond tried not to stare at her huge belly and round breasts bound in his Aunt Louie's faded, flowery dress. 'I just wish it could all be over and our lads come home,' she added, betraying her worry.

'It'll come soon,' Raymond encouraged, 'and you'll have a bairn for Joe to be proud of an' all. Just think of that.'

Sara felt a stab of affection for the lad who had befriended her ever since she had come to the village. 'I think it's on its way now,' she said softly, pressing her hand over the dull pain in her side.

'What is? The bairn?' Raymond was aghast.

'Aye,' Sara laughed, 'I've been having these

571

twinges for the last hour. I thought they would pass off, but now I think it's the real thing.'

Raymond coloured with shock. 'Haway then, get yourself home. You can't go having a baby in the dene!' He stretched out his hands.

Sara took them and allowed herself to be hauled up from her seat. She felt so ungainly as Raymond led her back up the village, but he did not seem to mind her waddling progress and kept a protective hold. Delivering her safely back to Pit Street, Raymond left her to the fussing Elvira and no-nonsense Anna who scolded her daughter-in-law for wandering about on her own in such a condition.

Anna packed Sara to bed and the women gathered around to assist and encourage as the labour progressed, banishing Arturo and Bobby to man the shop below. But Sara's excitement waned as the half-dark night wore on and nothing happened, just the dull pains and an overwhelming tiredness. Then, as day came once more and Anna opened the window to allow in the cool morning air, Sara's contractions began in earnest. Rosa stayed by her side, wiping her face and body, while Sylvia kept the inquisitive children out of the way.

Sometime after her waters broke, Sara was aware of a commotion outside the bedroom and Anna disappeared to admonish her family.

'What's going on?' Sara asked weakly, exhausted with the pain and lack of sleep.

'Just the children wanting to be in,' Rosa said calmly, puzzled by the sound of her father's raised voice.

'It sounds like Mr Dimarco,' Sara panted, though she was past caring what the dispute was about, only desperate for her agony to end. There were moments when she felt she could bear the pain and then the contractions would seize her again and leave her crying for relief.

'Just you concentrate on the Dimarco who's taking such a time to come into the world!' Rosa teased.

'Lazy like its mother,' Sara whispered, with a weak smile.

Outside the room Anna stood rigid with fear at the sight of what her husband was holding. Sylvia was trying to quieten the children.

'Open it,' Anna whispered.

Arturo fumbled helplessly with the telegram and Anna snatched it from his useless fingers. The message was brief and stark enough for even her poor English to comprehend.

'Santa Maria, please no!' she gasped, gripping the letter and closing her eyes in numb disbelief.

'Joseph,' Arturo asked hoarsely, *'E morto?'*

Anna nodded and handed him the message. Arturo let out a wail of anguish that shook Anna out of her stupefied state.

'Be quiet!' she ordered her husband, glancing at the closed bedroom door. 'Sara must not know of this until after the baby is born.'

'Anna!' Arturo sobbed and held out his arms to her for comfort. But she could not succumb to her grief now, else the young girl in the next room would guess the worst.

'Stop it, Arturo!' She forced herself to be sharp. 'If Sara hears you, the news might kill her – or

573

the baby.'

Elvira stepped between them and guided the helpless Arturo back down the steps. Anna said a silent, desperate prayer for courage and went back into the bedroom.

Somehow she managed to keep the pain from showing as she helped Sara bring her child into the world. What a sorrowing world it is that welcomes you, little one, Anna said silently as Sara, screaming, finally pushed her baby from her womb.

'It's a boy,' Anna said, her eyes brimming with tears.

'Paul Joseph,' Sara cried happily as her mother-in-law laid the querulous bundle in her arms. Anna turned, choking back a sob and hurried from the room. Sara looked at Rosa perplexed.

'She's always emotional about babies,' Rosa smiled and leaned forward to kiss her new nephew.

But later that day, when they had both slept, Sara and Rosa learned that Joe was dead.

Chapter Twenty-Nine

Sara's grief was so profound that even Joe's family could not bring her comfort. Her joy at Paul's arrival turned to hysteria at losing her husband and those summer weeks, when the country was gripped by the fortunes of the Allies in France, were the blackest Sara had ever known. The successes and setbacks of the invasion through Europe passed in a blur as she was beset by periods of bitter anger and limp depression.

Most distressing of all was her inability to find solace in her young baby. Almost immediately her milk had dried up and she was unable to feed him and his constant crying jarred on her torn nerves. It was Rosa who showed the greatest patience and nursed baby Paul through the night and prepared his bottles of milk every day.

Anna and Arturo arranged for their grandchild to be christened at St Teresa's that August and strangely, while Sara mourned, it was to Arturo that the boy's arrival gave a new purpose in life. It was as if the young Durham woman's deep grief had frightened him out of his own self-absorption.

'I never realised how much she loved our son,' Arturo whispered to Anna one night, as they lay in bed listening to Elvira's even breathing. 'I'm glad they went against our wishes and married –

575

at least Joseph had that brief happiness before...'

The clock ticked loudly on the small chest of drawers.

'And they gave us Paul,' Anna murmured. 'He is like our Joseph with his black hair.'

'His hair is brown, Anna,' Arturo contradicted.

'His eyes remind me of Joseph.'

'His eyes are green like Sara's.'

'But they are big like Joseph's,' Anna protested.

Arturo sighed. 'Why can Sara not be happy with her *bambino?*' he asked. 'Paul came like a gift from heaven at the very time Joseph was taken away.'

Anna leaned her head on her husband's shoulder. 'Perhaps that is the reason,' she whispered. 'She would rather have our Joseph.'

'But Paul needs his mother's love!' Arturo grew agitated.

Anna was more philosophical. 'Give Sara time, Arturo, she will grow to love her son. And we shall love him until she is ready.' She kissed her husband on his leathery cheek.

The late summer brought news of the liberation of Paris and then Brussels, and Anna and Arturo decided Sara's depression might lift if she were to go home before the autumn set in. She had been once before, shortly after Joe's death, but had returned almost immediately, as if being close to Joe's family brought her a modicum of relief. This time Lily Pallister came down to Whitton Grange to fetch her daughter and meet the Dimarcos. Lily stayed overnight with her brother Alfred who displayed little sympathy for the traumas the Dimarcos had undergone.

'Old Dimarco's not had it so bad,' Alfred pontificated at breakfast, 'for one of the enemy. He's got a well-paid job at the ordnance factory and his business seems to have survived. He's not the only father to lose a son in this war.'

'Two sons,' Lily reminded her brother curtly, finding his indifference hard to stomach.

'Well we all have our crosses to bear,' Alfred said piously.

Lily looked across the table at Ida's taut face, so anxious to please her husband she would allow him to say anything. Their gawky daughter Marina sat round-shouldered in her chair, her face a permanent mask of petulance. She did not seem to care about Sara's bereavement, either. Lily could touch no more of her breakfast and, with a perfunctory goodbye, hurried to Pit Street and away from the dispiriting house at South Parade.

In contrast, the encounter with the Dimarcos was less strained than Lily had imagined and she found herself welcomed courteously into Sara's adopted home. She saw at once how they cared for her daughter and young grandson, though she was shocked to see Sara so thin and grey-eyed. The baby Paul was fussed over by everyone except Sara, and Anna took Lily aside before she left.

'She cannot show her love for the baby,' Anna told her. 'I think in some way she is frightened to show her feelings.'

'Frightened?' Lily was puzzled and a little annoyed by her daughter's lacklustre state.

'She loved my son,' Anna said proudly, 'then she lost him. To love again so deeply might hurt, too, I think,' Anna explained, surprising Lily with her perception.

'But that's nonsense,' Lily remonstrated, 'Joe would have wanted her to love his son just as much.'

'We know that,' Anna was patient. 'But Sara is too much in the black mood to see it.'

But the trip to Stout House did seem to alleviate some of Sara's pain and she drew strength from walking around the timeless moors and sharing her grief with the remote beck and the desolate, swirling curlews.

'I want this pain to go away!' she cried to the raw wind – but half of her did not, for to lessen the grief was to let slip her hold on Joe's memory. She found herself seeking friendship with Beth and her cousin Colin, who surprised her with his gentleness and concern.

'I'm that ashamed of my part in mucking things up for you and Joe,' Colin told her one evening. 'I should have tried to stop Marina handing over your diary to me father. But I was full of hate at the time. I'm sorry.'

'It makes no difference now,' Sara said wearily, 'your dad didn't succeed in keeping us apart, did he? In a strange way it made us more determined to be together.'

'Aye, but that's not all,' Colin went on, fidgeting with the ears of his sheep dog. 'I know me father went to Sergeant Turnbull with your diary.'

'What on earth for?' Sara asked in astonishment.

'It was when there was all that talk about spies in the village after Dunkirk. Father was certain the Dimarcos were part of the fifth column. Anyway, I was in the house when Turnbull called and father handed the diary over. I don't know how much use it would have been...' Colin shrugged uncomfortably.

Sara thought of the names of Dimarcos listed, their relationship to Joe, the mention of relations in Italy, the fascist club in Sunderland, all innocently recorded for her own interest, yet welcome evidence of enemy aliens to the vigilant and merciless Turnbull. No wonder her uncle had refused to hand back the diary. She felt a wave of shame that her trivial writings could have been used against Joe's family. Yet it all seemed so long ago and she saw Colin's remorse; she could not feel anger at him any more. He had not handed over the diary and Sara saw now that she had been too ready to condemn Colin and blame him for her troubles.

'Turnbull would have known all there was to know about the Dimarcos without the help of my diary,' Sara answered kindly.

'That's what *I* kept telling you, Colin,' Beth added, 'and Sara's not one to hold a grudge – not like old Cummings.'

Sara saw the relief lighten Colin's sombre face and the diary was never mentioned again.

Before Sara left Stout House, her sister Chrissie surprised everyone by announcing her engagement to Sid Gibson and Sara hurried away before the family party to celebrate the event.

She wished them well, but their happiness only increased her aching loss.

Back in Whitton Grange, Sara found herself going through the motions of living, doing small, mindless jobs around the house or shop to occupy the empty hours, while Rosa did most of the caring for Paul. She was filled with guilt at her lack of feeling for her baby and sensed that the Dimarcos' patience towards her was tiring.

Strangely, it was at the Ritsons that Sara found herself most at peace, sitting at Louie's scrubbed kitchen table with the smell of soup warming on the old black range and the men blacking up their boots or talking about sport. She yearned for their company because Sam had been Joe's mentor and Louie and Raymond had been his close friends. Sara found she could talk about Joe with the Ritsons, whereas she was afraid of mentioning him at home without opening up the deep wounds her parents-in-law bore. But Raymond and the Ritsons talked about Joe with affection and could make Sara smile with stories from Joe's past.

It was shortly before Christmas that a turning point came in Sara's life. Louie suggested that she went into Durham to look round the shops.

'Buy something for the bairn,' Louie encouraged, chucking Paul under his plump chin. She never chided Sara for her lack of interest in the baby or made reproachful remarks as her own mother had done. 'Raymond's going in with Malcolm to watch a football match – you could go with them.'

Sara was unenthusiastic, but Rosa persuaded

her it was a good idea and offered to go with her.

'We'll take the bairns to hear the carol singing,' Rosa said excitedly. So wrapping up baby Paul in woollen clothes, hat and blanket, Sara allowed herself to feel a fraction of Rosa and four-year-old Mary's anticipation at the rare trip.

Raymond and Louie's lodger, Malcolm, came to meet them and walked the family to the bus. The cheerful Mr Parker, who had first brought Sara to Whitton Grange, was driving and she found herself reminiscing with Parker and Raymond, telling the amiable Malcolm tales of the village as if she had lived there all her life. Sitting back watching the frosted countryside slip silently past the grubby windows, Sara realised how fond she had grown of the pit village and its people. Even without her beloved Joe, Whitton Grange would always be her home now, she thought.

The men went off to support their pit team, while Sara and Rosa wandered around the town and treated themselves to a cup of tea. Sara wanted to go and visit Eb and Eleanor, but could not bring herself to do so. There would be too many reminders of happier times there with Joe. Perhaps in the New Year she could face them, Sara made excuses to herself. However, when Raymond met up with them again, he insisted that they at least call on his grandmother. It seemed she could not evade the visit to the Ramshaws at the Market Inn, where she and Joe had spent their first night of marriage.

'We might get a drink out of me grandfather,' Raymond grinned at Malcolm, 'if he's got more than tap water to offer.'

'Come on, what are we waiting for?' Malcolm agreed, blowing on to frozen hands and winking at Rosa. Sara was aware of the young Scotsman's attraction to Rosa, although she seemed indifferent to his attentions.

Sara's reluctance was over-ruled and the cold chased them indoors. Mrs Ramshaw was overjoyed to see her grandson and made a fuss over him and his friends. The portly Ramshaw brought up a glass of watery beer each for Raymond and Malcolm and Rosa sat chatting with Raymond's giggling Aunt Nora. But Mrs Ramshaw's failure to mention Joe nearly reduced Sara to tears and she could not bear the older woman's coddling of Paul, which made her feel so inadequate.

'Please, just leave him!' Sara snapped finally which drew an awkward pause in the cheerful banter.

Raymond looked at Sara in concern. 'Listen, I can hear the Sally Army playing outside. Want to go and hear them?' Without waiting for an answer, he pulled baby Paul from his grandmother's hold and thrust him into Sara's arms. Taking her by the elbow, he guided her down the stairs, nodding at Rosa and Malcolm to stay in the warmth of the Ramshaws' flat.

It was almost dark and only the pale glint of brass instruments could be seen under a crisp, icy moon. But their joyful music seemed all the louder, filling the marketplace as shoppers hurried past. Paul began to cry in the cold air.

'He shouldn't be out here,' Sara said petulantly. 'It's too cold and I want to go home.'

Raymond turned and looked down at them both then, without a word, cautiously lifted the baby, pulling the blanket tighter around his head and face.

'You're all right, bonny lad,' he smiled and rocked him like he had seen Louie do with babies. The small infant responded to the firm hold and his crying lessened to a rhythmic whimper as Raymond talked to him in a calm, friendly voice.

Sara stood riveted to the icy cobbles, quite overwhelmed by the flood of feelings she experienced at the sight of a young man holding her baby and not just any man, but her husband's good friend. It struck her suddenly that this was how Joe would have treated his son, with loving, humorous words and tender affection.

Raymond turned and caught sight of Sara's distraught face. 'I know you love the little lad,' he said quietly, 'so don't be afraid to show it, Sara. It doesn't mean you loved Joe any less.'

Sara felt winded at the gentle reproof. Convulsions of tears seized her as she realised Raymond knew how she felt, understood her guilt towards Joe for wanting to love Paul and letting the past go. Only the caring, affectionate, sensitive Raymond could have shown her that this was the way Paul should be loved.

Speechless and sobbing, she stepped towards Raymond and her baby and allowed the tall friend to put an arm about her shoulders. Together they cradled Paul and each other as the hopeful sounds of carols drowned Sara's distress.

Shortly afterwards they all caught the bus back to Whitton Grange and Raymond did not repeat any shows of tenderness in front of Rosa and Malcolm, but the warmth that Sara had experienced in the frosty darkened marketplace remained with her.

Sara saw in the New Year of 1945 at the Ritsons', with Raymond clashing on the piano and Hilda and the Parkins adding their voices to the singing. Increasingly, as the late winter turned to spring, she found herself relying on Raymond Kirkup's company, frequently calling round to Hawthorn Street to help Louie with her clippy mat or helping out in the shop in the hopes he would call with mates from the pit during their free time. For his part, Raymond felt it a day wasted if he did not see Sara and he was growing fond of baby Paul with his large, dark green eyes and soft brown hair, who smiled when Raymond came near.

But when Albina came home for a week's leave she wasted no time in criticising Sara's behaviour.

'I don't know how you can let her gad about with that pitman, Aunt Anna,' Albina needled her aunt. 'She's a disgrace to the family. It makes me wonder if she cared for cousin Joe at all,' Albina added waspishly, noticing the effect her words were having. 'Perhaps she was only ever after his money.'

Anna Dimarco was furious at her niece's bitching and did her best to ignore her. But the seeds of doubt about Sara and Raymond took root and Anna could not deny she was upset at the blossoming friendship and said so to Arturo.

'How can she look at another man when our Joseph has not been gone a year? It's shameful the way he calls for her all the time – treating Joseph's son as if he were his own.'

'Anna, you have been listening too much to that meddling Albina,' Arturo tried to calm her fears. 'Sara and Raymond have always been friends and he at least is making her smile again. You must not make Raymond feel unwelcome – he was a good friend to Joseph.'

'How can he be a friend of Joseph's when all he wants to do is take our son's place?' Anna cried bitterly.

Arturo retreated into the shop, leaving his wife to wash up in the backshop, no longer having the strength to argue with her. The traumas of the war years had left him feeling an old man, drained of the vitality and bonhomie that had made him such a good patron of the cafe and head of his family. Arrest and captivity had undermined his sense of authority and he no longer had the confidence to run the shop without the advice of his strong-willed wife.

Who would have thought that the timid Anna he had coaxed from his mountain village would have shown such fortitude through all their hardships? Arturo mused. But both he and Anna were ageing and he worried at the future of the business with Paolo and Joseph gone and Bobby's interest only in bicycles. The burden would fall on the young women of the household, Arturo supposed.

The Home Guard had been disbanded and March brought news of the Allied push across the Rhine into Germany. That spring, there was a buoyancy of spirit that infected Sara with some of her old optimism after the months of depression. She and Rosa organised a picnic on Whitton Common at Easter for the children and invited Raymond and Malcolm along. They spent a happy day, rolling two rationed, painted eggs down the slope, eating Aunt Elvira's special currant bread and watching the men play football with Peter and Bobby.

'Paul wants to be after you,' Sara laughed, encouraging her son's attempts to pull himself up from crawling across her legs.

'We'll sign him up next season,' Raymond called and side-stepped Malcolm with the knot of rags they were using as a ball.

'Malcolm's asked me out to the pictures again,' Rosa told Sara as the men ran out of earshot.

'Good,' Sara smiled.

'I said no,' Rosa sighed. Sara waited for her to explain. 'I know he's canny, but how can I trust him? This war'll be over soon and he'll be off back to Scotland and out of my life, just like Emilio.'

'That's not fair,' Sara reproved. 'Malcolm's *not* like Emilio. He really cares about you, I'm sure of it. You can't go on treating all men as bad just because Emilio was.'

Rosa hung her head and mumbled, 'Well, if he asks me again, I might say yes.'

Sara resolved to pass this piece of information on to Raymond in the hopes that the fair-haired Malcolm would not give up, discouraged.

'And you, Sara...' Rosa slid her a look. 'What

586

about you and Raymond?'

Sara was startled by the question.

'I'm not looking for anyone to replace Joe,' she answered abruptly. 'Nobody could. I just like Raymond as a friend.'

'He loves you,' Rosa said quietly.

'Rubbish!' Sara cried, going hot with embarrassment and got up to help Paul take steps on his chubby eager legs.

Despite her annoyance at Rosa's words, the afternoon passed contentedly, but Sara returned to find her mother-in-law tight-lipped with disapproval. The young men sensed Anna Dimarco's coolness and left swiftly.

'What's wrong?' Sara asked later, after Paul had been put to bed. A tenseness had crept into her relationship with her mother-in-law in recent weeks that puzzled Sara. They had been so close since Joe's death that this recent growing apart was hurtful.

'I think you are seeing too much of that Raymond,' Anna said, her feelings erupting at last. 'People are talking. It's not a year since...'

'Go on, say it,' Sara replied, stung by her mother-in-law's condemnation. 'It's not a year since Joe was killed.'

'A respectful wife should still be in mourning,' Anna said with indignation.

Sara was aghast. 'A few months ago you said I mourned for Joe too much – you said it was making the baby unhappy! I miss my husband more than you'll ever know,' she answered forcefully, tears stinging her eyes, 'but what use is it shutting myself away for the rest of my life like one of your old Italian widows? I'm only twenty-two – I can't wear black for ever.'

'Don't be disrespectful!' Anna snapped. 'You are Joseph's widow and a Dimarco and you should behave like one – like Sylvia does.'

Anna could not explain that she had felt so close to the grieving Sara, wanting to protect her in her sadness, but now she felt distanced by this new liaison with Joe's old friend. It irked Anna that Sara should have sought comfort and a new happiness outside the family, however much she deserved it.

'Are you telling me I can't see Raymond?' Sara fumed.

'You should wait.' Anna coloured at the young woman's hostile face.

'Well, there's nothing to wait for!' Sara shouted. 'Raymond is just a friend who's shown me more understanding than you have.'

She ran into her bedroom and slammed the door, waking Paul from his sleep. Rocking her crying son, Sara felt remorse at her blunt words as well as anger at the attack. Her mother-in-law had no right to dictate whom she saw, yet Anna had shown her great patience and kindness during the black weeks after Joe's death. Was it any surprise she was hurt to think Sara might love another so soon after her son's death? Sara reasoned.

Sara was suddenly struck by the truth. Anna was right. She did care for Raymond – not in the passionate way she'd loved Joe, but differently. She felt a deep affection for the Ritsons' nephew, for his kind humour and cheerful company. She could not have borne the pain of these last months without him and she realised it was not just because Raymond had been a friend of Joe's; she loved him for who he was. She wanted to carry on seeing Raymond but did not want to hurt Joe's family by doing so and Anna's criticism brought on a new wave of guilt that she was being disloyal to Joe's memory. Sara bowed to her mother-in-law's pressure and began to see less of him, declining to go out to the pictures or the park when Malcolm called for Rosa.

'You shouldn't worry what my parents think,' Rosa told her, no longer inhibited by their disapproval at what she did. She was a working woman at the pit canteen and she was at last enjoying her freedom and courtship with the young Scot.

But Sara did worry. The Dimarcos' distress at her seeing another man filled Sara with guilt, too, and Raymond's hurt confusion at her rebuff only made her feel worse.

'What's changed, Sara?' he asked in desperation, catching her outside the parlour one day.

'Nothing,' Sara replied irritably. 'You just expected too much from me.'

'I don't expect anything,' Raymond said, 'but I care for you and I don't like to see you unhappy like this. You seemed to be – you know – getting over...'

'I'll never get over Joe's death!' Sara snapped.

Raymond looked at her with wounded blue eyes, his handsomely wolfish face colouring.

'No, you won't,' he said quietly. 'I was daft to hope you might.'

Sara looked at him unhappily, wanting him to be angry and not to give in to the pressure under which she had bowed. But he went, hunched in sadness, and did not call at Pit Street again.

On May 8th Sara did not go out to celebrate the joyous news that the war in Europe was over and the Germans had surrendered. While Rosa went out to join in the street parties and stand over the bonfires of blackout material, Sara stayed quietly at home with the other Dimarcos and shared a toast to absent friends over a bottle of Arturo's bitter homemade parsnip wine.

'To the partisans who strung up Mussolini!' Arturo gave another toast.

'To the end of Hitler!' Elvira joined in, already tipsy.

'To the return of Davide and Domenica,' Anna said quietly.

Sara exchanged looks with Sylvia and saw the sadness on the small woman's face. Only they, of all the family, knew what it was like to be widowed. It was clear the next few weeks and months would bring a flood of husbands and sons and daughters returning to their families in ecstatic reunions, but they would only relive the pain of losing Paolo and Joe. Sara got up abruptly and went over and kissed Sylvia on the cheek. Before anyone could question her gesture, Sara retreated to bed, snuggling down beside her sleeping son for comfort, thankful for his warm, peaceful, trusting presence.

Wilfred Parkin was one of the first prisoners to

return to Whitton Grange at the end of the war, his camp liberated by the 9th battalion of the DLI. A welcome-home committee was set up by friends and neighbours and a party laid on at his home in Hawthorn Street which was bedecked in patriotic bunting. A thin, bewildered, but cheerful Wilfred was greeted by his family and neighbours and a nervous Hilda.

'What if we don't get on?' Hilda had asked Louie fearfully that morning. 'I hardly remember what he looks like!'

'Stop worrying,' Louie retorted, 'and make the lad feel at home.'

To Louie's relief, Hilda and Wilfred at least put on a show of being happily reunited, however awkward they felt in private. She was more concerned about her subdued nephew Raymond, who had lost his cheerfulness in recent weeks and spent his free time up at the allotment instead of with his friends. She knew his unhappiness was due to his parting with Sara and Louie wished there was something she could do to cheer him up.

'You'll be looking forward to your mam coming home,' Louie smiled, handing Raymond a plate of drop scones to take next door to the Parkins. 'She'll be bringing that American with her, will she?'

'Aaron?' Raymond grunted. 'I suppose so.'

'He must be special if he's passed Iris's inspection,' Louie said wryly. 'I've never met an American before. What's he like?'

'Canny,' Raymond answered, 'and he's got plenty money, so Mam's happy twice over.'

Louie gave Raymond a playful cuff. 'Don't be cheeky about your mam,' she scolded, but was pleased to see a smile return to Raymond's drawn, handsome face.

In July, Iris returned to Whitton Grange the day after the General Election and was annoyed to find the Ritson household more concerned with the Labour landslide than her dramatic appearance with her sophisticated American. She had not seen Sam Ritson so galvanised with excitement for years.

'Labour have taken every seat in the county, every bloody seat!' he cried, cock-a-hoop. 'By heck, it's the dawning of a new era for the working classes.'

The easy-going Aaron showed his surprise. 'I can't believe you Brits have kicked old Churchill out after he's won the war for you. You're all crazy.'

'He was the right man for the job in wartime,' Sam admitted, 'but God help us if he'd ended up running Britain in peace time. The country's had enough of Tory bosses putting us down. And Churchill's one of them, after all.'

Aaron looked bewildered as he passed around his cigarettes.

Louie explained. 'Churchill was no friend to the pitmen when he broke the General Strike in '26. He and the other Tories supported the coal-owners and we suffered for years as a result.'

'Aye, but now we've got Attlee and a Labour government who'll nationalise the pits. It's the beginning of a golden age for British coal and us pitmen – an industry worth working for.' Sam's eyes shone with joy as he looked across at Louie, still intoxicated by the news. Louie smiled back fondly, so happy for Sam and their own people.

'Aaron hasn't come here for a lesson in British politics,' Iris said testily, 'we've got something more important to celebrate.'

Louie put down her mending and saw Raymond pause in his game of cards with Malcolm.

'What's that, Mam?' Raymond asked.

'Aaron and I are going to be married. Isn't that wonderful?' Iris's attractively made-up face beamed at them all.

'Congratulations!' Louie spoke first and gave her sister-in-law a kiss.

'Aye, all the best,' Sam followed, shaking the American by the hand. They all turned for Raymond's reaction. For a moment he hesitated, then stood up and went to hug his mother.

'I'm pleased, Mam,' he smiled and kissed her, 'I really am.' Still with his arm about her he said to Aaron, 'I hope you'll make me mam happy – she deserves it.'

'She sure does,' Aaron smiled at Iris. 'But she'll only be completely happy if you agree to do something too.'

'What's that?' Raymond asked.

'Come with us to America,' Iris urged excitedly. 'Raymond, we'll start a new life together just like I always promised we would.' Iris laughed at the gawping faces around her. 'I mean it – and Aaron wants you to come, too.'

'Yeah,' Aaron nodded. 'I'm not short of a bob or two, as you English say. We could start something up together – a family business – while your mom becomes a famous movie star,' he joked. 'The climate's good in California and my family live near the beach – you'll love it. What d'you say, partner?'

'You'll never need to work underground again, Raymond pet,' Iris smiled and ruffled his auburn hair.

Raymond was astounded by the suggestion, quite speechless at the dream life being waved before him. It would mean never having to labour underground again in the dark and wet of a cramped pit, not seeing the daylight for hours on end. His mind filled with glamorous images of America gleaned from films at The Palace. It was more than tempting. He looked at Louie and Sam for their opinion.

'It sounds a grand offer,' Sam grunted.

'Aye, why don't you sleep on the idea?' Louie suggested, not wanting to show her dismay at the thought of Raymond going so far away. But if that was what he wanted to do, she would never stand in his way, Louie told herself firmly. She loved him like her own and all she wanted was that her nephew would be happy.

'Well, don't take too long,' Iris wagged a finger, ''cos Aaron's going back home shortly and I'll be following him out.'

Sara sat in the sheltered backyard on Nonna Maria's old bench, peeling carrots and watching Paul tottering around Elvira's vegetable patch after his cousin Peter, while Linda attempted to teach Mary to skip. Rosa sat beside her, fidgeting with a piece of crochet, the perfume of late summer roses filling the air.

'When shall I tell them?' Rosa asked. Sara put down her knife and raised her face to the late afternoon sun, sensing her friend's nervousness.

'You should tell them soon, Rosa. No point putting it off,' Sara advised, wondering how Anna and Arturo would respond to the startling news that Malcolm and Rosa had decided to marry. She was pleased for them, but worried that Malcolm would experience the same resistance from Rosa's parents as she had.

There had been a rash of weddings that summer as men returned to the village and started new lives in the euphoria of victory. Sara was thankful that at least Malcolm wanted to stay on at the Eleanor and train as an engineer, so Rosa would not be leaving Whitton Grange for the moment – unless the Dimarcos' attitude drove them away. For Sara was sure of one thing, Rosa would not allow her parents to stand in the way of her happiness this time. She herself felt set adrift and aimless now that all the war work had stopped and people were already building new lives for themselves. Elvira had returned to Sunderland to prepare a homecoming for her husband Davide, finally released from captivity, and for Albina and Benito returning from their army jobs. Domenica had written to say she and Pasquale would be returning to Britain as soon as they could, making Anna impatient with excitement to see her two unknown grandchildren.

Brother Tom had written from Greece to say he would be demobbed and home before Christmas and was longing to see her again. Sara treasured her brother's letters, but knew the reunion would be a painful one as he was a last tangible link with Joe, a comrade who had seen him before he was killed.

'We'll live nearby, I promise,' Rosa said, watching Sara's pale, taut face framed by her fair hair, glinting gold in the sunlight.

Sara turned and gave her friend a wan smile. 'I know – and I'm glad. I'd hate to think of you going away. Paul would miss you so much, too.'

'That's not what's worrying you is it?' Rosa said quietly. 'It's the thought of Raymond going away.'

Sara gulped, trying to hide her sadness. Rosa was right; the news from Louie that Raymond was going to emigrate to America with Iris and her new husband had come as a heavy blow. She could not blame him for wanting to start a new and exciting life away from the grimy pit village of his birth and she had heard stories of America's vastness and wealth, a land of opportunity for the young and eager. She had given him no reason to stay.

'I've no right to be so miserable over him, but I am,' Sara whispered. 'He's been such a good friend.'

'Tell him how you feel,' Rosa urged, 'before it's too late.'

Sara shook her head. 'I couldn't stand in the way of such a chance,' she replied, 'it wouldn't be fair. If that's what he wants to do, I'll not be the one to stop him.'

Rosa sighed with impatience, but their argument was cut short by the appearance of a man at the yard gate. He was square-shouldered with a weathered, bronzed face, cracked in the centre by a bushy moustache. He wore an old-fashioned suit and his hair was cropped short under a battered trilby hat.

'Is it Domenica?' he queried, beaming at Rosa.

'Rosa,' she answered, half rising. The children gathered round to stare.

'It's no?' he cried. 'You've grown that bliddy much since I seen you. You were just a wean. D'you no mind me?'

A half memory stirred as Rosa stammered, 'Sorry, I don't remember...'

'Your Uncle Gino, that's who I bliddy am!' he laughed and swung her into a firm embrace.

Gino's appearance had the effect of a minor earthquake in the Dimarco household. Arturo clung on to his long-lost brother as if he were a ghost who might dissolve into thin air once more and Anna forgave all his past misdemeanours and prepared a feast of pasta and fresh vegetables. Gino explained how, after the sinking of the *Arandora Star*, he had been picked up in the Atlantic and returned to Liverpool, only to be shipped out almost immediately to Australia, where he had spent the last years as a lumberjack.

'I wrote once,' Gino insisted, 'but I'm no bliddy journalist.'

'Why didn't you try and come back sooner? Did they keep you interned all this time?' Arturo asked.

'I was no going to risk another bliddy voyage,' Gino was scornful. 'The first time the Nazis blow us out the water, the next we end up wi' dysentery. Soldiers treated us like pigshit, d'you ken?'

Anna gave him a disapproving look.

'Awfy good pasta, Anna,' Gino smiled and let Sylvia help him to some more.

They spent the evening exchanging news and stories and Arturo and Gino stayed up half the night talking while they emptied two bottles of wine. Arturo told his brother he could stay as long as he wanted, but by the end of the following week, the women were tiring of his raucous presence. The wayward Gino was eating and drinking away their meagre rations with no signs of wanting to leave.

Rosa and Malcolm chose this moment to declare their intention to marry.

'Another stranger in the family!' Anna protested to her husband once they were alone.

Arturo sighed. 'At least this Scots boy wants to marry our Rosa and give Mary a proper father. It's more than that devil Emilio Fella was prepared to do.'

'He might still return...' Anna was stubborn.

'Ah, Anna!' Arturo lost his patience. 'You would wait for ever for that terrible man? I would not have him under my roof – and neither would Rosa.'

Anna covered her fraught face with her hands. Just when life appeared to be getting back to normal and she was full of anticipation at Domenica's return, the wretched Gino had turned up to disrupt their lives and now Rosa's sudden announcement... Anna shook her head as if she could empty it of problems. But deep down she was not surprised that Rosa and Malcolm wanted to marry, she had witnessed their growing tenderness for each other and she knew the fair Scotsman loved her daughter and young Mary. She would accept him, if only because he would make Rosa's situation respectable again.

'Perhaps we could ask them to wait a while longer...' Anna said.

'That young man knows his own mind, Anna,' Arturo said sternly. 'He will not wait. Do you want our Rosa to blame us a second time for standing in the way of her marrying?'

Anna shook her head. Arturo was silently thankful to see his wife capitulate over the drama. He was far more concerned about the aggravation his brother Gino was causing among his family. So, distracted by the domestic crisis caused by Gino's continuing presence, Arturo gave his consent to the marriage without protest.

'You will have to tell him to go,' Anna told her husband in bed one night, kept awake by the wireless music Gino was listening to.

'He's my brother, he saved my life,' Arturo protested, half-heartedly.

'And he has a home in Glasgow and that woman he's been living with who must think he's dead,' Anna reminded him sharply. 'He's taking advantage of your good nature, Arturo, as always.'

Arturo sighed. He had been overjoyed to see his brother return from the dead, but he knew Anna was right. They all had to try and rebuild their lives as best they could and for Gino that meant returning to Glasgow. If not, the fragile regrowth in his own business and family happiness might be blighted beyond repair.

'I'll speak with him soon,' Arturo promised and buried his head under his pillow to muffle the strains of Vera Lynn singing about meeting again.

A deluge of rain caused the opening match of the new football season to be cancelled and Raymond returned home, thwarted from playing his final match. He had handed in his notice at the pit and worked his final shift. In a couple of days he would be travelling to Liverpool to meet Iris and sail with her for America.

Louie occupied herself making him a pair of dark trousers out of an old coat of Jacob's for him to travel in. She looked up as he tramped across the uneven doorstep, soaked and stony-faced.

'Match off?' she guessed.

'Aye, I told you it wouldn't be worth coming to watch,' he grumbled.

'Don't look so twisty faced,' Louie said. 'You won't be bothered by the rain in America. Iris says it's sunshine all the time where Aaron lives.'

'Aye, well that makes no difference, 'cos they don't play football either, according to Aaron,' Raymond snorted. 'Least, not what *we'd* call football.'

Louie put down her sewing and looked hard at her restless nephew. It was just a hunch, but she decided to speak her mind before it was too late. 'You don't have to go if you don't want to,' she spoke gently. 'Iris would understand.'

'I've burned me boats now,' Raymond answered ruefully. 'Packed me job in, said me good-byes.'

600

'You haven't said all your goodbyes,' Louie persisted. 'What about Sara? You can't leave without seeing her.'

Raymond fought to control his emotions. 'I'll write a letter when I'm on my way.'

'Don't be so daft!' Louie replied roundly. 'If you care for the lass go and see her instead of moping around like a wet rag.'

Raymond looked up in astonishment at his aunt's sudden attack. 'That won't change anything,' he defended himself. 'She's made it clear she doesn't want me. I'm not Joe and I can't stand in a dead man's shoes. I'm not like me father who didn't think twice about going after any woman he fancied. I care for Sara too much to treat her like that.'

'Don't you criticise your father,' Louie said angrily. 'He had more guts than you're showing, Raymond Kirkup. He stood by your mam when she was pregnant with you and unmarried. He may have had his faults but our Davie had a loving nature – he was one of the best. He'd have gone to Sara long ago and shown her that he loved her. Of course she thought the world of Joe – but he's dead and he's never coming back. That lass is too loving not to marry again – and if it's to someone else and not you, Raymond, then it'll be your own doing.'

Raymond jumped up in agitation. 'All right!' he shouted. 'I'll go and see her, even though I know she'll turn me down. But I'll risk being made a fool of just to keep you happy.'

Still in his damp football clothes, Raymond stormed out of the kitchen and slammed the door. Louie looked after him with a long-suffering sigh.

'You're as stubborn as any Kirkup when you want to be,' she said aloud. 'I just hope my instincts are right and you're not going to get hurt again, bonny lad!'

Raymond found the Dimarcos in the middle of a family squabble over Uncle Gino who was out buying fish and chips for the children with Bobby's wages from the cycle shop.

'I'm looking for Sara,' he said at once.

'Come in, Raymond.' Arturo was glad of the diversion. 'She's here in the backshop.'

Anna and Arturo followed him in, and Raymond realised he was not going to be left alone. Well, what he had to say was for them all, he thought, steeling himself for the ordeal.

'Sara, I've come to say goodbye,' he said, his voice tense.

'Raymond!' Sara's delight at seeing him evaporated at his words.

Arturo clapped a hand on his shoulder. 'You are going to America, to make your fortune, eh?'

Raymond ignored him. 'If I thought I had a chance with you, Sara, I would stay, even now.'

Sara felt her throat drying as she tried to respond. His blue eyes in the lean face regarded her intently. She could not find the words to answer him.

'You must not throw away your chance of going to America,' Anna chided him. 'Sara is not ready to marry again. Perhaps no one will take the place of our Joseph.'

Sara saw the look of pain crossing Raymond's

face at Anna's words but he stood his ground.

'She can speak for herself, can't she?' Raymond replied shortly to the grey-haired woman. Turning back to Sara he said, 'I want to marry you, Sara, and I'll wait until you're ready, if there's half a chance you'd say yes. Do you want me to go?'

Sara looked into his anxious face. For a moment Joe's laughing visage came into her mind, but she forced herself to banish it. Raymond's intense blue eyes, watching for her response, were far more vivid now.

'No,' Sara found her voice at last, 'I don't want you to go. I've only kept away because I thought this chance of going to America was what you wanted.' She stepped towards him and put out her hands. 'I love you, Raymond,' Sara said shyly. Raymond grabbed her to him and their arms went around each other protectively.

'Oh, thank God for the common sense of Auntie Louie,' he laughed and kissed Sara on the lips.

Anna burst into tears. 'How can you do this?' she sobbed. 'Have you no respect for Joseph's memory?'

'Of course we have,' Sara replied, controlling her temper. 'But I know Joe would have wanted Paul to have a father to care for him. Raymond was one of his closest friends – he once said he would've liked Raymond in his family.'

'No, that cannot be!' Anna was almost incoherent with distress, 'Raymond is not one of us.'

'Neither was I, once,' Sara reminded her mother-in-law.

'But that is different,' Anna protested. '*You* gave

us a grandson.'

'Stop it, Anna!' Arturo trembled with emotion, finding the courage to intercept at last. 'How can you speak to Sara and Raymond in this way? Raymond is our *friend* – he has helped around our shop since he was at school – he came to protect us when the village turned against our family. Do not say that he is not one of us. There must *never* be such divisions again, else our boys will have died for nothing.'

Behind them, Rosa and Sylvia had appeared on the doorstep, silenced by the raised voices, listening to the heated exchanges.

'Papa is right,' Rosa spoke in support. 'It would be wrong for any of us to stand in the way of Sara's happiness after all she's been through. If you try and stop her she might leave with Raymond anyway and you'll lose both her *and* Paul.'

Anna gawped at her youngest daughter, astonished at the unheard-of criticism to herself.

'I agree,' Sylvia spoke up unexpectedly. 'Only I know what Sara has gone through losing her husband and it is a terrible thing. Let her be happy now, Mamma.'

Anna was silenced by Sylvia's quiet plea, feeling the stirrings of remorse for her churlishness towards Sara and Raymond.

'Raymond,' Arturo turned to the young man, standing protectively beside Sara, 'I have a suggestion. It is not necessary for you to go away from the village. You can stay and work in my shop. I have no sons to help me run the business – Bobby has no interest – and my daughters are making their own lives. Anna and I cannot go on for ever – we are getting old and need the help of strong arms to make the ice-cream, do the fetching and carrying. You worked in Sergeant's for long enough and know about business. When the time comes – and if you are up to it – you can take on the shop – with Sara's help.'

'What are you saying, Arturo?' Anna said bewildered.

'It will suit you too, Anna,' Arturo assured her quickly, 'because I shall tell Gino I have a partner and there is no place for him in the shop. He will have to go back to Glasgow. Does that make you happy?'

'Of course,' Anna mumbled, blushing.

'And Raymond?' Arturo asked.

Raymond and Sara exchanged looks.

'Please say yes,' Sara urged, gripping his hand. She felt an answering squeeze as he smiled at her tenderly.

'I'd be honoured to work with you, Mr Dimarco,' Raymond replied and stepped forward with an outstretched hand.

Arturo clasped his own rough fingers around Raymond's in acceptance.

'Then I am happy, too,' Joe's father smiled, his eyes shining. 'Welcome to our family.'

Sara felt a surge of joy at the words. As she reached towards Raymond, he turned and their arms went around each other in a fierce hug and they kissed roundly, not caring what anyone thought. How near she had come to losing him! Sara shivered with fleeting anguish, then succumbed to the wave of happiness washing through her as they clung together.

The publishers hope that this book has given you enjoyable reading. Large Print Books are especially designed to be as easy to see and hold as possible. If you wish a complete list of our books please ask at your local library or write directly to:

Magna Large Print Books
Magna House, Long Preston,
Skipton, North Yorkshire.
BD23 4ND

This Large Print Book for the partially sighted, who cannot read normal print, is published under the auspices of

THE ULVERSCROFT FOUNDATION